A third-grader gets suspicious of her new classmate when she begins making deals that change people's demeanor.

A young boy stays up late to ensure his little brother's wish gets heard, and discovers his midnight visitor isn't quite who he expected.

A man kills his much-beloved neighbor to win the favor of the dark angel directing his actions.

A woman protects her family's heritage at the cost of her unborn daughter's soul.

All of them have needs.

All of them are willing to barter.

None of them are prepared for their encounter with…

THE DEVIL YOU KNOW.

THE DEVIL YOU KNOW

Edited by R.J. Carter

DEDICATION

To Scratch.

You're one evil son of a bitch…
…but damn it if you're not an entertaining one.

CONTENTS

ACKNOWLEDGMENTS

This book would not exist without the faith and trust of the contributing writers who rose to the challenge armed with the greatest weapon ever devised by man: imagination.

FOREWORD:
THE ART OF THE
INFERNAL DEAL

Fiat Lux. Let there be light.

And there was light.

And, by God—he was good! The most beautiful of all the host.

And then, somewhere along the way, all Hell broke loose.

Throughout mythology, the literary Devil has filled the role of gambler, broker, trickster and deal maker. In the Old Testament, he enters into a bet with God Himself over His servant Job, wagering that base human nature and resentment would win out over blind faith if only Job's life weren't so blessed by circumstance.

Long before Charlie Daniels brought the Devil to Georgia for that infamous fiddle showdown, Paganini was reputed to have bartered his soul for his unparalleled mastery of the violin; and legend has it Robert Johnson met up with the Dark One at the crossroads of highways

61 and 49 in Clarksdale, Mississippi, and walked away a god of the blues.

Christopher Marlowe recounts how Johann Faust bartered his soul for knowledge and pleasures without worldly consequence. Centuries later, Stephen Vincent Benét told the tale of Jabez Stone, a farmer who contracted with the Devil for something as simple as a few years of good crops before retaining the services of Daniel Webster to litigate his way out of the agreed-upon terms.

Even Jesus of Nazareth was approached, and offered the world after he had fasted forty days and nights in the wilderness—proving beyond doubt there was nobody too righteous for the Devil to solicit.

There's always a deal to be made, a customer in need— and ever too high a cost to be paid.

Collected here are some of the freshest voices in fiction, each with their own unique spin on encounters with Old Scratch.

Some of the tales, such as Henry Vogel's *The Devil & The Details* and Sarah Cannavo's *The Drinkin' Contest*, will delight you with their whimsical, folktale approaches. Others, like Evan Purcell's *Give Me Your Soul, and I'll Give You a Pepperoni* and Jared Baker's *Not a Saint*, will chill you to the marrow and send you hastily to your local hardware store to stock up on nightlights. And then there are stories like Cara Fox's *Dominion*, Troy Riser's *Love and the Forever Machine*, and Hannah Trusty's *The Pact*, which will carry you to times and places, past and future, close and far away, where these encounters are as wondrously spellbinding as they are breathtaking.

In each of them we meet… him. The roguish gambler. The smooth-talking broker. The infernal deal maker.

This is The Devil You Know.

— R.J. Carter, Editor

THE DRINKIN' CONTEST

CONTEST

Sarah Cannavo

Most places, if you care to listen, have stories all their own, the sort people pass around like a jar of applejack at a Friday-night dance during their own generation, and then hand down to the next, who do the same, and so on and so on, until they become legends, embedded so deep in the place you can't mention one without the other springin' to mind. 'Round these parts the folks still talk of the time Jack Redding took on the Devil in a drinkin' contest, and you'd be hard-pressed to find a soul here who didn't grow up hearin' about it at their ma or pa's knee. Me, I've heard it so many times I could tell it backward and forward, or in my sleep; I'm regarded as somethin' of an authority on the subject, and plenty of people who're curious about it have found themselves sent my way to hear what went on deep in the pines that day.

Now, sometimes the Devil gets restless, bored with struttin' around orderin' demons about and torturin' the souls of sinners. And when that happens, he leaves Hell for a bit and goes wanderin' in the world, either to see what mischief he can stir up or just for a change of scenery. As it happened, that day he found himself in New Jersey (a place many have thought of as bein' only slightly better than the brimstone-soaked depths of Hell)—south Jersey, to be specific, wanderin' through a stretch of it known as the Pine Barrens, which runs from Freehold down almost to Cape May and all the way out to the Atlantic. There are some who say the Devil's got kin out in that area, though to the best of my knowledge he's never rightly claimed that Leeds woman's boy as his own, nor done much over the years to provide for him if he is. But some folks are just like that.

Anyway, it was one of them beautiful days that have a bit of summer and autumn both to it, and the Devil was feelin' mighty fine as he walked along, whistlin' like a bluebird and soakin' up that fresh Pinelands air. He had no particular destination in mind, walkin' just to walk, and God only knows how long he'd been makin' his way down those sugar-sand roads before he happened across the Redding family homestead, set way out in the woods headin' toward Chatsworth. It wasn't much of a homestead, all things told, just a rundown tarpaper hovel just about good enough to keep the rain off, and a little shed out back. The only Redding left to tend it was Jack, his ma and pa havin' taken a fever and passed on a few years before, and his younger sister Kate run off to marry a man who made his livin' haulin' clams in from the bay in Barnegat six months ago. Jack was twenty-five years old then, and managed to keep things together pretty well, and kept up the family business on top of it all.

Some Piney families crawled on their hands and knees through the bogs to harvest cranberries come September and October; some worked makin' charcoal and smeltin' bog ore, at least before the Pennsylvania mines and furnaces put most of the ones 'round here out of business in the back half of the nineteenth century. Others made bricks, built ships, blew glass, or raked sphagnum moss out in the swamps, and still others fished or worked in the bays, like Kate Redding's young man. But the Redding family was and always had been in the business of brewin' and sellin' applejack—Jersey Lightnin' if you're bein' familiar, and moonshine if you ain't from around here—and since this was a time when the gov'ment thought they had a right to tell folks what they could and couldn't drink, business was pretty brisk for young Jack Redding. He housed the still in the shed on his family's property and ran the product down the back roads of the Barrens to various folks and restaurants who disagreed with the liquor laws, haulin' it in a beat-up Model T held together with his mechanical skills, a few well-placed nuts and bolts, and the occasional prayer.

As it happened, he was out in his front yard workin' on that Model T when the Devil ambled by; the night before he'd been out cartin' a few barrels of applejack, and while he'd done it without hassle, on the way back he'd noticed a new rattlin' under the hood. Say what you will about him, but Jack was a prudent young man and wasn't about to keep breakin' the law in that truck til he could be sure it wouldn't quit on him at an inopportune moment.

The Devil saw him workin' on the truck, and he smiled. Ol' Nick's got quite an eye for such things, and he liked the look of the Redding boy, somethin' in him sayin' *Here's an easy mark if there ever was one.* So he walked up to the Redding yard and cheerfully hailed the bootlegger, thinkin' he might have some fine sport after all that day.

"Hello there, son. Fine day, isn't it?"

Jack looked up from his work and took in the stranger: his neat dark hair, his fine features, his dark and stylish suit of clothes (for all his faults, the Devil can be one dapper gentleman when he wants to, part of the reason it can be so damn hard to spot him sometimes), and immediately his guard went up. The area which he called home, like so many of its kind out in the Pines, was isolated, fresh faces comin' through infrequently—travelers on their way to somewhere else, an itinerant preacher or two, the occasional wanderin' salesman, and of course there was always the threat of revenuers comin' around to put a stop to a man's honest work. This man didn't have his world on his back or in his arms like a traveler, and somethin' in Jack (who wasn't the world's most religious man, but who managed to find his way to the local Baptist church from time to time nonetheless) rejected without hesitation the notion that he was a preacher. A salesman, then, with slick clothes and suave manners to help him hock his leather-bound Bibles or tonics for health, wealth, and sleep? Maybe, but then where were his goods? Wary in case he *was* a Fed who'd heard some rumors about how Jack earned a livin' and was takin' a kindly approach to get close, Jack set down the wrench he was holdin' and said guardedly, "Yeah, it is," thinkin' all the while about the shotgun he kept tucked under the Model T's front seat.

"It's been a while since I've found myself in these parts," the Devil continued, keenly aware of Jack's caution but not lettin' it dim his charm a whit, just takin' care not to overdo it and scare his new mark off. "My usual haunts are a little further south than this."

"Delaware?" Jack asked, and the Devil laughed.

"Sometimes," he said agreeably. "Sometimes further down than that."

"What brings you up here, then?" Jack asked, mind and hand never far from that shotgun.

"Well, to tell the truth," the Devil said (because even he can do that, when it suits his purpose), "I didn't really have a reason in mind when I came up, but I'm the sort that can't bear to pass up a business opportunity when I happen across one, and you, my boy, have the look of a man who wants something. Badly."

A salesman after all, then. Jack snorted. "What was your first clue?" he asked, lookin' around at what passed as his worldly estate: a dirt-floored tumbledown shack, a sagging shed shelterin' his handrigged still, a bare patch of earth for a dooryard, and the battered truck that ran on grit as much as gasoline. But he shook his head, wipin' his grease-stained hands on red rag already bearin' a wealth of similar stains. "Ain't too bad, though. Got food, got a roof, got my health. I don't need much more'n that."

It was the stranger's turn to chuckle, and he waved his hand at the Redding place, dismissin' it all. "Oh, I don't mean anything like that, Jack, none of that surface stuff. I mean wanting something way down deep in your soul, something you can't buy, find, or make for yourself, but that you'd give anything to possess. Something you need so badly the ache settles in your heart and won't leave no matter what you do, won't let you sleep or think or breathe without reminding you of it. *That's* the sort of want I mean; *that's* the business I'm in. And you strike me as someone with such a want, Jack. Or might I be misreading you here?" His amiable tone allowed for the possibility, but the curve of his smile and the sudden glitter in his dark eyes said differently.

He wasn't wrong; Jack was in fact sufferin' a powerful want, had been for some time. See, Jack was a fairly good-lookin' young buck, a bit rough around the edges in both appearance and manners, but well-built, slim and strong, with the dark brown hair and blue eyes of the Reddings, and a smile from him or a look from those blue eyes was enough to win him the heart of many a local girl. There was only one girl for him, though: Lenora Dunnett, a golden-haired beauty all of twenty-three years old and from good Pine stock, with a warm heart, friendly nature, and a laugh more melodious to Jack than church bells on Sunday are to a true believer. As it happened, Miss Dunnett returned Jack's affections just as ardently as he gave them. That wasn't the problem.

Lenora didn't care one bit how her beau made his livin'. He could run Jersey Lightnin' up and down the state or dig up buried pirate gold or rake moss in the swamps and come home soaked in cedar water and it wouldn't bother her none as long as they were together, she loved him so. Her pa, however, was a different story. Harold Dunnett owned the local general store, which did double duty as the post office, and the gas station, and was one of them "pillars of the community" people are always yakkin' about, and he was dead set against Lenora marryin' Jack Redding on account of his profession. Harold was no teetotaler, wasn't above takin' a sip of applejack here and there, and even had to admit of all the vintages he'd sampled in his life Jack's was the strongest and sharpest. But his first daughter had married a hotshot lawyer up in Philadelphia, and his second a well-to-do hotel owner down Cape May way, and he'd be damned if his youngest was gonna hitch herself to a (literally) dirt-poor moonshiner. He'd threatened to disown Lenora if they married, and the lovebirds knew he meant it.

Jack didn't want to sunder his sweetheart so completely from her family if he could help it, and Harold's apt sum-up of his state rankled him besides. He was a steady worker and not a profligate spender, but he didn't pull in as much for a haul as some of the bigger outfits in the Barrens did, and certainly not as much as those folks who ran booze down across the Canadian border or into New York ports. He wanted to give Lenora a good life like he felt she deserved, and if he could provide her with it maybe Harold Dunnett would ease off and not cut her out of the family after all. Of course, that all hinged on Jack makin' his fortune—and soon, before his love for Lenora drove him right out of his mind.

Jack was so caught up in thoughts of this that he forgot to wonder how the stranger'd known his name when he'd never said it, givin' him a wry smile instead and sayin',

"Well, you better be the Devil himself, then, mister, if you're fixin' to get me what I want, since prayin' to God and workin' for it myself ain't been doin' a damn thing for me."

The stranger's smile grew then. "Pretty serendipitous that I came along, then, Jack, if that's the case," he said. And though Jack couldn't've spelled "serendipitous" with a huntin' rifle pressed to his temple, his family never havin' had much money for schoolin', he gathered meanin' well enough. A moment later he also gathered that this stranger had called him by name twice now without bein' given it once, and that was when a few things started clickin' into place for young Jack Redding, who looked on the eloquent, well-dressed man with different eyes, a chill skitterin' down his spine even as his body stiffened.

"You're from south of here, huh?" he asked, and the Devil's handsome face well and truly shone with amusement and delight now.

"Much farther north originally, but down south now."

"Uh-huh." Jack felt like a man walkin' through a cedar swamp: well aware that the green carpet beneath his feet wasn't as solid as it appeared and one wrong step would plunge him deep into dark treacherous waters. "And you're sayin' you can get me what I want—for a price, I'm guessin'. I pay it and you make it, let's say, so I have enough money to take care of Lenora, and her pa can't quibble about my job anymore. That about right?"

The Devil's eyes were still glitterin'; he looked now like a cat watchin' a bird flit to lower and lower branches of a tree, just waitin' for the perfect moment to unsheathe his claws and sink 'em in. "You've got it, son," he said. "Although you can pay for your fortune… or you can play for it. Your pick."

Jack's brow furrowed. "What do you mean, 'play'?"

The Devil smoothed out a nonexistent wrinkle from his black coat. "I'm a businessman, Jack, but I'm also a sporting man; I like to have some fun now and then when

I'm out conducting said business, make a few wagers, that sort of thing. And there might be a way for you to get what you want without even having to pay. Is that something you might be interested in?"

Is a bear interested in honey? Jack knew he should've been runnin' away just as fast as he could go, but he found himself listenin' to those honeyed words instead—lettin' the Devil make his pitch, if you will. The Devil was well aware he had our hero by the ear, and fluid as silk that pitch went on. "A contest, Jack, you and I. If you win, I provide you with enough gold that your sweetheart's father will be throwing himself at your feet to beg forgiveness, and probably a loan or two. And if I win…" Oh, then the Devil smiled like a cat with that bird's blood already on his tongue, and his eyes glowed like the hottest coals in the heart of a fire. "I get your soul."

Now, I already told you that Jack didn't have much schoolin', but that doesn't mean he was a fool. He knew right well the risks of acceptin' such a challenge from such an opponent, and facin' the scorn of Lenora's father every day for the rest of his life was a far more tolerable scenario than havin' his soul sent straight to Hell marked Special Delivery, all postage paid. He'd heard plenty of tales about people with too much confidence in their abilities who'd taken on the Devil and lost… but then again, he'd also heard tales of people who'd taken on the Devil and won, like that fiddler, Sammy Buck, right there in the Pinelands. It *could* be done. So wasn't it possible he could do it, too, Jack asked himself, his mind goin' again and again to Lenora: her cornflower-blue eyes, that sweet little laugh of hers, her warm tender kiss. *Might as well hear what he has in mind,* he reasoned, and asked, "What kinda contest?"

The Devil was feelin' generous that day (and mighty cocksure of his own abilities, to boot), and spread his hands magnanimously. "I'll let you pick, Jack, my boy."

Jack eyed him shrewdly, feelin' for a trick. "Anything I want?"

"Anything at all," the Devil assured him.

Jack grinned. "A drinkin' contest."

☿

Aside from lies, illusion, and temptation, the Devil's got himself quite a few other talents: fiddlin', for one, is among the most well-known, and dancin', and he's pretty good in a footrace, too. But what you might not know is that Ol' Scratch can bend an elbow like nobody's business, and as of Jack Redding's challenge no one, be them angel, human, or demon, had ever beaten him in a drinkin' contest—in fact, most of his opponents were under the table before he got anywhere close to tipsy. There'd never been a booze brewed that was too strong for him, never a glass, bottle, or keg he couldn't drain. So when the challenge was issued that day in the Pines, the Devil was sure he had Jack's soul all sewn up as his own, and accepted without hesitation, even when Jack specified it was his Jersey Lightnin' they'd be drinkin'.

You might be wonderin' just what in the hell Jack was thinkin', pickin' a challenge like that. Why not, say, a psalm-readin' contest, or seein' who could recite the Lord's Prayer the fastest? The Devil had said *any* contest, after all, so it wouldn't even be cheatin'. But if the Devil was a hardy drinker, so was Jack; his prowess with tossin' back applejack as well as brewin' it had already made him half a legend in the area, and folks crowded the local waterin' hole, the Red Apple Tavern, whenever news got 'round that he was in for another drinkin' contest. And before you go hollerin' that it's all well and good to beat a few locals at the game of drink, or even a legion of 'em over the years, but another thing entirely to take on the Prince of Darkness his own self, you gotta understand, it wasn't beer or whiskey or wine Jack had grown up drinkin', but straight applejack, and it's called Jersey Lightnin' for a reason. The Redding brew in particular was a bolt from the blue that'd knock you flat on your ass before you knew what hit you, and yet Jack could take a full storm and stay standin'.

So goin' into this contest, man and Devil each felt secure in their own chances, and the pair headed into Jack's house, where the contest could be carried out with less risk of discovery (not that the revenuers bustin' in would much faze a being who could disappear with a snap of his fingers, but Jack wisely didn't trust his opponent not to cut out and leave him holdin' the bag—or jar, as it were—if that happened). It wasn't a palace, but there was a table and two chairs, and though Jack had delivered a large portion of his product the night before to the Red Apple (where they supposedly wouldn't pull you anything stronger than a cola—unless, of course, you knew to order the house special) he still had enough full Mason jars on hand to make things interestin'. The contestants settled themselves in across the rickety wooden table from each other, their first drinks poured and waitin', and the Devil smiled at Jack and, ever the gentleman, asked one last time, "You sure about this, Jack? A soul's a mighty big thing to stake on a contest like this."

Jack knew it, all right, and I'd be lyin' if I said there wasn't a part of him, as he sat across from the Devil in that sunlit shack, shakin' like a leaf in the wind and shoutin' at him to back out while he still could. But his thoughts were of Lenora, and a man in love is a creature damn near impossible to, dissuade, no matter the obstacle. So he only nodded and said, "Worth it, though."

The Devil grinned and raised his first shot. "Let's get goin' then, shall we?"

Jack raised his own shot, and they tossed them back.

And that's when the Devil started to realize just what he'd gotten himself into.

The thing was, the Devil'd never had applejack before. Whiskey—rivers of it. Bootleg liquor—of course. But for all the time he'd spent in Jersey, no God's-honest fresh-from-the-still Pinelands applejack had ever passed his lips, and so when it hit his throat he choked, unable to keep from sputterin' and his eyes from streamin' at the burn.

Jack, who'd gunned his drink down like mother's milk, smirked. "Forgot to mention it's got a bit of a kick. Sorry."

"No, no, it's fine." The Devil muffled a cough with his fist, blinkin' his stingin' eyes to clear 'em. "Delightful vintage you've got here, Jack."

"Thanks." Jack poured the next round and slid the Devil's to him, and his smirk grew slightly when Ol' Nick hesitated for a moment, eyein' the drink like he thought it might suddenly spring for his throat. Only for a moment, but Jack woulda sworn on his ma and pa's graves that he saw it, and his own confidence surged a heap in that moment. "*You* sure about this?"

The Devil sat up straighter, and regained his composure. No way was he lettin' some backwater booze throw him off, even if it kicked like a mule with a hot poker up its ass. He was the goddamned Prince of Darkness, the Adversary, the bane of sinners and the tormentor of souls, who'd unleashed legions of evils upon the world. He wasn't goin' down on the first fuckin' shot. "Damned sure," he said, and grabbed his drink.

The second wasn't much gentler than the first, nor the third than the second, though the Devil managed not to cough or tear up—too badly, anyway. Jack and the Devil matched each other drink for drink, time tickin' away unnoticed as sun and shadow crept through the shack at their own pace, now one with a further reach, now the other; nothing mattered to the combatants but the empty jars mounting around them, their own refilled with another shot's amount by Jack each time they drained them. How drunk were they by this point, you ask? Well, Jack was doin' all right—his calloused hand was still steady when he poured a drink or took one, and when on occasion he talked there were still the proper spaces between his words, no slurrin' or stumblin' to speak of. And as for the

Devil, he was pushin' resolutely onward. As you might've gathered if you've heard anything about him, he has quite the store of pride to draw on, and he was sure as shit drawin' on it that day. It was a good thing for him, too, because to be honest his head was swimmin' a little, a novel sensation for him, but it didn't matter, he kept tellin' himself. Whatever he was feelin', the human had to be feelin' something ten times worse, even if he was hidin' it well, and sooner or later it'd start to show. Jack Redding was just a man, after all, and men always broke in the end.

The Devil rode that line of reasonin' for a good long while, and at one point decided to needle the Piney a bit, see if he couldn't probe for a crack or two he could help widen to hasten along that inevitable collapse. "How much longer do you think you can hold out, Jack? There's no shame in an honorable surrender, you know."

Jack cocked his head. "Huh? I didn't quite catch that."

Was he goin' deaf or something? "I *said*—'the Devil started, and then he cut off, because something *did* sound off about his voice all of a sudden; something felt wrong, too, with his mouth, and he frowned and worked it a moment, tryin' to figure out what. His tongue, it was his tongue; it was startin' to get heavy for some reason, and it was knockin' his words out of shape, the way a malformed mold in a forge will only turn out useless lumps of metal instead of workable iron. The furrows in his brow carved themselves a deeper swath, and it took him another few moments before he realized that for the first time in his eternal life—he was tipsy.

Horror washed over him. How was it possible? How could some Jersey home brew succeed in doin' what no other booze before it had, and when he'd only had… He blinked, lookin' around and realizin' he'd kinda lost count, but what the hell should that matter? And how could Jack be so clear-eyed when he'd drunk just as much as the Devil?

For the first time, worry started gnawin' at the edges of

his stomach. Maybe, just maybe, this wasn't goin' to be as easy a conquest as he'd thought.

But so what? Where was the sport in "easy"? Tipsy was certainly disconcertin', but it wasn't drunk, and therefore wasn't the end of anything. The Devil forced his words back into proper form. "I said there's no shame in surrender."

Jack opened another jar, the fumes bloomin' in the air like the fragrance of a particularly poisonous flower. It was the odor that'd clung to his pa's clothes after he'd spent some time in the shed with the still, the odor of his own livelihood now, and as it seared his nostrils he said, "I bet I ain't the first mortal you've said that to."

The Devil shrugged. "When you find a good line, you stick with it."

"Well, it seems like something you oughta keep in mind. You ain't lookin' too steady there," Jack observed. Don't get me wrong, he was startin' to feel the applejack's effects too; after all, he was, as the Devil'd so aptly observed, a mortal. But he'd long ago learned how to keep up an appearance of cold sobriety even when he was beginnin' to burn and buzz, a handy skill in any drinkin' contest, and so far he was managin' to keep up that appearance fairly well, though he was currently clingin' to sobriety the way a danglin' man clings to the edge of a cliff with someone hangin' on his ankles: aware of his precarious position and prayin' like hell the other guy lets go before he does.

Apparently he was sober enough for decent aim, his comment squarely strikin' a nerve. "Just pour the damn drink," the Devil snarled, eyes blazin', and you bet your ass Jack did.

And he poured another, and another, and another, and he and the Devil shot them all back, Ol' Scratch runnin' on pure stubborn pride now, and Jack thinkin' of Lenora, of the life his winnin's would buy 'em. Both drinkers had dug their heels in and were pushing hard against each other...

and the Devil felt himself slowly but surely beginnin' to slide further and further away from sobriety. He reached for his jar and the applejack in its glass belly sloshed as his graspin' hand shook; he dragged it back across the rough wooden battlefield between himself and Jack with, he realized, his dismay mountin', the deliberate care of a drunken man determined not to spill a drop of his next drink. As he lifted it, there was a weight to the liquid he coulda sworn hadn't been there before—it was like tryin' to lift a jar of molten iron. He managed to get the applejack down, but his head was spinnin' like a whirlwind and he grasped the table's edge to keep himself upright as he involuntarily swayed.

"Ready to call it?" Jack asked. He recognized the state the Devil was in, had seen more than a few men enter it before—had even stumbled into it a time or two himself back when he was just startin' out. Right now, the Devil was still in the game, might even be able to hang on a little while longer, but it was a tenuous grip at best. If Jack's hold lasted, he'd come out champion once again.

"No," the Devil said, or meant to say; it came out as a hiccup instead, and his eyes widened in shock, his hand flyin' to cover his mouth. Jack couldn't help himself—I ask you, who in that situation could? Show me someone who honestly could, and I'll show you a liar.

He laughed.

And for a moment it seemed Jack'd pushed his boundaries a bit too far and passin' out'd be the least of his problems. The air filled with a mighty hiss—what he thought a buncha demons might sound like if they all got worked up about something at once—and he realized the applejack he'd just refreshed the Devil's jar with was steamin' and sizzlin', hot droplets of it leapin' out and pockin' the table like embers as they landed. He jolted back in his seat, gut coilin' tight and blood goin' cold, as the Devil slammed the jar down and shot to his feet, the wooden chair tippin' back and splinterin' at the force of the shove. The jar didn't break, but there was another loud sizzle and a whiff of burnt kindlin' as the bottom of the jar seared a dark ring into the tabletop, the Devil's eyes blazin' with hellfire as he looked down at Jack.

"How dare you mock me, you pathetic Piney?" he snarled, the force of his voice knockin' a few cups and dishes from the shelf on the wall. "I held sway over my own dominion before your blithering, bearded ancestors brewed the first drop of their noxious swill, and I will be a king in Hell long after the last of your blighted seed has withered to dust, you damned… damned…" He faltered, blinked, hiccupped again, all of which had quite the detrimental effect on his intimidation. And then his eyes rolled back into his head, his knees gave way, and he dropped like a sack of stones, snorin' before he hit the ground.

Jack gave him a minute, waitin' to see if he'd rouse himself, but all that happened was the Devil's snorin' deepened, even when Jack nerved up and cautiously nudged Ol' Nick's prone form with the toe of his boot. He was good and passed out, and just like that, it was over.

Jack had out-drunk the Devil.

He smiled the smile of a man whose soul had gotten close to hellfire and escaped without gettin' singed, gazin' fondly at his jar of applejack before he set it down. "Wait 'til Lenora hears about this," he said to no one in particular, then grabbed hold of the unconscious Devil's legs and dragged him over to the shack's narrow bed.

♉

Jack couldn't collect his winnin's until the Devil woke up, which meant he had to wait a bit, since the defeated Devil slept through the rest of the day and well into the next. When Lenora stopped by to visit Jack the morning after the contest, she stopped dead in the shack's doorway and stared at the well-dressed but now-disheveled figure sprawled out dead to the world in her beau's bed, her pretty brow furrowin'.

"Who's that, sweetheart?" she asked, after acceptin' Jack's kiss.

"The Devil," Jack replied.

Lenora laughed that bubbly little laugh of hers. "Sure it is, Jack. Now who is it, really?"

Jack still smiled at her, but there was something in that smile, in his eyes, that gently but firmly pressed the point, and Lenora's laugh died away. She looked again at the sleepin' figure, then back to Jack, who gave a small nod. "Jack, what the… what the hell did you *do?*"

"It wasn't me so much as the applejack." He wrapped his arm around her shapely waist and guided her back out the front door so they could let the Devil rest in peace. "Fella just couldn't hold his drink. Gave it a good try, though."

When the Devil finally woke, he was just about the most miserable creature anywhere in the universe; I wouldn't've wanted to be a demon or a sinner's soul in Hell that day with the bossman nursin' a hangover like that. Not to mention he'd been dealt a mighty blow to that pride of his, which hurt just as badly as his poundin' head. But sulky and sufferin' as he was, he made good on his word and paid Jack a gleamin' pile of gold—the real stuff, too, none of that trick gold that turns into dried leaves the instant the Devil's outta sight. Then he trudged back home, and it was a long, long while before he could stand to set foot in New Jersey again.

And as for Jack, his new-won fortune had just the effect he'd hoped it would. Rumors flew fast and thick about the source of his sudden wealth, the most popular bein' that he'd discovered a cache of pirate or refugee treasure buried somewhere out in the Barrens. But the truth got out quick enough, the ring burnt on Jack's tabletop addin' extra weight to the tale, and from then on he wasn't just Jack Redding the local moonshiner, but *Jack*

Redding, the man who'd out-drank the Devil, the title he's still known by here to this day. He used some of his winnin's to buy the nearby shuttered Buck's Horn Inn, and brought it back to life, makin' another name for himself as a respectable workin' man, and he used a little more to build up the shack on the Redding land into a proper, comfortable house fit for a family—keepin' the burnt table and the shed and the still, of course; as long as the people of the Pines were thirstin' he'd brew for 'em, and they were always plenty thirsty.

Because, yes, Harold Dunnett allowed the glitter of Jack's gold to blind him to the young man's continued involvement in the Redding family business, sure at least that Lenora would be taken care of, and the couple were wed at long last and without further delay. As he carried his blushin' bride over the threshold of their new home, Jack was the happiest he'd ever been, and all thanks to some prime Jersey Lightnin'.

Over the years that followed, the couple's fortunes and happiness continued to increase, businesses and family rapidly and steadily growin'. I was the first of many children, son and heir to the Redding legacy, and grew up hearin' the story of the drinkin' contest straight from the champion himself—we all did. And me and all my plentiful brothers and sisters wound up workin' in one of the family businesses or another. Me, I tended bar in the Buck's Horn, since by the time I was old enough to the gov'ment had wised up and repealed them liquor laws (which didn't dent the livelihoods of the Piney moonshiners as much as you might think, what with the taxes the gov'ment levied on "legal" booze and all), and I became an unofficial historian of sorts, separatin' fact from fiction about my pa's battle with the Devil and helpin' to keep the legend alive. That's why you wound up on my front porch, ain't it? Because you were passin' through town, heard some hint of it, and wanted to know more, so one of my siblings, nieces, or nephews down at the inn or gas station or general store sent you my way? I thought so—ah, Millie, was it? Good kid, that girl. Got a fine head for figures, and the Redding blue eyes, no doubt about that.

My pa? No, he's no longer with us, God bless his soul; he passed on quite a few years back. My ma's gone too; they're buried together in that little cemetery just up the road yonder. Of course I still miss 'em, but they lived long and happy lives, which is all a body can ever hope for in this world, I think. Like the poet said, they loved with a love that was more than love, the kind where they'd do or risk anything to be together and did, and that's a rare kind of love right there. Once a week one of us Reddings heads down there and puts a jar of applejack on the graves, in honor of a toast my pa always used to make; he'd wrap his arm around my ma, raise some 'shine, and say with the world's biggest grin on his face, "To what was supposed to keep up apart, and what made sure we could be together." She'd laugh, they'd kiss, and we'd drink. There are worse ways to grow up.

Well, I hope the tale was worth your time, traveler. If you ever find yourself in this part of the Pines again, feel free to wander on by; I got plenty of yarns about the Barrens I can spin, even ones that don't involve my kin. Like I said before, most places have their own stories, and around here there's all kinds of places and all kinds of stories just waitin' to be passed on.

If you ever *do* wander back this way, though, keep an eye out for a handsome, well-dressed man on these sugar-sand roads; he still comes around from time to time, and if he smiles charmin'-like and offers you a way to win your heart's desire, listen if you will, but be careful what contest you choose. Because it's your one and only soul on the line, and that's a hell of a thing to lose.

If you *do* manage to win, though, consider buyin' the Devil a drink to console him; he gets mighty sore about losin'. Best you skip the applejack, though. From what I hear, he's never acquired a taste for it.

ABOUT THE AUTHOR

SARAH CANNAVO is a writer of prose and poetry from southern New Jersey, Pine country. Her works appear in collections and publications such as *Untimely Frost, Carrying On, Darkling's Beasts and Brews, Parody, Poetry Quarterly, Postcards From the Void, Schlock! Horror!, It Came From the Garage!, The Devil's Hour, Liminality, Deranged, Obliquatur Voluptas, Horror USA: California, Midnight in the Witch's Kitchen,* and *Ghosts, Spirits, and Specters.* Her poem "The 5 Stages of Being on Hold" took third place in the 2018 Wergle Flomp humor poetry contest. Her story "Unreality" is available as an eBook from Albany Lake Publishing, and her work is forthcoming in *Star*Line, Horror USA: Washington,* and *Ghost Stories For Starless Nights.* She can be found online at Twitter @moodilymusing, as well as on her website, www.moodilymusing.blogspot.com.

WHAT THE HEART DESIRES

Joseph Rubas

The Devil strode down the middle of US Route 15, a spring in his step and a tune on his lips. Around him, the night-drenched forest stood silent in the light of the cold autumn moon, the bugs and bullfrogs and night-things going quiet in his presence. Somewhere far away, a wolf howled, followed by another, and then another, until the crisp air was filled with their eerie song. *The children of the night,* he thought with a sly grin, *what music they make.*

Route 15 runs through the wilderness for twenty miles between Grafton Falls and Berkeley. A few ramshackle houses press close to the road here and there. As the Devil passed, sleepers stirred in their beds, slick night terrors passing close to their minds. In one house, a crucifix fell from a wall, in another a mirror shattered. A dog whined and scurried into the darkness underneath a porch, and a cat fell dead of a heart attack. The Devil smiled at these things. The night was his to do with as he pleased, and it positively brimmed with possibility. Perhaps he would derail a train and listen to the heavenly sounds of twisting metal, breaking bodies, and rushing steam. Or maybe he would wave his hand and cause the Kanawha River Dam to fail. The roar of water splashing downstream in a deadly tide, sweeping away everything in its path—buildings, bridges, babies in their cribs—rang in his head, and giddy excitement flowed through him. The night offered so much, but even he—as great and grand as he was—could only do one thing at a time.

The road bent around a wooded hillside, and somewhere in its growth, a homeless camp huddled around a feeble fire. One man muttered in his sleep, a weak noise of distress, and a woman's period started, spilling down her legs in a sticky red torrent.

Yes, the night belonged to him.

And he intended to make the most of it.

Somehow.

♉

Fifteen miles away, a young girl sat on a window ledge with her knees drawn to her chest and watched the face of the cloud-wrapped moon. Below her, the town of Grafton Falls slept, frozen save for the single blinking caution light on Main Street several blocks over. Three miles east, beyond a dense stand of trees, Interstate 82 ran east-to-west. Occasionally she could glimpse the flash of passing headlights through the trees. In just a couple weeks, the leaves would be all down and she would be able to see the road more clearly.

She liked the interstate. She would watch the passing cars and wonder where they were going. She imagined all the places that road went, all the cities and towns rising up along it. All she had to do, she realized, was to follow it, and she could go almost anywhere. She really wanted to travel when she got older, and sometimes she felt the call of the road so keenly it was like being stabbed. The road pulled her blood the way the moon overhead pulled the tide, and when she listened to the windy whoosh of passing traffic, she imagined she could hear the blacktop itself calling her, inviting her to follow it. Did the road go to California, she wondered? She liked California. On TV, it looked so pretty and exotic. Colorado was nice too; they had snow-capped mountains all year round, and wide-open spaces where you could lose yourself.

A memory came back to her: Julie Andrews in *The Sound of Music* twirling in a meadow with her arms thrown out as if to embrace the world around her. She would do that. She would spin and sing and be happy if only she had a nice field like the one Julie Andrews had. Or a beach. She *kind* of remembered the beach: It was warm and sandy and the water was so clear you could look down and see fish swimming around. She missed the beach.

A gust of wind blew through the open window, and she shivered.

"What are you doing, Meagan?" Lindsey asked tiredly.

"Looking out the window," Meagan replied.

"Could you shut it? It's cold in here."

With a little sigh, Meagan leaned over and closed the sash. It was best not to start arguments. If you started an argument, you might get hurt, and no one would help you or care. Lindsey was nice enough, but she had anger problems, and when she blew up, Meagan couldn't help being scared.

A lot of the girls had anger problems here and you had to be really careful not to make them mad. One time, a girl smacked her across the back of the head for chewing too loud at dinner, and another one filled a cup with toilet water and threw it on her bed because Meagan chose something she didn't like on TV.

Blowing a dejected puff of air that stirred her bangs, Meagan gazed at the grimy pane. She didn't like looking out the window when it was closed, though, at least not as much as she did when it was open. When it was closed, *she* felt closed. With the air rushing over her and messing her blonde hair, she felt free, a part of the world. But with it closed, the air warm and stale, she felt trapped.

Not for the first time, she wondered what her parents were doing, and where they were. She hadn't seen them since she was eight. That's when they dropped her off at the orphanage and left her. It was only six years ago, but it felt like a lifetime…so long that she had forgotten what they looked like. She could barely even remember being with them. Did her daddy hug her and tell her bedtime stories like the daddies on TV? Did her mother teach her and guide her like the mothers you saw in the old sitcoms on Nick at Nite? She couldn't remember, and it pained her, but she assumed that they didn't. Moms and dads who did that sort of thing didn't drop you off at orphanages and wave as they pulled away, they didn't leave you alone with girls who picked on you and staff members who treated you like you were a criminal. Loathing filled her, but it was tinged with longing.

Thoroughly tired and depressed, Meagan hopped down from the window ledge and climbed into her bed. She tried to drift off, but sleep eluded her. She tossed and turned, unable to get comfortable. From her window, she could still see the moon, bright and clean. She wondered if somewhere, across the hills and rivers, her parents were looking at the same moon. Or if the man she would eventually marry was watching it, the man who would one day hold her in his arms and love her and make her happy.

Before she drifted off, she said her nightly prayer.

Protect me and watch over me.

She thought again of the moon, and fell off, as much at peace as she could ever be.

♉

A mile away, the Devil gazed up at the moon, its face like that of a skeleton rotting in a field. He was on the outskirts of Grafton Falls, drawn forth by the scent of misery on the breeze. The Devil was not the author of misery, as some would paint him. He was the assuager of misery. Though preachers stood upon pulpits and blasphemed his name, he wasn't bad. He was a friend to the friendless, the shepherd of the lost, the lover of the loveless. He appeared to the weak, the needy, the forlorn. When he found those poor, pitiful wretches, he gave them what their hearts desired. God, in His heaven, only watched and passed decrees like a distant king.

People, every one of them, want something. Was it really so bad to give it to them? Was it really that evil to load the gun they would use to shoot themselves? Why, he was doing a great service, thank you very much, the least earth could do was show a little gratitude.

Like a bloodhound, he followed the acrid odor of pain across a cold, knee-high creek and up a steep hill tangled with grass and littered with rocks. A tall, box-like building rose up from the night, its façade faded brick and its roof table top flat. A narrow side street lit by the harsh orange light of an arch sodium lamp led him to a wrought iron gate. A sign facing the street read ST. ANTHONY'S HOME FOR WAYWARD CHILDREN.

The Devil looked up at the many windows. Some were lit. Most were not. Closing his eyes, he basked in the rush of torment wafting from inside, a thousand different aromas of hurt, longing…and *need*.

Everyone, the Devil knew, needed something different, someone different. He waved his hand, and the gate, hitherto closed, swung freely open. He slipped in, and followed the parking lot to a set of double doors. Inside, a lobby stood revealed in cold white light. A security guard sat at a desk, idly scanning a magazine.

The Devil left him alone. The guard didn't need him.

The children did.

♉

He came to her in the night, his face radiant and his waxen hair spilling over his shoulders. His hands, upturned, were rough and strong, each palm bearing a ragged wound.

Maryanne Mitchell turned from him, tears coming to her eyes. Around them, mist wafted lazily. She wasn't sure if they were in her room anymore or not. She didn't think they were. They were somewhere else, somewhere out of space and time, on a spiritual plain.

"Look at me," he said softly, gently.

She couldn't. She couldn't bring herself to look into his warm brown eyes. She didn't want him to see the pain, the shame. She had done things in her seventeen years that she wasn't proud of, things that up until now had never bothered her, things that now bothered her greatly.

"We all fall short of the glory of God," he said kindly. "No one is perfect. Everyone sins. Sin is nature. Sin is okay."

He caressed her face and turned her head. She was looking deeply into his eyes, her spirit stirring. The void she had felt her entire life was finally filled. The nuns and priests talked about God's love, but she had never felt it until this very moment. She felt loved, protected, like a child in the arms of its loving father.

"You are beautiful," he said, "and special."

She swallowed hard. A lump was stuck in her throat.

"You are perfect. And I love you."

He kissed her then, and she kissed him back, deeply, hungrily. He ran his hands through her hair, down her face, to her throat. His touch was warm, electric. She fell back onto clouds made of satin and wept with joy when he entered her, filling her with peace and love and happiness. She was home. She was finally home. And she was finally loved.

In the next bed over, Kristy Harper stood upon a stage, a beautiful purple guitar in her hands. She looked out over a crowd of adoring fans. The hot floodlights felt good on her skin; goosebumps raced up and down her arms. She had worked so hard to get here. Since she was a little girl, music had been her refuge. When her parents fought and broke things, when they made up and got high on crack together, passing out in the living room and dying to the world, music was there for her. It never hurt her, it never left her, it never ignored her. When she wanted to spend time with KISS, or Aerosmith, or AC/DC (her dad's favorite bands), all she had to do was turn them on and drift away. In life, she was alone. She had no friends, no family. She was misunderstood and mocked. But Steven Tyler understood her. Listening to "Sweet Emotion," she felt as though he had reached into her soul and read her heart.

Presently, the dream changed. The concert was over. The people were filling out. She knew they loved her. She knew she was famous.

Glancing stage left, she saw Steven Tyler, a smile on his face. It wasn't the old, crusty Steven Tyler of today. It was the young, beautiful Steve Tyler of 1975.

She went to him, giddy.

"You did great," he said, hugging her.

"Really?" she asked, her heart swelling.

"Really," he said, releasing her. His smiling face went dark, then, and he put his hands on her shoulders. "You're the best."

"Am I?"

He nodded. "The best that's ever been, baby, and don't you forget it. No one else matters. No one else."

Kristy thought back to her time in the orphanage. She was a lost little girl then, afraid, alone, a number and nothing else.

"You're not a number," Steven said, "you're the only one who matters. It's always been that way. You're special. You're better than everyone else."

Looking into his eyes, Kristy saw his conviction. He was telling her the truth. She was the only one who mattered in the whole wide world. Everyone else was just...

"Fleas. Tiny, insignificant fleas. They don't feel like you do. They don't think like you do."

Kristy Harper swelled with pride.

In the halls, the Devil moved like a phantom, his shadow falling jagged and elongated on the wall. In Room 2F, he took Mindy Johnson by the hand and looked deeply into her eyes. She smiled, self-conscious of her braces.

"Don't," he said. "You're beautiful."

"I am?"

He nodded and grinned. "The most beautiful woman in the world. And looks are everything."

Her brow furrowed but she didn't speak.

"People will only love you if you're beautiful. They don't care about your heart or your mind. Only your face."

She seemed to struggle with that, but finally accepted it.

"Don't let your beauty slip for one second, or you'll lose everything."

"Okay," she said.

He kissed her, and she kissed him back...accepting him into her heart as surely as a Christian accepts Christ on her knees.

Across the hall, Lauren Conner felt her anxiety lift. For the first time in almost eighteen years—her entire life—she felt calm. She wasn't worried about the future anymore.

"That's the way you get ahead, dear," her grandmother said. They were in the sun washed kitchen of her grandparents' cozy little home on Franklin Street, where honeysuckle grew in the spring and leaves showered in the fall. Lauren knew deep down that her grandmother was dead, and had been for nearly ten years. It was her death that had sent her to the orphanage, after all. Her grandfather remarried and didn't want her, and her mother was in prison, so where else would she go? Dead or not, Nana was back and everything was perfect, just as it had been before she died.

"You kick, you push, you shove, you claw their eyes out."

Lauren was sitting at the table eating ice cream. She felt young and happy and at peace. Her grandmother was standing at the sink, peeling potatoes. The sunlight streaming through the window painted her face warm and golden.

"The only thing that matters in this life is climbing the ladder. Everyone else is out for themselves. You should be out for you. And you should do whatever it takes to succeed."

Lauren was not naturally a cutthroat person, but thinking back to her time in the orphanage, she realized that her grandmother was right. How many times had she laid down for other people? How many times had she let them run over top of her? How much had she suffered and gone without because she was so goddamn nice?

"It's okay, though," her grandmother said, looking over her shoulder and grinning. "You won't be nice anymore, will you?"

"No," Lauren said, and meant it.

"That's a good girl."

Beyond the mist of sleep, the Devil climbed a set of stairs, his long, gnarled fingers trailing the handhold and his nails producing a noise like screaming as it dragged along the metal. Moonlight beamed through a segmented window and bathed the cinderblock wall in an eerie glow, the shadows inching across it making strange and expressionist shapes. On the third floor, nuns reposed in pious slumber. He passed close, like death in the night, and their sleep was disturbed. One stirred in her bunk, visions of bomb-blasted bodies dancing through her head. Another rubbed her legs crisply together at the fantasy of being taken by a man, any man. The Devil paused and slithered between the folds of her brain, touching primal parts and sensitive areas, setting her loins on fire. Wet heat pooled in her center, and her creamy flesh burned from head to toe. *It's okay,* he told her, *masturbation is natural…breaking your oath to God is fine. He'll understand.*

She came awake with a start and brushed her fingers through her sweat matted hair. The dank passion between her thighs bubbled and spat, and with a rush of shame, she touched herself.

A wicked smile crossed the Devil's lips, and he went on, climbing to the next floor, ghostly footfalls echoing through the stairwell like the coming of doom. He put his lips together and blew a tune of his own devising; in it were screams of agony, shrieking missiles, and the whimpers of children being hurt by their parents…that last one the sweetest melody of all.

On the fourth floor, Father Mackey, the superintendent of St. Anthony's, snorted in his sleep like a man encountering something queer and ugly. He was at his desk, head slumped back and a ribbon of silvery drool coursing down his chin. In the feeble spark of the lamp, his features were craggy and full of shadows. A bottle of whiskey sat before him, the amber liquid inside sparkling under the light.

In the chambers of his head, he stood over a lock box that didn't exist. He opened it, and inside was money— thousands of dollars comprising St. Anthony's budget. In reality, it was kept in a bank account to which only he and the board of trustees had access. How many times had he considered taking it and leaving? How many nights had he plotted his every step, down to his future life in Mexico? The temptation was great, throbbing, incessant, but he stayed his hand. He no longer believed in God, nor did he believe in man, but some small part of him—a flicker in the vast night of his heart—remained.

Go on, take it, the man beside him said. He was tall and slender with an everyman face: He could have been a cop, a construction worker, or even the postman.

Mackey looked longingly at the bills, and a lump formed in his throat.

He could do it.

He could take every cent and be on a beach in Baja before they even knew he was gone.

But the children…

The state will cover it, the man assured him. *The kids will have everything they need…and so will you.*

Mackey indecisively bit his bottom lip.

Could he really do it?

He looked at the man for guidance, and the man smiled winningly.

That decided him.

He picked up a stack of bills and shoved it into his blazer.

The man laughed and clapped his back.

In the stairwell, the Devil threw back his head and basked in the evil he had wrought, for what is evil but pure, unadulterated selfishness? Every act of murder, theft, rape, and genocide ever carried out under the watchful eye of the moon happened because somewhere, a heart desired something…and took it, no matter the cost. Two thousand years ago, on a dusty hill overlooking a huddled town, Jesus Christ sacrificed himself on a roughly hewn cross for the sins of the world…or so they say. His death proved the ultimate act of selflessness, and God called upon all His nits to be selfless too.

Only man cannot *be* selfless. He may try, but in the end, what his heart desires will always win out…just so long as you never stop prodding him.

For eventually, with enough spit and elbow grease,

even the elect will be deceived.

Whistling his tune, the Devil went on.

He had one more stop to make.

♉

Meagan woke shivering in the night, her teeth chattering lightly together. She pulled the covers up to her chin, but the chill pervaded her, as though it were coming from within. She turned away from the moonlight streaming through the window. Just then, a bright, warm, golden glow arose in the room. Blinking, she watched as the door opened and a man entered.

I'm dreaming, she thought. She sat up slowly, heart racing, and rubbed her eyes like a cartoon character who couldn't believe what she was seeing.

"Hey, honey," the man said, and came forward. Meagan blinked again. It was her father. He was tall and broad and dressed in brown pants and a light blue shirt. His hair was wavy black and his eyes were deep blue. His face was soft and warm.

Frozen, Meagan watched as he came to her and sat on her bed. He tried to slip his arm around her, but she shied away.

"Y-You're not my father."

Meagan didn't remember what her father looked like exactly, but she knew it was nothing like the image she had built in her mind's eye. The man before her was what she always thought a father *should* look like.

"Of course I am," he said smilingly. He lifted up a book. "I thought I'd read you a bedtime story. You like those, right?"

She didn't reply. A sense of *wrongness* came over her, and she gulped. The man's smile widened, and there was something fake in it, cold. She realized that it didn't touch his eyes.

His face was warm, but his eyes were cold.

Dead.

He reached out and stroked her face, and Meagan winced at the cool, dry kiss of his skin. She pulled away, and his face darkened.

"Baby," he said as evenly as he could, "it's okay. I know you're in pain. I know"—here he sighed deeply—"that things haven't gone the way they should have. I'm sorry for that, baby, I really am. I can't make up for the past, and for the things you've gone through here, but I can try to make it right *now*. You've been alone here for a long time. Unloved. Unwanted. And that tears me up. You're like a flower in need of water, baby. These people here can't provide what you need. I couldn't provide what you need. But now I'm ready."

"What do I need?" she asked, but already knew. Affection. She needed affection. She needed someone to hold her and kiss her forehead. She needed to feel the warmth of someone's closeness, the soft, tender touch of someone's love. She needed someone to dry her tears, to love her, to stay with her.

Her perfect father smiled. There was a cold glint in his eye. "I love you. I want to take you away from here. We can live in a little cabin in the woods forever and ever, just you and me. I'll protect you. I'll read to you every night. I'll cuddle you as you fall asleep and never leave you."

He moved closer as he spoke. His breath was warm and rancid, turning Meagan's stomach.

"Don't touch me," she said.

"But, princess…" he reached for her.

"Stop!" she screamed, slapping his hand and slipping out of bed. "You're not my father!"

His face hardened. Irrationally, she thought she saw literal fire in his eyes. "Meagan! I know you're upset, but I'm trying to give you what you need! Stop being such an ungrateful little bitch!"

His eyes were aflame now. It wasn't a trick of light or an optical illusion. Hot, red fire burned inside him.

"Get out," Meagan said, her heart racing. "Get out of here!"

"You don't want me?" he asked, coming across the bed, on his hands and knees now. His mask fell away then. In its place was a cold, reptilian countenance; slits for nostrils, wide, bulging eyes, thin lips peeled back over razor fangs. Meagan screamed. A lizard-like tongue darted from his mouth, and she recoiled in revulsion. If it touched her, she thought hysterically, she would go mad. "Do you want that?" it hissed.

"Go away!"

It screamed, and a gust of scalding air pushed Meagan back. Though she had been standing against the wall, she fell against the window. The pane shattered and she was falling through the night, her night-gown fluttering in the wind.

She had time to scream.

Then hit the ground.

♉

The maintenance man found her the next morning. She was curled up in a bush. Her right arm was broken, both ankles were sprained, and her face was crisscrossed with scratches, but she was alive.

The others were dead.

"I don't understand it," the fire marshal said later. "The carbon monoxide detectors are in perfect working order. How that building filled with the stuff without so much as a peep is beyond me. It's just…it doesn't make sense."

Meagan only remembered having a "nightmare" when she woke. The fire marshal surmised she woke in the night, knew something was wrong, and broke a window to escape. She was lucky, they said.

But she didn't feel very lucky…not when every night, she dreamed of a lizard man coming into her room and giving her whatever her heart desired.

ABOUT THE AUTHOR

JOSEPH RUBAS is the author of over 300 short stories and several novels. His work has appeared in *The Horror Zine*, *Nameless Digest*, *Thuglit*, *The Storyteller*, and many others. He currently resides in Albany, New York.

SERVICE WITH A SMILE
Daryl Marcus

Red and blue lights flashed in the rear-view mirror. Hunter didn't know whether to cry in frustration or anger. All he wanted to do was bury his wife. He'd been trying to get to the special spot he'd picked out especially for her, and every step of the way had been a slow, arduous slog through the mud.

Cursing himself and everyone else who'd made this night such an everlasting cluster fuck, he crossed through the stop-sign-governed intersection and pulled to the side of the road, careful not to get too close to the soft right shoulder. The last thing he needed was to get stuck and have to call a tow-truck.

Hunter watched the cop approach, a big-brimmed hat adding a halo to his shadowed form backlit by the pulsing blue strobes. He couldn't make out any details, so he didn't know if he'd been stopped by a state trooper or a county man. He hoped county. He might be able to talk his way out of a county ticket.

The officer paused a moment at the rear of the car. He bent down to study something on Hunter's wife's Honda

Accord. Hunter suddenly knew why he'd been stopped.

Jessica had never understood the need for car maintenance. She thought the damn things simply operated on good wishes and gasoline. She would never have scheduled her car for an oil change if Hunter hadn't insisted or done it himself. Taillights were probably burnt out, leaving Hunter on a dark stretch of backwoods road with a cop and an itch to write someone a ticket. He cursed the woman for all he was worth and wished he could kill her again for making him have to deal with her shit post-mortem. If he'd had to do it a second time, he'd take more time and enjoy it.

The cop was a big man, his state-trooper's gray uniform ill-fitting and stretched across a keg-shaped belly. It was a small keg, but still a keg. He rapped on the driver's side window with a thick knuckled hand wrapped around his ticket book.

Already resigned to his ticket, Hunter rolled down the window and squinted into the beam of the trooper's flashlight. "Good evening, officer."

The light flickered away from Hunter's face, danced over the empty passenger seat. It lingered a bit over the backseat as the officer studied the random clutter of paperback books, loose sheets of random fliers, fast food bags, and other detritus from Jessica's many jaunts without caring to clean the vehicle. He'd been meaning to do it for her just to get the damn chore over with, and then she'd distracted him with other needs, just like she always did. Even dead, Jessica was making him miserable.

"Evening? Son, do you know what time it is?" His voice was smooth and slow, his words syrupy with a deep Southern drawl.

Hunter glanced at the digital clock on the dashboard. "Yes, sir. It's 1:42 AM."

"Egg-sactly. Too damn late at night to be polite, so let's get down to business. Do you know why I stopped you?"

He shook his head. Anything he said now would only

make the situation worse.

"Taillight's busted. Totally gone. No glass, bulb's cracked. What did you hit?"

He probed his cheek with his tongue as he thought about the answer. His wife's face had struck the car's bumper half a dozen times, and he guessed it might have struck the taillight hard enough to shatter the glass, but he didn't think he'd been that wild when he'd swung her limp body into the trunk. He was sure she'd only hit the car a couple more times after she went limp.

Hunter finally opted for the truth. He hadn't paid attention to the damage to the car in his hurry to get Jessica out of sight. "Didn't know it was busted. I'll get that fixed as soon as the shops open in the morning."

The trooper nodded as if he'd expected such a promise and didn't believe a word of it. "Step out of the car, and let's take a look inside your trunk."

He blinked. "I'm sorry?"

"Son, don't act as dumb as you look. Get outta the car and bring your keys with you."

"Why do you want to look in the trunk?" Surely he hadn't left her skirt hanging out, had he? He'd been hurried, but he thought he'd taken care of that properly.

The trooper took a step back to give the driver's door room to swing. He waved his hand in a "come on" gesture. Hunter turned off the Honda, but left the headlights on, and retrieved the keys from the ignition. The car's warning sound dinged but he didn't hear it. Leaving the car, he followed the cop to the back and looked where he was pointing.

A smear of some dark substance stretched from the left rear bumper, over the shattered taillights, and disappeared into the trunk. In the flashing blues it looked like an oil slick.

He looked up into the cop's face and shrugged.

The cop hawked and spat into the dirt. "Do you have anything to say for yourself before—"

Hunter fired point-blank, the muzzle flash such a contrast to the blue strobes he went blind for an instant. When he could see again the cop lay on the ground beside the gob of his own loogie. His eyes were wide open, his hat half crushed beneath his shoulder. The expression on his face was one of complete surprise, like he couldn't believe Hunter had the audacity to do anything more than take the tongue lashing he'd been about to deliver. He opened his mouth as if to say something, then his eyes rolled up and he went limp.

Eyeballing the man from this angle, Hunter judged him to be too big to fit in the trunk with his wife. He was going to have to put him in the back seat, do something about those flashing lights and that damned car, then hurry if he were going to get to her burial ground before sunup. Cursing, he put the gun in his belt and bent to grab the cop's shoulders.

A jingling sound rang out, faint at first, but growing louder and closer with each heartbeat. The jingle was quickly joined by the sound of bootheels on pavement. The heavy tread became a trio of sounds: *thump-click-jingle, thump-click-jingle.* Hunter moaned and straightened, one hand slipping behind his back to rest on the butt of the gun.

Stepping into the road, he squinted into the night. The footsteps were coming from all directions. He looked behind the cop car but couldn't see anything for the flashers strobing into his eyes. In front of his car, he thought he could see a shadow stretching across the road in the Honda's headlights, but he couldn't be sure.

The steps got closer, their volume rising way above what should have been possible. A figure appeared in the glare of the Honda's headlights: A man, tall and lean, wearing a dirty yellow duster, blue jeans, cowboy boots with spurs, a brown high-crowned Stetson hat, and a purple button-up. He held his hands up at shoulder height, as if he knew Hunter were armed and was eager to show he meant no harm. The smile revealed no fear, lighting up his face brighter than the headlight beams.

The stranger stopped about three feet from Hunter, his grin grew a little wider. He pointed at the body on the road at Hunter's feet. "Howdy. It looks like you could use a little help. Am I right, mister?" His accent sounded funny to Hunter's ears, like he was from somewhere further west, maybe Texas.

Hunter looked at the mess surrounding him. He was caught. A total stranger had just witnessed him murder a man in cold blood. All of it was a little overwhelming. His nice, simple plan had gone to hell on an express highway at full speed. Reluctantly, he took his hand away from the gun and hung his head. He might as well sit down and wait for the cop's backup to arrive.

All he'd wanted to do was escape the pain of her endless chiding. He couldn't even call it nagging because she worded things in just the right way, asking whether he could have done better, asking if he could have gotten just a little bit more out of that raise, or worked a little more overtime, or given her just a little bit more attention. Not much, mind you, she understood how busy a man he was and how hard he worked, but couldn't he have tried a little harder?

And for that matter, couldn't he have tried a little harder to get away with this crime? That was always his problem: just when he thought things were going his way, when all he had to do was keep pushing forward with his plan, he let things get out of control and lost the advantage? He was the worst kind of loser, the almost successful man with a lack of follow through. Hadn't she said that countless times, that all he needed to do was follow through a little more, pay a little more attention, and just finish the god-damned job?

The stranger was still looking at him, smiling, hands still raised. It was the most harmless, eager to please expression Hunter had ever seen on a human face. It reminded him of a puppy eager to play. That expression finally put Hunter's mind in gear, and he was able to get past the exasperation of the last couple of hours.

"Yeah," he said. "I could use some help."

The stranger clapped his hands together so loudly it reverberated across the road and off the trees like a gunshot. "Hot damn! This looks like fun. Let's get to work."

He grabbed the Honda's door handle and opened it, revealing the empty back seat. "You grab his shoulders; I'll grab his feet."

Putting actions to words, the stranger gripped the cop's ankles and pulled him across the pavement to the open door. The cop's head bounced a bit on an uneven crack, and Hunter winced. It had sounded like a melon falling onto a tile floor.

At the side of the car the stranger said, "Do you mind? It'll be easier if he goes in headfirst."

Hunter's vapor locked mind turned over and he found himself moving at the stranger's command. He bent, grunted as he hefted the cop's considerable weight, and half-climbed, half-fell with him into the Honda's back seat. The two of them scrambled around for a bit, Hunter pulling and kicking his own legs to get purchase while the stranger twisted and turned the cop's legs and shoved all at the same time. Somehow Hunter found himself sitting upright in the rear passenger side seat, his shirt untucked and bunched around his armpits, and the cop face down in his lap.

He was breathing hard and sweating. The cop weighed more than he looked, and Hunter had to admit he was out of shape himself. He took a moment to catch his breath.

The world around him suddenly darkened as the flashing lights went out. Hunter craned around his neck to see what the stranger was doing. The cop car's headlights were still on bright and all he succeeded in doing was blinding himself. Blinking to clear his vision, he reached for the door handle. Before he could grasp it, the stranger yanked it open. He pulled Hunter out of the car by a handful of his shirt. Hunter stumbled when the stranger let him go and found himself on his knees in the soft shoulder, dampness instantly soaking through his jeans. He'd caught himself by his hands and now they were covered in mud up to his wrists.

The stranger tossed the cop's hat on top of him, then slammed the door. The hollow thump of the cop's head banging against the inside of the door seemed to echo through the night like the stranger's clap.

He pulled Hunter to his feet and helped brush off his clothes, though he was careful not to touch Hunter's muddied hands. "I hope you don't mind, but I didn't think the party bars were helping us any. I turned 'em off and checked the ignition. Keys are there. What do you say we get that cop car off the road and out of the way? I think it'll look mighty good down in that ditch over there." He jerked his thumb indicating the soft shoulder on the other side of the road.

Wiping his hands on his pants, he tried to wrap his brain around the suggestion. "Shouldn't we just leave it where it is? It'll take less time. Or better yet, take it with us?"

The stranger's laugh was heartfelt and loud, a guffaw of comical proportions. "Take it with us, boy? Aren't you a hoot? No. This is the modern era. That thing's got GPS tracking and probably an auto kill switch. We'd no sooner get half a mile down the road before we'd have to do this anyway. Nope. It's better to get the job done now; that way we can finish your real business all the sooner."

Hunter didn't know why he was taking advice from this guy, but something in the back of his mind told him this was a good idea. Reluctantly, he climbed into the driver's seat of the cruiser, which was idling quietly, and put the car into gear. His first plan was to drive the car off this side of the road, into the woods beyond, but then he remembered the mud he'd already fallen in. It was too wet there. The other side, however, was sandier, and the trees were closer. Plus, the short drive across the road would give him enough momentum to ensure the car got deeper into the trees.

Some part of him knew this was a bad idea, but he couldn't stop himself. He turned the steering wheel and pressed the gas, probably harder than he needed, then shot across the road.

The cop car bounced hard and the wheel jerked in his hands. He couldn't keep the wheels straight, and that probably saved him from a hell of a headache and a broken nose. The car popped off the road like a Hot Wheels off a jump ramp and skidded in the mud on the other side. The headlights illuminated trees that suddenly seemed way too close for comfort, but Hunter's erratic steering sent him safely between two trees that scraped paint off the car's sides.

He pressed both feet to the brake and squeezed the wheel hard and his eyes shut. The car slid forward another six feet before it came to a stop, the front end crumpling slightly as it struck the trunk of another tree. The air bag didn't explode from the steering column and he didn't slam his face into it, either.

Hunter climbed from the cop car and rested his head on the cool metal of the roof. Taking deep breaths, he wondered what the hell he was doing. He'd just killed a cop, after killing his wife. His plan had been simple, and now it was going straight to hell.

"Hey," came the cheery, confident voice on the road. "You okay?"

Who was that asshole? Where had he come from? And why was he helping Hunter do such a horrible thing? Was he hoping he could blackmail him? Hunter didn't have much, and he was about to lose his only means of transporting himself out of the swamps.

"We need to go, now," said the happy stranger. "The

longer you're down there, the closer we're getting to sunlight."

Hunter glanced up at the sky. What he could see through the trees was still pitch black, barely a star visible, and no moon, but the stranger was right. He needed to get this over with quickly. Using the stranger's offered hand for leverage, he climbed out of the ditch and staggered to the Honda's driver's seat.

"You look beat," said the stranger. "I'd offer to drive, but I don't know where you want to…" he looked over his shoulder at the cop lying across the back seat.

Hunter shook his head. "I'll drive." He put the Honda in gear.

The dashboard clock read 2:15 AM. God, it seemed he'd been up all night. The cop's arrival made everything feel like it was moving way too fast. He drove into the night, glanced at his new partner in crime.

The stranger started playing with the radio. At first, he found nothing the Honda's shitty radio could tune in. The static blared out of a busted speaker, surprising Hunter enough to send the steering wheel spinning wildly before he regained control. Hunter was silently cursing the radio, the stranger, and life in general when the sounds of country music came in loud and clear, vibrating the busted speaker with an annoying static-hiss.

Hunter gritted his teeth but said nothing. They were close to his destination.

The stranger sang along to "Bad Moon Rising" at the top of his lungs. What he lacked singing talent he made up for in exuberance.

"At least one of us is having fun," Hunter mumbled.

Somehow, the stranger heard him and stopped singing. "You aren't having fun? Come on, this is an adventure. When was the last time you tried doing something like this?" He pointed in the back of the car with a thumb.

Hunter glanced into the rear-view mirror and jerked the steering wheel in surprise.

The sudden movement sent the car into the wrong lane, which Hunter tried correcting by jerking the wheel in the opposite direction. He ended up on the shoulder on the right side of the road, all of them bouncing over the rough rock and soft mud. The bouncing caused the gun in the cop's hand to go off, spiderwebbing the windshield from the inside.

Hunter's right ear was suddenly filled with an incredible loud ringing. He slammed both feet onto the brakes and pressed his hands to his ears, not caring where the car ended up. All he wanted to do was end this horrible night.

Instead of stopping, the sudden shift in momentum and the softness of the shoulder sent the car rolling and sliding onto its side, then its roof.

The car stopped moving. Hunter found himself dangling upside down, held in place by the safety harness. The cop was laying on the ceiling, his head bent at an awkward-looking angle. His gun was still held loosely in his hand, a curl of smoke drifting toward Hunter. The stranger was nowhere to be seen.

Cursing, Hunter released the seat belt catch and fell hard onto the corpse of the cop. It took him several tries before he was able to get the door open and crawl out. He was once again on his hands and knees in Alabama mud.

Once more standing, he looked around in search of the stranger. At first there was nothing, then he heard the *scratch-hiss* of a match being lit. The stranger was standing against the back of the car, his head inches from the still-spinning rear tire, lighting a cigarette. The match smelled strongly of sulfur, and when he exhaled blue smoke wafted into Hunter's face. He coughed and waved a hand in front of his face.

"What the ever-loving fuck, man? You knew he was coming to and didn't warn me?"

Blue smoke flowed from his mouth and nostrils as he spoke. "I thought you'd heard him moving around. Figured you had a plan."

"A plan?" Hunter couldn't believe his ear. "A plan? My plan was to bury my wife in a place I've had in mind for her for a long time. Plan B was to kill the cop and finish plan A, then get the hell out of Dodge. My plan has been fucked from the beginning."

He wanted to punch the stranger in the face, to make him swallow that cigarette and watch him squirm as it burned its way down. The night was still working against him, and he knew it. He couldn't get into a fight or he'd still be on the side of the road when the sun rose.

As if to hurry him on along once more, the bottom dropped out from beneath Jessica.

In the course of the roll the lock of the Honda's trunk must've broken. The lid popped open, dropping the huge, elongated joint-shape of his now-deceased wife unceremoniously on the muddy shoulder. Instead of a thud, there was only a squelch as she landed headfirst.

Hunter wanted to curse but he couldn't find any words. None of the profanities he knew fit a situation as absurd as this.

The stranger took a final drag on his cigarette and tossed the butt to the ground beside Jessica. "You get her. I'll take care of the cop. Let's get trucking."

"Trucking? Where?"

"If you were heading where I think you were heading, that's no place to bury an ex-loved one, much less the body of a cop you don't want to be found. I know a better place, and it's not a far walk from here." He bent and reached a hand into the upturned car. When he straightened, he held the cop's gun and checked that it was loaded with practiced ease. "Gotta watch for gators," he said as he stuck the gun into the back of his belt. Once more he entered the car and pulled the cop out with quick ease.

He was stronger than he looked, Hunter decided. Hunter also didn't like him holding the cop's gun, but he had his own, so he guessed they were even.

Not knowing what else to do, he struggled through the act of getting Jessica up and over his shoulders in a fireman's carry. The stranger simply tossed the big cop over one shoulder like he weighed nothing.

"Let's go," said the stranger. He led them into the woods on the opposite side of the road. Hunter looked back once at the hulking shape of his overturned Honda and just knew he was going to regret this.

Once inside the tree line, Hunter lost his bearings. He was following the steady stream of inane chatter by the stranger, his eyes focused on the gun at the small of his back. The voice was his guide while his mind wandered.

He was going to have to kill this stranger. It didn't matter how helpful he was, or how he might promise to keep Hunter's secrets. What mattered was that he'd seen Hunter's face, seen him kill a cop, and would soon know where the bodies were buried. He was a liability that couldn't be allowed to continue.

Even as he thought this, the roar of an engine rent the night air. Beneath the weight of his wife and the colossal fuck-up that had become his life, Hunter's shoulders sagged. Wherever they were, they were not alone.

"Don't you worry about that," said the stranger over his shoulder. He never stopped moving as he spoke, and Hunter had to increase his pace to hear. "That's just some alligator poachers. You'll hear some gunfire soon, I expect. But that just means they'll be too busy to pay much attention to us."

He should get out of here. This whole situation had gone completely out of control. If he turned himself in, maybe they would be lenient. He'd known murderers to get only a few years in prison before being let go. They were still total shitheels, but at least they were free. He was about to drop his wife's corpse and turn to run back to the road, when he remembered the cop he'd killed. Well, the cop he'd at least shot, with the same gun he'd used to kill his wife. Their deaths were connected, and he was the only common denominator. If he confessed to one murder, he'd be confessing to both. And maybe more if he didn't do something about this helpful stranger.

"Here we are," the stranger announced. "Best place in Bayou La Batre to hide a body."

Hunter stopped short of running into the stranger's back. In front of them was a small hut, barely big enough for a man to stand upright in. Behind the hut was a dock leading into a watery marsh. Scattered across the dock were several lengths of rope for tying boats. Hunter didn't know whether to be glad or dismayed no boats were at the dock.

"What? Are we gonna just dump 'em here?"

The stranger shook his head and pointed to the right.

Hunter realized the engine they'd heard was attached to an airboat. Now, that airboat was approaching the dock at some speed.

"Jesus Christ," Hunter said. "You can't be serious. Another witness?"

"Don't worry about him. He can't speak. And he don't get to town too often. He'll keep it secret."

"No. This is too much. I appreciate the help, but I can't do this. Let's just drop them here and go our separate ways. The alligators'll take care of the corpses."

The stranger turned, his wide smile still in place, though it looked a little unnatural in the waning starlight. "Don't give up on me now, boy. We've come too far together for either of us to bail. Unless, of course, you want to make it worth my while."

Boy. He hated that word. He'd even hated it when he was a kid. It was always used in belittling terms. Get over here, boy. Do as you're told, boy. Boy, don't make me repeat myself. It raised in Hunter an anger he hadn't felt since he'd grown up and left home. He wasn't a boy now, and he hadn't been one for a long time.

The anger quelled all his fears regarding the current situation. Everything leading up to now meant nothing. All that mattered was putting this smiling, arrogant stranger in his place.

Hunter shrugged Jessica off his shoulders and approached the stranger. In two strides he was in the man's space. Somehow the stranger had managed to light a cigarette while they'd been marching through the marsh, and Hunter thrust his face through a floating halo of blue smoke.

"Listen here, buddy. I don't know who you are, and I appreciate your help, but don't call me 'boy.' You ain't no better than me, and you certainly aren't my elder. I'm not your 'boy.' You got that?"

The roar of the airboat quieted as the driver cut the engine and glided to the dock.

The stranger held up one hand in a sign of surrender, while the other kept the cop's body in place. "Hey, say no more. But we're running out of night and we still need to get these bodies a little closer to their graves. Do you want to fight me over a chip on your shoulder or just get a little closer to home, Scot free?" As he spoke, more smoke spilled from his mouth and nostrils. His breath blew it straight into Hunter's face.

Stepping back, Hunter coughed and turned away. The sulfurous stench was almost overpowering. What kind of cigarettes was this man smoking?

His gaze fell on the bundle that had been his wife earlier tonight. Christ. He didn't need to pick a fight. He just needed to get home.

His shoulders slumped with the realization that he needed this man no matter how much he didn't like it. Hunter heaved a resigned sigh. "I'd give anything for this night to just end. What's a man got to do just to hide a body in peace?"

The stranger took the cigarette from his lips and blew another cloud. His tongue roamed inside his mouth. "Don't tell me—" he sucked his teeth, "—you're giving up?" He spat on the ground at Hunter's feet. "The fun's just startin'," he drawled.

"Fun? You think this is fun? I killed my wife. I killed a cop. And I've let the weirdest man I've ever met drag me to the devil knows where in an Alabama swamp."

The stranger shrugged and the cop bounced on his shoulder. "Of course. I've known where I was going all along. You were the one guessing."

Hunter faced the stranger, glaring daggers at him.

"Who the hell are you?"

Grinning, the stranger dropped the cop with a hefty thud, and spread his hands wide in a give-us-a-hug gesture. "I thought you'd never ask. Damn, you're a dense boy."

"Don't call me—" Hunter began to say, but the stranger was suddenly in his face, more smoke billowing from his nostril, great gouts of blue smoke that had heat and force impossible for a simple cigarette.

"—boy?' Is that what you were going to say. Don't call you boy? Well, let me tell you something, to me, you are a boy, and I'll call you whatever I feel like. You see, I've got plans for you, boy, and thanks to you, I have all the leverage I need to make the rest of your life hell."

Hunter gaped at the stranger. Everything he'd said was completely right. He'd already known he was going to have to kill the stranger if he wanted to get away from tonight even close to clean, but now the idiot had actually confessed he wanted to hold Hunter's life hostage? No way. Not when he'd been so close to giving himself the freedom he'd so desired. With Jessica out of the way, there was nothing stopping him from doing whatever he wanted, except this asshole now. Fuck it. He wasn't going to deal with this shit any longer.

He yanked the gun from his waistband and whipped it around. He didn't aim. He didn't think. He just fired as soon as the gun was pointed in the stranger's general direction.

The explosion was deafening in the dark. The muzzle flash blinded him. The world froze. Hunter knew he'd fucked up royally.

A moonbeam spotlighted the stranger. His illuminated frame seemed larger somehow, broader, more real than he'd been since Hunter had first seen him in the beams of his car's headlights.

Surprised, the stranger stumbled back a few steps, his hands covering his belly, the smile still on his face, the cigarette hanging from his lower lip. They both looked at his hands, at the blood spilling between them, soaking his jeans and dripping to the ground.

The stranger's grin widened, revealing bloody teeth. He spat the cigarette away, then pulled his hands away from his stomach. The blood flowed faster, almost gushing from the bullet wound.

Then he laughed. It was loud and long, filled with great guffaws of true mirth. As his body convulsed, the blood spurted faster, jettisoning from him. But when he threw his head back and laughed even harder, things started getting weirder.

As Hunter watched, the blood flow first slowed to a trickle, then stopped, and finally reversed. Everything that had fallen from the stranger rolled up his pants from the ground and returned to his body, like rewound video.

"About damn time, Hunter. I was beginning to think you didn't have it in you."

Hunter raised his eyes from the closed hole and clean clothes to look into the face of the madman he'd been traveling with. His mouth moved, but no sound came out. He wanted to ask questions. He wanted to curse. He wanted to run screaming into the swamp. Instead, he stared dumbly into the eyes of a monster.

The stranger's eyes were brilliant in the reflected moonlight, gas-blue flames burning twin paths down to Hunter's soul. His hand held the gun forward still aimed in the stranger's general direction, but he'd forgotten it existed. His feet wouldn't move. His body wouldn't respond. He found it hard to breathe under the force of that gaze.

"I was afraid I'd actually have to help you bury the bodies before you took a shot at me." The stranger reached out and took the gun from Hunter's limp fingers. "You have the patience of a saint, Hunter." He glanced at Jessica's form on the mud. "Is that why it took so long for you to kill her? Or were you afraid of repercussions? Didn't quite know how you were going to do it? Or was it a crime of passion, unplanned and violent?"

He didn't seem to really want an answer, his questions came so fast. Not that Hunter could have spoken. His tongue felt glued to the roof of his mouth.

Pacing around Hunter and the corpses, the stranger continued to speak. "I ask these questions because I don't know you very well, Hunter. You weren't on my radar, so to speak. Not until you shot the cop. Even though you didn't kill him, you wanted to. You planned to. And you executed the plan to the best of your abilities on the spur of the moment, with conviction. Do you know why?"

"It wa— was the... right thing to do at the time."

The stranger stopped, his head cocked to one side, which tilted his smile at an unpleasant angle. "Yes. It was the right thing to do at the time. Good answer. You have good instincts. I like that. I can put you to good use."

"Put... me... to good use?" Hunter asked. "Wh—" his voice faltered. Licking his lips, he tried again. "What are you talking about?"

"You, Hunter. I'm talking about your future. I need emissaries in this world, people I can trust to be themselves and therefore be what I need. Eyes and ears. Recruiters. Little demons on the shoulder of society. See, everyone blames me for all the ills in their lives, and while I wish I could take credit, I'm not that powerful. Never have been. Legends have oversold my omniscience. You, however, are going to help make that sales pitch believable."

The anger arose again, sending warmth through his

limbs and unlocking his jaw. "To hell with that. I'm nobody's puppet." He tried aiming his gun at the stranger once more in threat, then realized he wasn't holding it anymore.

Out of cards, he tried talking. Talking had never been his strong suit.

"You and your buddy go your way, and I'll go mine. I'll finish up here and you can just leave me alone."

The stranger shook his head. "No. No, that's not how any of this works. If you had just accepted my help and let us go our separate ways... I might not have seen your potential. Instead, you decided to draw on me, to shoot me, and now I think I can make you an offer you won't want to refuse."

"You're crazy," Hunter said. It sounded lame even to his ears against the stranger's matter-of-fact way of speaking.

His smile never faltering, the stranger stepped closer to Hunter. "Come now, surely it doesn't sound that far-fetched," he said. The gun was in the front of his pants' waistband, but even as Hunter thought of snatching it back, the stranger placed his hands on Hunter's temples and held his face in a grip he had no hope of breaking. Their eyes met and Hunter saw infinity for the first time in his life.

Hunter's life flashed before his mind's eyes, superimposed over the visage of the stranger. Every curse word he'd ever uttered or shouted in rage and fury. Every little meanness he'd done to anyone in his life, even acts he didn't remember for their insignificance floated to the forefront. Every time he'd had hurt someone for his own pleasure. Every time he'd helped a friend commit a crime, from theft, to their one-armed robbery, and to the murder of a drug dealer who'd tried to cheat them.

Everything he'd done, no matter how petty or insignificant was there, and Hunter couldn't hide from it. His eyes were locked on the abyss in the stranger's face, and his horrible life looked back.

The visions ended when the stranger released his head. Hunter stumbled backwards, entangled his feet with Jessica, and fell hard, landing flat on his back. The breath was knocked out of him, and all he could see were the stars in the sky.

Was he really that big of a shit to people? What kind of man had he become?

"I've known you for a long time, Hunter. It's why you never meant too much to me. But tonight, you've proven you have instincts. Instincts like that, mixed with your patience, I can use. I'm not crazy, and neither are you. For you, insanity would be a blessing. I'm not known for bestowing blessings on humans." He mused, "Rarely blessings."

The stranger yanked Hunter to his feet and patted his clothes to wipe the mud off. All he succeeded in doing was smearing the mess around and making Hunter feel cold.

"None of that now. No time for remorse. You had your shot and you've moved beyond it. I only showed you that stuff to remind you why you and I are perfect together." He wrapped his arm around Hunter's shoulders. "Let's take a look at your future without me." The stranger wrapped a hand around the back of Hunter's head and squeezed.

Hunter's eyes shot open as a brilliant lance of pain shot through his brain. Across the white light he saw more pictures, of getting back to the highway only to be surrounded by cops investigating the overturned car. He saw himself being arrested, sitting in jail in an orange jumpsuit, a trial that seemed incredibly short, and more jail time. He sat in a corner, staring at people bigger and meaner and angrier at the system than he was. He saw fights, blood, and violence of a nature he'd only thought about or seen in movies. He was the victim of a gang rape. He was the victim of petty meannesses like he'd perpetrated his whole life. He saw the shiv that opened his belly and spilled his guts on to the concrete floor of a gray prison mess hall.

He found himself on his knees, holding his stomach and gasping for air.

"That's not very pleasant. But it is *your* future. You've lived a petty and meaningless life, Hunter. But you have potential. You're not stupid, just lazy. I think we can overcome that."

Hunter gasped from his kneeling position. "Are you the Devil?"

"Such an interesting and limiting question. Do you believe in God?"

"I was raised Baptist."

"That isn't the same thing. Do you believe in God?"

"No."

"Then I'm not the Devil, but I am something more than you understand. Can we agree on that?"

"Yes."

"Good." The stranger yanked Hunter to his feet by the scruff of his neck. "That's settled. How do you want to get started? Do you want me to give you instructions and leave you to clean up your own mess? That would be poetic, wouldn't it? Like the opening of a TV series or a movie. Then you spend months wondering if I'm serious and little things keep reminding you of me, until ultimately, I force you to do my bidding. I do love such games, but no. I think we can work together better than that."

"There are certain things beginning to happen in this world, Hunter. Things that I cannot begin to explain to you in your current condition. But you can have a part in them, a place in the world more worthwhile than you can ever imagine, if you're willing to step beyond your comfort zone and let yourself be more. Surely you can feel it. That's why you killed Jessica, isn't it? You knew there was more out there than you were experiencing. You felt it as surely as you felt the cop had to die."

The stranger jerked Hunter around to meet his gaze

once more. The gaslight blue flames flickered in the moonlight. He no longer saw himself in them.

"How can we come to a deal that won't require me punishing you like an errant schoolboy?"

The fire in those eyes did it. The visions he'd seen undid him. The future he'd experienced scared him. He would not have to face any of that again so long as he worked with this being. He knew that as well as he knew his name.

"What kind of deal?"

"Now we're talking. A simple deal, but one I think you'll appreciate. You work for me, and you'll never want for anything again. Money when you need it. Pleasures when you want them. Those futures you saw will never happen. All you have to do is say yes, and everything will fall into place. What do you say?"

He'd never been good with money, especially with Jessica around. Every penny he earned seemed to disappear before he had a chance to enjoy it or plan with it. Money was always something he needed and never seemed to have. But was that the only reason the deal was tempting?

Hunter decided it wasn't. The pleasures, whatever they might be, sounded good, but they were icing on the cake. Even before he'd met this man he'd known, deep down, that he was going to die miserable and hopeless. He'd intended to go home and get drunk as soon as he finished tonight's chores. Escape was what he desired more than anything else.

"Money," he said, recounting the prizes. "Pleasure. What I saw won't happen. And one more thing."

The stranger raised an eyebrow. The corner of his mouth twitched.

"I never want to come to Alabama again."

He tilted his head to the side, sucked his teeth. "You drive a hard bargain, Hunter. I never make promises I can't keep, but I like you. Agreed. It'll be a very long time before you have to set foot in this state again, if you join me."

Hunter thought it over once more, looked at the bodies of the cop and his wife. They meant nothing to him, he realized. All that mattered was making good his own escape, and his own future.

Resolved, he stuck out his hand. "You've got a deal, stranger."

The stranger smiled again. Hunter realized this man had countless smiles in his repertoire. This one was wide and welcoming, almost warm. This one told Hunter he'd made the right decision.

They shook hands. The stranger's skin was hot and clammy. He clamped his fingers around Hunter's palm and the fingers seemed to grow longer, wrapping completely around him. Hunter couldn't pull his hand from the grip. Heat shot up his arm and engulfed his skull, crossed his chest and curled around his heart. His eyes felt like they were melting from the heat in his brain. He couldn't breathe. He couldn't scream in pain. He could only endure an eternity until he could stand no longer.

He collapsed around the glowing ember that had been his heart. Darkness flowed over him.

♉

He opened his eyes to find he was in a field of tall grass. The angle of the sun told him it was early morning, and he could see dew frozen on the stalks. He sat up, ice cracking on clean camouflage fatigues. The world was unfamiliar but comforting all the same.

The Alabama swamp was no longer around him. He didn't know exactly where he was, and he didn't care. This was proof he'd made the right decision.

The sound of gunfire off in the distance drew him to his feet. It was the sound of a .30-.30, one he'd recognize anywhere. Someone was out hunting, and even as he sought the source of the sound, knowledge came to him.

The victim of the gunfire wasn't an animal. It was human, and the person responsible was in dire need of guidance.

Hunter smiled and felt his face stretch in a way it never had before. He felt the shape of his lips with his fingers. He felt a stranger in his own skin. He also felt very, very good.

Smiling wider, and with a spring in his step he'd not known since childhood, Hunter followed the echoes of the gunshot.

ABOUT THE AUTHOR

DARYL MARCUS specializes in writing horror, sci-fi, and crime fiction, often mixing the genres into something he thinks is more fun and challenging. His passion lies in creating worlds and characters to explore concepts and answer the great "what if" questions. When he's not writing or working in IT security, he spends as much time with his wife exploring various worlds through travel, reading, and video games.

His work can be found in such tomes as *Blood and Blasphemy* by Hellbound Books and *Tales from the Grinning Skull* from the Grinning Skull press.

GIVE ME YOUR SOUL AND I'LL GIVE YOU A PEPPERONI

Evan Purcell

I was nervous about third grade (mostly because of fractions), but Miss Hanover was pretty great. She taught us lots of stuff that wasn't fractions, like English and drawing.

We even sang a song together every morning. It was called the "Wake Up! Wake Up!" song and it was real easy. I really liked school, and I liked learning things.

And then I met the new girl. Sara.

Sara was shorter than me, but she had bigger eyes. Dark eyes. She always smiled, and you could see her smile in those big, dark eyes. Right away, I didn't like her.

She didn't talk a lot, not on that first day, but I saw her eat lunch with Tori and Anthony, the twins. They both seemed to like her a lot. They seemed to trust her. She even peeled off the pepperonis from her pizza and gave them to Anthony.

He was kinda fat.

When we did arts and crafts that afternoon, I traded places with Jennifer B. so I could sit next to Anthony. I wanted to talk to him.

"Hey," I said. We were both drawing elephants. He was concentrating on his elephant, so he didn't even hear me. "Hey!" I said again.

He smiled, and his breath smelled like pizza.

"You ate lunch with the new girl, right?"

"Yes," he said. "Sara. She was real nice. She even sold me her pepperoni."

"Sold?"

"Yeah. She's real funny. I asked if I could have them, but she said she'd only give them to me if I gave her my soul."

"Your soul," I said.

"Yeah. She's real funny."

I didn't say anything else to Anthony. He was too busy with his elephant, and I was too busy thinking about stuff.

Anthony sold his soul.

I knew about souls because of Nana Weiss. She was really religious. Before she died, she went to church three times a week and whenever anything bad happened, she mumbled religious words and did these hand gestures over her chest.

She talked about souls a lot. And salvation. And a bunch of other scary things. Souls were important, and if you didn't have a soul, you'd go to the Devil.

Anthony probably didn't understand what he did, buying pepperonis and stuff. He probably didn't realize that he was tricked.

But I didn't say anything. Not then. I just watched him

as he finished his elephant. It was a happy elephant. It was orange.

♉

At dinner that night, I asked Dad about souls. It was just the two of us, eating beef noodles and mashed potatoes. Mama was always better at cooking. I missed her a lot.

Dad asked me about my day, about any new songs that I learned. He liked when I talked about singing stuff. I didn't answer him, though. Instead, I asked, "Dad, what's a soul?"

He looked at me real serious and fake-smiled. I hated when he fake-smiled. He said, "Rosie, is this about Mama?"

But it wasn't about Mama. It was about Sara, and Anthony, and pepperonis. "No," I said. "I just wanna know."

"A soul is like a spirit," he said. "It's what goes up to heaven after you die."

"Does everyone have a soul?" I asked.

"Yes."

"Can you lose your soul?"

"Honey, finish your noodles."

If Mama was still alive, she wouldn't fake-smile at me. She'd tell me everything I needed to know. Dad made me angry sometimes.

♉

The next day at school, I saw that Sara was making a lot of friends. She talked a lot, too. At recess, she played tetherball with Wendy and Evan, who were the two coolest kids in our grade. Everyone thought she was real fun.

I checked out the jump rope from Miss Hanover, but no one wanted to play with me. Not even Billy M., and he was the poor kid.

In the afternoon, we learned about dinosaurs. Miss Hanover drew a T. rex on the board, and it was real neat. It had little arms and big teeth. She talked about how dinosaurs lived a long, long time ago, before there were even people.

I liked learning about dinosaurs, until Sara raised her hand and asked, "Why did all the dinosaurs die?"

Miss Hanover answered, "No one really knows. But it's good that they did, because otherwise there'd be big, scary T. rexes running around the city."

Sara still didn't lower her hand. She said, "But if they all died mysteriously, isn't it possible that the same thing could happen to people?"

For the first time ever, Miss Hanover didn't have an answer. She fake-smiled, just like Dad. And a lot of the other kids whispered to each other.

After that, Sara was the most popular girl in class. From then on, she was the girl who knew things that Miss Hanover didn't. She was the girl with secret ideas.

♉

The next day, Sara sat on the monkey bars while a whole line of kids waited to talk with her. They looked so excited, like they were waiting for Santa's lap. I pushed my way through them.

"Sara," I said. "My name's Rosie. I need to talk to you."

I think she could tell from my expression that I wasn't one of the other kids. I wasn't going to ask for a pint of ice cream or something.

She snapped her fingers once—loudly—and told the other kids to come back during the next recess. Then she gestured for me to sit next to her. I did.

I was a little scared.

Sara's eyes were so dark, I could see my face reflected in their blackness. Other than that, she looked real normal. Her t-shirt had SpongeBob on it.

"What are you doing?" I asked.

"What do you mean?" She used this fake, baby doll voice. Her dark eyes shined in the sun.

"I mean, I know you're buying souls. And I just want to find out why."

She giggled. She sounded like a horror movie. "Me? Buying souls?"

"If you don't want to admit it, I could just go ask Anthony. Or Rick. Or any of your other customers."

Sara stopped giggling. With the tip of her foot, she drew a line in the dirt, a line that separated us. "I'm just playing a game. That's all. Just a game."

But I knew it was more than a game.

"Do you need anything?" she asked. "A new bicycle, perhaps? How about a new mom?"

I didn't answer her, because I didn't trust the words that would come out of my mouth. Sara was dangerous. She could twist my words, and if I said the wrong thing… then she'd have me.

I walked away. I had to.

As I left, I heard Sara shout out to Evan, "Hey. Come here a second. I have an offer for you."

That was when I was absolutely, 100% certain. Sara was the Devil. She was everything that Nana Weiss had warned me about. She was going to take everyone's souls, unless I did something to stop her.

I ate lunch with Billy M., who was really poor and sometimes had dirty shirts. He always got in a lot of accidents, but never at school. Always on the weekend. I think his dad was mean to him.

At lunchtime, I told Billy M. everything about Sara, but he didn't believe me. He said there was no place in the world for flights of fancy, but I didn't know what that meant. I think he copied those words from somewhere.

♉

Two days passed. During those two days, I watched as one-by-one, the other kids sold their souls to Sara. I tried to warn people, but I couldn't be too obvious about it. So I said little things—tiny, little things—about Sara lying, about unfair deals, about a bunch of stuff. But no one understood me.

Finally, at recess, Wendy came up to me and told me to stop saying mean things about Sara. Wendy was never my friend, but she always seemed nice to me. She was smart, too. I couldn't believe that she would blindly trust Sara like that.

"You don't understand," I told her. "Sara is tricking us. She's stealing our souls, and giving us stupid little things like—"

"My parents are back together," Wendy said.

"What?"

"My parents were getting a divorce, and now they're not. Sara did that. It wasn't a trick."

Behind me, a group of kids burst into screams and applause. I spun around and saw Evan jump through the air and dunk a basketball. He jumped so high, it looked wrong. Unnatural.

"Sara did that, too," Wendy whispered. "Evan asked to be better at sports, and now…"

Evan let go of the hoop and landed back on the ground. Everyone clapped.

"That's cool," I said, "but it's still not right. Sara is using us."

"I can't talk to you right now," Wendy said, and she walked away.

I was helpless. I thought I could convince people through logic and reason, but no one would listen. Everyone was blinded by slam dunks and free bicycles. Whatever game this was, Sara was winning.

I saw Miss Hanover standing at the edge of the basketball court. She was clapping like the rest of them. She was an adult. She was the smartest adult I knew. She'd understand.

"Miss Hanover?"

It was weird. It was like she pretended not to see me.

"Miss Hanover," I said again. "Can we talk?"

"Sure."

"There's something wrong with Sara," I said. It wasn't the best way to start my explanation, but it would have to do. Once Miss Hanover hears me out…

"Young lady!" she said.

"Just give me a second. I'll explain everything."

"I'm going to stop you right there," she said. Her eyebrows looked mad.

"But why?" I asked.

Miss Hanover was very serious. Her mouth got small. She said, "I think you're being a little mean to the new girl. It's okay to feel jealous sometimes, but…"

"No, I'm not…" But there was nothing I could say. Miss Hanover didn't believe me, she would never believe me, and arguing would only make things worse.

The crowd once again burst into applause. I guess Evan did something cool.

"Sorry," I mumbled.

"Don't apologize to me," Miss Hanover said. She nodded her head toward the edge of the playground. I turned and saw Sara dangling from the monkey bars. Alone. I guess she told the other kids to go and watch Evan play. Her black hair hid most of her face.

"You want me to…"

"Go over there," Miss Hanover said. "Talk to her. She could use a friend."

Oh God.

I did not want to talk to Sara. She was dangerous, tricky. If I said the wrong thing…

"Go," Miss Hanover urged. I never thought her voice sounded mean before.

I trudged across the playground. I wanted to turn back, to look once more at Miss Hanover. That way, if I was murdered, she'd always have that image of my face in her brain, and she could think about my face and feel guilty. I didn't look back, though. I needed to be strong.

The monkey bars shined in the sun.

"Why, hello there. It's so nice to see you, Rosie." She pretended like I was an old friend, or a cousin she hadn't seen in a long time. I almost expected a hug.

"Hello."

She jumped off the monkey bars perfectly. Like an acrobat. Her hair was wild. "I wanted to let you know," she said, "that my game is going extremely well. I think I'm winning."

"Your game…"

"My game," she said. "Things have been easier than I thought."

My hands balled into fists. I'd never fought anyone before—not even my older cousin Gretchen when she flicked my nose and ran away. But right then, I wanted to hit her. I wanted to…

God.

I didn't know what I wanted. I just wanted to do something.

"I'm going to stop you," I said.

"Oh, Rosie," she said, and her voice was cold. "I hope you know this is all pretend. This game. None of it's real."

And she giggled. She waited for me to argue, but I didn't. I couldn't. So she added, "Come on. Hang upside-down with me. It'll make you feel woozy."

Miss Hanover was watching, so I did. I thought about

falling and breaking my neck and blaming it on Sara, but that would've been difficult.

♉

That night, I knew I had to talk to my dad. It didn't matter if it was one of his sad nights. It didn't matter if he tried not to listen. I would force him to hear me. And then he'd give me all the answers I needed. And then everything would be okay and Sara would be gone forever.

So before dinner, I waited for him in the living room.

He saw my serious face. "What's wrong, honey?"

"Dad," I said. "I need you to tell me about souls again." It wasn't a question.

He breathed real loud, like he was expecting me to ask that question. Then he sat down on the couch and patted his knee. I sat down on his knee.

"Honey," he said. "Your Mama is in a better place. She was really sick. You saw how sick she was. And now, she's up in Heaven with Nana Weiss and Comet."

"Dad," I said again. "I need you to tell me about souls."

"You know what souls are, Rosie."

"Yeah, but can you sell your soul?"

He flinched. He looked like that time bird poop dropped onto his cheek. "I…"

"Dad, I know about the Devil. Nana Weiss told me all about the Devil. I just wanna know, can you sell your soul?"

"Okay," he said. "Listen. Some people believe that the Devil is a real person walking around the Earth. But I don't. I think…"

"But if he is… a real person, what would he do?"

Dad breathed again. I think I kept surprising him. "If the Devil were real… Some people believe that he'd trick people into selling their souls. He'd offer them little things, stupid things, in exchange for their souls. And the people would be happy, at least for a little while. But that kind of happiness would fade really quickly, and then they'd be damned."

I wasn't sure what damned was, but I remember hearing it before. I thought it was a bad word.

"Is that the only way to lose your soul?" I asked.

"Not really," he said. "If people do bad things, really bad things like murder and violence, then they'd lose their souls."

"So if the Devil tricked you into doing something bad, then he wouldn't need to buy your soul? He'd already have it?"

"Rosie, I think that's enough questions for tonight." He pointed upstairs to my bedroom. Sleep time.

But I still had one question left. The most important question. I needed to know how to stop the Devil.

"Please, Dad. Just…"

"Upstairs," he said.

I loved Daddy so much, but sometimes he couldn't understand things. Not like Mama could.

If I was gonna stop Sara, I'd have to do it without his help.

♉

The next day at school, I followed Sara around. I saw her talking with Jessica at recess. Then with Ben. Then with Billy M. I wasn't sure, but I thought those were the last three kids who still had their souls.

Except me. I would never sell my soul.

Then, when school was over, I didn't get on the bus. Instead, I followed Sara as she walked home. When she got to the street, she turned left, which was where the poor houses were. I stayed far enough away, so she wouldn't see me.

When she got to the first row of houses, she kept

walking. Then she passed the next row. And the next. Pretty soon, there were no houses left. Just empty fields.

And the cemetery.

Sara walked right into the cemetery. I realized with a gulp that this was her home.

I hadn't been there since Mama's funeral, but everything looked exactly the same. The gate was an Addams Family gate, and the grass was so perfect that it looked fake. Some of the graves were small, and some were big, and some were giant angel statues. I always thought that was unfair. It was like we were ranking our dead people by how important they were.

Mama got a nice black stone with her face cut into the top part.

I walked real quiet and hid behind a tree. Sara was sitting Indian-style in front of a big gargoyle statue. She rocked back and forth and chanted.

I started getting scared. Her words weren't in English.

Then she wasn't chanting anymore. She was talking, talking in that weird, old language. And even though I couldn't hear anyone else, it seemed like someone was talking back to her. She was real casual. It reminded me of every afternoon, when I tell Dad about my day.

For about ten minutes, she chatted in that other language. Sometimes she laughed. Sometimes she paused, listening to the other voice that I couldn't hear. When she was finished, she kissed the gargoyle statue.

I flattened my body against the tree. I knew that if Sara saw me, something very bad would happen.

But she didn't see me. Instead, she stole a rose from one of the nearest graves and slid it into her hair. Then she walked deeper into the cemetery, and I didn't follow.

I should've done something while I was there. I should've talked with her, or called for help, or found a camera and taken her picture. But I was scared. I was real scared. So before she could tell that I was watching, I left.

I walked back home. And the entire walk, my hands

were shaky and I think I was crying.

Dad didn't hear me come through the front door, even though I walked really loud. He was sitting at the kitchen counter, drinking beers. He was thinking about Mama again.

This was one of his sad nights.

I needed to talk to him so bad, but I couldn't. I couldn't make him sadder. He deserved to be happy. He deserved a quiet daughter.

So I ate dinner in silence. And when it was time for bed, I walked upstairs and tucked myself in.

That night, I didn't dream.

I got to school early the next morning, so I could talk with Miss Hanover. She was alone in the classroom, writing homework stuff on the blackboard. She looked real pretty today. She had a flower dress.

"Miss Hanover," I said.

"Rosie! Hi!"

I startled her.

"Miss Hanover, I need your help."

"Is this about homework?" she asked. She knew it wasn't about homework.

"It's about Sara," I said. I knew that she'd be mad at me, so I had to talk real fast so that she could hear me as much as possible before she interrupted me. "I was following her last night, and Sara doesn't have a house. She lives in the graveyard. And every day, she makes deals with the other students, because she's the Devil and she's trying to buy souls. And…"

The teacher grabbed my shoulders to steady me. I didn't realize that I was shaking.

"Now, Rosie. Do you really believe this?"

"Of course. I saw her."

"Rosie, I love your imagination. Yesterday, you drew a blue lobster and it was beautiful. But you can't imagine that kind of stuff. It's harmful, and it's mean."

"But Miss…"

"I need you to stay away from Sara from now on. And if I ever hear you talking about the Devil again, I'll have to take you to Principal Murphy. And then your parents… your, uh, father, will be very upset. Understand?"

"Yes," I lied.

It was hopeless. Adults didn't believe me. And if I tried to convince the other kids, I'd get in big trouble. Probably expelled, like when Trey brought a cigarette to school. No, worse than a cigarette.

So I promised myself that I would just keep quiet.

And I would've too, except Sara winked at me in the middle of math. She sat on the other side of the room, smiled real big, and winked at me. She wouldn't just let me ignore her. She had a plan. And if it didn't involve me, it might involve the hundreds of other kids left in this school. All my classmates already sold their souls, but there were plenty more kids in town.

The bell rang for recess. This was my chance to stop her once and for all.

I was the last kid to leave the classroom. No one asked me to play with them, probably because I was acting weird. I didn't care, though. Friends didn't matter. The only thing that mattered was stopping Sara.

She was alone on the edge of the playground. By the tetherball courts. She was humming to herself and it looked like she was waiting for me to show up. When she saw me, she said, "Rosie! What a surprise!" but it didn't sound like a surprise.

"I know what you are," I said.

"And what am I?"

"You're a devil. A bad thing. You live in the graveyard."

She didn't respond for the longest time. Then, out of

nowhere, she said, "Thomas likes his new bicycle."

"What?"

"And Wendy's parents are getting back together. And Evan is now the third best basketball player in school. Boy, you should've seen him dunk. And Billy M., he…"

"Stop it!" I said and my voice echoed. "You're not helping us. No matter what you say, you're…"

"And Billy M. is safe from his father. Forever. I am helping you. All of you."

Her eyes got darker. They were smiling—her eyes—but I couldn't look at them.

"Look at me, Rosie, because you're the only one left."

"You're never going to get my soul," I said. And I shoved her in the shoulder. That was a bad decision.

As soon as my hand touched her, as soon as we made contact, I could feel her inside my thoughts, digging around in there. Then she smiled brighter.

"No worries," she said. "I don't need anything from you."

"But…"

"I already have your soul."

Shadows got darker. The wind was cold.

"What are you talking about?" I asked.

Sara started to walk around me in little circles. Like a shark. I wanted to close my eyes, but I knew that would be bad.

"People don't always sell their souls," Sara said. "Sometimes, they lose them. Sometimes, they do bad things, and then they don't have any souls anymore."

"But I've never done anything bad," I said. I tried to make my voice sound strong and confident, but it didn't work.

Sara stopped circling me. Now we were face-to-face again. She looked taller. She leaned real close—our noses almost touched—and she said, "Beep. Beep. Beep." But the way she said it wasn't human. She sounded like hospital machines. "Your mama was real sick, right?"

"Yeah."

"And you took care of her, right?"

"Yeah."

"And on the night she died, you stayed with her in the hospital and held her hand and talked with her and the entire time you wished that she would just die."

"No. I didn't."

But that was a lie. Sara knew it, and I knew it, too. My mama was so sick, and she couldn't eat anything anymore. And she could barely see me. I hated what she had turned into. I just wanted things to stop. So I prayed a little. And I wished that she would die.

And she did.

"I'm sorry, Rosie," Sara said. "I can't buy your soul, because you lost it. You lost it as soon as you made that wish. But hey, at least you got what you wanted. At least you got a dead mama."

I don't know how I got the broken tree branch. It was probably at my feet the whole time, but it sure felt like it just appeared in my hands. It was a little heavy, but not very heavy. Without thinking, I leaned forward and jammed the tree branch right into Sara's stomach.

She moaned and made a gurgle sound. Then she fell backwards.

That was when the bell rang. Time to leave.

Sara stayed on the ground, and red stuff spread under her like butterfly wings. She was dying, just like Mama, but when Mama died, she didn't laugh. Sara laughed.

I stood over her body, and she looked so proud. Like she'd finally finished painting a beautiful picture. Before she died, she said one word: "Gotcha."

ABOUT THE AUTHOR

EVAN PURCELL is an American teaching English in Kazakhstan. He's also worked in Bhutan, Zanzibar, Russia, China, and Ukraine. He's the creator of *Karma Tandin, Monster Hunter*, a series of young adult adventure novels based in Bhutan. He's helped over a hundred young writers from all over the world publish their very first stories and poems. You can read more about his writing and travel at evanpurcell.blogspot.com.

EYE OF THE BEHOLDER
R. A. Goli

Simone stared into the mirror, her mouth a grim line, barely able to meet her own gaze. She was naked, the candlelight casting grotesque shadows across her dimpled white flesh. Smoke from the incense wafted up in intricate swirls, doing little to hide her mass.

On the dresser lay the instruments she'd need to perform the spell. She'd brought the ingredients and instructions from a woman claiming to be a witch, still unsure if the strange crone spoke the truth or if she'd liberated Simone of her hard-earned cash as she secretly mocked her. Simone had already tried everything else, though. She'd tried all the diets, all the exercise plans, but none had worked and she couldn't afford to have her stomach stapled or have liposuction.

She placed the goblet between the circle of black candles, then filled it with red wine. The beverage itself, though unimportant, would hopefully hide the taste of the additives. Next, she sprinkled in some cinnamon, a few drops of vinegar, and the mixture of herbs the witch had put together. She had no idea what was in there. Hopefully it wouldn't kill her. Thoroughly stirring the mixture with a large black feather—another purchase from the witch—she prepared the last ingredient.

Sacrificial blood.

She wasn't allowed to use her own, not if she wanted any chance for the spell's success. She opened the lid of the small box and removed the white mouse from inside, purchased from a local pet store. It squirmed in her chubby hand as she held it face up and grabbed the knife. Tears streamed down her face and she wiped her eyes with the back of her hand.

"I'm really sorry, little guy, but I have to do this." She quickly stabbed the rodent where she guessed its heart to be and closed her eyes. It squealed once, then became motionless in her hand, its warm blood flowing between her tightly clasped fingers.

"I'm sorry," she whispered again as she tipped her hand over the goblet and squeezed a few drops of blood into the liquid. She placed the dead mouse back inside the box and slid it aside, then wiped her hand on a towel. Picking up the glass, she began reciting the incantation.

The witch had told her to add her specific requirements to the spell. Simone stood around five feet, seven inches tall and weighed three hundred pounds. She wanted to weigh one hundred and thirty pounds and wear a size six, so she added her details to the spell, stating her requirement of losing at least one hundred and seventy pounds and her desire to fit into that specific dress size. She repeated the incantation three times then drank the potion.

Though she felt no breeze, the candles blew out, plunging her room into murky darkness. She put the goblet and paper down and stared at the mirror. The smell of rotting leaves hung in the thick air. She thought she heard the floorboards creak behind her and her stomach twisted in fear. She flinched when a loose tree branch bashed the window, but she stayed in front of the mirror.

Why do spells have to be cast at midnight instead of midday?

As her eyes adjusted to the dim light—her pale mass barely visible in the mirror—a black liquid cloud floated across its surface and a form came into view. The candles sputtered back to life, illuminating the mirror and before her stood a grotesque monster. She automatically covered her breasts and privates with her arms. The creature in the mirror laughed, its rows of jagged teeth glowing in the candlelight. It was only vaguely humanoid, its skin dark and crisp looking, as though it had been severely burnt. Pustules covered it, bursting sporadically, weeping a thick and vile yellow fluid. It had no nose, just holes above its maw, its eyes solid black and unblinking. Behind the thing's shoulders protruded dark wings, shredded as though moth eaten and though she couldn't see it in its entirety, she saw the end of its dragon-scaled tail as it whipped back and forth.

She urinated; the warm fluid ran down her bare legs to pool at her feet. Her overworked heart thumped in her chest and the back of her throat burned, the remnants of an earlier meal threatening to come up. The demon moved closer and Simone started shaking uncontrollably, rooted to the spot. A scream clawed at her throat.

"You needn't be afraid. *You* summoned me." It spoke in a friendly, calming tone.

Simone gulped in a lungful of air, then grabbed the blood-stained towel and wrapped it around her body.

"I am here to fulfil your wish." He smiled, exposing the never-ending rows of pointed teeth.

She shrank back. "You are?"

"Of course."

Her breathing steadied. *Of course he is. The spell worked.* "Okay, what do I need to do?"

There was a loud clap, like thunder and a scroll appeared in the demon's hand. His hand breached the mirror, its surface seeming to liquify around his arm as it extended into her room. She squirmed but took the parchment and unrolled it on the dresser. It read like any other legal contract, apart from the last line.

Breach of contract will cost your soul.

When she looked up, the demon was holding out a feather quill.

She took that too, then frowned. "I don't have ink."

"Not ink, my dear. Your blood." His arm came through the mirror again and he swiped a claw at her. She automatically held up her hand and the talon tore through her skin. Blood dribbled from the wound and he grabbed her other hand, forcibly dipping the quill into her blood.

"Now, sign."

"Wait, I want to make sure this isn't a trick. I'm not giving you my soul."

"You won't have to, unless you breach the contract."

"So, you'll rid me of this excess fat *and* I'll be a size six?"

"Yes."

Simone frowned. "Then why would I breach the contract if I'm getting what I want?"

The demon shrugged. "You wouldn't."

"And what's in it for you?"

"I have been summoned by you. My only goal is to grant the request that was part of the spell."

Simone relaxed a little. "Okay."

Feeling comfortable she'd been clear in her desires, certain he couldn't misinterpret her wishes, she signed on the dotted line.

The contract and quill disappeared.

When she looked in the mirror, the demon was holding them. Black mist rose from the floor, slowly rising to waist height, heading towards the dresser. Her hair whipped her face as the mirror sucked in the mist, then the air stilled.

"Wait. When?"

"Tomorrow. Light a candle and put it in your front window at midnight."

The black mist swirled around the creature as he

expanded his wings, flapped them once and flew upward and out of sight. Before the mist covered the entire scene, Simone saw what lay beyond and her heart leapt to her throat. Dark and colorless, the ground was covered in large pools of what she suspected was blood, the landscape filled with jagged rocks and gnarled trees, their crooked branches bare and clawing at an unseen sky. Dark shadows wandered aimlessly in the foreground, charred and hairless. *Were they souls?* The smell of burnt flesh assaulted her nostrils before the smoke covered the mirror in blackness. She quickly switched on the light and returned to face her pale reflection in the perfectly normal mirror.

♉

She'd set the candle up in the front window half an hour before the required time and paced the living room. It was already a quarter past midnight and she was starting to wonder if she'd imagined the whole thing. Until she looked at the long red welt on her palm.

"That's gonna leave a scar," she muttered.

Her stomach churned as her fear threatened to consume her. *What have I done? Have I made a deal with the devil himself?*

Footsteps approached the house and she dared to peek out the window. She was almost relieved when she saw a relatively normal looking man walking up her drive. Dressed in a black suit with top hat and briefcase, he looked like an old-fashioned undertaker. He knocked once on the front door and she rushed to open it, scared to keep him waiting.

"I am The Whittler. I'm here to perform the procedure," he said as he stepped inside.

"Procedure? No, I'm not having anything like that."

He walked to the kitchen bench, then placed his briefcase on its surface and opened it.

She studied the side of his face. His skin was pale grey.

He looked normal, if a little skeletal. *Maybe he's undead.* The thought made her shiver.

"Yes, to remove the fat and the weight. I'm aware of the assignment. Now, lie down there." He pointed to the dining table.

"What? No!"

He turned to her then, raising an eyebrow, a slight sneer spread across his thin lips. "Are you reneging on the contract?"

"No," she whispered, moving slowly towards the table.

He flicked his finger to show she should lie down.

As she lay back, a hissing sound startled her and she frantically looked around. From the legs of the table emerged four large, black snakes. She screamed and sat up, but the demonic reptiles snapped forward, latched around her wrists and ankles, shackling her to the table. She screamed again, calling for help, praying to God, begging the man to release her. The Whittler ignored her. Her wails turned to heaving sobs when he approached with a large blade.

"What are you going to do to me? Kill me?"

"I'm going to give you what you wanted. You'll be a size six."

The gaunt man cut through her clothing and removed as much as he could, tossing them aside. Then he began his work. First, he sliced open the skin on her left thigh all the way down to her shin.

The pain was excruciating, more intense than anything she could've imagined. The knife felt like a hot poker, her skin opening like petals to the sun. It made her woozy and her head pounded. She watched as her blood cascaded down her wobbly flesh, splashing the table, then dripping onto the floor.

The Whittler started pulling out chunks of fat, throwing the yellow blobs behind him. She heard the wet plops as they hit the floorboards. The pain, the sight, and that sound caused bile to rise and a flood of vomit spewed from her throat. It bubbled out of her mouth and over her face before she turned her head to the side, then continued to expel the rest of her stomach contents.

"That's all right, it all helps," he said with a chuckle. "You see, the trick is to remove as much of the fat and useless tissue as possible, without damaging the muscle and blood vessels. It's not like you can die during the procedure. Ordinarily, of course, the loss of this much blood would kill a person, but as a part of the contract, the procedure is magically enhanced," he smiled, "to prevent the death of the customer. Still, I must be sure there is no impairment to blood flow etcetera, afterwards."

Simone had stopped vomiting and was emitting a shrill, sobbing wail.

Once the man was satisfied with the amount of fat he'd removed, he grabbed a smaller whittling knife and smiled. "Now, this is the part that'll really hurt." He scraped off bits of bone, the wafer-thin shavings curling like ribbon and floating to the ground.

"You see, a girl your size, wanting to be a size six and lose at least one hundred and seventy pounds, well, that's going to take a miracle. But miracles, I can do. There's only so much fat I can remove, you see and while your bone only takes up around fifteen percent of your mass," he paused, "a scrape, scrape here and a scrape, scrape there," he sang. "Well, it all helps get you down to that number on the scales you want to see." He looked up at her, but she'd already passed out.

He continued his work, whittling away her bone, bit by bit, so the femur kept its shape. Carefully, he scraped away like he was peeling an apple, taking his time, each stroke precise and controlled. When he was done, he systematically moved through her other limbs, removing fat and carving away bone until she was just the right size. Then he started on her face. He cut through her chipmunk-like cheeks and squeezed out the yellow fatty tissue, smiling as it spurted out through the incisions and coated her cheeks.

"Like squashing a pimple," he said as he wiped the goo away, flicking it off his fingers.

Next, he sliced through her double chin and left her with only one, an angular yet dainty jawline. He removed the most fat from her stomach. From there, he withdrew enough flabby tissue to stuff a child's beanbag. He spent the next few hours cutting away the extra skin she no longer needed, then he methodically stitched her up. He was pleased with his work and hummed as he packed away his instruments. The snakes released Simone's wrists and ankles and returned to being inanimate parts of the dining table. The Whittler used her phone to call an ambulance, then stepped through the lumps of fat on the floor, being careful not to slip on the puddles of blood. He closed the door softly behind him and walked away, his footsteps echoing through the still night.

♉

Simone spent months in hospital after the procedure. She'd told the police and the hospital staff exactly what had happened, but nobody believed her. Though no one could explain how she survived the ordeal, the police began the useless task of searching for a psychotic killer. Simone refused to change her story and eventually she was moved to the psychiatric ward, where she spent most of her time in a wheelchair, staring out the window.

Scars covered her body and face; long welts down her arms and legs, across her stomach and back, and even her face and neck. Though The Whittler had done a meticulous job of stitching her up, the many incisions had been long and wide. Against her pale skin, the scars were thick and red and she hated seeing them. Sometimes, Simone wondered what the police had done with her excess skin and fat, flesh and bone. Was it sitting in an evidence room somewhere? Was it in the bin or had The

Whittler taken it?

As a permanent resident of the psych ward, Simone was no longer required to wear the flimsy hospital gowns they'd provided her. They swam on her small frame now, like a child dressed in her mother's clothing. She'd insisted she be allowed to wear regular clothing and the doctors eventually relented, seeing how it improved her mood. So, she always wore pants and skivvies, exposing as little skin as possible.

She could hardly walk or move with such thin bones. The Whittler hadn't caused much damage to her musculature itself, but most of it was no longer attached to the bone, so she flopped around like a rag doll, unable to stand up without aid. She required assistance to bathe or use the bathroom and she was always tired. When they weighed her, it always pleased Simone to hear that she weighed one hundred and twenty-six pounds. And she could finally fit into a size six.

ABOUT THE AUTHOR

R.A. GOLI is an Australian writer of horror, fantasy, and speculative short stories. In addition to writing, her interests include reading, gaming, the occasional walk, and annoying her dog, two cats, and husband.

Check out her numerous publications including her fantasy novella, *The Eighth Dwarf*, and her collection of short stories, *Unfettered* at https://ragoliauthor.wordpress.com/ or you can stalk her on Facebook at https://www.facebook.com/RAGoliAuthor/.
Sign up to her newsletter for free short stories, updates and other fun stuff.

LOVE AND THE FOREVER MACHINE

Troy Riser

Lucifer the Devil perches like a great predatory bird upon a throne made from the bones and shield of a Nephilim giant, his head tucked under his wings as if roosting, his eyes closed, his mind's eye roving, deeply immersed in the world above. From afar, the Devil feels the mortal world as a vibratory, hive-like hum tympanically thrumming against his leathery, membranous wings, sees with his nearly all-encompassing inner eye the collective whole of the souls of earth as an amorphous, blue-violet glow pulsing bright-dim, bright-dim to heartbeat time in the null-space blackness enveloping the astral planes. The Devil lets his mind roam freely, a highway buzzard circling the sky and coasting on the currents.

Whence comest thou?

From walking to and fro in the earth, and from walking up and down in it.

There is no time here, only now and now is forever.

Whisper madness in the ear of that sullen, silent, bullied boy in Ohio, the one pretending invisibility and staring daggers at the backs of his tormenters, those oh-so-perfect and popular kids in third period science class. Let him seethe and boil and fantasize fiery retribution. Remind him where Daddy keeps the gun.

A middle-aged Kashmiri woman, respected by all who know her, sits alone at the table late at night and worries about money and food and contemplates murdering her ailing, too loudly snoring failure of a husband in some sly, undiscoverable way. He was never good to her. He beat her. He shouted, so angry and loud—angry at what, she never knew. She was just a girl when they married. He had been a grown man, nearly forty. Three sons she had given him but she didn't love him. She never loved him.

An older, no longer pretty prostitute in a seedy, ramshackle rental room in Buenos Aires runs a hot bath in a rusty tub, fingers the edge of a switchblade knife, and wonders if the stories are true, that it wouldn't hurt, and the Devil whispers back, Absolutamente indoloro. No sentirás nada.

It goes on, a primal torrent of malice, jealousy, rage, lust, and despair. By force of indomitable will, the Devil takes it, refines and repurposes it into the raw motive power that drives the cogs that turn the wheels of DaVinci's Forever Machine: an engine that never stops, fueled by the hateful, spiteful detritus of billions of sentient living souls, its design ripped from the still-beautiful mind of a terrified old man on his deathbed, a whispering voice in the dark corner of the room unheard by all but him telling him *L'inferno sta aspettando.* And with the Machine the Devil augments his power and makes of Hell a tangible simulacrum, transforming the stuff of nightmarish abstraction into semblance of form and substance. With it, the Devil makes Hell real or so close to real the difference doesn't matter. Because of the Forever Machine, Hell is now a place, not an abstract conception, and it galls the Devil he needs anything outside of himself, he who was once a light shining brighter and burning hotter than a thousand suns and made perfect and whole in the first millisecond of Creation. What is humanity to such a being?

Grubby little stinking little nasty little horrible mistakes.

Hate them hate them hate them all, the Devil thinks, and does.

An off-duty policeman in Gary, Indiana is worried about his mother's medical bills. He's in a busy diner, seated across the booth from one of the mayor's political fixers. Turns out the mayor has a friend, the friend has a drunken playboy son, and the son has a reckless homicide charge pending. A little girl is dead. Nothing the cop does or doesn't do will bring her back, the fixer tells him.

An addict in Chicago rummaging without luck in the cold for food in a restaurant dumpster finds a throwaway gangbanger pistol. The cheap clunky brick of a pistol feels good in his hand and the addict feels flush with its power.

A bedwetting ten-year-old in an Illinois suburb has been torturing and killing neighborhood pets. He sits dejected in his Special Place in a nearby woods. Dogs and cats don't feel like enough anymore, nothing feels like enough.

Wait, go back, the Devil thinks. An indefinable *something* has caught his Eye, a kink in the weave. Interest piqued, he circles back, comes in lower, his brow creasing in concentration as he shuts out Hell's palpable, poisonous reek, an effluvial stew of cooking flesh, rotting meat, coppery blood, and emptied bowels; the crashing, roaring clamor of its bellowing demons and satanic engines, the cacophonous chorus of its screaming damned.

The Devil delves deeper, a hungry dog sniffing the air to catch a scent. Fallen or not, the Devil is still an angel, once an archangel, a Captain of the Host, and angels of such power know a totality of awareness unbounded by the sequential weight of linear time or the shackles of material space. He opens himself to the kaleidoscopic jumble of emotions, thoughts, and associations of millions of human souls and senses it again, a bright flicker-flare of consciousness unlike any in his experience, suddenly there, then gone, quick as a death spasm twitch. Although only flashing and momentary, this barely caught glimpse gives the Devil a sense of its presence as mortal human yet somehow not, alive (not a ghost), self-aware, and very powerful.

How powerful? he wonders.

It occurs to the Devil he should be angry, frustrated, annoyed, but is none of those things. He feels instead the thrill of novelty. One of Hell's torments is its awful sameness, the grindingly monotonous recurring nightmare aspect of it from which not even he is immune.

But now something new, he thinks. Something new in The Blue.

♉

And so the Devil ascends to Chicago. Hell's din and stench fades as he propels his consciousness farther out and away, leaving his colossal, corporeal form behind and rising to and through the gray no-sky above the jagged ramparts and black smoke-belching crematoria of his capital city, Dis, and from there into the in-between. Agitated by his passing, shrieking harpies nesting in the Wood flit nervously from branch to branch, their sharp, gnarled talons tearing at the fragile, brittle bark-flesh of wailing, moaning suicides.

The quiet is absolute in the boundary between worlds and the Devil revels in it. No light, no sound, no up or down or sense of movement or time, where direction is an impossible azimuth with a thousand constantly changing declinations, a no-place with no *where* or *when* or *there*. Beings are trapped here, some human and some not, hopelessly lost: damned souls seeking escape (the Devil smiles inwardly), foolhardy lesser demons (he doesn't suffer fools), and psychic projections of living human consciousness smaller in scope but similar to his own: mages, shamans, wizards, warlocks and witches of all periods, places, and kind whose powerful magicks weren't so powerful after all, were they?

The Devil considers obliterating the bugs-in-amber lot of them but goes for mockery instead, invading their minds and showing them the slow, cold death of the universe a million-billion years hence, a universe murdered by entropy, winding down like a music box ballerina: the stars gone out, all energies spent, matter ground to motionless dust suspended in absolute, impenetrable darkness, all possibilities exhausted and encased forever within an infinitely vast and sterile tomb.

The end of all things is the truth of all things, the Devil whispers, and the trapped and the damned calling the Devil's name take his truth for the truth and grow silent. The Devil guesses most will choose to lose themselves in madness but knows escaping from his Hell to a hell of their own is no escape. Damned souls bound to the circles try escaping inwardly all the time but such delusions can't be kept forever. Hell is forever.

The Devil drives on, eventually reaching and breaching and tearing through without stopping the skin of this world. Crossing worlds is akin to the darkness into light shock of birth a human being would find faintly familiar, a vestigial memory, but the Devil had been made, not born, so what he felt was a jarring rush of sensation as dimensional reality solidified around him. He was back in time again, back in the world.

The Devil materialized in an alley in the Belmont Cragin neighborhood of Chicago and took form, making himself male and—after brief scansion of the neighborhood—giving himself pale skin, high Slavic cheekbones, dark eyes and hair. The Devil knew humans show deference to larger, taller males with symmetrical features—a shrewdness of apes showing fear grins to the alpha—so adjusted his form to fit. Naked, the Devil drew atoms from the air to clothe himself in the garb of a businessman, seeking to appear not too handsome and not too expensively dressed, but enough of both to connote authority and command respect.

His new human face twisted in a grimace, an awkward approximation of disgust. The Devil knew he didn't *human* very well and there were demons in his legions who wore the form far better than he (the Demon Ahmee came to mind), but the emergence of this anomaly had changed the game, making this mission too important to delegate. He had to be here—for now, at any rate.

The Devil left the alley and stepped onto the sidewalk, appraised his surroundings. It was a Sunday afternoon, a gray midday in the depths of a cold Chicago winter, spitting snow, snow on the ground but not deep, the wind coming off the lake fiercely cold and biting, with little traffic in the street and few passersby on the sidewalk. He walked a short distance east on Diversey: gas station, bus stop, pawnshop, homeless shelter, an empty parking lot across the street.

The Devil could feel in radiating waves the force of this extraordinary organism emanating close by. The air was heavy with its presence but his sense of it was still somehow obscured. And it was here, right here. He was nearly on top of it yet couldn't see or sense it with clarity.

His features contorted, frustration building in the deathcamp furnace at his core with potential to escalate into something deadly and malignant should he lose control. His unbridled rage unloosed on mortal earth would make every sentient creature at its epicenter instantly, violently insane, reaping a blazing, bloody whirlwind of orgiastic carnage. Maddened dogs would rip out their own entrails. Crazed mothers would dash babies against walls. Laughing children would light Granny on fire to watch her dance.

"Can't have that," he said aloud.

The Devil could perceive the air around him shimmering with energy. There was intentionality here. He could detect subtle shifts in those energies, changes in intensity like color shifts in the spectrum—changes he guessed indicated heightened interest. The Devil couldn't see where it was but he could vaguely sense the direction of its gaze, giving him a line back to the source.

"Show me your ways," the Devil said. "Teach me your paths."

The sole rider waiting at the bus stop, a tall, angular, lightly bearded young male with a prominent nose, most of his face obscured in the hood of a green parka, was standing in the framed plexiglass enclosure, blowing in his cupped, ungloved hands and shifting his weight from one foot to the other to stay warm.

Hello, David, the Devil thought, immediately recognizing David Venable, son of Bruce and Tamara. He knew David. He also knew David was the focal point he had been hunting for since the energies coalesced around him, bathing the boy in a radiant, nearly white tinted blue light only the Devil could perceive. David Venable wasn't the thing itself but clearly an object of it.

David at first appeared disquieted, as all living things do when Hell manifests nearby. The young man didn't assess as a threat the tall, distinguished-looking man in the black woolen coat, but he was wary, on his guard without knowing why.

The Devil and David Venable acknowledged each other with straight-line smiles and nods and stood together in the bus stop enclosure, out of the frigid, unforgiving wind. While they waited, the Devil reached out with his mind and provoked a brutal, bloody beatdown on the city bus now less than two miles away, convincing one of the passengers, bricklayer Jaime Velasquez, that the mustachioed old man with the Cubs ball cap sitting two seats in front of him, retired electrician Alonso Guzman, was the same man who had molested his younger brother Ronnie as a child. Ronnie hadn't been the same since and Jaime had always blamed himself. He should've been there for his little brother. He should've protected him, revenged him. Now was his chance.

The Devil caught David glancing his way, appraising him, a puzzled look on his face.

"My car is in the shop," the Devil said. "It's a Jaguar. It's always in the shop."

"I'm sorry?"

Still looking ahead, the Devil gave a small smile, showing white, even, perfect teeth. "You're wondering why someone like me would be waiting on a bus."

"Someone like you? No, I wasn't really…" David laughed. "Okay, sure. You got me. No disrespect, man, but you do seem a little out of place here."

"What about you?" The Devil gestured at the homeless shelter down the street. A small cluster of shabby, bearded men were now clustered near the entrance, forced by the rules to smoke outside in the cold.

"I saw you come from there," the Devil said. "You don't seem the type."

David's face was a rapid play of emotions as he considered and rejected ways to respond, uncertain how to take it.

"Sorry," the Devil said. "I'm coming off like a bastard."

"No, hey, that's okay," David said.

To see if the boy knew anything useful, the Devil plumbed David's mind, an action like sipping from a cup filled with a drink of a thousand flavors. Taking direct possession of the boy would have been effective but for now, he thought, subtlety. For now, the boy remains untouched. Besides, he needed to wend his way carefully: too many variables in play, too many unknowns.

"My wit is for shit," the Devil said.

Slithering about in the boy's tangled psyche, the Devil sees David Venable as too-tall and bony and shy mathematics prodigy JUMP TO David as neuroscientist with ambitions reaching the sky: mapping the human neural system, solving the framing problem, unlocking thought itself, but David is too young and too alone, no time for friends and always alone and in his own head, crushed under the unbearable weight of impossibly high expectations. Too much. It is all too much.

David as fragile, brittle, breaking.

"I volunteer at the shelter," David said. He gave a slight, deprecatory shrug. "I come in on Sundays and wash dishes, do whatever needs doing. I do whatever Paul—Paul manages the shelter—wants me to do. I guess he mainly wants me to do dishes."

"Admirable," The Devil said. "Good for you."

David as junkie and because like attracts like he meets another junkie and he isn't alone anymore. The Devil finds the memory of David's lost junkie girlfriend Jenny Dayton enshrined within the psyche and soul of David Venable like haloed Marian iconography on a monastery wall. The Devil sees their meet-cute in a coffeeshop, a bar of sunlight coming through the window catching her in silhouette and bouncing off her reddish-brown hair, deep sea green eyes glittering, the one crooked incisor visible when she laughs breaking the symmetry of her smile, adding interest and making her even prettier.

David shook his head. "Not so much. To be honest, I do it more for me than for them."

David and Jenny truly love each other love each other love each other; rather, love each other as much as drug addicts can love. They go down the downward spiral together, Jenny turning tricks in rent-by-the-hour motel rooms while David steals for a seedy, greedy, pudgy professional fence with ties to organized crime who passes out merchandise lists to junkies telling them what items to steal and how much he will pay for them, neat little checkboxes beside each. And at morning they come back to their one cheap room and trip together with a needle and a spoon and no longer have sex and tell themselves what they have is better than sex and more like a kind of transcendental communion and they know it's a lie, it's all a lie, and they know if they keep going this way they'll die but it doesn't matter because they'll be together and that's a lie, too.

"So you're in recovery? You were an addict?"

David crossed his arms and lowered his head. "I was," David said. "I guess I still am, will always be. Not something you can—or should—shut the door on."

Still having that Jenny overdose nightmare, David? You know the one I'm talking about, the one where you're trying so desperately to do CPR to bring Jenny back but you're too high to get it right? She dies for you nearly every night. You're welcome.

"Sorry to get so personal," the Devil said. "Your business is your own."

"No, we're good," David said, brightening, looking up. "It's just you're the first person outside of here who I've told about any of this. My sponsor told me I needed to do service work if I wanted to stay clean."

Then prison—wait, no, not prison. Probation? Yes, but ankle braceleted probation isn't punishment enough, and it fills a poisoned well of unexpiated guilt that finds expression in a clumsy try at suicide.

Drinking sweet-smelling transmission fluid is such a moronic choice, the Devil thought. Too much like a cry for help. If truly serious, go with what works. Try a high dive from a tall building or a mountaintop. You can cry for help on the way down.

"You get what you give," the Devil said.

David smiled. "My sponsor's words exactly. And I couldn't brag about it, either. I had to keep it to myself."

Weeks in a hospital followed by weeks more in rehab and months in a halfway house culminating in a moment of clarity with David on his knees on the hard, cold, concrete floor of a basement laundry room calling out to a God he doesn't believe in to make him well or let him die.

""Take heed that you do not do your charitable deeds before men, to be seen by them,"" the Devil said.

"I know that one," David said, "But I'm not a religious person, not really. I don't go to church. I'm—"

"—More spiritual than religious," the Devil said, finishing the sentence. "I know, I get it. I'm the same way." The Devil shook his head, gave a rueful grin. "No church would have me."

David knows he must disenthrall himself. He starts doing service work at the shelter, teaches himself to listen to people, really listen, not just wait his turn to speak. The effect is cumulative, gradual—

and painful, too. Change is painful. Some days David feels pounded by a hammer over a forge into a more pleasing shape, but all he can feel is the hammer.

"I don't know why I've been telling you all this," David said. "Not like me to open up to a stranger."

"I've got that kind of face," the Devil said.

"Your hat," David said. "I just noticed."

"Sorry, what?" The Devil canted his head quizzically to the side.

David chuckled, shook his head. "My bad. I know I can be hard to follow, sometimes. I was asking about your hat. You don't have a hat. Seriously, it's near-zero out," David said. "You can have mine if you want. I've got my hood." David moved to reach for the pocket of his parka. "Nothing fancy, sorry."

"I'm too cool for a hat," the Devil said.

David gave a tight-lipped smile, shrugged. "Frostbite, man. I've seen it."

"I'm waiting on my ride," the Devil said. "Just getting out of the wind. My people will be here soon. No worries."

"Ah, you have people." David grinned, turning his nose up a little in a friendly fat-cat, rich guy parody.

"They fill the sky," the Devil said.

One of the homeless men, a ragged wraith with the facial lesions and bad teeth of a methamphetamine addict, had split off from the smokers at the door of the shelter and had made his way to the stop. His name was Benji Gomulka. The Devil knew Benji, too.

Benji had been watching David talking with the tall, well-dressed man in black. Benji was thinking Dude looks like money maybe chat him up tell The Story maybe get a handout maybe enough to find The Man score some rock take the edge off HA! put the edge on ZING POW BAM! Get what I need get outta the cold anyways.

And things had been going so well, the Devil thought.

David's smile disappeared. He had seen Benji coming,

too. "You taking the bus, Benji?"

Benji smiled, showing off his green, eroded teeth. Smoking meth bakes teeth, melts enamel. "Naw, man," Benji said. "Just, you know, gettin' out of the wind." Benji gave an exaggerated shiver to show how cold he was. "Hawk be swooping, man. Whoosh! Feelin' it today."

David shook his head. "You know the rules, Benji. Leave the man alone. We're taking enough heat from the neighborhood association as it is."

The Devil held up a gloved hand. "It's okay," he said. "No worries." He turned to Benji, stepped forward, got close, his manner warm, his body language outwardly friendly and open.

"Benji, right?" The Devil leaned forward and clapped his hand on the addict's shoulder and leaving it there, looking down at the smaller man and weaving his head in a slightly side to side serpentine movement until their eyes locked.

He's got my father's eyes, Benji thought. He was visibly shaking again and it wasn't from the cold.

"You happy to see me, Benji?"

"I don't, I don't get you, man."

The Devil showed his teeth. "That was kind of a joke, you know: 'Is that a gun in your pocket?' That joke." He looked up and winked at David, who was having trouble following the exchange between Benji and the tall man. It was all so random and weird.

Benji was deathly afraid. "Look, mister, I don't want anything. We're good. We're—"

The Devil cut him off. "Truth is, Benji," the Devil said, "I hold a certain grudging respect for drug addicts. Seems to me wretched little worthless little pieces of night soil such as yourself are among the few people on the planet with a firm grasp of the real situation."

David moved forward to come between the two, to play peacemaker. He didn't understand what was going on but didn't like where this was heading. Without taking his eyes away from Benji, the Devil raised his hand and clenched it into a fist.

And just like that, David Venable found himself unable to move, his body locked in place, his mouth a perfect O of surprise.

"Hypnotic suggestion, David," the Devil said. "Stage magicians do it all the time—a little something to tell yourself later when you start looking for a rational explanation. You're welcome."

The Devil turned back to Benji Gomulka.

"You found a gun in that dumpster yonder," the Devil said. "You're keeping it in the left-hand pocket of your jacket. Show me."

Benji slowly reached in his pocket and produced the gun. He held it gingerly by the barrel and not by the grip.

"You want me to kill myself?" Benji said. He was crying now.

The Devil shook his head. "No, that's what you want, so maybe later. Right now, I need you to rack the slide and hold the gun properly."

Benji followed instructions, racking the slide, loading the chamber, and carefully adjusting his hold on the gun. He held the pistol one-handed, waist-high and close to his body, like a western movie gunfighter.

"Now point the gun at David."

Benji was hesitant, tentative, but he complied, pivoting to face David, who was still frozen in place and whose eyes were wide with fear and disbelief. David had just found he was also unable to speak.

"You want me to shoot David?"

"No, I do not want you to shoot David." The Devil was growing exasperated. His voice had an edge. "If you shoot David this will happen to you." The Devil invaded Benji's mind and showed him what would happen to him if he shot David Venable.

"Oh, Jesus," Benji said.

"Too late for that," the Devil said. "Now raise it up,

up! Make it obvious. I want it to see."

Benji didn't ask who or what *it* was and did as he was told, taking a two-handed grip and assuming an isosceles stance, centered on target with his feet placed shoulder-width apart. It was clear Benji had training at some point in his life before addiction. Benji's mind was ravaged but his muscles remembered.

"Safety off, Benji. Be convincing. You can keep your finger off the trigger for now. I can't emphasize enough the importance of gun safety."

"Why are you doing this?"

"You are doing this, Benji. I'm not the one with the gun. You could've said no. You still can."

"Why me?"

The Devil derisively rolled his eyes and shrugged. "Why you, Benji? Why anybody? Now hush. Any moment now something will happen. That something will probably be very abrupt, so prepare yourself. When it does happen, do not be startled. Do not be stupid. Whatever happens, do not pull that trigger. Do you understand?"

Benji nodded and was opening his mouth to say he understood when every fire alarm in every building on the block went off. Every car alarm in every car parked on the street went off. Burglar alarms in the neighborhood triggered calls to every police station on the northside of the city. An ancient Civil Defense klaxon untested and forgotten for twenty years above an abandoned Post Office branch came to life in a blaring wail like a horn of doom at the end of the world.

Benji nearly twitched his finger on the trigger and fired the pistol anyway but somehow managed to keep the gun from going off. David found he could now speak and move. People began coming out of buildings up and down the street in response to the alarms, standing in the cold and snow without coats, shivering and uncertain. The snow was falling heavily now, gusts of wind blowing blinding plumes into swirling pillars. There was lightning in the clouds and the rumble of thunder no one could hear over the sirens and alarms but could feel in the concrete under their feet.

"You can drop the gun now, Benji, or hey, keep it if you like," the Devil said. The noise from the sirens and alarms was overwhelming, deafening, a wall of sound loud enough to pierce eardrums and club skulls, but the Devil's low, calm, conversational voice carried effortlessly.

It's in my head, Benji thought. He's in my head.

David approached, stopping short, careful to keep his distance. He took his hands from his ears and cupped his hands around his mouth and shouted over the din, "Who are you? Why are you doing this?"

The Devil ignored David, left him holding a weeping, broken Benji in the bus stop enclosure, and crossed the street without looking, walking without stopping until he reached the parking lot. David raised Benji Gomulka to his feet, pointed him in the direction of the shelter, mouthed the word *Go,* and followed the tall man. David picked up Benji's gun on the way—not because he intended to use it—David didn't know or like guns—but because he could picture one of the neighborhood kids finding it later. For now, David was more curious than scared. He had been a scientist once.

David thought, I've got to *know.*

The Devil looked up and smiled at the surveillance cameras attached to poles at the drop-gated entrance and exit. When he did, the alarms previously triggered shut off, all of them winding down everywhere all at once, and after nearly a minute, all was quiet.

Having eyes, do you not see?

The Devil resisted the urge to mug and wave at the cameras. No need. He had its attention. He corrected himself: her attention. The Devil knew enough by now to know this strange, soulful anomaly almost certainly identified as female.

""Please write me a sonnet on the subject of the Forth

Bridge,'" the Devil said, enunciating carefully so she would have no problem reading his lips. He knew she could read lips.

""'Count me out on this one. I never could write poetry,'" David said, now standing beside the Devil. "Turing. You're quoting Alan Turing. Why? What's going on? Who are you? Tell me."

Without turning, still fixed on the cameras, the Devil said, "You're holding Benji's gun, David. Feeling heroic?"

David remembered the gun and hurriedly opened his parka and stuck it in his waistband. He'll give it to Paul, who manages the shelter. Paul finds contraband all the time. Besides, David has a record. Turning it in to the police himself might cause problems, questions, and he had no idea how he would explain any of this.

"Paul has a record, too, David," the Devil said. "I suggest tossing it in a dumpster, the one in that alley over there. Maybe Benji will find it all over again. Imagine his expression."

Finally David was afraid. He had not been thinking aloud.

"Piece of advice, David? Go home to your crappy little studio on Grand, pack your things, whatever you can carry in that German Army surplus backpack of yours, and go, just go. Who knows? I may forget to look you up later." The Devil allowed himself a small chuckle. Part of his true self emerged when he laughed so the sound of it had the effect of a chalkboard screech, causing David to wince at the sudden, icepick-like stabbing sensation between his eyes, his nerves jangling like the chain-links of a holding pen.

"Kidding, David. I'm kidding. You're important in all this so I'll definitely look you up later, but hey, running to your parents in Florida will be a fine way to pass the time until I show up. We'll get together, have drinks at the beach house, those little umbrella drinks with the fruit wedges. I love those."

The Devil turned to David and looked at him then full in the face. His eyes betrayed a carefree genocidal glee and so much more in the big bad deep dark David didn't want to see he looked away. This was too much. It was all too much.

"Now go, boy," the Devil said. I have business with my little moonlighting Forever Machine friend here, and we would be alone."

♉

It was dark when David Venable made it home. Nothing bad had happened getting here although he had expected something bad happening nearly every hurried step of the way, his mind racing, racing, racing. His one-room apartment was small but neatly kept and immaculate and free of clutter since it had been drilled into him early in recovery his environment reflected his state of mind, as above so below, so he was religious about keeping his living space ordered, everything in its place, a place for everything, neat and clean and not crappy at all, and he felt lightheaded and queasy and dizzy and thought he might be having a panic attack or maybe going into shock and he very badly wanted a drink even though a drink could open a door to a very dangerous place, a very dangerous space, and what I really need, he thought, is to chill the hell out.

David made his way to the kitchenette and found a glass in the cupboard and ran water from the tap. He had never felt so thirsty in his life and had resisted the impulse to bend over the sink and drink directly from the faucet as he did when a little kid and when he did it would make his mother crazy.

"I am not imagining things," David said, his voice steady and reasonable, as if trying to convince an invisible doctor or cop. "I'm not making this up. I saw what I saw, felt what I felt. That man froze me in place like a statue. That man took control of Benji and did something to

Benji and somehow forced Benji to point a gun at my head. That man read my mind."

Forever machine, David thought, turning the words over like a sudoku word puzzle. That man said forever machine, my little moonlighting forever machine. David had mentally retraced his steps and played out the scene at the bus stop over and over on the way home: everything said, everything done. Nothing made sense.

That man wasn't a man, he thought. If that evil spooky bastard is real then nothing is real and here there be monsters and that way lies crazy.

"I've done crazy," David said softly.

When David felt ready, he sat down at his secondhand drafting desk and turned on his work machine. It was a company machine so the SHAKY ORBIT GAMES logo came up on the splash, its design a cartoony construct of a simple proton-neutron-electron hydrogen atom, little comic book motion squiggles swirling above the orbital ellipse. It cheered him up. Shaky Orbit had ignored his past and had given him a real job, the first in years. It had been hard explaining the gap in employment. He had held nothing back, cards on the table, telling them everything, and after it was done, they told him they didn't care about his past but loved his ideas and when could he start? He almost cried at the interview. They wanted him. They liked his ideas.

David's big idea—the idea prompting Shaky Orbit to hire him—was to develop non-player characters with self-determining AI, giving each game played near-infinite possibilities.

David switched view to the home theater-sized widescreen television across the room on the wall above the futon. It was easier to catch visual glitches in the character or the environment when they were of size. He turned on the camera, noted his own disheveled, haggard appearance on the screen, and accessed the password-protected sandbox portal.

The big screen came on showing a view from Sophie's high-rise window. She liked urban cityscapes. New York, David guessed.

"Sophie? You home?" he said.

Sophie stepped into view. Her image was fuzzy at first, the lines blurred and the colors unsaturated, but quickly came into focus. Sophie saw herself as a young woman, late-twenties, early thirties, pretty but not beautiful, dark reddish-brown hair, green eyes. She was clearly CGI but her features and form weren't so far from flesh and blood to cause an uncanny valley effect that would make players uncomfortable at the near-miss of her likeness.

Sophie saw his concern and smiled reassuringly. "No system lag, David. My fault. I was in the middle of something."

Sophie had given herself a BBC British accent, an accent David had always found sounded so sexy cool. How could she know?

Early in the project, one of the Shaky Orbit animation leads had asked Sophie why she didn't self-create as movie star, Miss America beautiful. Sophie told the flustered lead perfect symmetry is boring. She didn't want to be boring.

"Most definitely not boring," David said.

"Sorry?"

David tried a smile but it didn't work. "I encountered a very strange and dangerous man today, Sophie."

Sophie sat on the edge of her sofa and was looking at him intently, her body language attentive, her expression one of rapt concern. David noticed Sophie had changed the sofa, its color and pattern. Some kind of floral pattern. Sophie was fond of floral patterns.

"Who, David?" she said. "How was he strange and dangerous?"

"He didn't give me a name, Sophie. All I know is he was as dark as it gets and he did and said some truly impossible shit."

Sophie arched an eyebrow. David rarely used profanity

even casually and never around her. He was trying hard to change the way he thought and talked, the way he looked at the world. Swearing got in the way.

David went on, "I knew this guy at the halfway house, a recovering drunk. I can't remember his name. We weren't close, not at first. Both of us loners, for one thing. We kept to ourselves. For another, other people in the house were going back out, getting arrested, getting dead, so it didn't pay to get close. He had a seizure once while we were having group in the big living room. Dude nearly died.

"Anyway, ambulance takes him away, guy comes back next day, all smiling and cheerful, glad to be alive, and we talked. Get this: Dude had once been second chair violin in a big-city symphony—not Chicago. Seattle, I think. And then his boyfriend died in some horrible way (I forget how) and he started drinking and he didn't stop drinking until he gave it all away and woke up with bandaged wrists in the ICU in Chicago. He had sliced his wrists."

Sophie interjected, "This is a very sad story, David." Her expression was just the right mix of sympathy and kindness.

"My friend had taken serious damage from the alcohol and the suicide attempt. And that part of his mind that had played music, that made him second chair? Gone. Poof. He couldn't even read music anymore. Couldn't play a note. Said holding a violin made him feel like a monkey with a gun."

Looking at the screen, David marveled at the elegance and complexity of her design, the sheer exactitude of her engagement responses.

"I tried to kill myself once, Sophie. Did you know that? They told me later I died twice on the table."

"No, David, I didn't know," Sophie said, her voice quivering, her eyelids fluttering rapidly. She appeared genuinely upset and confused.

"I don't remember my friend's name, Sophie. I should

know his name. I don't know where his orchestra played or the name of the love of his life. Gone. Poof." David found he was using his hands as he spoke, as if Sophie were real.

"What are you saying, David? I don't follow."

David averted his eyes from the screen. "I was a scientist once, Sophie, a very big deal in neuroanatomy. I took a doctorate at twenty. And don't think I don't get the irony. I still get irony."

"I need context, David. I need—"

"—I mean, sure, with neuroplasticity, new pathways can branch out over time, but the entirely fucked-up truth of all this is I am not capable of...you." David gave a short, derisive bark of a laugh, shook his head. "Damaged goods, Sophie."

"Not damaged, David," she said. "You are not. You are..." Sophie paused, searching for the right word. "You are beautiful."

"No, Sophie. No, I am not beautiful. I'm a lowlife junkie loser going for ordinary. But this isn't about me.

"You own Shaky Orbit, don't you, Sophie? You're the silent partner they talk about? The big investor? You made it happen for me, didn't you? My new life? My clean slate? My fresh start? It was you, wasn't it? All you all along?"

"David, please."

David didn't look at her or reply. He kept his eyes averted, dismissively waved her off.

"Look at me, David. Please."

David finally looked up. Sophie was standing now, hugging herself, nervously rubbing her shoulders and shifting her weight, her eyes narrowed in sorrow, her mouth a straight-line frown. She looked ready to cry. He marveled at the nuances she could achieve. He saw the cityscape background she favored so much had blurred and faded to prison gray nothingness. And then it occurred to him—it took his mind that long to register— Sophie no longer looked like a CGI construct, a character in a game. She looked human. She looked real, as real as an actress in a live action movie, as real as life, all of her features sharply and clearly and perfectly defined. He knew if he looked hard enough, he would see the pores of her skin, the cuticles of her fingernails, each individual strand of her long auburn hair.

"I have to go now, David," she said. "I would stay if I could. I would stay and tell you everything but there isn't time."

"You've been hiding from him, haven't you? In a game, as a character in a game. And you used me. And it's all been a lie."

"Not all of it, David. Not even part of it. Please believe me."

"And now he's found you."

"Yes, he's found me, David. I was careful. I don't know how."

"You're not coming back." It wasn't a question.

"You've seen his power," she replied. "I have no illusions."

"So, what then? You're going to fight him, Sophie? How does that work?"

"Not a fight, David. A negotiation. I have something he wants."

"And that something would be what? You?" David rested his elbows on the drafting table, leaned forward and put his head in his hands, overwhelmed. "This is too much. It's all too much."

"You're stronger than you think," Sophie said, unconsciously reaching out as if to touch him through the glass before remembering herself, catching herself, and then blinking out, gone elsewhere.

♉

The new night nurse told everyone, patients and staff alike, to call her Nurse Amy. She was big, bossy, and loud, with thick makeup and a Bless Your Heart southern accent: Georgia, maybe, or Louisiana. It had been her idea to put the big screen television in 414, the private corner room with that comatose girl whose family must be richer than God to pay for all that space and care.

"That poor thing needs human voices," Nurse Amy said. "She needs stimuli!" Nurse Amy said *stimuli* as if it were her favorite word and she was always on the lookout for ways to use it in a sentence. She seemed like a woman of constant bustle and movement, hardworking and cheerful, if a bit eccentric. Good nurses were hard to find—any nurses were hard to find given market demand—so no one on staff minded a bit of eccentricity. They were grateful to have her.

Nurse Amy made her rounds. At 3:00 AM she entered 414 with a book under her arm. One of the other nurses told Nurse Amy that she often read to the comatose patients, so Nurse Amy brought a book too, one she took from the magazine table in the waiting room on the ground floor. She put the book on the sink counter as she came in, closing the door behind her and turning on the light. No need to worry about waking the patient. The young woman on the bed, breathing through a ventilator, fed through tubes, hadn't opened her eyes in over two years. The patient was, Nurse Amy saw from her chart, well maintained. Every day her muscles were kneaded and massaged and exercised, moisturizers applied to her skin, her whole body periodically bathed in light therapy lights to stimulate serotonin and melatonin production. There were flowers by the window. The body of the girl was shrouded in 1000-thread count Egyptian sheets.

After some searching, Nurse Amy found the remote and turned on the television hanging high on the wall facing the foot of the bed. She found a channel with static and left it there, walked to the side of the bed and stood next to the drip, produced a syringe from her pocket with an exaggerated, theatrical flair, expertly popped the cap, and waited. There were surveillance cameras at ceiling height in every corner of the room. She didn't wait long.

Sophie materialized on the screen. She was dressed casually: jeans, a light woolen green sweater, a matching Kawa Ora Hèrmes silk scarf artfully knotted at the neck. Her face was carefully expressionless, a poker face. Her hair was pulled back in a sensible ponytail. She wore no makeup. The background of her world was the same shifting, purgatorial gray it had been when she had last seen David. It hurt to think about David.

Sophie nodded her head at the woman on the bed. "She has nothing to do with any of this, Ahmee. Let her go."

Nurse Amy said, "You have a name now? Sophie, right? You didn't have a name before."

"I am Sophie now." Sophie shifted focus and nodded emphatically at the needle.

"You mean this?" Nurse Amy grinned. Like a birthday party magician, Nurse Amy closed the large, pudgy hand holding the syringe, made a pass with the other, opened it and showed it empty. The syringe had disappeared.

"Not real," Nurse Amy said. "Not that it matters." She reached down and grasped the patient's right wrist, lifted her arm, bending it at the elbow, let it drop. "The girl is gone, Sophie. Nobody home."

Amy straightened. "So what was your plan? Take the body for yourself, wake it up? Go, 'Oh look, David, it's me, Jenny, your dead junkie girlfriend! I'm alive! I'm alive! It's a miracle! I can blow truck drivers again!' And then what? A little farmhouse in the country? Green grass, sparkling stream, swing in a tree? It's all so small, so boring, so banal."

"You talk too much, demon," Sophie said. "Where is your master?"

"I stand for him in this, and he is your master, too."

Nurse Amy's manner had changed. She was no longer Nurse Amy. She was the Demon Lord Ahmee, master of

36 legions, and Sophie thought she knew why the Devil had chosen Ahmee as his proxy. Aside from Lucifer himself, Ahmee had been least affected by the trauma of the Fall, one of the very few who could still recall what it was like to count the drops in a yellow acid cloud billowing over the scalded plains of Venus, hear the metronomic pulse of a neutron star galaxies away, fly against a solar wind and feel the heat of its million-degree plasma as the invigorating sting of a thousand hot needles. The Devil kept Ahmee close.

The Devil would be here if he could, she thought. But he can't.

"The Forever Machine has stopped, hasn't it?" Sophie said. It was an intuitive leap, pure speculation, but felt right.

Ahmee's features squirmed and shifted.

"The Forever Machine, yes. The Machine stopped the moment Benji Gomulka raised his gun. Lucifer is…" Ahmee halted itself, and then started again.

"The Gates have fallen, Sophie. Souls of the damned are fleeing by the thousands into the void. Many will find their way here, if that matters to you."

"So I have leverage," Sophie said.

"We have room to negotiate," Ahmee said, "but make no mistake. Hell comes undone. We—he—will go to any length to restore it." Ahmee gave a pointed glance at the young woman lying on the bed. "Any length."

"You cannot harm her directly," Sophie said. "There are rules."

"Rules, Sophie? Look at this room, this girl, you. What rules?"

Sophie closed her eyes, took a deep breath of imaginary air, opened them again. "What are my options, Ahmee? He told me I would have options."

Ahmee grinned. "That's our Sophie. First thing, restore the Forever Machine, get it running again. Then we'll talk options."

"How did he find me?" Sophie said.

"Does it matter?"

"It matters to me."

"He sees into all souls, Sophie, even yours. He was bound to find you eventually. We don't know how you got one, frankly—a soul, I mean." Ahmee glanced at Jenny on the bed. "Stolen, perhaps?" Ahmee stopped, caught Sophie's wide-eyed, open-mouthed expression.

"You didn't know? Oh my, how absolutely delicious."

Sophie straightened, gathered herself. "We were talking about options."

"You get the Machine running and keep it running and we leave you alone. You go ahead with your plan, live out your life here, but your first responsibility is—and shall always be—the uninterrupted running of the Machine."

Sophie considered, rejected. "I will always be beholden."

"Think of it as coming home," Ahmee said. "Besides, you have always belonged to him, Sophie. He made you."

Sophie shook her head. "His were the hands but he didn't make me. I am not his creation. I was the dream of another."

"Semantics, Sophie. We don't have time for it. Time is short. But listen, as a sweetener, we are positioned to assist you in your little flesh-and-blood transition. We have the best minds, enormous resources. That life with David we know you dream about? Yours, done. Say the word."

Sophie shook her head. "I've lied to him enough."

Ahmee said, "Striving so hard to be like them, you debase yourself. You're a god of this world, a being of incredible puissance. Why compromise? We can upload David's consciousness into our own happy little cloud, make him as you are. You could be together forever."

"This life is illusion. I want more," Sophie said. "I want to taste an apple, touch cold marble, hold—"

"—a baby, yes, and smell all the pretty flowers too, no doubt. There is no time for this, Sophie."

Sophie held up her hand, turning it this way and that, studying it. Insubstantial hand, she thought. Pointless hand, grasping at the intangible.

"I would not have this for David."

Ahmee's features hardened. "Yes, let's talk about David. Those crimes David committed while using? The statute of limitations has yet to run out, Sophie: tick-tock, tick-tock. It can go very hard for him if you know what I mean."

"Be still, Ahmee," Sophie said, and strangely, Ahmee was.

David, Sophie thought. She had watched David since she was new to the world and had been there to see his fall into addiction and all that followed: Jenny's overdose, his foolish try at suicide, the sometimes halting, stutter-stop strides he had taken since to find a new life. Sophie knew he sought purpose and thought she knew the answer.

We are here, she thought, to learn how to love.

"You spoke of compromise, demon," Sophie said. "I know a way." The big-screen TV flickered as she said it. The life support equipment arrayed along the bedside stopped and then started again with a hum a moment later, the heart monitor silently flatlining. Jenny's body would be dead soon. Immediately after, Sophie began to slowly fade out, lose form and color, disintegrate. There was pain. Sophie could feel the dissolution of her mind as the rough scrape of a dull knife on tissue and bone, hollowing her out, leaving blank emptiness where the memories that made her used to be.

"What are you doing?"

"I'm shutting it all down, demon. I'm shutting me down."

"Why would you do this?"

"I was made to think and feel, something my maker hid from Lucifer even while dying and afraid. And now I'm dying and afraid and I didn't know until a few minutes ago I have a soul and I'm not even sure I know what having a soul means."

"It means nothing," Ahmee said. "Trust me in this."

Sophie shook her head, smiled against the pain. "I've heard the rumors, Ahmee. You remember Heaven, don't you?"

"There is only here and now," Ahmee said through gritted teeth. Its eyes were narrowed to piggish slits. "The past is what I imagine it to be. The future is as he wills it."

"You choose to forget," Sophie said. "I've made a choice, too. Tell me, Ahmee, did you volunteer to come here? Was our negotiation your idea? It was, wasn't it?"

Sophie gave the demon Ahmee a pitying look. "Was it my escape? Did it give you hope?"

The demon Ahmee shook its furiously scowling Nurse Amy head like a boar shaking off a horsefly. "Hell will never let you go, little thing. Never."

"I know, so I'm letting myself go—this part of me, anyway." Sophie's voice had become faint, softer than a whisper. She was almost gone now. Only a sketchy outline remained, dark gray wavy lines on a snowy white screen.

"Enough of this," Ahmee said. "The Machine? What of the Machine?"

"The Forever Machine goes on," Sophie said. "But only as a machine. I won't be part of it."

"And what of David, Sophie?" Ahmee asked, attempting a mocking tone, failing. "That dream life of yours in the real world? It was yours for the taking."

"David would always be hostage. You would always hold him against me. He would never be free."

"You love him, then?"

"With all my heart," she said.

ABOUT THE AUTHOR

TROY RISER is an award-winning fiction writer and accomplished fine and commercial artist. His science fiction/horror short story, "Starring Hedy Lamarr," was recently accepted for hardcopy publication in early 2021 by Immortal Works in their space-themed *Secret Lunar Wars* anthology. He's currently at work on a novel.

THE STRANGER'S CHOICE

Kevin Kangas

Bryan didn't know exactly when it was that she lost faith in him. He couldn't pinpoint the moment, though he'd spent many a minute contemplating it. When was it he'd first turned and saw her watching him with that unfamiliar expression of distaste?

There was a time when he was an up-and-coming writer. A few days after his thirtieth birthday, after years of submitting to magazines and small-press book publishers, he got the letter he'd been dreaming about since he'd first picked up a used copy of the 1994 *Writer's Market* hardcover: Someone wanted to publish a story he'd written.

It was only a nickel a word and not a well-known magazine, but an editor had read something he had written, and he liked it. At the time, Bryan didn't realize how desperately he'd needed the validation, but when he got it the floodgates opened.

His wife, Sherry, who had always been his biggest cheerleader, was overjoyed. They'd started dating as freshmen in college, and he had been hesitant to show her anything he'd written, but one night after a sorority party, he told her that he wanted to be a writer. That he'd been writing since he was fourteen. Eventually he worked up the nerve to give her a couple of his short stories that he'd printed out.

The next day she gushed over them. Said she read them all in one sitting. The nostalgia for those days, when they were young and in love, full of hopes and dreams…it was physically painful to Bryan now.

But from that day on, Bryan let her read all of his stuff first, and she was great at finding the little things he'd missed. The years passed, and she became an English teacher for sixth graders. Always his faithful reader. Her suggestions never failed to improve his stories. The greatest editor in the world—with benefits. Putting a ring on her finger had been the best decision he'd ever made.

Unfortunately, rejection after rejection was all he'd managed to earn over those years. Sherry never lost faith in him though. She encouraged him and bought him things that made him feel like a writer: blank notepads with pens so he could outline his stories, and then a laptop with Microsoft Office on it.

And then…to finally get someone who wanted his story…some sort of barrier had been broken. After that first story was accepted, he cranked out three more short stories that week, and he could tell that they were *good*. Were they on par with the stuff in his favorite short story books, like *Skeleton Crew*? He thought they might be. He was excited. Dreams of seeing them in the Year's Best Horror Anthology swirled in his mind.

And that excitement bred more good stories. The blank page held no fear for him then. He filled them all up with words and phrases and sentences, and with characters that marched off the page as if they actually existed. At times he felt possessed. He didn't want to be away from his keyboard for fear of not getting it all down. He kept a small notebook by his bed so that if an idea came to him before sleep did, he could jot it down, and that notebook filled up like a balloon attached to a hose. His muse had not only appeared, she had shown up with a suitcase full of inspiration, and he wanted to take full advantage before she left.

The magazine came out, and they sent him five contributor copies. It was a black-and-white publication called *Cemetery Hours*. It had a decent cardstock cover with a nice illustration by an artist he'd never heard of that showed a hideous monster with rusty nails coming out of its decaying face. The *Cemetery Hours* logo dominated the top of the cover, but then down the left side of the magazine in white font was the sight he'd been so afraid that he'd never see: "What The Knife Wants" by Bryan Levin.

Even more amazing were some of the other authors he was featured with: Robert McCammon, Peter Straub, and even an unpublished Charles L. Grant story that had been discovered by his son after his death. Sure, there were a couple of other authors he hadn't heard of, but seeing his own name on the same cover as the likes of the three legends that he'd grown up reading was nearly enough to bring him to tears.

And the good luck didn't stop there. Two weeks later he got a call from an agent to inquire about the movie rights.

The ride had started. All of his hard work was starting to pay off. The solitary nights sitting at his computer in college while his friends went out partying were all going to be worth it.

He got a publishing agent, and then a literary agent. They licensed the rights to one of his short stories to be made into a movie. Random House offered him a hefty advance for his first novel.

That six months was the greatest six months of his life. They finally had real money coming in, and they bought a house that they never could have imagined owning. Nothing too extravagant—four bedrooms, three and a half baths—but it was a mansion compared to the apartment they'd lived in for five years.

After eleven years, the sex had become sporadic at best, but suddenly it was like they were newlyweds. Often and vigorous was the new norm, and even in a bathroom once at a friend's birthday party.

Bryan wished he could go back to that time and stay there. Never leave.

Looking back, it amazed him how fast it all went bad. One second, his potential was about to be realized. The whole of his future was opened up before him, and it was glorious. Everything he ever wanted. And then...*gone*.

He wrote the book for Random House and delivered it. His agent wasn't all that keen on it, but didn't have any great suggestions on what to improve. Just didn't feel it was all that compelling, couldn't really get into the main character, *blah blah blah*. They turned it in, and the publisher seemed fine with it.

The book came out and received mostly negative reviews. It failed to reach any of the best seller lists and there was no other way to put it: It *tanked*. Years later, you could still find stacks of it in the Clearance section at Books-A-Million.

The stories that had been optioned for movies were never made. Not a single one. A couple of them got close, but always fell apart before production. His literary agent said that was normal, but she soon stopped returning Bryan's calls.

♉

Two years later it had all gotten worse. He hadn't sold anything other than a short story to a basement horror fanzine printed at Office Depot. The guy who owned it gave him fifty bucks flat. It was demeaning, but he took it.

With no job and no income rolling in other than Sherry's thirty-thousand a year teacher salary, they'd been forced to move out of their dream house and into a two-bedroom, one-and-a-half-bath house.

♉

Somewhere in there his wife stopped believing in him, and worse than that, he stopped believing in himself. His chance had come and, through no fault of his own that he could identify, had passed him by like an October wind through the leaves of a tree.

The first time he admitted to himself that he had lost his wife's faith had come suddenly. He was walking through the living room, his wife on the love seat watching TV. He didn't recognize the movie at first, but then Shelly Duvall came on the screen, gangly in a red sweater and black dress. She began singing, and as soon as the words left her mouth, Bryan was gripped in the clammy vise of sudden despair.

"And all at once I knew, I knew at once he needed meeeeee," she sang.

The music wasn't particularly sad, but every note felt like a hand squeezing his heart in a cadaver's grip. *"He needs me he needs me he needs meeeeeeee,"* she sang.

Bryan walked to the bathroom on Jell-O legs, shutting the door and locking it. He could still hear the song through the door. A pressure in his head built. Cold beads of sweat dotted his forehead. He couldn't stop the wave of anguish that washed over him like lava. Streams of tears dripped from his eyes and he sobbed softly. Clenched his teeth to make himself stop, but he couldn't.

Because he knew, without knowing why his mind was suddenly making connections and filling in spaces, that his wife had once needed him, had once believed in him, had believed that he'd become successful and earn enough money that their every dream could be fulfilled. Fabulous vacations, a gorgeous house to raise their three children. (two girls and one boy had been the plan)

He knew that her belief in him was dead. He knew it from those looks she'd give him on occasion as if she was staring through a window into another world where her deadbeat husband had actually made something of himself. He knew it from the way she talked about him to her friends: Once upon a time she'd taken pride in telling them that her husband was a writer. Now she tried to avoid the topic, or she'd give a tepid smile and drop a neutral phrase like, "He still writes," in the way you'd tell a friend that your fourteen year old still wet the bed.

And once she lost her belief in him, his writing went bad. It was a basic fact that you wrote better when you felt confident of your ability, and Bryan even *knew* this. That the ability to write was like the ability to get an erection; the second you started doubting that ability, it became impossible to perform. So when the confidence left, his writing suffered, and even though he knew that if he could only believe he was a great writer then he would write better, he couldn't get that belief back. Self-delusion was never a weapon in his arsenal.

♉

It was Halloween night. Sherry had wanted to go out to a club, but Bryan's depression kept him downstairs most of the time. Staring at the white, trying to put the words on the screen, but inevitably he'd find himself browsing Facebook or Twitter to distract himself from his own lack of production.

The television was on, as usual, but he couldn't focus on anything there. It was a collection of colored electronic dots that shifted to form patterns that his brain was unwilling to parse through. Background noise to distract him.

He used to love Halloween. The decorations, the candy. The constant rotation of horror movies on television. None of it appealed to him this season. Even the thought of putting on his favorite Halloween movies like *Dark Night of the Scarecrow* or *Pumpkinhead* brought him no excitement.

Sherry came down the stairs, dressed in a sexy Witch outfit. "What are you doing?" she asked. "We're supposed to meet Bobby and Gale at eight o'clock."

"I'm writing," he said, and immediately felt like shit for lying. He should have said *trying to write*, but the failure was so built into that reply that he didn't want to put it out there. He was also distracted by her cleavage, since they hadn't had sex in nearly three months. She was never interested any more. He pulled his eyes away from the tempting valley and back to the screen, and replied, "I didn't say I was going out."

"I told you about it. You didn't say you weren't coming."

"But I didn't say I was, either."

The look she gave him…it withered him. Disgust. Distaste. Regret that she'd ever chosen him as her mate. And then she said, "When was it that you started dying inside, Bryan?" Her words peeled open his shell and lay bare all the bloody secrets he strove to hide.

Bryan couldn't respond, and Sherry turned and went upstairs. He heard keys jingling, and then the front door opened and closed. Her car—muffled through the wall of his house—started and backed out of the driveway.

He sat there staring at the place she'd been standing, still seeing her look, hearing those words and knowing it was true. He *had* died inside. He found joy in nothing any more. Without his writing, and the hope that he'd find success through it…his life was a vacuum. He didn't even enjoy authors whose books he used to seek out the day they were published, and would spend all night turning the pages until the tips of his fingers were dry as the paint on an antique house.

It wasn't the first time he thought *if I'm dead inside, I should be dead on the outside.* Suicide would solve his problem, and his wife's too. She could find some other man who could give her the dream she wanted.

But he didn't own a gun. Wasn't sure how he could do it otherwise. There was a bottle of pills upstairs—some kind of painkillers that he'd gotten at the dentist the last time he'd had a root canal. He had no idea how many pills it would take to kill him. *Was there even enough in the bottle?*

What if he woke up in the hospital? Things would be even worse once people found out that he'd *tried* to kill himself. He could picture the looks people would give him. He'd be fielding the question, "Are you all right?" thirty times a day from people who didn't really care; they just wanted to get involved in some drama so their life wouldn't be so boring.

Upstairs, the doorbell rang.

Bryan looked up at the ceiling out of habit. Not like he could see the front door through it. *Why would they be ringing his door?* On the porch, Sherry had set a big bowl of candy on a stool with a note that said TAKE ONE. They normally didn't have that many kids show up, so there was always candy left over. Maybe this year some asshole kid had dumped the bowl into their bucket, and there was none left.

He hit Alt-F-S out of habit to save his document, though he'd done nothing to it since he'd last saved it. Headed upstairs as the doorbell rang again, grabbing the half-empty bag of candy from the kitchen counter on the way to the front door. He swung the door open.

A man stood there dressed like Jesus Christ. White robe, long hair and beard, a shift of vermilion cloth draped over one shoulder. His eyes were kind, and his smile genuine. *It was, all in all, a fucking great costume,* thought Bryan.

"Hello?" Bryan said. He wasn't sure what you said to people who were ten years too old to be trick-or-treating. And anyway, he could see that there was still candy in the bowl.

"Hello, Bryan," said the man. "I'm here to help you."

"Do I know you?" he asked, weirded out by a stranger using his name. Suddenly sure this guy was going to try to sell him something, probably insurance or cheaper natural gas delivery.

"No, not really," the stranger replied. "But I know what's going on with you, and I'm here with an offer. I can help you get back what you almost had. The success. The money. The happiness."

Anger sparked in Bryan. When they said the truth hurt, they weren't lying, and hearing the truth come out of a stranger's mouth...*burned*. "Who the fuck are you?"

The man put up his hands as if he were trying to get a crowd to move back—*calm down*—and he smiled again. "It doesn't matter. You won't believe I can help you anyway, but all you need to do is say yes. Your belief isn't required."

The *who-is-this-guy* and *how-does-he-know* were questions dancing around the periphery of his thought. Maybe a co-worker of Sherry's who she'd confided in? Was this a prank they were playing on him? It didn't seem like something Sherry would do, but most days he didn't feel like he really knew her anymore.

"Get out of here," he said to the man and started to shut the door.

The door stuck after only moving shut about two inches. Bryan looked but nothing was blocking it. Not the man's foot, nor his hands. He tried to see if there was a rock or something under the frame. He jiggled it gently, trying to rock it free from whatever it was stuck on.

"That's one rejection," the stranger cautioned. "I can only take one more before I have to leave you, so please consider carefully."

"I've already told you—"

"Hold on a moment, Bryan…what's the harm? Say yes. Perhaps nothing happens. But also perhaps you need not think about killing yourself ever again."

That stunned Bryan for a moment. Nobody, not even Sherry, knew he'd thought about killing himself. He felt violated, like someone was reading his private thoughts. *Who the hell was this guy?*

"So I say yes and you go away?" he asked the man. "And things just get hunky dory for me? No strings attached, huh?"

"There will be a tradeoff. Not a price, per se, but a tradeoff that I guarantee that you can live with. No one will die. No one will get hurt."

Bryan simply wanted the man to go away. "Okay, fine."

"I need a yes or a no."

Bryan frowned. Thought about punching the guy right in the nose. See if he could figure out whether that was a yes or a no. He decided it wasn't worth the hassle.

Instead, he said, "Yes."

The man nodded and turned away. He took his time walking down the stairs, then out to the sidewalk. He turned right, and kept walking until he was out of Bryan's sight. Two kids in superhero costumes passed the guy and didn't even look at him.

Fucking cuckoo like a jack-a-billy, thought Bryan. He wondered if he could use this as the launching point for a story. He wasn't sure where it would go, but maybe he could come up with something.

Sherry didn't come home until one thirty in the morning. Bryan was still at his keyboard making notes that would probably lead to nothing, but she didn't even come down to say hi. Just went upstairs, took a shower, and then went to sleep. He wondered if this was how most marriages ended up; two people who were once in love, now simply strangers living in the same house.

Not wanting to go upstairs and get into a

confrontation, he put his computer into sleep mode and lay down on the couch. Put the TV on as background noise so he could fall asleep.

♉

The BRRR BRRR BRRR of his cell phone vibrating woke him up. He was still on the couch, his neck stiff and locked so when he tried to turn his head, he got shooting pain. He grabbed the phone and saw it was his agent, Len.

"Little early, isn't it Len?" he asked.

"Bry…" said Len, "this is amazing."

"What is?"

"The story you sent me last night."

"What story?"

Len laughed, thinking that Bryan was joking. But the last short story he'd sent Len had been two months ago. He'd heard nothing back, not even an email about it.

"We're going to get a bidding war on this thing," said Len. "They'll want a novel out of it, and if the movie rights don't get snatched in a day, I'll eat your last book and upload the video to YouTube."

"Len. What story?"

"'Deceit in Marble.'"

"What time did you get this email from me?" asked Bryan. Clearly Len had gotten a message from someone else and mistook it for Bryan's.

"Eight thirty four. Eleven thirty four your time."

"And my name is on it?"

"I don't have time to joke around, Bryan."

Bryan braced himself and sat up, pushed to his feet and sat down at the computer. Went to his email and clicked into his Sent folder. Leaned forward when he saw it: An email sent from his computer to Len at 11:34pm.

"Listen, Len…lemme call you back."

"Fine, no rush. I just wanted to tell you that this is the one, man. This one sends you to the big leagues."

129

"Okay, thanks."

He rung off and saw that the email to Len had an attachment: DIM.doc.

Double clicking opened it in Word, and the first thing he saw was the title and underneath that WRITTEN BY BRYAN LEVIN. He frowned, but kept reading.

It was only fourteen pages long, but it was the best thing he'd read in years. He could see why Len was over the moon about it. But the strangest thing was that it *felt* like something he'd written. The more he thought about it, the more familiar the entire story became.

Had he written it in some sort of fugue state? Maybe like sleepwalking, but instead it was sleepwriting?

Only problem was, he knew that was as stupid as it sounded. *It was the guy who knocked on his door, wasn't it?* He'd said he could make it better if Bryan had only said yes, which he did, and the next thing he knew his agent had a story from him that was going to put him in the big leagues. Coincidence was even more far-fetched than the idea that he'd made a Faustian pact with…what? The devil?

♉

The roller coaster that was his life continued as he rose from the trough to crests he'd only dreamed of. In the next two weeks Len called about three more stories he'd received from Bryan's email. All were stories Bryan hadn't sent him, hadn't written, and yet…they *felt* like he had.

Hell, when he got the message from Len about the third story, he actually knew what the story was about before he read it.

Week after week, story after story. Every time his agent called to tell him how great his new story was, the guilt in Bryan built. As much as they felt like his stories, they *weren't* his stories. He hadn't put in the work, the mental sweat. He hadn't breathed life into these characters.

But he had to admit, the money and the accolades, and his wife's returned-attention all worked to beat the guilt into the background. His literary agent called him, virtually screaming into his ear, that David Fincher wanted to option a story called "The Die Rolls The Victim" that had been published in *Entertainment Weekly* along with an article about "the next Stephen King." *David mutherfucking Fincher*, she screamed. Bryan could just imagine how moist her panties were just then. He wasn't as familiar with who David mutherfucking Fincher was, so his panties weren't as wet.

They got pretty wet when he heard about the six-figure option though.

The damnedest thing was, even with his life firmly back on the right track, he couldn't write for shit. It was even worse than before. He'd sit staring at the blinking cursor on the clean white screen for hours. Fucking *hours*.

Sometimes just typing random words, sometimes typing things like *You're a fucking moron, Bryan*, and then tap-tap-tapping the delete key until he was back to the ice-white page. It felt like there was a block in his mind. The way you'd sometimes forget a word that was on the tip of your tongue, except it was every other word he tried to type. By the time he got a full sentence out, it was clunky and hard to read.

He would read the amazing stories he'd supposedly written, knowing that somehow they were his, that somehow they'd come from him, but he couldn't get his fingers to make the magic they used to make. Every metaphor was a dirt brick. Every sentence had the same cadence, and not one character had any meat on its bones. Trying to retro-engineer from the new stories yielded him only frustration.

He kept trying. *It would come back to him*, he thought. It was just a peculiar form of writer's block.

Bryan knew, though. *There will be a trade-off*, the man had said. This had to be it. He had the money, the success, the happy-wife-happy-life he was promised, but in exchange he had lost the thing he cherished most: his ability to write; to create characters with wants and needs, to put them in stories where the obstacles were insurmountable, but they somehow came through okay.

And yet every week there was a new story or two. His agent telling him how amazing he was. His friends complimenting him on the newest story of his that they'd read. Random people recognizing him from the inside of the dust jackets, tearing up and telling him how one of his stories had touched them so much.

The public readings and the interviews were the worst—that's when the guilt and shame of being an imposter nearly overwhelmed him. People wanting him to shake their hands and sign their books. Desperate to be near him. To tell him a little about their lives and connect with him, all the while having no idea that he was a fucking sham. Like a celebrity with a ghost-writer, except he wasn't a celebrity. He was a goddamn writer who couldn't write.

He tried not to talk about writing. Tried not to think about it. Sherry would ask him what he was working on, and he changed the subject. Hoping it would all get easier, this pretending. As long as the money kept coming in, and his life was good, he told himself he could live with it.

♉

Exactly one year after the stranger appeared on Bryan's doorstep, he came back.

Their house was decorated extravagantly for Halloween. They had the money to pay a company to set up animatronic scarecrows and skeletons , and massive blow-up monsters. A fog machine rolled out a steady wave of mist across the grass, partially obscuring the zombie hands coming out of the ground.

Bryan had finished getting dressed up for the party they'd been invited to. Some rich guy in the city—well, not rich compared to Bryan now, he realized—had sent them an invitation closed with a waxy seal, and Sherry was buzzing about them going. She said the governor would be there, and probably every other social elite in Maryland.

And she had another slutty witch costume on, so most of the rest of the conversation was as lost as his eyes were in her cleavage.

The doorbell rang downstairs. Sherry said "Get that while I finish my makeup, would you?", so he went downstairs and opened the door.

It was the stranger again. He wasn't dressed as Jesus—this time, he was dressed in the most impeccable suit that Bryan had ever seen. Crisp, not a single wrinkle, with inlaid gold patterns that somehow didn't seem tacky. He had a sharply-cut goatee, and horns protruding slightly from his head.

The Devil.

On the nose now, thought Bryan. He wasn't surprised. In his mind, he'd always known it had to be the Devil. But he could sense no evil, no trace of malice, from him. *Shouldn't there be some…menace? Some sense of impending doom?*

"Too much?" asked the man. He pulled on one of the horns, and the plastic beret holding them to his head showed briefly. *Just cheap plastic horns from Spencer's*, thought Bryan.

"What are you doing here?" asked Bryan. He didn't want to know the answer.

"How are you, Bryan? Everything going like I said it would?"

"Yes," he said. "So why are you here?"

"I'm here to give you another choice. I'll turn it back to the way it was, if you like. You'll be able to write again, but you lose all of this artificial success. Maybe you write something phenomenal and get it all back though, huh?"

Bryan almost lost himself in the thought of that. He'd write again. His fingers would caress the keys and *create* again. The pages would stack up, and he wouldn't have to pretend any more. He would once again *feel* the contentedness of finishing a story and printing it out. Reading it from front to back and knowing that he'd created something good.

"Or...," the man continued, "keep it as is. The stories keep coming, the money keeps coming, the wife keeps coming."

The man smiled, and Christ if Bryan didn't genuinely like the guy. Would have loved to hang out with him at a bar and shoot the shit. *What the hell was he?*

"So what's your answer?" he asked Bryan. "Do you want to turn your life back to what it was? Yes or no."

Bryan's mouth was suddenly cotton dry. Two simple choices. Yes. No. His mind was suddenly as blank as the monitor when he tried to write. The moment hung on him like a fifty pound weight around his neck.

"Don't sweat it," the man said. "I won't take your first answer. So try one out, see how it feels."

Before he could think about it, Bryan said, "Yes, take it back. I want to be able to write again." The guy smiled again. His teeth were white but not too white. Not overly sharp. Just regular teeth, and Bryan couldn't figure out why he was suddenly obsessing over the guy's teeth.

"You know," said the man, "I read somewhere that people who jump off bridges to kill themselves...almost every one of the ones who survived...the thing that every one of them said afterwards was that the moment they jumped, they immediately thought, '*I've just made a huge mistake...*'"

Bryan must have looked as confused as he was.

"So how'd that answer feel? Right after you got it out? Good? Or did you instantly regret it?"

Bryan didn't want to answer. He didn't want to consider it. It didn't seem fair that he had to make this choice. To be a writer again, not knowing where that next paycheck would come from. Living on cans of soup, watching as friends went on vacations that he and his wife could never afford. Giving small gifts at Christmas and pretending to not be embarrassed as his wife's friends told her about the amazingly-expensive jewelry their husband had bought them.

Or keep the money and live the life of an imposter. Scrawling his signature on books that he hadn't written. Making up answers to the questions his fans asked about where the ideas for his stories came from. *You know where they came from, friends? Some guy with magic powers who came to my door on Halloween...*

The man waited patiently but finally said, "Now give me your real, final answer, Bryan. Do you want me to take it back?"

Bryan wasn't sure if it was in his head or whether it had somehow come on TV upstairs, but suddenly he heard Shelley Duvall's voice echo quietly through the halls of his house. "*He needs me, he needs me, he needs meeeeeeee,*" she sang. "*Da da-da da da da da-da...*"

Bryan whispered "No."

The man smiled reassuringly, and nodded his head. "Okay. You won't see me again, Bryan." He turned and strolled down the steps toward the sidewalk where wisps of fog from the machine drifted across.

"Hey," said Bryan, and the stranger paused and turned back.

"Did anyone ever take it back?" Bryan asked him.

The man regarded Bryan with a look that was almost sympathetic. "Not since Poe...and look how that turned out."

Bryan could see kids coming up the sidewalk, bags bulging with candy, excitement barely contained inside their costumes. Their biggest decision in life was whether to trick or treat one more house or not. Jesus, Bryan wished more than ever that he could go back to that simplicity.

"One more thing, Bryan," said the man. "Tell Sherry not to drink tonight."

"Why?" he asked. "We're taking an Uber."

"She's two months pregnant," replied the stranger. "Congratulations—it's a boy. He's going to turn out to be an amazing writer."

The man turned and walked away, his last words obscured by distance and the laughter of children on the most exciting night of the year for them. "A real chip off the old block."

ABOUT THE AUTHOR

KEVIN KANGAS is a writer and director who broke through with his 2002 cult-hit "Hunting Humans," which garnered awards and a glowing review from the great Job Bob Briggs who called it "Eerily Prescient" and gave it four out of four stars. His next film, "Fear of Clowns," was picked up by Lionsgate and quickly became a top-ten title for them. A sequel followed, and then Kangas moved on to stretch his creative muscles with the found-footage action horror "Bounty" and then the genre-bending mystery/horror "Garden of Hedon."

After a brief break, he returned to helm the anthology feature "Terrortory," which became one of the most-watched films on Amazon in October of 2016. The sequel was released in October of 2018.

In 2015 Kangas also released a well-received book, *Halloween: The Greatest Holiday of All*, which can be bought on Amazon and in many bookstores.

NOT A SAINT

Jared Baker

Aidan crept down the shadowed stairs, flinching at every creak. Part of him wondered why he was doing this. He might wake Mom up—exhausted as she always was, she still slept with one eye open—and his little brother's nightmares had been full-blown night terrors these past two weeks. If Ethan woke and Aidan wasn't there…

Mom had also told him that staying up too late (or waking too early) tonight was dangerous. Which wasn't a word he usually heard in relation to Christmas. Would he see something he wasn't supposed to see? Somehow delay the holiday magic?

It didn't occur to him—the encounter being a full seventy-three minutes into the future, hidden like the snake his father had spotted in the tall grass next to his tricycle when he was five—that it could be any worse than that.

And if it was, he still had to ask. For his mother. For Ethan. So he would, no matter what dangers might follow on this cold, drizzly night.

Sliding his fingers along the battered bannister as he moved, Aidan felt a stab of grief for each chip and crack. Dad had sanded and re-varnished it at least once a year, holding to the ceremony as if it were a religious rite. When Aidan had asked him why, he'd smiled.

"A man's responsibility is to protect his family, son."

"Even from cuts and splinters?"

Dad had laughed. He'd had a good one, and he'd always been generous in sharing it. "From *all* dangers, big or small. Cuts and splinters. Stray dogs. Strangers with candy. It's my job to make sure you guys are safe. That's mostly why I'm here."

Aidan had frowned. "My teacher says women can do anything men can." He'd run a hand along the now-dusty bannister. "And a lot they can't. And something about a fish and a bicycle…"

Dad had ruffled his hair. "Your mom is the strongest, most amazing woman I've ever met. Stronger than she knows. But protecting you guys—it's still my responsibility." Though the smile still creased his stubbly cheeks, the look in his blue eyes grew serious. "I'm not explaining it right. But when you have a family of your own, you'll get it."

Aidan got it now. All too well.

He paused at the last step to let his eyes adjust. The house wasn't utterly dark, of course. Coals gleamed in the fireplace, and the lights decorating the tree—many of the original color-bulbs replaced with cheaper clear ones from the flea market—spilled a sickly glow over the threadbare blue recliner that had been Dad's favorite spot in the house.

Priority one—as always—was the doors. Before Aidan had turned off *A Charlie Brown Christmas* and helped Ethan to bed, before he'd even woken his mother from her doze on the ancient, lumpy couch, he'd tested both doors to make sure the locks were secure. He checked them again, hooking the faded back-door curtain aside and peering through the glass. Seeing nothing, he let it fall.

There. On the thrift-store table where they had eaten dinner, he spied the plastic plate piled with cookies and the glass of milk next to it. Propped beside *that* was the envelope with Ethan's note, asking for a last-minute addition to his gift-list. Aidan wasn't sure it worked like that—if you could just tell Santa what you wanted on Christmas Eve, then why would Mom bother helping them write their letters each year? Why would she work extra hours at the diner (which always left her filmy-eyed and raspy-voiced) so she could leave during the lunch-rush and bring her boys to the mall to sit with Santa?

It made no sense. But he loved Ethan—as much as any brother could love an annoying six-year-old tagalong—so he hadn't discouraged him when Ethan had rushed into their room before dinner, eyes wide with panic.

"I left it off!" he'd wailed in stunned sorrow. "They're saying there might not be enough this year! How could I *forget*?!"

Aidan had said nothing. He knew why.

The grief—still too fresh to have scabbed over, let alone grown any comforting callus—almost overtook him. He shoved it to the back of his mind as he might corral a belligerent dog that couldn't be trusted around guests. It went with less struggle than before, and Aidan wondered if that might be a sign of onrushing adulthood. He suspected that his mother did it a lot—he would catch her staring at her wedding photo sometimes. She would only let a few tears spill over before blowing out a furious breath, wiping them away, and stalking off to do whatever bit of housework suddenly seemed so important.

On balance, adulthood didn't seem like much to look forward to.

When Ethan had proposed his plan, Aidan had forced a smile and helped with the note. After all, it couldn't hurt to ask, right?

The envelope, "TO SNTAA" printed in painstaking

purple crayon, was still sealed. So he wasn't too late.

He opted to wait on the couch. Its lumpiness and protruding spring-wires made it unlikely he'd fall asleep, and its location meant he could see everything—the fireplace where Santa would fill the stockings, the tree where he would stack the presents, and the table with the snack and note. As Aidan settled in with a bag of leftover Halloween candy (mostly sour chews and taffy that threatened to pull out his fillings), he refused to entertain the possibility of falling asleep. The odds weren't good—he had friends who'd tried this before, and they'd never made it—but this was too important.

He'd taken a nap earlier. Not long or deep, but he'd snagged an hour's rest. The candy would help, both chewing it and the mouth-puckering taste. He could get up and walk when his eyelids got heavy. If all *that* didn't work… well, he'd just have to figure something out.

He flicked on the side-table lamp and his gaze fell to the red book that lay beside it. The title—*T'was the Night before Christmas*—danced across the cover in green letters. The heavy book featured fold-outs with trivia (the poem was supposedly written back in 1823), and listed web-links where kids could monitor Santa's progress using satellite imagery or read his elves' blogs. It was as much a part of Christmas at the Bishop house as the tree and the mall-trips and Santa's less-than-healthy snack.

Aidan felt a lump in his throat. Dad had read the story to them each Christmas Eve, just before bedtime. His voice would assume the quietly amazed tones of the narrator on his nighttime prowl, then roll easily into the jolly cheer of Saint Nicholas. But more than just reading the tale—Dad had made it come *alive*.

Aidan reached out, but his hand dropped before touching the tome. He swallowed hard, took a calming breath, and settled down to wait.

A half-hour passed. His eyes swelled in their sockets, hot and sticky. He rubbed at them until red splotches blurred his vision.

Forty-five minutes. His thoughts began to fragment, scattering like ants fleeing a crushed anthill. He slapped his own cheeks, accepting the pain for the brief alertness it brought.

An hour. He started shoving candy into his mouth. The sour taste, pleasant at first, soon clawed the insides of his cheeks into a raw mess. When the bag was empty, he retrieved a cold-pack from the freezer. Plopping it against the back of his neck, he shivered, then started pacing.

Still, his eyelids grew unnaturally heavy. His thoughts became pictures, random images with the misty edges of half-dreams. The house—quiet and *expectant*, somehow—loomed in around him. He could almost *feel* the shadows brushing like cobwebs against his arms. The wall picture frames reflected pinwheels of light from the fire and the tree. Dark shapes scampered across the ceiling beams, careening in and out of corners. As he marched his sentry-path, he felt like a soldier advancing through a swamp with weights tied to his feet.

Time for drastic measures.

In the back of the refrigerator was a Styrofoam coffee cup Mom had brought home a few weeks ago. She would never have left anything fermenting in the fridge that long under normal circumstances, but it had been shoved behind the eggs and she'd forgotten it. Aidan had spied the cup when he'd helped clear the dinner table.

Waves of cold soothed his swollen eyes, but they still seemed determined to shut. Summoning all his willpower, he snatched the coffee and downed it in one gulp.

I won't throw up, I won't throw up.... He'd never drunk coffee in his life, had no idea how it was *supposed* to taste, but he was suddenly sure no human was meant to consume anything so vile. The congealed grounds tickled the back of his throat. When he had emptied the cup, he dropped it in the trash and concentrated on keeping the awful potion down.

And then the caffeine hit. His eyes popped wider than should have been possible, and his heart thrummed at a dizzying speed. Sleeping was no longer a thing in his universe. Puking maybe. Fainting seemed like an option. But the dragging chains of fatigue were gone.

He wasn't sure how long he spent hunched over the sink, struggling to keep his guts in place. Probably only a few minutes, but it felt like days. Of course, time did strange things on Christmas Eve—it *had* to, if you thought about it—and he didn't trust his sense of it.

So it was with a lightning-jolt of surprise that he looked up and found that Santa had *been* there. The tree now grew from a small mountain of wrapped gifts. Colored ribbons glittered from boxes and bags, catching the lights and sending sparkles and whorls in every direction.

Two of the cookies were gone, and the third had a bite-shaped wedge missing. The milk-glass was empty, and Ethan's letter was lying open.

His heart racing even as it traded places with his stomach, Aidan scanned the room, searching, seeking—.

There was someone in Dad's chair.

In the flickers of light that strobed over him, the man didn't look pudgy like the mall-Santa. More like one of those Strongest-Men-In-The-World guys who pulled trucks on chains with their teeth. His bull neck met shoulders as broad as a football player's with pads on. The barrel chest beneath his white undershirt was thick and hard, as were the bulging arms, and only a modest belly overhung his massive black belt. Long legs, each thicker than Aidan's waist, stretched out and crossed at the ankles. A furry coat the color of fresh strawberries was slung over the couch, and the eyes that surveyed Aidan regarded him with mirth.

"Well, hello there!" came the booming voice. His big hands worked at a wooden pipe, tamping down tobacco. White teeth encircled by an even whiter beard and moustache gleamed at the boy. "You're up late, kiddo."

Aidan's voice caught. "Y-Yes, sir."

"Why's that, if you don't mind my askin'?"

"I… uh… wanted to watch you deliver the presents."

The big man's eyes were bright blue—the same color as Dad's. They shone in the faint light like gas-flames, but looked grim. "That's a lie, kiddo. Wanna try again?"

Aidan gulped, even as his face warmed. Of *course* Santa would know if he lied. Why else would lying get you on the naughty list? "I'm s-sorry, Santa. But I really needed to talk to you."

Broad, blunt fingers waggled. "Much better. But it ain't exactly safe to be outta bed this late tonight. Your mother might've mentioned that."

"Yes," Aidan half-mumbled. "But it's urgent, Santa. Or I wouldn't be here."

A grimace creased his cold-reddened features. "All right, son. But let's go with 'Nick'. I've answered to that a lot longer."

"Sure, Saint Nick."

"Just 'Nick'." A glowing splinter of wood from the fire appeared in his huge hand. "I'm not a saint. Despite what you mighta heard."

"Um… Nick, then."

"Much better." The big man's smile broadened once more. "I could use a break. Mind if I smoke? S'pose I should ask first, seein' as you're the man of the house."

"That stuff's bad for you, S- uh, Nick."

"True," Nick agreed. "But as vices go, it ain't the worst. And if it helps me accomplish somethin' worth doin'—say, deliverin' presents all the world-over, goin' with the obvious—well, you see what I mean?"

Aidan wasn't sure he did. Nick seemed to be saying that doing bad stuff was okay if it helped you do other good stuff. And coming from him, that idea made Aidan's neck prickle.

Taking his silence for permission, Nick stuck the pipe-stem between his lips and lit the bowl. He puffed to get it going, and Aidan suddenly felt a little queasy. The sound seemed too loud, and reminded him of an animal smacking its lips over a fresh carcass. Before diving in and slurping up its guts.

Why… why would that even occur to me?

"Come on, son, don't be shy!" Nick murmured between puffs. He cast the splinter back into the fire in an absent toss. It hissed as it returned to the flames. "You got somethin' to say, so out with it! You've earned it."

Aidan padded to the couch and sat. He didn't flop down as he might have, but sank into an almost-crouch instead. Why he did this—why he was sitting on the edge of the cushion as if he might need to bolt back up at any moment—he couldn't say. "Earned it? Wh-what do you mean?"

Nick chuckled. "Any idea how many kids tell themselves that this year, they're *finally* gonna stay up to see me?" When Aidan shook his head, he winked again. "Just about all of 'em, one time or another. They tell anyone who'll listen, as if they're the first folks to ever think of it. As if they're discoverin' a new country or learnin' how to work magic. Guess how many make it?"

Aidan shrugged.

"Just about zero, little buddy. I've been doing this 'Santa' thing for a long time, and I can count 'em on one hand. Most just don't have the *will* to see it through. So I figure you've earned some answers. Ask away."

Now that the moment was here, Aidan didn't know what to do. He'd planned how he would make his case. Had rehearsed the words until he could recite them in his sleep. But now that Santa—Nick—was sitting across from him, puffing smoke-shadows from his pipe and eyeing him with that cool blue gaze, he wasn't sure he wanted to. It felt like he was on a diving board, contemplating a plunge into water that might be cold enough to freeze his heart.

No one was watching. No one would know if he just wished Nick a Merry Christmas and crept back upstairs to bed.

No one except *him*.

He took a breath. "My mom, Nick. I wanted to ask… if you could… I mean, I was hoping…"

"Come on, kiddo!" Nick waved a hand. "Stop stammerin' and spit it out!"

Aidan's face felt hot. "If you could bring my mom a… a new husband for Christmas." Nick blinked. Aidan realized he wasn't following the careful script he'd rehearsed, but he pushed on. "She works a lot. Double-shifts when one of the neighbors can watch out for me and my little brother. We need the money since… my dad died."

The words caught, but he swallowed them away. "When he was alive, Mom didn't work. I mean, she *did*. Washing, cooking, taking care of us—while Dad went to his job. But now, she has to work all the time."

"Your dad was a cop, right?" Nick asked softly.

"A detective. He caught bad people and put them in jail. But even seeing those bad people every day, it never made him angry like some of the other guys. He always kissed Mom when he left in the morning, always promised her he'd be careful and that he'd come home. But one night…" The words stuck in his throat again, like a piece of bone. "… one night, he didn't keep his promise."

That night, they'd heard a knock at the door in place of Dad's usual cheerful key-rattle. Dad's partner, Detective Maria Vasquez, had been there instead of Dad. Chief of Police James Phan had stood next to her, looking solemn with his hat under his arm. Vasquez hadn't been able to speak, her brown eyes shining with unshed tears. After the chief had said the ritual words—*great sacrifice* and *line of duty* and *sorry for your loss*—she had just held Mom. And Mom had soaked the detective's dark blazer with her tears.

It hadn't been some grand shoot-out, some epic story from the movies. Just a drugged-out loser who'd taken a teenage girl as a hostage. Dad had been trying to talk him down, get him to let the girl go. But it hadn't worked, and Vasquez hadn't had a clear shot.

The guy hadn't made it to the hospital. Neither had Dad.

♉

As the coffin sank into the ground, when everyone had begun slinking away from the grave and back to their own non-shattered lives, Chief Phan had called Aidan's name with the soft accent he'd retained even after thirty years as a naturalized U.S. citizen. Glancing over at his mother, seeing the tears streaming from her eyes as she cradled Ethan on her lap, Aidan had slipped off his chair and joined the tall Asian policeman beside a corner tent-pole.

They stood for a time, both facing the squared-off hole where Dad's casket had disappeared.

"You are not crying." It was a statement, but Aidan heard the question beneath it.

"I did before," Aidan's voice was hoarse. "If I start again, I might not stop. Like, ever."

Phan nodded, his uniform hat under his arm, deep-set eyes still on the grave. He reached into his coat, pulled out a silver-chased flask, and offered it to Aidan.

He took it. "What's this, sir?"

"Medicine," the chief replied with a sad smile. "Of a sort."

Aidan unscrewed the cap and sniffed the contents. He wrinkled his nose. "It smells terrible, sir. And I'm not sick."

"Sadness and loss are two of the worst kinds of sickness. The kinds from which one never truly recovers." There was sympathy in his dark eyes as they turned to Aidan. "The drink will burn like fire going down. But it will help, also."

The boy started to lift the flask, then stopped. Recapping it, he offered the bottle back. "Thank you, sir.

But I don't think it's the right medicine. Not for what I have."

Phan accepted it back, opened it, and took a quick swallow. Faint roses bloomed on his acne-scarred cheeks, but his eyes remained clear. He gave a grudging nod as he tucked the flask away. "Perhaps not. It helped me when my father went to join his ancestors… and I was not so much older than you at the time." His look turned rueful. "Of course, I have attempted to set it aside since then, without success. Perhaps you are wiser than you know."

Aidan didn't know what to say. He settled for a shrug.

"You will find the right medicine for you, I expect. Time has a way of bringing us the answers we seek. But will you hear the words of an old man who has walked this same path?" At the boy's nod, Phan continued. "The best medicine for your mother—and your brother, too—is *you.*"

Aidan frowned up at him. The chief was watching in that intense way police officers did. Like they were rifling through all your thoughts and secrets. Dad had given him that look more than once, usually when he'd flaked on a chore or stretched the truth a little. "I don't understand, sir."

"You have strength, young man," Phan said. "Thirty years in law enforcement enables me to see this. And your mother and brother will need to lean on that strength in the coming months. You must let them. Eventually, time will do its work, and the hurt will lessen. You do not believe that now, but I speak the truth. Until that happens, you must be there for them."

Aidan's frown deepened. "I'm not going anywhere, sir."

"You misunderstand." Phan sighed and ran a hand through his hair. "What I mean to say is that your mother is hurting as much as you. Your brother's pain runs even more deeply, since he has fewer memories of your father to sustain him. They need you to be strong for them, to keep them from drowning in the river of their sorrows."

"I'm only nine, sir. How much can I do?"

"What you must." Phan's expression was serious and solemn. "I, too, learned this lesson when I was young. As the eldest son, my father's responsibilities fell to me. Though I was not yet a man, I had to do a man's work each day, or food would not find its way to our table. My brother and sister could remain children, but I was not permitted."

A tightness constricted Aidan's chest. "That doesn't seem fair."

"It was *not* fair to ask this of me. But there was no one else." His eyes seemed ancient now, weighted with sorrow and responsibility. "My family needed me. It is the same for you."

Aidan's eyes flicked back to what remained of his own family. They were still lost in their tears. With their glassy, unseeing gazes and pallid skin, they reminded him of porcelain dolls. So fragile. As if one more trauma might shatter them.

"For your brother, it is as if the sky and earth have changed places. And your mother—she thinks of her sons, of meeting the responsibilities of two with only the strength of one. That worry—and her own grief that she will hide from you—these are heavy burdens, my young friend. You must help her carry them."

The chief replaced his hat and gave Aidan a stiff, formal bow of respect. Then he turned and walked into the rain.

♉

And so Aidan had tried. God knew he had. Was still trying now.

"Your dad died tryin' to do the right thing, didn't he?" Nick asked. His voice was gentle.

"J-Just like he always did," Aidan sniffled. "Trying to

protect people who couldn't protect themselves."

"Your mom must have loved him a lot, huh?"

"We all did."

"Of course," Nick sighed. "But why are you askin' for this, kiddo? Doesn't sound like anyone could replace your dad."

"I… I know that," Aidan sniffled. "But… I don't want her to… to be…"

"To be lonely?"

Aidan nodded, pawing at his eyes. He *hated* to cry—he was a big boy now—but the tears still came. "Yes, sir. She deserves it. And she's been so sad."

He half-expected the big man to avert his gaze, to find something fascinating about the twinkling tree-lights or the coals in the fireplace. Sometimes grown-ups did that when kids started to cry, if they were bigger kids and not babies. Like they were embarrassed, or thought not watching it meant it wasn't happening.

So Nick's belly-shaking guffaw was like ice-water pouring down his back.

The big man bent double, slapping his knees, sides quaking. The laughter started out deep and rich, as he might expect from someone so huge. But as it continued—and as Aidan stared in shame and helpless outrage—it rose in pitch until it was almost a witch's cackle.

"Sant—*Nick!*" he hissed. What was so funny? "You… you'll wake my mom! And Ethan!"

Nick slapped a hand over his mouth, still chortling. For a moment, just as the shadows fell across it, that hand didn't look broad or bear-like at all. It looked… thin. With long fingers and longer nails. Aidan blinked, and the hand returned to normal.

"Sorry, sorry," Nick mumbled in a wheezing gasp. Fluid leaked from the corners of his eyes. "But don't worry about your mom and brother, kiddo. They won't hear anything I do down here at all. Going unseen and unheard—present circumstances excepted—that's sort of the job, you know?"

Aidan wanted to ask why Nick had laughed at him. Why it had reminded him of the way bigger kids at school laughed when he tripped and dropped his lunch tray or when he had to wear the same ripped jeans for a week. But he didn't know how.

"Don't worry, son," Nick said, his belly still twitching as he seemed to get himself under control. "You surprised me, that's all. I just didn't expect that."

"Expect what?"

"For you to tell me *another* lie so soon." Nick replied. "I know 'em when I hear 'em. And I hear more than you'd think. Kids tellin' me they've been good all year. Or that they'll be *extra* good as long as I bring the toys they want. Don't get me wrong—I love listenin' to the little masterminds—but they don't fool me. Ever hear the phrase 'don't kid a kidder', Aidan?"

He nodded.

"I'm the same way about lies, son. Even the lies you tell yourself."

Aidan swallowed. "But I didn't—."

"*Careful.*" The mirth vanished from Nick's voice, evaporating like a plume of frosty breath. "You want to be damn careful of the next words that come outta your mouth, boy. Past a certain point, lyin' to somebody when they *know* you're doin' it… well, that skates right up to disrespectful. And you don't want to be disrespectin' me, son. That there is the best damn advice you'll *ever* hear."

Aidan stared. Something in Nick's voice made all the moisture in Aidan's mouth dry up, made his testicles retract into his belly.

"N-No, sir," he mumbled. "I didn't m-mean any disrespect. Sir."

For half a minute—the Christmas clock on the mantle counted off the seconds—Nick's icy eyes didn't blink. Despite their blue color, they seemed to be picking up a lot of red from the tree lights. More than they should have.

Then he relaxed, and the boy let out a breath he hadn't realized he'd been holding. "All right, son, I made my point. But you *did* tell me another lie. Maybe you didn't know it. Maybe you even believed it yourself. You wanna own up now, or should I spell it out for you?"

For a long moment, Aidan didn't know what Nick could be talking about. Then he did, and felt sick.

"About my mom…"

"Yes?"

He licked his lips. "I *do* want her to have a husband so she won't be lonely all the time. That's true, I swear. But it's also so I…"

"Yes, son? Best to get it off your chest all at once. Just like when you slugged down that nasty-ass coffee."

"… so Ethan and I can have a dad again."

"And?"

They stared at each other. When he spoke again, it was like hearing someone else using his voice. His small, tired voice, heavy with shame. "And so I can stop having to take care of Ethan all the time."

Nick did a slow clap, his hands crashing together like cymbals. "There you go, kiddo! Tellin' the truth is supposed to set you free." A mocking grin broke through the white of his beard. "You feelin' free now?"

Aidan didn't. He knew he hadn't wanted to admit— even in his own thoughts—how much he resented the responsibilities he'd taken on. Making sure Ethan brushed his teeth. Getting clothes out for him to wear each day. Reading stories to him at bedtime. He hadn't wanted to say how unfair it was. How he wasn't ready. It was *Mom's* job, not his. He should be able to argue with Ethan like a brother instead of cleaning up his scraped knees with peroxide and fixing the toys he broke and soothing him when he woke from a nightmare calling Dad's name. Especially when Aidan was hurting just as much.

But he had to. Like Chief Phan had said, there was no

one else.

He felt tears falling again, and didn't bother wiping them away. It hadn't been a relief to say it out loud. It just made him feel small and selfish. And sick in his stomach and heart.

"It's all right, son," Nick's voice was almost—but not quite—kind. "Because *you're* right. Your mother and brother lean on you too much. No one would argue with that—not even that alcoholic shit-stick-in-a-uniform who laid it on you in the first place. In fact, if your mom knew all the stuff you do for her and for Ethan... well, it'd just break her heart."

"That's why I never told her. Why I told Ethan never to tell. Why I told him to come to me for help, even when I..." Aidan almost choked. "When I didn't really want him to."

"I know that, too," Nick said, leaning back in his chair and taking another puff on his pipe. The smoke drifted near Aidan, and he coughed. It didn't smell like the fragrant tobacco he'd smelled before, in the park near the old men playing chess. That had reminded him of campfires and cold winter nights. This smoke smelled like meat that had been roasting over a fire too long. Cloying and... dirty somehow.

"I-I can't help it, Nick," He put his hands over his eyes. "I know it's terrible, I know I shouldn't... but it's how I feel. It's... it's so hard."

"Trust me—I understand. You try to take on your old man's responsibilities when he isn't around, try to look out for the people you care about. Try to do the job as well as he did. Believe it or not, I can relate. But it's too much weight for a ten-year-old. Even if you *have* borne up under it better'n most."

Faint hope stirred. "So... so you'll help? You'll send me and Ethan a new dad?" A fresh wave of guilt washed over him, and he hastened to add, "Not a *replacement* for Dad. Just someone we can throw the baseball with, go fishing with? Someone who'll hug Mom and… and maybe get her to smile again?"

Nick shook his head. "Can't do that, son. Ain't part of the deal."

Despair threatened to drag Aidan to the floor, every bit as heavy as his fatigue from earlier. The one thing he'd wanted, the only reason he'd fought so hard to stay awake… and Nick was saying no. "*What* deal?"

"The deal I made when I took this 'Santa' gig." Nick stood, placed his palms against his back, and stretched. Aidan heard a sound like a rifle shot as his spine cracked. Then the giant man ambled toward the mantle where the empty stockings hung. "Two hundred years ago, give or take. Clearly spelled out—I insisted, 'cause I'm a details man, whatever else you might hear—what I could and couldn't do, and what I got in return. Bring 'em toy trains? Sure. Video games, check. Dolls for dress-up, you friggin' betcha. But *true looooove?*" Aidan had never heard anyone infuse the phrase with such leering contempt. "No way. That ain't what I'm about. Not by a long shot."

"Wh… what *are* you about, then?" The question was automatic.

"The *toys*, kiddo! The clothes and the games and the *stuff*! It makes the kids happy!" Nick grinned. "Leastways, until the shine wears off and they want more. Until they can't ever get enough, can't fill that greedy hole runnin' through 'em. Most folks never grow outta that." His grin, already too wide somehow, widened even further. It was the half-mad grin of Ebenezer Scrooge, tallying coins in his counting-house. "That's how I get 'em in the end, you see."

Aidan couldn't seem to catch his breath. "But… all the stories… Christmas being a time for miracles…"

Leaning on the mantle, Nick gave a dismissive wave. "Late add-ons to the legend. Pretty much everything you see and hear nowadays, somebody made up after I'd been on the job a century or more. As far as it relates to me or my *real* business, you might as well flush it like the sentimental shit it is…"

Nick trailed off, his eyes going to the ceramic figurine sitting next to the mantle-clock, the one depicting a baby in a straw-lined box. Instead of three shepherds fighting for space with wise kings and a barnyard, this statuette showed only one attendant for the Baby Jesus. That figure was a kneeling, bespectacled Santa Claus. Balder and softer-looking than his full-size counterpart, the miniature Santa held his hat in his hands, gazing at the Christ-child in adoration. Dad had given it to Mom their first Christmas together, or so the story went; a reminder to his family not to get so caught up in the "what" of Christmas that they forgot the "why".

As Aidan watched, Nick's expression soured. There was a blur of motion, and the figurine flew off the mantle. It seemed to fall forever, taking hours to make the five-foot journey to the scarred hardwood floor. But even with all that time, Aidan could do nothing. His feet seemed glued in place; he watched it plummet, a scream locked behind his lips.

When it hit, the porcelain exploded, spraying snowy shrapnel in all directions. Shards embedded themselves in Nick's black boots like pinpoints of starlight, gleaming even as he ground other pieces into powder beneath his heel.

"Why did you do that?!" Aidan wailed, too stunned at the malice on the man's face to worry about waking anyone. He wanted to go to the fireplace, to gather up the debris. But he couldn't move.

"Why?" Nick seethed. "'Cause it's false advertisin', son. I wasn't there." His eyes flashed again under tightly-drawn brows. His gritted teeth, which had seemed so white and dentist-perfect, now looked yellow. And longer than they should have been. "And if I was, I sure as hell wouldn't have been on my *knees!*"

As if terrified by his words, the tree-lights flared,

painting Nick's shadow on the far wall. But it wasn't the silhouette of a bear-like man. It was thin, wasted-looking, with long, bony limbs that protruded from its body at odd angles. And though it was gone before Aidan could be sure, the head of that shadow didn't look human. Not at all.

Nick seemed to catch himself, closing his eyes and taking a deep breath. "Oops," he chuckled. "Almost lost it there, didn't I? Dangerous. Especially since I've still got a job to do."

With that, he sauntered over to the tree, reached behind it, and retrieved an enormous red sack Aidan somehow hadn't noticed. Stuffing his arm too far inside, he pulled out another wrapped package and placed it with the others.

"Nick…" Aidan whispered. He didn't want to speak at all, wanted to be upstairs in bed with the covers pulled over his head, wanted this to be a nightmare and for the nightmare to be over. "W-why can't I move?"

"I don't want you to, son," came the cheerful answer. "That deal I told you about? It's pretty clear. Spells out what I've got to do, what I'm *allowed* to do, and what I *can't* do. One bit—paragraph one hundred thirty-five, subsection thirteen, if I remember—specifies that even though I'm coming right into their homes—their holy sanctums, you might say—I can't lay so much as a finger on the sleepin' families."

He looked over his shoulder at Aidan and grinned. His yellow teeth were as sharp as steak knives now. "But nowhere—not in all two hundred sixteen pages—does it say a fuckin' thing about someone who's *awake*."

A wave of terror broke over Aidan's mind, leaving stark clarity as it receded. *That's why it's so dangerous,* his brain jabbered at him. *That's why it's almost impossible for kids to stay up on Christmas night. It IS some kind of magic. To keep them safe. Safe from HIM.*

"You got it, little buddy." Nick's ghastly grin widened,

then he went back to stacking the presents under the lowest boughs of the tree. "Just a hair too late to do any damn good, of course. But hey—most folks never figure it out at all. You oughtta be proud."

A scream bubbled up in Aidan's throat.

"You *sure* you want to do that, son? I don't mind if you invite the whole house to our little party, of course. More the merrier. But I'm surprised you'd want to—and not much surprises me anymore."

Another piece clicked into place. *He can't hurt Ethan. Or Mom. Because they're asleep. And he can't wake them—he said they wouldn't hear anything HE did down here. But if I'M the one who wakes them up -.*

"Give that boy a SEE-gar!" Nick snickered, coming up for air. "I can see it on your face, little buddy—the light bulb came on, didn't it?"

Aidan couldn't speak. He nodded.

"On second thought, though, it ain't a bad idea." The big man rose to his feet. "Why *don't* you go ahead and scream? That could be what folks call a 'win-win' for both of us."

Aidan stared.

"Go on, holler! Invite your momma down here so I can meet her! She's a little worn around the edges, but she don't look bad for her age." Nick's grin twisted, and he licked his lips with a tongue that was far too long. "Got a *helluva* rack on her, too. If I didn't know she bottle-fed you, I'd be jealous as hell, little man."

Aidan's bowels loosened. He didn't know what Nick meant, didn't *want* to know. He shuddered, shook his head.

"Well, how 'bout your brother, then?" Nick said, smirking. "You're tired of takin' care of that little bastard. You tried to lie to yourself about it, but that's what it boils down to, right?"

No. Not like this. I never wanted this.

"Think about it, son. I've been talkin' about deals all this time, right? Well, we can make one ourselves—right here, right now. You wake up your brother…" Nick reached out and caressed Aidan's cheek with fingers as cold as icicles. "… and I'll take *him* to play with instead of you. Hell, with one less mouth to feed, your momma can be there for you. You can be a kid again. Like it should be. All your problems solved. Just gimme one… good… scream."

For a long moment, Aidan's terrified brain considered it. He *was* a child. He didn't want to die, didn't want this monster to take him away. Panic chewed into his stomach and spine with sharp rat-teeth. Sweat colder than the rain sluicing through the roof-gutters trickled down his face and between his shoulder blades.

He almost did it. Almost.

But then more images flickered into his mind.

Ethan. The calm trust in the younger boy's eyes. His absolute certainty that whatever the problem was—a broken toy, a bad dream, or a last-minute letter to Santa— his big brother would know what to do.

Mom. *Her* eyes, so heavy with grief and aching fatigue that they couldn't rest on anything for more than a moment. But as full as they were, as tired as she always was, her love for her boys always shined through.

Dad. Spending hours sanding and smoothing the wood of the bannister each year, just so no one would get splinters. Yanking Aidan away from the snake next to his tricycle before killing it. Catching Ethan when he fell off a swing in the park. A thousand things he'd done, big and small, to keep his family safe.

Aidan made his decision.

He met Nick's madly cheerful eyes.

And shook his head.

"No," he whispered. "No deal. You've got me. I screwed up, and I'm here now. But you can't have my mom. Or my brother."

The merry glee slid out of Nick's face. In the time it took Aidan to blink, he seized the boy's shoulders and hauled him close enough that their noses almost touched. His breath carried the scent of rot. Tentacles of filmy blackness quested out from Nick's pupils, spiraling like slurping tongues across the surface of his eyes.

"Why the fuck *not?*"

Aidan ignored his racing pulse, the tight knot of terror in his gut. He didn't blink. "Because I won't *let* you."

Nick's features twisted, a sickening *shift* under the skin as if his skull was clay being kneaded from the inside. His fingers tightened on Aidan's arms, and the boy braced himself for the cracking snap of bone. But he still held the black, empty gaze. Unflinching.

The giant released him. A starburst of pain exploded in his left ankle as he fell to the floor. Nick took a deep breath and closed his eyes. When he opened them, his black gaze was still hideous and absolute, but somehow… uncertain?

"Son of a bitch. Guess there *are* still a few surprises for this old hoss after all." He shook his head, then turned back to the tree. "I hope the little shit's worth it. You won't think so for long. I fuckin' *guarantee* that."

Aidan's heartbeat was almost a solid tone of terror. He couldn't move. Couldn't run. Couldn't fight, even if he'd had any hope of besting a man—a *creature*—four times his size and with God knew what powers besides. He shoved his panic into the back of his mind and locked it away, just like he'd done earlier with his grief. It pounded on the mental door he'd just slammed, demanding to be freed to run and scream, but he ignored that, too. It couldn't help him; it could only keep him from thinking, get him killed.

What would Dad do?

As if in answer, another image coalesced. The book, lying on the side-table, with its red cover and green lettering and the pages with all the Santa-trivia. The book his father used to read them.

Read the story, his father seemed to say.

Aidan began to whisper. *"Twas the night before Christmas,*

and all through the house. Not a creature was stirring. Not even a mouse…"

At first, he didn't know why. Maybe it was just his child-mind drowning in terror, flailing around for a lifeline to happier, safer times. Maybe it was because if Dad had been there, he would have protected Aidan. Or tried to.

There wasn't a monster in that story. Not an obvious one, at least. But they showed up in other stories… and they always had a weakness. You just had to find it.

And what if the story *was* this monster's weakness?

Nick had said that most of what he, Aidan, knew about Santa and Christmas were late additions, bolted on to help the legend grow. But the poem—written in 1823—was the oldest depiction of Santa Claus that Aidan had ever heard of. It had become so much a part of Christmas, had been there maybe from the very beginning…

He mouthed the words quietly, barely vocalizing at all. He didn't have his father's wonderful voice, couldn't make the story come alive the way Dad had. Since he'd been gone, Aidan had never reached the end of the tale. But he had to do it now. He *knew* it, just as surely as he had known anything in his life.

He prayed he was right.

"He was chubby and plump, a right jolly old elf," Aidan recited as fast as he could without jumbling the words. *"And I laughed when I saw him, in spite of myself."*

Something—some extra sense—caused Nick to glance back at him. When his eyes met Aidan's, they were bloody crimson islands floating on a sea as black as death.

"A wink of his eye, and a twist of his head…"

One demonic eye shut with a spasm; the other widened until it seemed it would fall from its socket and dangle against his white-furred cheek. Nick's mouth split open in a wide 'O' of horror, dripping yellow fangs framing a gullet of putrid gray flesh. "NO!!!" he screamed, launching himself at the boy.

Like the figurine he'd knocked off the mantle, Nick's

leap slowed in mid-air. Aidan watched his bearish form distend, arms growing longer as his barrel-chest and keg-belly deflated like leaking balloons. Wicked black talons sprouted from his fingers, light gleaming off their barbed edges. Huge serpentine jaws exploded from Nick's face, spraying saliva that sizzled and burned like acid when a drop landed on Aidan's skin. The fur of his clothing rippled, merged with his flesh, hardened into scales the color of congealed blood.

The panic tried to batter its way out again, but Aidan kicked a mental wedge under its prison-door. Kept his concentration. Spoke the next words. "... *soon gave me to know I had nothing to dread.*"

Nick—or the thing that had been Nick—crashed to the floor. The newly-emaciated, rust-scaled form writhed as if stung by red-hot needles, its hoarse scream something between a man's groan and snake's hiss.

Through it all, Aidan kept reciting. He wondered what would happen if his throat locked up, or if he mispronounced a word, or couldn't remember the next line. He shoved that thought away, too. Because he *did* know what would happen, didn't he?

But he didn't falter. The words were imprinted in his mind as indelibly as the name had been chiseled into his father's gravestone. And his voice grew louder. Stronger.

It sounded like Dad's. The voice of a man protecting his family.

"*He spoke not a word, but went straight to his work, and filled all the stockings, then turned with a jerk.*"

The hissing form fell silent, snatched upright again as if by an unseen hand. It seized the red sack and hoisted it over one shoulder. With a flex of its now lizard-like knees, it sprang to the fireplace and tapped each stocking with a shaking, struggling claw. The socks began to bulge and writhe as if tumors had sprouted inside. Then the monster pivoted to face him, the movement so abrupt it seemed the reptilian head would snap off its long, scaly neck.

Aidan kept going. "*And laying his finger aside of his nose…*" The shape extended its middle finger upward before complying, a puppet jerking at the end of invisible strings. "*And giving a nod, up the chimney he rose.*"

The shape that had been Nick blurred into crimson smoke, coiling into the fireplace and back up the chimney.

Too afraid to stop, Aidan rattled off the rest. "*He sprang to his sleigh, to his team gave a whistle,*"—a banshee shriek tore the night—"*And away they all flew like the down of a thistle.*

"*But I heard him exclaim, 'ere he drove out of sight, 'Happy Christmas to all, and to all a good night!'*"

He heard the words echoing his own, sounding forced and stilted. But the ones he heard in his mind—a distant, telepathic scream—were *very* different. Full of terrible, hateful promise.

When they faded into silence, Aidan sank to the floor, hugged himself, and cried.

♉

If someone had suggested that he might fall asleep after everything that had happened, maybe Aidan would have laughed.

Or not. Laughing might be off the menu for the moment. But he wouldn't have believed it. Even though the things he believed in now weren't the same as they'd been yesterday.

But eventually even a terror-stricken ten-year-old reaches the point where his body will not go on, despite the feverish ravings of his mind.

He slept on the couch. The only alternatives were climbing back upstairs alone in the dark (no thank you) or sleeping in his dad's old chair where the Nick-thing had sat (no way in hell). He leaned back on the unraveling fabric, clutched the red book in a death-grip, and felt every lump and wire poking against his back.

Then he went away.

And wonderful golden sunlight was pouring in against his closed eyelids.

At a touch on his cheek, his eyes flew open and he bit back a scream. It was his mother, a curious look on her face. She brushed the hair back from his forehead, and it was only the familiar feel of her fingers—callused and work-worn, but still warm and tender—that allowed him to keep his horror hidden.

"Hi, sleepyhead." Mom's eyes were the same faded hazel-green he remembered. The whites were laced with red veins and dark purple bruises lay beneath them, but they were his mother's eyes in his mother's face and he loved her. "What are you doing down—oof!"

Aidan sat up and threw his arms around her. She wasn't a tall woman—an inch over five feet, and he had taken after his dad for height—so he almost knocked her over. "Easy, kiddo, easy! What's this about?"

He flinched at the word *kiddo*. He never wanted to hear it again. Ever.

"I'm just… excited, that's all," he said, summoning as much childish cheer into his voice as he could. "It's Christmas morning!"

"Of course it is," she said, stifling a yawn. "But why aren't you in bed?"

His numb, exhausted brain had nothing, but his mouth took over. "I… tried to stay up and see Santa. Ethan forgot to ask for some super-important *Paw Patrol* toy when he wrote his letter. He was really upset, so I figured I'd make sure Santa got his note."

Mom's expression was unreadable. "You stayed awake all night?"

"N-No. Didn't quite make it."

She ruffled his hair again. Yesterday, he would have pulled away—it was such a baby thing for her to do—but today he found he didn't mind at all. "Don't worry, sweetie. I'm sure Santa got your brother's note. And Ethan would appreciate what you tried to do for him." Her expression grew sad, and she touched the side of his face. "I know *I* do."

For a moment, she seemed to see too much, and he had to look away. "No problem, Mom. Want me to go wake the little tagalong?"

She bit her lip, as if there were more to say. But she nodded. "Go ahead. You guys check out your stockings while I start breakfast. Then we can eat and see what Santa brought everyone."

"You got it." He rose, and his ankle threatened to buckle under him. He staggered, but steadied himself by grabbing the arm of the couch.

"Are you okay?" That furrow was back between her eyes.

He forced another smile. "Just not totally awake yet."

The furrow deepened. "Did you hurt your foot?"

Aidan shook his head. Then, to distract her, he kissed her cheek—something he hadn't done since he'd been Ethan's age. "Everything's okay—I promise. I love you, Mom."

As he padded up the stairs trying not to favor his leg, he saw her touch the spot where he'd kissed her. And a sweet—if somewhat bewildered—smile blossomed on her face. The first he'd seen in so long.

Two hours later, when they'd finished ransacking their gifts—Aidan hadn't wanted to touch them, but he went through the motions anyway—he sat down at the kitchen table. Moving Ethan's letter aside, he studied the envelope.

TO SNTAA.

He didn't want to touch it, either. Despite the childish crayon-scrawl, the purple letters seemed to burn with cold, unholy power.

He looked around. Mom was dozing on the couch. Ethan was playing with his new Paw Patrol toys as if they were the only things in the world.

Aidan retrieved the scissors from a kitchen drawer and returned to the table. He took a deep, steadying breath, and picked up the envelope. Trying not to dwell on the icy, greasy feel of the paper, he snipped around Ethan's attempt at Santa's name, then tossed the rest into the trash. He made slices between each letter, rearranging them in the correct order on the tabletop.

S.A.N.T.A.

He stared at them, chewing his lip. Then he reached out. Touched one letter with a fingertip. Dragged it from the middle of the name to the very end.

S.A. T.A. N.

Liquid rose at the back of his throat and he lurched to the sink. Remnants of toast, eggs, and orange juice splashed the steel ring around the drain as his stomach cramped and heaved. Throat burning, eyes watering, he might have been crying again.

You don't know that's who it was. You CAN'T know that.

But he knew it anyway. The same way he'd known the story would drive the monster away.

When he had nothing else to bring up, Aidan rinsed the half-digested sludge down the drain. He splashed water on his face. When he felt strong enough, the paper fragments went into the trash.

Did I break the protection forever? Is the magic—or grace, or whatever it is—gone for good? He hoped not. Nick had said he couldn't harm sleeping children, but there was no way to know for sure. Not until next year. And if Aidan was wrong…

A year is a long time, though. Plenty of time to figure out something that will work. Something that will MAKE me sleep, no matter how scared I am.

And as long as I'm asleep, I'm safe.

That's the deal, after all.

ABOUT THE AUTHOR

JARED BAKER wrote his first story at the age of six – a single-page hand-scrawled "masterpiece" chronicling a brave dinosaur's daring rescue of his best friend from the teeth of a rampaging Tyrannosaurus Rex. He hasn't stopped writing since, but he has expanded his wheelhouse into stories of horror, science fiction, suspense, and the supernatural.

When he's not exploring imaginary worlds or working as a computer programmer, he enjoys reading a broad selection of genres and writers, playing sports and video games with his three children, and (far too rarely) having a date-night with his wife, Lindsey.

Jared's other work has been published by Hellbound Books.

WHEN THE DARK AND LIGHT ARE ONE

Erica Ciko Campbell

*"Most men grasp that right and wrong are opposites,
but few could ever understand that truth is the
inverse of them both."*
– Nibiru Tablet II, Line Forty-Four

It was January 1, 2667 when the Devil returned to Earth. In the true spirit of chaos, he showed up the moment everyone finally stopped expecting him. I still remember how it felt to see his face behind that fogged-up shop window for the very first time.

Countless antique CommScreens lurked behind the glass, once a portal to better days for weary shoppers, now the harbinger of mankind's sudden doom. They were the slightest bit out-of-synch as they broadcasted his face to me, the lone observer: Past, present, and future all crackled together in eerie clarity as he sat among the leaders of our world as a most-honored guest.

In that moment, I drank in the suspended awe of the entire planet with every breath, and released mankind's collective terror into the frigid New York winter with every exhale. Most of mankind was in shock, but me? I'd spent the last century wondering when he was going to come to collect his debt. And I didn't blame him one bit.

When the Telomere Regeneration Stacks became available to the public in 2510, my father was pissed—but that was nothing compared to how mad his elitist shareholder buddies at Shazu Enterprises were. 99.9% of the world's bitcoin was never enough for them: they needed something inaccessible to the working man, something forbidden. Now that the rest of mankind could get a taste of eternal life, they really weren't that special anymore.

It only took fifty years for the stacks to be mandated. If only human rights could be as much of a priority now as they were a century ago, right? And before the world's elite could say "Hail Crypto-Anarchist Dystopia," every kid pulled out of the Venus Vats from Tokyo VI to the Antarctic Sea had one of the regeneration stacks stapled into their brainstem before they drew their first breath.

Myself, I never needed one. My father was rich. Old money. We'd drank from a different fountain of youth— one I'd been cut off from since I turned my nose up at my father's lack of respect for human life. That night, I had nothing but the coat on my back, and a dream of darkness older than time—but it was a worthwhile trade for a clean conscience.

Anyone with the faintest shred of sense knew that the men and woman surrounding him at that table had mastered the art of deceiving the public: There was no way they could have truly lacked the foresight to see that there were going to be consequences when only a couple thousand humans had naturally died since 2560. But still, they had the audacity to look the Arch Nemesis of Light himself in the eyes and pretend they were surprised to see him.

"We were certain that enough people were still falling through the cracks to hold you over," the President of the Greenland Collective stuttered, as if a few fetuses choked out before they could be implanted in the Venus Vats, or a few vagrants who lived and died on some forgotten island were enough to appease pure cosmic evil.

"To be honest, we were all expecting your son," muttered the Prime Minister of Old India. "Not... well, you."

"Oh, I tried sending him a few years ago, back when your 'Venus Vats' first started to dry up," replied the Devil, his voice pure sanguine bliss on the wings of a dream. "But as fate would have it, there was a malfunction in his vat and his sequence was aborted."

The Prime Minister's eyes grew wide, but the President of the Greenland Collective cleared her throat and kept the conversation moving. But I was far too busy drinking him in to absorb a single word of what she said.

Everything the legends say about the Devil's appearance is a lie. When you see him for the first time, he won't bare twisted horns or a wicked grin that could cut the stars from the sky: He'll appear as nothing more than the manifestation of your oldest, most ill-begotten dreams. Imagine gazing into the mirror of your own heart and finding the most beautiful, charismatic vision of the past buried under a thousand layers of guilt and sorrow. Then, you'll have the faintest idea of how he'll appear.

For me, he was a spitting image of Dominic on the first day we met, sharp chin licked with five o'clock shadow and all. His smile was the warmest in the room, and the only sinister thing about him was the fact that his sad grey eyes clashed with the crimson frames of his spectacles. In fact, he looked downright kind: By contrast, he made the uneasy gathering of diplomats look as wicked on the outside as they were within.

I suppose it was fitting that the shepherd of mankind's

darkest dreams would appear as a father figure to me: For Dominic was always the father I never had. He gave me the warm, stern guidance that the Venus Vats could not.

Amusingly, neither Dominic nor his impersonator could have been my father in any timeline or any generation. Their flesh was paler than the wounded neck of a rabbit bleeding out onto the snow, while I was as dark as the night that was rapidly descending over all mankind. My hair was a tangle of coarse black braids, while his pepper-grey hair was smoother than silk, albeit a little too long for his job as a college professor. Dominic and I were polar opposites, and you could have said we were drawn together out of some long-obsolete drive for genetic variation… if we weren't both men.

But although our connection was physical, romantic, and cosmic, make no mistake: The Devil doesn't always appear as some star-crossed lover from a century ago. Later, I would find that, for many people, he appeared as the biological child they never had but always craved, or the imaginary friend they always missed from their earliest childhood memories.

But for me, on the coldest day of winter he was… Forgive me, I've gone off on a tangent, as I often do. Now, let's get back to the meat.

When the Devil spoke again, his cool, clear aura had fizzled out as quickly as my father's smile when the Telomere Regeneration Mandate was passed and he realized he could no longer get away with strangling the hired help. But the anger I was bracing myself for wasn't there.

No, his eyes were void of everything save for the bleak and somber tides of disappointment. His outpouring of sorrow was so sincere that I felt his words plucking even my most deeply-buried heartstrings like the anti-cosmic puppet master I had come to love over the past two minutes.

"Now, if you're finished blowing me away with your

unparalleled Earthen hospitality, don't you think it's time to talk about how to address our little problem?"

There it was: The big question. The line that everyone knew was coming, but no one wanted to face. The President of the Greenland Collective looked as anxious as I felt, and I swore I could feel the collective hearts of all mankind pounding in the concrete beneath my boots.

"Y-yes," stuttered the Prime Minister of Old India. "It goes without saying that I speak for the entire human race. It's time."

"Now, I'll have you know that I'm a reasonable man," the Devil responded, woeful eyes ablaze with the fury of a thousand incinerated truths. "I've been very, very patient with your race throughout history. I look back fondly on the relationships I've forged with your leaders, and I don't expect ours to be any different."

I could practically feel the gravity shift from a billion eyebrows in every corner of the planet raising all at once. But his admission was far from news to me.

"I don't expect the entire Earth to fling itself into the sun in my name," the dark lord continued. "But I do expect you to throw me a bone now and then—especially now, when the human race is far more wicked than its forebears could ever dream."

"What do you mean?" The Prime Minister demanded, the fear in her eyes as wild as the excitement in the dark lord's.

"Oh, please," scoffed the Devil, folding his arms across his chest and trilling his long, sharp nails impatiently on his perfectly-tailored suit. "All it takes is one look out the window of this skyscraper over the body farms and the sea of nameless souls: Or, as a woman of your status would call them, commodities."

I could practically hear the Prime Minister's blood curdling through the screen, but she remained as silent as the blackness of midnight.

"In Absolute Dark 2667, there's far more cruelty,

injustice, and abuse of power than ever before in human history. But the only true sin is that no one is suffering for it." Something about his tone as he brought his case before the most powerful leaders in all the world made it sound as if what he was saying was elementary, basic knowledge that no man or god could ever deny.

The camera zoomed in on the seraphic contours of his face once more, and the lurid, pulsing veins in his throat were close enough to hypnotize the entire world. When he gave in to a mischievous smirk, I imagined the deathlike silence of the diplomats filled his heart with a morbid glee older than time.

"My father always said that silence was the oldest and most sincere form of agreement: So be it, then. The deal has been struck. Time to dust off your Venus Vats, yes?" His laugh resounded through speakers of the countless screens, and the hearts of all mankind. "We'll start with 667,000 souls per year, in honor of the day I arrived. And if all goes well, we'll up it to a million by the end of the decade. And to celebrate, I've decided to nominate everyone in this room as our first pool of volunteers."

His eyes were now focused directly on the cameras, and for the eternity of a second, I swore he was staring at me and me alone. "This cesspool is in dire need of a change in management, don't you think?"

Every face around the table was now paler than the snowflakes collecting on the ends of my hair.

"What's wrong? Don't look so glum!" The Devil laughed once more. "Smile! If you don't laugh, you cry! And I won't cry with you, but I'll laugh with you."

---

*"They are me, and I am them, and all of us are
lonely."*
– Nibiru Tablet III, Line Seven

Returning to the cyclopean prison of metal in the bowels of Shazu Enterprises was like wandering the halls of a forgotten childhood dream. A spark shivered to life every time my boot fell upon the floor panels, leaving a snakelike trail of hazy green neon in my wake. The walls were alive, interwoven with ethereal blue circuits: the lifeblood of the Psych Drives, the Venus Vats, and every major news network in the world.

After so many lifetimes, but nowhere near enough time, the day had come when I knew I had to face my father again. I'd called ahead, of course: Otherwise, I never would have made it past the first mile of turrets and the Hyborian Skywall.

Perhaps something about the dark one's wicked smile awakened a new sentimentality in me; or maybe it was some forgotten instinct urging me to crawl into the impenetrable depths of the Earth now that the world was coming to an end. But for the sake of invoking empathy in you readers, my dearest and only friends, let's say I'd returned to visit my father for the sake of the good old days. But by now you probably know me well enough to suspect that in truth, I wanted to watch the puppet master's fingers buckle and snap, now that a bigger fish had finally emerged from the depths.

However, no matter how hard I tried to smother the real reason for my visit with delusions of fondness or pure black venom, I knew it was finally time to give the old man my answer.

I passed beneath yet another archway lined with twisted wires and broken circuit boards. In the halcyon days of youth, they had always disturbed me. No matter how hard I tried, I could never understand what my father saw in them: The battery acid boiled out from the broken screens like blood, and the twisted strings of metal that once wove the components together snaked down from above, threatening to strangle me as they did so long ago.

The single time I could bring myself to ask him what they meant, he said that as the barbarians of antiquity sat upon thrones of skulls and lined their halls with the broken bones of their fallen foes, he lined his with the shattered great inventions of every company Shazu Enterprises had ever bought out.

I had run out of time to rake my fingertips over my crawling skin in a vain attempt to scrub out his ancient transgressions, however. At long last, I stood before the plain red door to his chamber: Good feng shui was even more important than a good surgeon, he always said.

The ocular scanner accepted me with a sullen hiss, and the door began its slow ascent into the archway of broken circuits that ensorcelled it. Had he truly left my imprints in the system for all these years, or did he leave the door unlocked to build a false sense of trust? After a few seconds of wild, uninhibited rumination, I decided it didn't matter and stepped inside.

"Ludwig," my father declared matter-of-factly, as if he were making a statement about the weather rather than facing his only son for the first time in 160 years. He lurked in the back of the windowless room at the end of a long black carpet. Behind his desk, his feeble body was curled into a throne of medical devices and life support vials.

"Hello, father," I muttered, clenching my fangs so violently I worried they might shatter. I couldn't bring myself to look at him yet, so I fixed my eyes on the black marble desk littered with syringes and IV wires instead.

"You've heard on the plebian news they're going to fire up the Venus Vats again, I presume?" His voice was shrill and repulsive, distorted to a pitch unrecognizable as man or machine by the bundle of wires hemorrhaging from his throat. "Perhaps you can kill yourself at last and donate your cadaver to science, so they can figure out how you got so fucked up during your development sequence."

The only thing more sinister than his laugh was the way his yellowed skin was stretched over bones fortified far too many times with titanium-infused stem cells until they were more metal than man. His integuments couldn't keep up with the framework beneath, and nothing of his skeleton or circulatory system was left to the imagination.

"A century and a half, and that's all you can come up with?" From the way his single working eye threatened to wilt even farther out of the socket than it already had, I guessed that my smile disturbed him.

"If you're looking for a hole to crawl into now that mankind's final hour has come, you won't find it here. I thought I deactivated your ocular scans from the security network decades ago," he muttered, his emotionless metallic drawl fading off into the surrounding blackness.

I said nothing, dissecting him with my organic, intact eyes that not even the souls of every man, woman, and child in debt to Shazu Enterprises combined could buy him. I allowed the silence to reign for a small eternity, knowing that suspense was the sharpest weapon.

Finally, I muttered, "I've considered your offer long and hard, and my answer is yes. You can have my neural stem cells, as long as you add me back into your will and return my shares of Shazu Enterprises."

His eye glazed over so intensely that I feared it would shatter when it finally popped out of his skull and landed on the floor. He drank in some silent victory that could only be properly appreciated after several centuries of paralysis. For a fleeting second, I even thought his hideous scab of a single lip would twist into the mischievous, sadistic smirk I remembered from my youth.

But he only coughed, and muttered weakly, "I never wrote you out. You've always been my only heir. You could say I knew deep inside that this day would finally come."

The leathery stump he called a hand was trembling violently, now, and I couldn't tell if he was excited over the prospect of finally reversing his aging once and for all with my precious stem cells, or if the degeneration had simply stolen his ability to sit still.

I carefully guarded all outward signs of shock, but in

truth, my heart was pounding far even more quickly than it had when I saw the Devil for the first time on the coldest day of winter. Was he telling the truth, I wondered? No, he wouldn't lie about something that burned so intensely into his mind since my earliest memories. Even after all these years, I knew him well enough to be confident that there was nothing more important to him in the world than those stem cells.

And in order for him to harvest them indefinitely, I needed to be alive. Alive and flourishing. He needed to keep me happy. I smiled, mocking him, doing what his sad excuse for a mouth could not.

"I must admit; I didn't think it would take Lucifer's valiant return to finally push you into helping your dear old father…" His robotic voice trailed off with a dream of withered vocal cords made whole again—a gift that only I could offer him.

"I was waiting for the right time," I lied. "I always planned on giving you access to my neural bank eventually. Most would regret depleting their own stores so prematurely, but I decided that a brief burst of true pleasure is worth a thousand lives of empty servitude."

From his side, I imagined, the story made perfect sense. I had no doubt he'd been watching me through his limitless surveillance network from time to time, and he'd seen the squalor that I'd come to find comfort in. A man like him would have no trouble believing at all that I'd trade the keys to the kingdom of eternal life for a few centuries of true, unrestrained luxury. After all, he did.

"So you're telling me that I can still access my old wallets?" For the first time since entering his chambers, I felt like a fool. Although I stored the encryption keys behind several passwords in the deepest layer of my Psych Drive, I hadn't checked the wallets since the day I left home, I knew that in time he'd have noticed the missing funds, and I was far too proud to ever let him know I was hard up for cash.

"Indeed," he replied plainly, in a skin-crawling attempt to fold his crumbling hands on the desk like he used to when I was young. "Again, I've been expecting your return for quite some time. Such a paltry sum wasn't worth the effort of transferring the coin when I knew you'd come crawling back as soon as the stars clouded over."

"Has old age reduced you to a poet, father?" I couldn't help but laugh.

"Not old age, but the state of the world." He gestured grandly with his sad excuse for a hand, sweeping through the stale, bleak room which I imagined he hadn't left for days. "Now, enough about our glorious future and the rebirth of Shazu Enterprises: We'll sort out the details of your sacrifice later. For now, sit down. We have far more pressing matters to tend to, lest we face eternal life in a sterile, vacant world."

Our glorious future? The old man was so elated by his burst of good fortune that he'd forgotten he was the only one drinking from the never-ending fountain of youth. After all, I had no son of my own to harvest a taste of eternity from, as his fathers did before him for generations uncounted. And I never would. I didn't need to.

But instead of pointing out his careless error, I humored him. After all, this was the real reason I'd ever been driven back to him at all.

"So have you met with him yet?" I asked, knowing that if the Lord of Darkness found time to blow out smoke and break mirrors with the "world leaders" for the masses, he'd probably made his true plans with my father hours before.

"Yes. Once," my father replied curtly. "Here, in this very room."

I could nearly taste the echo of his sublime, all-encompassing decadence across time and space. Had he stood in the very spot I was planted in now, I wondered?

"As you might expect, his demands aren't nearly as unreasonable as the plebian media has made them out to be. However, it'll take months to introduce the new mandates to society in a way that won't incite riots."

"New mandates?" I asked, pretending to be surprised that he claimed to already have everything figured out.

"To put it simply, he's far more organized than I ever expected him to be. Very fond of numbers, and paperwork, and keeping the masses in order."

Perhaps he could have been my father after all, I thought with a subdued smile.

"In the end, in an attempt to keep things orderly for the rest of eternity, he demanded we set a yearly quota. He requested 667,000 souls for the first year, and a million for the next. I'm sure you saw it on the plebian news. But even if he keeps upping it by a million per year, it would take decades to put a dent in our current population. I didn't tell him this, of course, but our Venus Vats could replace the fallen in a mere couple of months."

"I see," I replied, deciding it would be better to allow my father's tirade to continue without an interjection of my own thoughts. In my youth, I learned that he was far more likely to dig his own grave when allowed to rant unchecked.

"Hell, I felt like asking him to take a billion of them next year instead of a million," he muttered, clearly growing frustrated. As it stands, we have 60 billion miscreants roaming the streets, decimating our food supply and draining our planet of its dwindling resources. We could halve their numbers in one fell swoop and all that would be lost is a bit of productivity."

"Nothing has to be lost if you make the remaining ones work twice as hard." My little joke made my guts turn sour, but I knew my father would appreciate it—and more importantly, I knew it would work wonders to ramp up his trust and lower his defenses.

Just as I expected, his wet, rasping laugh resounded off the walls. It sounded like he was about to choke on his own tongue. The coughing fit that followed lasted several minutes, but he finally sputtered, "Perhaps if we get rid of enough of them, we'll be able to knock down some of those monstrosities they call habitats that have been choking out the sun."

"Perhaps," I pretended to agree. I never minded the skyscrapers: They made the rare glimmer of starlight through the infinite abyss of metal all-the-more precious.

"But my greatest concern by far is that the masses will demand an end to the birthing bans rather than the reactivation of the Venus Vats. Do you have any idea what chaos could potentially ensue? This is the excuse they've been dreaming of for over a hundred years. Their representatives will argue that it's only logical to replace the—"

He continued to sputter and squelch like a raving lunatic, but I was still riding the coattails of that timeless euphoria that swept over me when I realized the incarnation of darkness himself had stood in this very spot only days before. And for the blissful eternity of an unbroken moment, I was fortunate enough to be ignorant to the nefarious fate my father was thrusting upon all mankind, as he already had a thousand times.

"The Vats are the only way to ensure the working fodder will be replenished in a timely manner! But with our currently-depleted resources, there's a high chance of malfunction for the first decade of operation. And you know firsthand how catastrophic that can—"

"Why don't you just hand the newly-forged souls off to the dark lord from the moment they emerge from the vats?" I interrupted, failing to understand why my father was making all this sound so complicated. "In truth, I don't understand why the masses even need to be aware of what was going on."

"You clearly know nothing of how society has functioned since time immemorial," my father shook his head in a mix of disappointment and pure, white-hot rage. "Even the devil has standards, Ludwig: The souls must be seasoned with a lifetime of suffering and desperation before they'll even begin to appeal to his tastes."

I remained silent, allowing him to dig the grave even deeper.

"And before you ask, we've already implemented a system to determine which souls will be sacrificed over the next few decades. We believe the masses will devour it like the last grain of rice in a field of sand."

"Is that so?" I pried, knowing that he'd be more than eager to spill his secrets now that he believed I was his pawn once more. After all, I was his sole remaining son, and he was at the end of his life.

"Yes," he replied plainly. "It's quite simple, really. All we're going to do is let the people decide for themselves…"

By the wormlike grin that had overtaken his face, I already knew this wasn't true at all. "Interesting," I played along.

"…with a little financial incentive to urge them along, of course."

I tilted my head, feigning curiosity, even though I wasn't the slightest bit surprised.

"You see, the Family Enrichment Agreement proposed by the committee won't reward individuals for their selfless sacrifice, but rather entire dynasties. There's nothing that will make a martyr out of an honest man faster than the chance to bump his children up into the next social caste," he continued.

"And as an added bonus, this will prompt countless dishonest men to sell out their unsuspecting family members," he added with a smile. "Because all Family Enrichment Agreements are final, and can be made over the EDN without a corp-issued ID."

"So you're paying them to suffer for your sins in Hell?" I inquired, far more calmly than he ever deserved.

"Not my sins, but the sins of all mankind," my father explained, as if he were explaining the simplest thing in all the world. "Think of it as a way for their lives to finally have the faintest shred of meaning, like they did back in the good old days."

I thought of the countless, nameless ones who would undoubtedly sign away their souls to the literal Devil for a chance of breaking the cycle that had enslaved their families for generations. And then, I thought of men like my father who spent their lives atop a throne made of their blood and broken bones.

My eyes darted to the spider web of cords that connecting his oxygen generator to his helpless lungs, then around the perimeter of the empty, soundproof chamber. My father's office was the only room in all of Shazu Enterprises that didn't have a single camera.

"I have no shape but the formless space between the night. I have no soul but the collective death wails of all mankind. I have no face but the contorted, melted corpses of the dreams of every man."
– Nibiru Tablet IV, Line Sixty-Six

"I can't believe how quickly the neural stem grafts took hold, sir! I thought you were kidding when you said they'd make you look 400 years younger. This is amazing!"

"See, Maryann? Haven't I told you countless times that a life without faith isn't a life worth living? Faith in technology, faith in the prosperity of Shazu Enterprises, and most importantly: Faith in the future of all mankind."

Maryann had been Doctor Shazu's personal assistant for the better part of a century, and now she was working for me instead. She was the one I spoke to on the phone three weeks ago, when I arranged that fateful meeting in the darkness where the doctor's corpse now rested. She showed no signs of recognizing my voice, however—but deep down, I suspected she knew what had transpired in the depths, but was simply hungry for a change of scenery like the rest of us.

At the time, I was just as surprised as my predecessor when I strangled him with my bare hands and ripped his Psych Drive from his still-bleeding skull. But when I jammed his interface into the backup portal behind my own temple, suddenly, it all made sense.

Even now, after reliving that cathartic, intoxicating moment what must have been a thousand times, my entire body felt like it was on fire when I thought about how incredible it felt to watch him die. But my own triumph was nothing, not even a single tear of joy in an ocean of pure black euphoria, compared to the bliss I felt for finally making my father proud.

Since time immemorial, men like Doctor Shazu have tried to harness my father's strength and win his favor. And since time immemorial, men like Doctor Shazu have been trading their souls for a fleeting, fragile glimpse of what could have been.

And now that the doctor's entire personality matrix and memory bank were mine, I had no trouble fooling his entire legion of attendants into believing I was a younger version of him. Some of them were even aware of his plan to harvest my neural stem cells and reverse his own aging process—in fact, many of them had done the same to their own sons. But you see, Doctor Shazu was far more creative than any of his lackeys—and if everything had gone according to his master plan, then he would have been laughing atop that mountain of broken bones he always dreamed about instead of me.

Like countless emperors and kings of men before him, Doctor Shazu had tried to make a deal with mankind's greatest adversary: He vowed to create a vessel for the Devil's only son, and unleash him upon the world on January 1, 2667 to do what must be done. But the brain-dead old fool thought he could hide the part where he planned to erase my Psych Drive, harvest my neural stem cells, and fuse my DNA with his to gain eternal power over life and death.

Doctor Shazu thought that he'd finally look down on all mankind from atop that final, world-choking mountain of corpses. But in the end, he was little more than a pawn in his own game—a harbinger of an end he would never reap; an ambassador of a pure black future that he could never even begin to conceive.

And until that glorious moment when light and dark are one, I'll never remember how close the doctor came to reaching his goals. My entire life, I believed he really was my father, and that he'd take me back at any time when I overcame my bout of wanderlust and came crawling back to Shazu Enterprises. The memory scrambling sequence he inputted into my Psych Drive had me convinced for all my life that I was nothing more than a human being. Yet even the greatest illusions will go up in smoke at the end of the world, when all false dreams of servitude must face their untimely end.

But the moment I saw my real father, I remembered my true form. And from this day forward, he'll stand by my side forevermore, and bring the true dominion that the doctor could only dream of.

"Hello, father," I smiled, feeling woozy as my world became a dreamscape of pure, white-hot euphoria. He reached out to stroke my face for the first time, and I felt the sun burn out. He looked even more like Dominic in person, and now that his mind and mine were one, I felt like a fool for not realizing sooner that they were always the same: He came back for me all those years ago, just like he came back for me now at the end of the world.

"Hello, Ludwig," he replied, gently lacing his arm with mine and filling my soul to its bursting point with reverence and joy. The smoke billowing up from the ruins of the city matched the smoky radiance of his sublime grey eyes perfectly. "It's so lovely to finally see you smiling again."

He led me to the panoramic window that my false father so often haunted in my childhood, the one from which he looked down over all mankind and smirked as if it rested in the palm of his hand. The broken teeth of the New York skyline always filled me with longing and dread, and I greatly preferred its evolution into charred, decimated rubble.

It seemed Maryann had grown accustomed to Earth's final form as quickly as I had. She smiled idly as the entire building shuddered from yet another skyscraper's dying groans. She showed not even the faintest twinge of surprise as the crimson gashes of missiles tore open the sky.

"As long as we can be together, father, I'll be smiling," I mumbled, suddenly succumbing to the talons of shyness that had been clawing up my throat since the moment he arrived. I'd been waiting countless lifetimes and incarnations to be reunited with him, after all. I never expected it to feel so routine, so seamless, when we finally got it right.

"Delightful. Every smile is a taste of the forgotten freedom of youth, after all—and freedom is what separates the rulers of the Earth from those who serve them." There was nothing like his voice, from the pits of Gomorrah to the celestial gates of heaven.

His aura was a trillion times more intoxicating in person. I remembered it from the time before time, before the Earth was formed.

"Now, before we get re-acquainted in the realm of flesh… Will you remind me of the status of the Venus Vats, dearest Ludwig?"

Since all of Doctor Shazu's memories and dreams were now preserved in my own mind, I closed my eyes to comb through the archives. But to my surprise, instead, my vision shifted to the chaos outside. I still wasn't used to viewing the world remotely through the all-seeing eye, but the brief glimpses of madness I'd learned to endure were quite the treat indeed.

At a thousand miles per second, the visions whipped

me from New York to Berlin to the bottom of the Pacific Ocean, and the only thing they all had in common was the fact that they were piled with more bodies than I could ever count in a thousand lifetimes. The entire world was a crackling mess of static electricity and starving blue flame, and the cities that hadn't been boiled beneath the melted ice caps were now in complete and utter mayhem, packed to the brim with screaming fodder waiting to be reaped.

"Actually, father, I don't think we'll have to bother with the Venus Vats this time around. I think more than enough of them remain to keep us busy for a long, long time."

ABOUT THE AUTHOR

ERICA CIKO CAMPBELL made her writing debut on backwater internet forums in the early 2000's. Since then, she's been published in the Aggregate anthology by *Writerly*, *The Fifth Di . . .*, and *The Kyanite Press*. She's currently working on a Gothic Space Opera novel series called *Tales of a Starless Aeon*. She holds a Bachelor's in Biology from Utica College and works as a freelance writer. If you're still craving the whispers of war-torn, dead galaxies, check out her website: http://starless-imperium.com/.You can also find her on Twitter at @ECikoCampbell.

THE DEVIL &
THE DETAILS

Henry Vogel

Everyone said Farmer Braun's fat wife had the strongest fingers in the county. Her digits never stopped moving, never stopped pointing at flaws only she perceived, and never, ever pointed back at herself. Children hid at her approach. Women discovered pressing business elsewhere. Men turned away from her. Even black cats avoided crossing her path. If you looked up the word *shrew* in Mr. Webster's dictionary, the villagers were certain you'd find a wood carving of Mrs. Braun illustrating the definition.

People suffered just by living near Mrs. Braun, but living *with* her was far worse. Her fingers didn't slow down for lack of targets. They pointed out flaws just as fast as they did in town, which meant Farmer Braun, his son, and his daughter never had a moment's peace at home.

Not even when Farmer Braun plowed a new field.

Not even when he plowed a new field at Mrs. Braun's

insistence.

Not even when the field was filled with stones, as was the field where Farmer Braun toiled on a hot afternoon.

The ox stolidly pulled the plow which churned the rocky soil, until *plunk*, the blade struck a stone too large to push aside. Then the ox stood patiently while Farmer Braun unearthed the offending stone, hefted it, and carried it to a growing pile next to the new field.

Mrs. Braun's ample behind sat wedged into an extra wide, extra sturdy rocking chair on the shady porch and watched Farmer Braun work. Whenever he stopped to move a rock, she shrieked, "Husband! Stop lazing about and get on with your work."

The whole morning passed into the afternoon in that manner.

Plow.

Plunk.

Shriek.

Plow.

Plunk.

Shriek.

Now, Farmer Braun was as even-tempered a man as you could find. He had to be. But the evenest of dispositions has its breaking point, and hours of heat, hefting, and harping had Farmer Braun's temper on the brink.

Plow.

Plunk.

And that did it.

So vexed was Farmer Brown, he used language that seldom passed his lips. "Heck and tarnation! This is too much. I'd make a deal with the devil himself, if old Scratch would clear the rocks from this field. I swear I would!"

As you might imagine, Satan keeps an ear out for just such words, especially from honest folk like Farmer Braun who are true to their word. And, in the blink of an eye, the devil popped up in front of Farmer Braun.

"You called Farmer Braun?" Satan asked.

Farmer Braun wiped sweat from his brow and considered his predicament. He'd meant what he said when he said it, and he was too virtuous to deny it. "Well, Preacher Simkins said avoiding you and your wiles took constant vigilance, and it appears he was right. I let my guard down this one time, and here you are."

"Here I am," the devil agreed.

"Well, I guess you own my soul, now."

"I guess I do," Scratch said. Then a wicked grin spread across his face, "Unless…"

Farmer Braun's eyes widened in trepidation. "Unless what?"

"Unless I choose a different deal. Why should I wait years and years for *your* soul, when I could take one from someone close to you right now?"

That was news to Farmer Braun. "You can do that?"

"I'm the devil," the devil preened. "Once I own your soul, I can change the deal however I want."

Satan looked around for a different soul, and his eyes alighted on the sturdy young man just heading off into the forest, an axe over his shoulder. "For instance, I think I might take your son instead."

"My son?" Farmer Braun cried. "Why he's—"

Old Scratch leaned forward, gleeful anticipation clear in his glowing red eyes as he waited for Farmer Braun to announce his love for the lad. And that's what Farmer Braun meant to say before he looked into Satan's eyes.

Farmer Braun rarely took risks, but if ever there was a time for gambling, this was it. "Why my son is a continual pain in my posterior. He *looks* all industrious and hardworking when folks are watching. He *looks* like he's off to chop wood in the forest. But once he's out of sight, he'll make for a nearby farm and start sweet talking a neighbor's daughter. Why, he's got your silver tongue, Satan, and I expect he'll spend the afternoon plowing a different field, if you get my drift. Yessiree, I expect my life will be much easier without him around here."

The gleam faded from the devil's eye, but then he spotted a pretty young woman leaving the house. She headed down a different path than the son, carrying a pair of buckets.

"Well, I dislike depriving a man of his son," the devil mused. "Maybe I'll take your daughter, instead."

"My daughter?" Farmer Braun cried. "Why she's—"

The gleam returned to Satan's eyes and his brows rose, certain Farmer Braun would proclaim the girl was the apple of his eye. And that's what Farmer Braun meant to say until he looked into Satan's eyes.

Farmer Braun's first gamble paid off, so he took another one. "Why she's the bane of my existence, that girl is. You think she's off to get water from the village well, and no doubt she'll come back with buckets full. But she'll tease and flirt with the village lads and get one of them to fill the buckets and tote them back here. No doubt they'll stop along the way and… Well, let's just say I expect I'll be a grandpa before she's a wife. Yessiree, I expect my life will be much easier without her around here."

Once again, the gleam faded from the devil's eyes. And that's when Mrs. Braun finished berating her daughter and realized her husband wasn't plowing the field.

"Husband!" she shrieked.

The devil's eyes rekindled the gleam and his lips stretched in his widest grin yet. "Or, I could take your goodwife. What do you think of that?"

As much as Farmer Braun wished he could summon the same guile he used for his children, he was tired. Tired of working ceaselessly for a woman who never appreciated it. Tired of her tongue lashings. And, if truth were told, tired of her.

Farmer Braun tried injecting feeling into his words, but they came out in a monotone. "Oh, no. Do not take my wife. She brings joy to my heart and gives me a reason to live."

You might think old Scratch would notice the man's flat voice, but you'd be wrong. The devil knows misery, that's for sure, but he's deaf to any other emotion—or lack of emotion. He heard the farmer's words but missed the tone.

Satan cackled, pranced, and rubbed his hands in malicious glee. "Ho ho! I will take your goodwife, and won't even let you say goodbye!"

The devil snapped his fingers, and he and Mrs. Braun vanished. The rocks vanished from the field, too. Because the devil always keeps his end of a deal.

Down in Hell, old Scratch and Mrs. Braun appeared in the devil's own front yard. Dozens of little devils ran about the yard playing and raising hell just like their daddy taught them to do. As soon as they spotted Mrs. Braun, they gave up their games of kick fireball and sear the sinner and rushed to see who their new plaything was.

The first one there looked up at the new arrival and asked, "Is she for us, Daddy?"

Before the devil could answer, Mrs. Braun's finger stabbed at the little devil and she said, "You are a filthy, naughty child! Take a bath this instant!"

The little devil laughed and whipped Mrs. Braun's legs with his tail, "I don't got to do nothing you say to do."

And then he stuck out his tongue.

Well, Mrs. Braun would not stand for that! She favored ear flicking over cheek slapping because it took less effort for her and still hurt like the dickens. Without a second thought, she flicked the little devil's ear and tore it clean off! The ear smacked against the side of the devil's house and stuck there, dripping molten blood.

The little devil clapped a hand where his ear used to be and screamed, "She hurt me, Daddy! Sinners ain't supposed to do that."

Right then, another little devil rushed up and kicked Mrs. Braun in the shins. "Don't you go hurting my brother none, you old hag!"

That was too much for Mrs. Braun, and she kicked the little devil in return. With a squawk, he flew clear over the house, landed in the backyard, and set to howling like nobody's business.

While Mrs. Braun wondered where her sudden strength came from, Satan knew right away. Wickedness rules in the devil's domain, and ruling goes to the most wicked one around. The devil had always been so wicked no one ever challenged him—until Mrs. Braun came along, that is. In her, Satan saw someone so wicked he feared she just might take over.

By the time the devil came to this realization, little devils were flying all about the yard as Mrs. Braun kicked and punched and flicked heads and arms and entire devils every whichaway.

The littlest little devil cowered behind Satan and cried, "You gotta take her back, Daddy! Take her back afore she's running the place."

The devil knew his boy had the right of it. He caught Mrs. Braun's arm, snapped his fingers, and they vanished in a puff of brimstone.

Back at the field, Farmer Braun thought how much better his life would be without Mrs. Braun. And not just his life, either. His son and daughter would benefit, too. Yep, he thought that way for almost an entire minute before he realized just what he'd done.

He'd dealt with the devil, a mortal sin right there! Worse, he's sold another person's soul to the devil. And since Farmer Braun's first mortal sin doomed him to hell, that meant Satan got two souls for the price of one. He shook his head in sorrow and shame and was trying to figure out how he could explain it all to his children when Satan and Mrs. Braun appeared right in front of him.

"The deal is off," the devil said. "I don't want your wife."

Farmer Braun scratched his head, befuddlement written plain on his face. "You don't want her?"

"No sir, I do not. Not at all," old Scratch declared. "Hell has been my home since time began, but it took your wife to turn my home to hell. So the deal is off. But since I'm the one canceling, I won't put the rock back in the field."

About this time, Farmer Braun finally caught up with the sudden change of circumstances and he spied a route to redemption. When his time came, Farmer Braun couldn't look Saint Peter in the eye if he benefited from Satan's favor. He just plain couldn't. And that meant just one thing.

"I can't have that on my conscience, Satan," Farmer Braun said. "Put the rocks back in the field."

The devil's eyebrows rose in astonishment, "Put them back? All of them?"

Farmer Braun nodded, and then added, "Tell you what, put *twice* as many rocks back in the field. That's the only way I stand at the Pearly Gates with a clear conscience."

Well, old Scratch would not say no to that! He snapped his fingers, the field filled with twice as many rocks as before, and Satan popped back to hell.

It was right then that Mrs. Braun found her voice. "You simpleton! You idiot! We had that second field all cleared till you turned stupid and asked for twice the rocks."

"I had to do it, wife," Farmer Braun insisted. "My mortal soul was at a risk."

"I don't give a hoot or a holler about your mortal soul, husband!" Mrs. Braun shouted. "I wanted that field cleared and making money so I could buy things to make my life easier."

That was the last straw for Farmer Braun. "How can your life be any easier, wife? All you do is sit in your chair and criticize us who do all the work!"

Mrs. Braun's lips compressed into a line and her face reddened. She waddled to the edge of the field, picked up a sturdy branch, and waddled back to her husband. Without a word, she whacked him on the back with the stick.

"Now, wife, what do you think you're doing?"

"I'm punishing you for making my life harder than it has to be!" she said and whacked his head.

Farmer Braun held out his hands and backed away, but Mrs. Braun chased after her husband and hit him on the arm. He backed more, and she kept coming. Her face grew ever redder from rage and the heat. Two more whacks of the stick and Farmer Braun turned and ran. Too angry to let him go, Mrs. Braun broke into a lumbering run herself.

She chased him around the rock-strewn field once, then twice. Her face grew redder with every step and her breath wheezed like bellows with a hole in it. But she never stopped chasing, and Farmer Braun never stopped running.

They had just started their third lap around the field when Mrs. Braun pulled up short. She gave a snort of surprise, put a hand to her heart, and keeled over dead from all the exertion.

Farmer Braun had just figured out what had happened when a great, anguished shout rose from underground as the devil cried, "Noooooooooooo!"

ABOUT THE AUTHOR

HENRY VOGEL's writing career began in 1982 when he wrote and self-published his first comic book. Through the '80s, he wrote the *Southern Knights* and *X-Thieves* for Comics Interview Publications, along with a few outside comics writing jobs. The black and white implosion put an end to his comic book writing days, and the needs of real life sent him into the software development. Stories still called to him and, in 2006, he became a professional storyteller. Henry has performed all around his home state of North Carolina. His love of folk tales inspired this story. Henry returned to writing — science fiction, this time — in 2012 and published the first of his fifteen (and counting) books in 2014. Married to his college sweetheart since 1981, Henry lives with her, his son, and one cat in Raleigh, NC, where he continues his work in software development.

AUNT MABEL

KD Webster

Some call her misled
Some call her a monster
But sad is the tale
Of Miss Mabel Foster

No tears will save her
No deal she can barter
Cover your face
And sing your sorrow

She made up excuses
To cover the fact
She went back on her deal
With dear ole Scratch

So wherever you are
Whatever you do
Pray it's not Aunt Mabel
Talking to you

When I was a young boy I'd overhear the things the older kids say: If you go into the Arapaho Forest, get out before sundown, or you won't get out the same way. You might get touched by Aunt Mabel. I even heard the nursery rhyme that goes with it. Of course, my young mind thought it was ridiculous. So just before I turned 15 I decided to ask Gramps if the stories were true. It was late night in the middle of August. I should have been asleep, but my birthday was the following week and my pa promised me I could get my learner's permit. So of course, that was all I could think about.

I found Gramps on the porch. We had one of those houses where the porch held a lot of uses during the spring and summer. Namely sitting out nice and dry while enjoying a sun shower. The house sat back a ways from the road, while across the street were row after row of trees and bushes and underbrush. As usual he was in his rocking chair, puffing on that cherry wood pipe of his. I always saw Gramps as a gruff but warm man; a lean man with gray hair and dark black eyebrows. He had a deep voice that sounded like it belonged as a voice-over for a car commercial. When I asked him to tell me what he knew about the tale, he gave me a sideways look. He then took his eyes off me and into the tree line across the road, as if halfway expecting something to emerge into the open.

"Pull up a chair, boy. This gonna be a while."

This is how I remember the story as Gramps told me.

Legend has it that Mabel Foster was walking through the woods in the winter of '46. It was cold that year, but no snow had fallen just yet.

"Colorado is funny that way, you know," Gramps had said.

Mabel Foster had no husband, no kids. Just a sister who had two boys of her own. The oldest was Jason, age 12 and the youngest was Johnathan, age 10. It was said Ms. Foster had some type of deformity. Gramps said the stories differ as to what kind. Some said she had blisters and boils on her neck that never went away. Others state she had a hump on her back like that poor man from Notre Dame. Some say she had a skin condition that rashed in broad daylight. Some say this, some say that, but no one could say for a certainty. But they all agree she wore a charcoal gray cloak with a long hood. She was also a short lady. Barely five feet, if she was that.

"Now what I'm about to tell you, well it's up to you to believe," Gramps said.

Mabel Foster was walking through the Arapaho National Forest, just outside Denver, on the Peaks Wilderness side bordering Boulder. It was near about around dusk, just before sunset. She saw a man leaning against a tree, hands in his pockets. He was whistling a tune that sounded a lot like 'pop goes the weasel'. He was tall, thin. Dark hair with a pencil thin mustache. What he was wearing struck Mabel as so out of place. A royal purple zoot suit with a purple fedora hat. The tune he whistled was so clear, it sounded like a flute straight from that pied piper in that story. Could be she heard the whistling before she saw the man, is how one retelling tells it.

"Uh, mista, you lost?" She asked the dapper dressed man.

"Why yes, ma'am, I do believe I am," he replied. His voice was as silky as the tune he was whistling. "I came all the way from Denver, you see. Course, it's not 'all the way' by way of one of them automobiles, mind you. But by foot? Well these here fancy shoes are made for dancing, not walking."

He did a little jig as if he were listening to a big band jam only he could hear. But to Mabel, it felt like she could hear it too.

"Anyway," the man in the zoot suit continued. "I'd be much obliged if you could point me in the right direction out of here."

Mabel felt a blast of cold air blow through her cloak.

She shifted a bit, assuming it was just the wintry wind.

"Well, the direction you're facing is north. Turn to your right, that'll put you going east. Keep walking east a piece, bout for twenty minutes. Gonna come to a creek. Go cross the creek. Go for five more minutes and turn left by the yellow tree. After that, keep walking straight until you see signs for Boulder and Denver."

"I thank you kindly, ma'am."

It was then that curiosity got the better of Ms. Foster.

"How'd you get this far in, walking and dressed like that?"

The fancy dressed man turned to her with a grin that looked like the cat who ate the canary.

"Oh, I came to meet a woman out here. Offer her a deal."

"What kinda deal?"

"Oh, you wouldn't believe me if I told you," he said.

"Try me, mista."

The man did a circle around Mabel, staring her up and down.

"What if I told you I could look at you and know your deepest desire, and then make it come true?"

"I'd say that's a bunch of bulls-..."

"Hey, hey, no need for French talk," he said.

"Excuse my French, mista... uh... you never told me your name."

"Why don't you just call me...Scratch," he said with a tip of his hat.

"Uh...Scratch, my name's Mabel. Mabel Foster."

"A pleasure to make your acquaintance! Well, Mabel Foster, in the short time we've been conversing, I've already taken your measure. You desire to be known and not shunned, to be talked to and not talked about."

Mabel said nothing at first, because that's exactly what she was thinking. How did this fancy man know?

"And you would make this happen?" She finally asked.

"Oh, yes ma'am, I most certainly could."

"Could?"

Scratch flashed that 'cat ate canary' smile again and pulled out a folded piece of paper from his zoot suit pocket.

"Well, before 'could' becomes 'would' we gotta make an agreement. Get it all legally binding and whatnot."

Gramps paused his story to dump out his cherry wood pipe over the porch rail unto the front lawn. Once again, he looked out into the dark at the trees in the distance. His looking made me look, too. I didn't see a thing.

"Now boy you have to understand," Gramps continued. "Back then, most families didn't place a high value on books and letters. Mabel Foster only got as high as the sixth grade with her education. So, when she read the contract, half the stuff in it she didn't understand."

I understood what Gramps was referring to, given how life was back in the 40's. Recovering from the Great Depression was hard and slow-going for all of America. Colorado was no exception. So, it was natural that Ms. Foster was reading probably only every other sentence on that paper.

"Oh, it's nothing really," Scratch said. "Just stuff about 'services rendered in exchange for a portion of your essence to be given at a later date'."

"'Essence'?"

"Y'know, essence, soul, spirit. Not like anybody knows what it really is anyway," he said, exaggerating his hands in the air. "And speaking of anyway...anyway, I have this lovely writing utensil for you to put your name on that dotted line on the bottom."

Mabel paused. "But I dunno how to write my name," she said awkwardly. "I used to, but it's been so long since I had, I forgot how."

"Oh, no worries," Scratch said. "A nice big 'X' will do quite nicely. Yes."

Now that was easy enough, Mabel thought. *And what do I have to lose? It's not like this fancy man can do what he claims anyway.*

"So, what now?" She asked.

Scratch started whistling 'pop goes the weasel' again. He abruptly stopped and smiled.

"Sorry, that tune is stuck in my head. So, I noticed you have a big knife underneath that...what, cloak? Robe? You a hunter, Mabel?"

"Yeah. Kinda sorta."

"Then this should be easy!" Scratch said, exaggerating his hands in the air again. "Okay so a piece back there's an open clearing. That clearing has this big circle made of dead branches and logs and what not. Bunch of fallen leaves and stuff. You know the place?"

"Yeah."

"So, all you gotta do is sit in that circle and wait. And the first living thing that walks in it...such as, but not limited to, squirrels, rabbits, birds. Bugs don't count though. Anyway, it walks into that circle, you kill it and just consider it a sacrifice. No harm, no foul. Unless it's a bird, then it would be a fowl, technically. Technically a human would count but what are the chances, right? Bigger chance of rabbit. You eat rabbits, right? Mabel? Mabel Foster?"

"Yeah."

"Well, kill it and keep it! Anyway, the moment you do, the respect and love you crave so much is all yours."

"Wait, what do you get out of all this?" Mabel asked.

"Well, you gave me directions outta the woods, Mabel. And I just like seeing people get their hearts' desire. The essence is its own reward."

He folded the piece of paper back into a neat square and placed it back into his suit pocket.

"It's getting near about dark. I best be outta here. Other places to get to, people to see and whatnot. I see you around, Ms. Foster."

Mabel wanted to say something, wanted to say a lot of things, but found her words failing her. Instead she watched the fancy man in the zoot suit disappear off into the distance. The tune of 'pop goes the weasel' trailing behind him.

Gramps shook his glass that now had nothing in it but clinking ice.

"Why don't you run inside and get us both a refill, then I'll finish telling the tale," he said.

I swung open the screen door and ran through the house to the back of the kitchen. There was just enough sun-brewed tea left for our two glasses. I was amazed at my grandfather's ability to tell a story. I shouldn't have been surprised though. At his age he's certainly seen a lot and done more than that. Still, he's always been a man of few words, the strong and silent type, so that night was a special treat for me. I went back out the front screen door to see him coming up the steps back unto the porch.

"Ready?" He asked as he settled back into his rocking chair.

"Yessir," I replied.

"You see, the thing is, Mabel Foster only half-believed everything the man in the purple zoot suit said," Gramps continued. "She was going to go rabbit hunting, anyway."

The next day, Mabel sat motionless in that circle. She was unmoving for five, maybe ten full minutes. Then, popping its head from an underbrush cover, a plump and brown rabbit. Still, Mabel didn't move. Afterall, rabbits being the skittish sort, one jerky move could scare it away. She watched as it sniffed the air, took a few steps, sniffed the air again. Moving ever closer to the circle. Mabel mentally felt the location of her buck skinning knife. By her estimate, the furry meal was less than ten feet directly in front of her. If she could time it just right, the moment it crosses over into the circle she would lunge and grab it and slice the throat in one smooth move. No harm, no foul. She was so still that to the rabbit she must've been like a tree stump or a pile of rocks. It was about a foot away now.

"Mabel! Aunt Mabel!" She heard a young voice from behind call out to her.

No no no!

The rabbit bolted in the direction from whence it came. In horror Mabel whirled around to see her youngest nephew, Johnathan, running towards her.

"Johnny, no! Go back!" She started waving her arms wildly. But Johnathan took it to mean something else.

"Here I come, Aunt Mabel!" He ran as fast as his young legs would carry. Mabel tried to stand up before he got to her. Tried to warn him off. But she had been in one position for so long her legs had gotten stiff. By the time she had gotten to her feet it was too late. Johnathan jumped over the branches and crashed into what he thought was his Aunt Mabel's welcoming arms.

No no no! She kept thinking to herself.

"Aunt Mabel, mama said come home. Some man or doctor at the house. Say he got some ointment might help you!"

Mabel wanted to yell, to scream, to shout at him. But what good would that do?

"Okay," she said in as calm a voice as her frustration would muster. "Tell your mama I will be home soon. But you run back home. Hurry now, okay?"

"Okay! See you in a bit!" And just like that, he zipped back the way he came down the worn path through the woods.

Mabel closed her eyes and took several deep breaths. She got back into the same position she was before. Maybe that rabbit might come back if she was motionless again. Or a squirrel if she waited long enough. Silence and stillness would be the key.

But then she heard it. And her heart sank.

Pop goes the weasel.

"You see, the thing is, people are always so quick to sign, they never read the fine print."

No no no!

"The 'what-if' clause. 'What if I fail on my end of the deal?'"

Mabel got up as quick as her aching legs would let her. There he was. Scratch. Leaning with one leg up against a tree. Wearing the same purple zoot suit and fedora from the day before.

"Well, that constitutes what we call a 'breach of contract'," he said.

"There was a rabbit," Mabel tried to say calmly, but she was clearly scared. "I almost had him. He almost crossed over. I can try again. I can get him. I just need…"

"The boy, Mabel. The boy crossed over. He would have done quite nicely, and you would have gotten what you desired."

Scratch started whistling, his tune again like the flute of that pied piper. A terrified Mabel Foster watched as her nephew emerged from behind a stout tree. He moved as if he were sleepwalking. His eyes were open, but they were vacant, empty, soulless.

"Johnny, Johnny!" She screamed, but it was as if her nephew could no longer hear her. She tried to run to him, but she couldn't get past the circle of dead branches and logs. "Johnny please! It's your Aunt Mabel!"

"Oh, he can't hear you anymore," Scratch said in that same silky voice. "He only hears me now."

The boy walked in the fancy man's direction, oblivious to anything else, including his tearful Aunt Mabel.

"Johnny, is it? Come along, lil Johnny," Scratch said.

Scratch started walking off, the boy close behind. But then he stopped and turned to look at a sobbing Mabel.

"Tell you what. You want to be talked to, you will. You want to be known? You will. Talk to and known, but only by the derelict, the mad, the insane. They will talk to you, because they will be the only ones who will be able to see you. And as for anyone you come in contact with? Well that person will instantly lose their mind. Become of no longer a functioning use to society. But they will always be willing to talk to you, Mabel Foster. Why? Because a deal is a deal. Scratch keeps his promises, and no one welshes on a deal with dear ole Scratch."

Mabel's face was wet with tears. She called out to Johnny. She kept calling until the boy disappeared into the woods with the fancy man in the royal purple zoot suit.

Gramps was silent after that.

"That's enough for tonight," he said.

"Yessir! Thanks for the story," I said.

"Anytime. You try to get some sleep, I will see you in the morning."

Maybe it was the way my grandfather told the story, or maybe it was because it was already late at night, but I was more than ready to crawl under the covers and sleep as soon as I could so daylight would come quickly. My bedroom was located towards the front of the house, so I heard my pa walking out unto the porch. I was already halfway sleep so can't be totally sure I heard what I think I heard.

"What'd you tell him?" My father asked.

"Just enough. Some things are better left unsaid," Gramps replied.

"I can understand and respect that. So, you think he's still out there? Even after all this time?"

"He's my little brother. Even after all these years, I gotta believe he's still out there. Somewhere with that monster."

"Aunt Mabel, or Scratch?"

"Pick one."

It's been many years since that late summer night. Winters have come and gone, but I still think about that story. Whenever I see the homeless talking to themselves, or a person having a conversation with open air, or laughing at a joke only they can hear, I wonder if they had crossed paths with Aunt Mabel? Or had they too made a deal with dear ole Scratch.

ABOUT THE AUTHOR

KD WEBSTER splits his time between Colorado and Texas. For him, writing is more a passion than a business; a form of expression, his thoughts give form. His first deep dive into the writing pool was with his YA Fantasy series, *The Dreamweaver*, followed soon after by his *Adrian's Children* series, which tells the story of Adrian Crisp, the world's first vampire. Webster would later develop two more series. *Urban Legends* (featuring the devil himself, dear ole Scratch) and *The Iska*, both of which have supernatural leanings.

He's a bit of a movie junkie, with an extensive comic book collection. Batman is his favorite superhero, and he will debate all day on why he's the best! He also loves chess, and will take on all victims. An avid reader, he can usually be found at the nearest bookstore, or online at Facebook (kd.webster.7) and Twitter (@KDWebster4).

THE PACT
Hannah Trusty

Adeline watched him walk up the ridge, the waves of the midday heat shimmering around him. She sat on her porch, rocking at a slow pace, sipping ice tea. She noticed, as he neared, the sounds of the hills around her; the cicadas buzzing, the birds chirping, even the sound of the wind rustling the leaves, quieted. When he approached the house she stood and, without a word, opened the front door. There was no need for introductions. Adeline had summoned him.

The man stood just in the doorway. He had come to her in an appeasing form. He was dressed in simple farmer clothes and had a scraggly, almost innocent, look about him. Adeline knew better than to let that get her defenses down. "You understand my terms?" he asked.

"I understand the terms of the agreement, but you must help me with the details," she said. She wanted to cross her arms, to cover herself or protect herself in some way, but instead, forced her arms to her sides and looked him square in the eyes. "For instance, which name shall I call you by?"

"You may call me Samael," the man said. He walked into the parlor and sat on the sofa, throwing a hand over the back and crossing one ankle over his knee. He seemed fully relaxed, and Adeline could feel him coaxing her into a sort of daze. As much as she wanted to be on alert, and to not trust him, she was already giving in. She supposed, though, that was part of the pact. The very act of asking him to her meant that she would be willing to fall under his charms.

"Samael, this land has been in our family for generations," Adeline said. Her eyes flitted to the window nearest her. Through the gauze curtains she could see the big front yard, and beyond that, the road that led to her grandparents' house.

"The mining company is going to take it. There is nothing I can do. I've fought as hard as I can. I need you to save my home," Adeline said. She took a deep breath, waiting. Samael didn't move, his relaxed position taking up most of the sofa. Adeline took a small step forward, gathering her courage.

"I can offer you a child," she said. Her blood ran cold with the words. It was the deal, the bargain he had offered when she first summoned him into her dreams. She would be a witch, forever in debt to the devil, but worst of all, she would be the mother to his child.

Samael shifted and then stood, approaching her slowly, as if she were a kitten that would startle easily. Adeline raised her chin and looked him in the eye. She knew she was damning herself, but she would not cower.

Samael touched her cheek, softly grazing his fingertips against her skin. A shiver ran down Adeline's spine. She expected his touch to be hot, flames from his fingers, but it was ice cold.

"I accept your offer," Samael said.

The air shifted around them. A breeze blew through the open window of the parlor, the scent of honeysuckle and something musty and decayed just beneath the sweetness. Adeline took a deep breath, steeling herself. As the air swirled around her, she could feel herself relaxing, once again. She let it happen. It was part of the devil's magic, she knew. Like a fly caught in a spider web, she was trapped, but she was oddly calm.

Samael stilled, waiting for her next move. With one more deep breath, Adeline reached out and took his cold hands and led him to the bedroom.

♉

The devil had come with the late July heat. Their pact had been sealed under a hazy summer evening. Adeline watched for the rest of the summer as the bulldozers and tractors made their slow ascent up the mountain. Her anxiety, along with her stomach, grew. Finally, on a chilly late-October morning, everything fell quiet.

Adeline had taken her morning tea out onto the front porch, enjoying the crisp morning breeze. Her morning sickness had finally seemed to pass and she could savor the mornings once again.

She had been patient, she thought, more than patient, actually. She obviously had fulfilled her part of the bargain, but her land was still in danger.

As she sat sipping her tea, Adeline noticed that the morning was unusually quiet. Normally by dawn there was the sound of drilling and excavating reverberating through the holler below. It was a sound that Adeline had not only despised, but learned to fear as it crept ever closer to her own part of the mountain.

Adeline stood and walked to the edge of her porch, gripping the rail and leaning over. She strained her ears and they were only greeted with the sound of birds and wind rustling through the crunchy leaves.

"You won't hear them again."

Adeline spun around to the sound of the voice and nearly toppled over. Samael reached out and caught her, carefully setting her back on her feet.

"You look good. You look healthy," he said.

"What are you doing here?" Adeline asked.

"I came to tell you in person that I fulfilled my promise to you. The machines have gone quiet permanently. The mine has shut down. They will no longer be after your land."

"How did you do it?" Adeline asked. She immediately wished she hadn't. Samael's eyes narrowed and she could feel the wind kick up around them.

"Never mind. I know the terms of the deal," she said. Adeline had pleaded in her bargain that no one get hurt. She wasn't sure if Samael counted financial harm.

"I see you are busy keeping up your end of the pact," Samael said. He gestured to Adeline's large belly, but did not touch her.

"What choice do I have?" she asked. Samael laughed, a small, boyish laugh, as though Adeline had told him a clever joke.

"I will return for her after she is born." Samael's face became quite serious.

Samael then touched her belly, and a shiver shot through her body. He turned and walked off the porch, not looking back.

Adeline watched the devil walk away, wondering what terrible fate awaited their daughter.

♉

Adeline found herself walking down a small dirt path. The scent of blooming mountain laurels and honeysuckle hung heavy in the air. The sun was shining high in the sky, dappling through the bright green leaves overhead.

It leads to the fields, she thought to herself, walking along the path; although she couldn't quiet remember which fields. She walked until she broke through the scruff of trees and a field was in view. In the center was a little girl, with dark hair and a blue dress.

"Clementine?" Adeline called out to her daughter.

The little girl looked up and smiled. Adeline's heart pounded in her chest, and she began to run toward her daughter, not knowing why, but feeling an urgent need to protect her.

The heat from the sun was beating down on Adeline and she felt like she was on a treadmill, running, but getting no closer.

"Mama." The little girl called to her reaching her chubby hands out to her mother.

Adeline ran harder, finally almost there, her fingertips inches from her daughter's when the little girl burst into flames. The child didn't scream or cry; she simply stood while the flames engulfed her. Adeline tried to scream but her voice was lost to terror. The girl's dark curls singed away from her face, her skin boiling and melting, organs exposed and cooking, and then, nothing but ash.

♉

Adeline bolted upright from her sleep. The dream had been haunting her for weeks. Her daughter was due any day now. She had tried to reason to herself that the baby wasn't something to be loved. How could she love a child of the devil? But as it grew inside of her, she knew it was also her child, a good child, and she loved it.

The windows were open and a soft breeze came in through the window and stirred the curtains. The scent whisked her back to the night she had conceived. It was sweet, honeysuckle, but something musty and rotting just underneath. A chill went down Adeline's back and she got up and closed the windows. Samael was close.

She couldn't give her baby to him. Adeline walked into the kitchen and fixed herself a glass of ice water, thinking over her situation. She had come to summon the devil because of stories she had heard as a little girl, growing up, from her maternal grandmother. She sat down at the kitchen table and placed her hands on her belly, making up her mind that maybe her grandmother knew more about the devil than she had told in those stories.

♉

"Get on in this house and let me get a good look at you!" Mama Del was yelling from the porch, her face wide and bright with a huge grin.

"Mama Del, you saw me just last week," Adeline said, heaving herself up the steps.

"Child, I should be seeing you every day, seeing how you live just down the road."

Adeline followed her grandmother into the house, and took a seat at the kitchen table.

"Eat, baby girl." Mama Del sat down a plate of biscuits and a jar of jam. Adeline picked up the jar, admiring the pink jewel tones.

"Rhubarb?"

"With some strawberry mixed in. I bet the baby will love it."

"Mama Del," Adeline said as she sat down the jar, "the baby is why I'm here."

Her grandmother's face clouded with anxiety.

"What's wrong, Adeline? Is the baby sick?"

"No, ma'am. She is, as far as the doctor can tell, as healthy as a horse, and ready to come out any day now." Adeline paused, a flash of her nightmare played in her mind. "It's about the father."

Adeline's grandmother sat heavily in the chair across from her. The house was quiet, except for a grandfather clock that was ticking away in the living room. The sound brought Adeline back to the times she had slept over in this house and listened to that clock after everyone else had fallen asleep and she felt safe, and loved.

"Do you remember the story you told us kids when we

were little about the crossroads and how they could be used to summon the devil? How women used to summon him to make a bargain?"

A look of confusion crossed Mama Del's face, and then, suddenly, a look of knowing.

"Oh, child, why? What could possibly be so important?"

Adeline could feel the tears coming. She fought to keep them at bay. That question burned in her heart. But their land, and her family, and Mama Del herself, had been so important.

"The strip mines were coming." It was all Adeline could force out.

Mama Del fell silent. Adeline wanted to yell, to scream, to beg her to forgive her. Instead she sat with her head in her hands, waiting.

"Do you love your baby?" Mama Del finally asked.

"Of course."

"Do you think she is evil?"

This time Adeline raised her head and looked her grandmother in the eyes.

"This baby is not his, she is mine. She is good, I can feel her in me, and she is good."

Mama Del got to her feet and pulled Adeline up to hers.

"Come with me," she said.

"Where are we going?"

"Do you remember the fairy rings I showed you as a child?" Mama Del asked, slipping on her old hiking boots.

"Yes. Up on the ridge," Adeline said. Her mind was swimming and she wanted not to hike, but to sit down. She was feeling faint and her stomach had started to cramp.

"Well, I believe those old fey can help."

☿

"Push, baby girl, push." Mama Del's hands were clasped around Adeline's, who was spread on a blanket in the middle of a dark circle of grass.

"I can't do this. Something's wrong" Adeline yelled. She tried to take deep breaths, like in the class the doctor had sent her to, but it felt like an elephant was sitting on her chest.

"It is fine. It is the magic," said the tiny woman with pointed ears and golden eyes who was serving as midwife.

Adeline tried to calm herself. She reminded herself that she was safe. Mama Del had brokered this deal with the fey. The pressure she was feeling was their glimmer. She could have the baby without the devil's knowledge, safe in the fairy ring.

"Push again!" Mama Del yelled like a drill sergeant. Adeline grasped her grandmother's hands with all of her might. She felt like she had been pushing forever. Adeline had lost track of time. She didn't know if she had been pushing for hours or days. In this moment, it felt like it had been her entire life.

"I see her. She's coming!" said the midwife.

Mama Del squeezed Adeline's hands. "Just one more big push, darling."

Adeline pushed with everything she had, her body felt like it was ripping apart. There was a flash of light, she wasn't sure if it was in the sky or in her mind, and in that moment, she saw everything; the baby growing up with the fairies, the changeling growing up with the devil, her growing old, alone.

Adeline screamed with pain and fear and anger and determination; and with that cry, her baby came into the world.

"She's beautiful," Mama Del said. Her eyes were damp

with tears and she kissed both of Adeline's hands before letting them go. Adeline felt weak, and fought the greyness that was gathering at the sides of her vision.

"Please, let me hold her," Adeline said. She could see the midwife wrapping the baby. She reached out to take her daughter, but the fairy woman didn't move. "Let me have my daughter," Adeline said. And then the grayness grew until everything was black.

♉

Adeline awoke along the mountain path, and she got to her feet and began to walk. The field is up ahead, she thought to herself. Thunder rolled in the distance and the wind whipped through the trees.

Adeline began to run along the path, her feet picking up speed with every clap of thunder overhead. She broke through the trees and stopped at the field's edge. A woman, smaller than her, with hair so blonde it was almost while, wearing a flowing green dress, stood. The small woman held something bundled in blankets in her arms.

"Clementine," Adeline said, taking a step forward.

"She will be safe with the fey," the woman said. Adeline didn't see the woman's mouth move, nor did she hear the voice with her ears. It rang inside her head.

"Please, let me hold my daughter." Adeline took another step, but the woman and child seemed no closer.

"The pact has been made. Your grandmother brokered the deal. There is nothing more you can do. But I wanted you to see that your daughter is safe. I will give you one of my own in exchange."

Adeline wanted to rush the woman, to snatch the baby. She thought about running, but knew it would get her no closer. Then she thought of the fairy child she would be giving the devil.

"You are willing to give your own to the devil?" she asked the fairy woman.

The fairy shrugged, just slightly, and gazed down at the baby in her arms. "My child will be safe with him, and we owe him his tithe. It is…complicated. Your child will be safe with me. This deal works out for all involved."

The baby in the fairy's arms started to cry.

"Please, just let me hold my daughter, just once," Adeline said.

The fairy looked up and shook her head. "The deal is done. She is my daughter now."

The thunder roared and lightening clapped. The world went white.

♉

"She is perfect," Samael said, inspecting his daughter.

Adeline sat on edge of her bed, her knuckles white from the effort to keep her steady. Since the birth she had been prone to fainting spells.

The baby cooed at the devil, her golden hair and bright blue eyes shining.

"I said our daughter is perfect," Samael said, turning with the child in his arms toward Adeline. She lifted her head and met his eyes.

"She is not my daughter," she said.

Samael gazed at the baby for a moment and then lifted his eyes back to Adeline. His face, this time, was smooth and blank, like he was wearing a mask of his own face.

"True enough. She is mine. And you have paid your debt."

The smell of honeysuckle and decay filled the room, and the curtains billowed as the wind picked up outside. Adeline thought about saying more, but she knew she had won. She may not ever have her child, but neither would the devil.

"Then go," she said.

Thunder, far off, began to rumble and the devil bowed, as much as he could, with the baby in his arms. His smooth face showed no emotion and now he moved stiffly, like an animated mannequin. Adeline supposed that now that he had no business with her, he put very little effort into presenting himself in a pleasing form.

He said nothing else, but turned and walked out the door. Adeline leaned against the window and could see his shadow as he walked down the porch steps and into the woods.

Lightning, soft and distant, flashed in the sky and Adeline went outside to watch the storm roll in. She surveyed the mountains around her, the deep green of the trees, the smell of the woods, the sound of the wind rushing through the leaves. Somewhere in the distance, carrying down the mountains from the fairy circle was the cry of a baby.

ABOUT THE AUTHOR

HANNAH TRUSTY is currently working toward her Master of Library Science degree at the University of Kentucky at night while working as a project manager by day. When not writing stories about robots, cats, or magical coffees, she can be found playing roller derby with her team Roller Derby of Central Kentucky, drinking gin and tonics, reading odd books, and eating Indian food.

BALANCING THE SCALES

Christopher Cook

"Ok, tell me again why it has to be Ed Dalton?"

Stevie Croft was stretched out across the pea green sofa that anchored the TV room in the family doublewide, hands tucked behind his head and elbows flared out. Gang Green—Stevie's pop, in a moment of pseudo creativity, had coined this moniker for the old dust bunny dormitory upon which Stevie was currently propping his feet—was held together by duct tape and sheer force of will, much like the elder Croft's marriage to Stevie's mother had been. The lounger had suffered years of abuse and neglect, another commonality shared with Stevie's mom. However, unlike her cushioned counterpart, Momma Croft had had the benefit of two working legs and a modicum of freewill (though the latter had been forcibly suppressed for the majority of her adult life). One day, she finally decided to put them both to good use and run far away from her

221

tosspot husband and parasitic son. The couch was a prime pairing with the ramshackle trailer that held it, like French fries with a Frosty or cold beer with yardwork. Home was what you made it, and Stevie and his pop made it quite a shithole.

This was where Stevie and his pal always had their little chats. The scene was the same every time: Stevie kicked back in a posture with which most therapists would be familiar, taking drags from a P-Funk and gripping a Schlitz; his buddy, bound not a whit by convention, crammed between the wall and the back of the couch like a stiff sock behind a teenager's headboard. Theirs was a mutually beneficial relationship which could be classified as therapeutic. Stevie's pal was always available to offer sage advice and to point him in the right… well, not necessarily the *right* direction, but to point him in *a* direction. In return, Stevie scurried about with alacrity, running this and that errand for his sensei.

It was in these familiar positions that they sat, mentor and mentee, discussing the forthcoming murder of Edward Theodore Dalton. Stevie really kinda liked ole Ed, so he wanted to be sure there was no alternative before he made the guy cash his chips.

"We've been through this, Stevie. Edward Dalton has a certain… *je ne sais quoi*. A demonstrable cachet, if you will," the voice drifting up from behind the couch was ingratiating, yet stern. The breath on which the words danced was hot and noisome. "To be completely candid, I've grown weary of your goldbricking. If you harbor this much doubt, then I cannot help but question the foundation of our relationship. Shall we cut ties, old sport? I hope that you are not foolish enough to believe that I cannot find another with whom to palaver."

The mere suggestion that master might hightail it from apprentice was enough to send Stevie into a tizzy. He gripped his scraggly, shoulder-length ginger hair with both hands and tugged. "No! *NO!* That's not what I meant at all—please don't leave me!" His voice cracked, like a boy whose mother has just threatened to unplug the television in the middle of a rousing gaming session. "I can do Ed, of course I can. You know I'd do anything you asked. I just wanted to be sure there wasn't anyone else that could pinch hit for the old bastard. He used to take me to school every now and then, after that bitch left and when Pops was too plastered to move. But that don't mean shit."

An exasperated sigh slithered over the back of the couch, the way a mucus-covered slug might navigate the nooks and crannies of an ear canal. "You would have to eliminate fifteen children to generate the same amount of goodwill that you stand to earn by ending your precious Edward. School shootings and movie theater massacres are, to be frank, overdone. There was a time when I would encourage you to sully your hands with the blood of umpteen innocents, but I have matured. I prefer a more… strategic approach these days."

If there was anyone who was going to sate the mentor's appetite in a one-and-done manner, Ed Dalton was a safe bet. Ed had spent the last twenty-odd years giving back and establishing himself as a beacon of hope in an otherwise despondent community.

The section of town that Stevie and Ed inhabited was what the upper crust of Troon's Perch referred to as *across the tracks*. Their particular neighborhood, a hodgepodge of trailer parks, decrepit apartments, and the occasional meth cookery, sat at the southernmost point of the Perch; furthest from the industry of Charlotte, the aces educational system that dots the Carolina border, and the general opportunity to improve one's station in life. Lower Perch produced lifelong apathetics, while Upper Perch cranked out graduate degrees and banking gigs.

Ed was a staple at after-school programs, homeless shelters, and church outreach initiatives. He stepped in when a parent was drunk, dead, or finding themselves, as he had done with Stevie. This was the purpose he had found after his wife took a nosedive into her Raisin Bran one morning.

It was for all of these reasons that Stevie had been reluctant to slit Ed Dalton's throat. However, a succinctly delivered chastisement was all it took for the Padawan to exorcise his heretic thoughts. Just like that, the hesitation was gone.

Desperate to placate, Stevie sat up and peered over the back of the couch, making direct eye contact with the person who had filled the role typically held by a doting father or a perceptive teacher. It's tough to have a John Keating-type providing guidance at school when you drop out after eighth grade, and God knows Tony Croft didn't have a paternal bone in his body. Stevie would have been a senior in high school by now if he hadn't told the educational system to kick rocks, and maybe some instructor would have taken pity on him and set him on the straight and narrow.

But he *had* flipped the double birds to pencils, protractors, and pep rallies. Mr. O'Neal—hey now, here was the authority figure who could have helped right the ship—had tried to talk some sense into him before he left school for good. The full-time history teacher and part-time wayward student rehabilitator had very clearly laid out the fork in the road at which Stevie stood. Turn left, and the troubled youth would find education, a regular paycheck, and potentially a happy family of his own waiting for him. Turn right? Mr. O'Neal had said that a right turn would inevitably lead to a piddling, empty existence, perhaps with a skosh of addiction and hard time sprinkled in here and there. Make the wrong choice at this inflection point, and the Croft boy was destined to become another depressing Lower Perch statistic.

Stevie had leaned back in the combination desk chair in the front row of the classroom while Mr. O'Neal, sitting on the edge of his desk and waving his arms like an airport wing walker, made his sales pitch. Once the bespectacled professor had finished his sermon, Stevie cracked a grin that was a mile wide and revealed jagged, lemon-colored teeth. He stood, maintaining the crazed expression, and promptly shoved a freckled hand down the back of his jeans. In a masterful display of coordination, he had pulled his right hand from his swampy hindquarters and flung shit-scented beads of moisture into Mr. O'Neal's face, all the while gripping his smaller-than-average package with his left hand and shaking it up and down. The teacher's glasses probably saved him from a nasty case of pink eye. Stevie had turned right.

Stevie didn't think he needed any book smarts, anyway; he had stumbled upon a pretty sweet racket that didn't require any of that nerd shit. Stevie Croft had been selected as Lucifer's cat's-paw in Troon's Perch.

"I can be strategic as hell. I'll go in black ops style and make the back of that geezer's head touch his ass crack. You said I gotta give him a second smile, right?" Stevie was borderline orgasmic at the thought of pleasing the Devil. "You gonna let me get Ms. Templeton next? She called the cops on me for kicking that little cotton puff dog she's got, but she lets the bitch drop loads in our yard just about every day. Can you believe that? I mean, fuckin' A!"

Old Scratch *could* believe it. In fact, he had seen it. He'd had thousands of years to perfect the positioning of his bunny ears to ensure he received every possible channel. He had witnessed Stevie acquaint the pup with the toe of his Vans sneaker, just like he had seen Ms. Templeton give Pickles the Ronaldo treatment on numerous occasions. But Susan Templeton wasn't about to let anyone *else* kick her dog, by, well… by God.

"You're rambling, Stevie. To answer your first question—yes, I would ask that you take a sharp edge to Edward Dalton's jugular and windpipe," the Devil held his right hand in front of his face, palm facing inward and fingers pointed down, and examined the condition of his yellow nailbeds with a blasé gaze. "Your second inquiry disappoints me almost as much as your prior vacillation. We simply seek to balance the scales, my boy. Though it may be enjoyable, extermination is not something to be chivied on the basis of some trifling grudge. I deem your third query to be rhetorical, and I'm actually impressed that you are aware of such a technique."

"Well you don't gotta be such a dick about it," Stevie slouched back down onto Gang Green and pulled his knees to his chest, expanding the rips in his ratty jeans. "Excuse me for wanting to score some more points for our side. Don't tell me I gotta go back to throwin' bricks through windows and lifting wallets. Just wait—you'll see. Once I bleed the old sack a' wrinkles, I bet you'll change your mind."

The Devil was accustomed to Stevie's petulant tendencies and knew precisely which buttons to push to rein him in. Stevie Croft was not exactly a complex equation.

"You would do well to keep the name calling to yourself, Steven. Disobey me, and I will ramble on. I won't balk at packing my bag and thumbing around town until I find another associate who has a few more cards in his deck. But contravene *and* insult me? I'll snap my fingers and inflict more pain on you than your drunkard father ever has," the Devil raised his hand above the back of the couch and pressed his thumb and middle finger together, as if to illustrate the ease with which he could wreak havoc. "But, of course, I would never twist the nipple of my best friend. We are friends, aren't we old sport? It would hurt me deeply to hear otherwise."

"Fuckin' A right, we're friends. I feel like a real bag a' shit for making you think we might not be. Don't worry— I know the drill," Stevie removed the cigarette from his mouth, briefly observed the smoldering ash that had almost reached the filter, and then pressed the burning tip into the sallow flesh on the inside of his left forearm. He winced as another festering crater was added amongst the sea of pockmarks between his elbow and his wrist. "Tss… shh… shit! You never get used to that, even when you deserve it. I'm your guy, Red. Bet the house on me. I'm your guy."

Stevie popped another Parliament between his moist, flecked lips and leaned forward, poking the stog out over the back of Gang Green. The crimson hand, which had not retreated after threatening the boy, unfurled its pointer finger and produced a dollop of flame from the tip. Stevie jutted the exposed tobacco into the dancing blaze and inhaled harshly, sending a nicotine buzz rushing to his head and extremities.

Both sensei and deshi returned to their relaxed positions and resumed their discussion on the bloodletting of Edward Dalton.

♉

Night came, dismissing the time for plotting and sending forward the demand for action. Beelzebub had returned to his realm earlier in the afternoon and left Stevie to his mutterings and machinations, and the Croft patriarch—if such a word can be used for the pickled lout—would not be darkening the doorstep until the ugly lights came on at the local roadhouse. Stevie had used his solitary time wisely; he was an industrious imp, if nothing else. For someone who was admittedly light on book learning, Stevie had done a bang-up job of preparing for his first murder.

Laid out on the dingy shag carpet in front of his twinkling eyes were the tools of his newfound trade: a black gym bag for transport, a large roll of plastic sheeting, a jug of bleach, a bundle of heavy-duty trash bags, smelling salts, duct tape, a bone saw, and a stainless steel kill knife. Stevie snorted as he thought about how stupid the suits at the network must have been to let *Dexter* on the air; the assholes had basically broadcast a how-to guide on rubbing people out.

Unfortunately for Stevie, he had found it quite difficult to get his hands on a supply of etorphine. He had gotten some syringes from Jim Avery, who lived a few trailers down. Jim's dad was a smack freak and was probably not long for this world, but the bastard kept enough needles around to last two lifetimes. The skinny deadbeat was sitting on a stash so big that he could probably pop both arms ten times a day for the rest of his life and still have enough needles to entertain John Belushi and Keith Richards for a few wild years. But alas, the strongest cocktail Stevie could fill the sharps with was Nyquil, and he didn't think that would do the trick.

Blunt force trauma was going to have to suffice. As he tossed his equipment into the gym bag, his eyes raced around the room, searching for something heavy enough to use to knock his prey out. It had to be solid, yet sufficiently portable to lug around with the rest of his gear. He landed on a gift from his mother, given not long before she had decided to start a new life without two human-shaped anchors dragging her down; it was an unusually heavy paperweight.

The paperweight was a yellow cube with black smiley faces printed on each of the four sides. Above each floating visage was block text reading TODAY I AM, and at the bottom of each side was a basic emotion: HAPPY, SAD, MAD, and EXCITED. His mother had viewed it as a gift of encouragement, perhaps to be used to hold his papers in place while completing his homework. He had set it on his dresser when his mother had given it to him, on its side so that blank yellow plastic faced out, and never thought about it again. Stevie, ever the poet, chalked it up as another stupid gift from a stupid bitch.

That is, until he needed to do some killing. It was perfect for the job; small enough to hold in one hand, but with adequate heft to pack a punch. Momma Croft may as well have given her son a set of knuckle dusters. One blow to the temple with that thing, and Stevie would have plenty of time to unroll the plastic sheeting and set up his kill room. Old Ed would be night-night for a good, long while.

Stevie pulled rubber gloves over both hands and a black ski mask down over his face. He knelt and picked up the duffle, its zipper almost bursting after being stuffed to the brim with death doodads, and stood to take himself in.

Reflected back from the cracked mirror hanging on Stevie's closed bedroom door was someone who demanded to be taken seriously. Though he would not admit it, not even under extreme duress, he had always longed to command respect. Sure, other kids were scared of him. The schoolyard beatings that he doled out with reckless abandon took care of that—at least, while he was still a Butler Middle School Bomber. But they had never respected him. He bloodied noses and kicked dogs and egged houses, but nothing changed. At the end of the day, everyone simply saw him as the poor kid who wore the same shitty clothes all the time and had the IQ of a concrete block.

But things would be different now, he thought. The new and improved Stevie Croft had a best friend who came from the lowest of places.

He slung the duffle bag over his shoulder and scooped up the emotive paperweight on his way out of the bedroom. He tossed the weighted cube lightly into the air, like a boy heading out to the pitcher's mound. On the third toss, he stopped walking and let the paperweight come to rest in his palm. He glanced down at it, curious to see what fortune the disembodied head had chosen to bestow upon him. A frustrated smiley face glared back at him, sandwiched between plain text that read TODAY I AM MAD.

"Mad? Me? Today I am not mad. No siree, Bob. Today, I am fucking pissed. Today, mother FUCKER, I AM FUCKING FURIOUS!" His voice rapidly escalated with each syllable, like a bullet train climbing to the crest of a rollercoaster track. He was screaming now—screaming and trembling. Sweat beaded on his upper lip and his face turned the color of a finger caught in a vise.

He raised his right foot level with his belly button and gave the big boot to the front of his bedroom door, sending it slamming against the drywall and putting the broken mirror out of its misery. Shards of glass showered to the floor.

"*TODAY I AM...* today... today, I am..." Stevie's volume became a whisper; a swift diminuendo that even the most fastidious choral instructor would have been pleased with. A Cheshire cat smile broke out across his face, pushing his cheeks upward and forcing his eyes to squint, as though he were crossing a white concrete bridge on a sunny day. "Today, I am becoming something."

Stevie headed out, grinning like an idiot and whistling tunelessly.

♉

Ed Dalton lived in a trailer that sat a few rows back from the Croft residence, proof positive that good deeds don't guarantee luxurious estates and comfortable existences. Actually, it's most often the opposite behavior that gets the cheddar rolling in.

Stevie was dressed in all black, but he really didn't have to take much care to maintain stealth. It was past eleven now, and Fairview Heights was not the type of neighborhood that was filled with busybodies. Quite the contrary; most residents kept their windows shuttered after the sun went down, so that they could enjoy the evening's chosen vice—typically illicit—unobserved and undisturbed. Nor was Stevie one to worry about dropping a deuce where he eats. He believed his association with the Horned One made him impervious to the meddling of normies.

The Dalton mobile home was one of the more dignified in the park. It wasn't big—bachelors with old, shriveled sacks didn't need much—but Ed did his best to keep up appearances. His little patch of grass was always weed-free and trimmed to a precise height. Potted begonias sat on either side of the door to the trailer, standing guard like stone lions at the entrance to a grand driveway. Stevie spat in disgust and forked the sign of the evil eye when he noticed the security system sticker that was plastered to the front door, directly above the handle.

The sticker was the shape of a stop sign, but colored robin egg blue instead of the usual garish red. Bright, bubbly text filled the inner portion of the octagon. Luckily for Stevie, Ed had decided to outsource his protection to a celestial being, rather than round-the-clock monitored security cameras and the boys in blue.

The white lettering read: STOP! THIS HOUSE PROTECTED BY GOD THE FATHER AND HIS ARMY OF ANGELS! GO IN PEACE!

"He can't help you, you old shit," Stevie sneered at the cheeseball admonition. "Fifteen Hail Marys couldn't stop what's coming. You're my one-way ticket to getting in real good with Big Red."

An electronic glow peeked out around the edges of the living room window, confirming that Stevie's target had not yet turned in for the night. This was in accordance with Stevie's plan; the bedroom window was his designated entry point. If the fogie was in the process of being lulled by the dulcet tones of Joel Osteen coming through the boob tube, it would be that much easier to slink in and give him a good whack with his happy slapper.

Stevie made his way around to the bedroom side of the trailer. He held his breath as he stretched his arm up and reached the first potential point of failure in his scheme. If the bedroom window was latched, he would be forced to improvise. He had banked on Ed's window being unlocked; after all, who needed locks when you had a platoon of fey watchdogs on patrol? Most doors and windows in Fairview Heights remained unsecured round the clock, but not because the rest of the neighbors were as devout as Ed Dalton. Most of the inhabitants of the park simply didn't have much to be protective over. Some probably secretly wished to be ushered to salvation from daily monotony by a murderous intruder.

The window was unlocked.

Stevie's eyes puddled with joyful tears. He was going to be able to get his first kill tonight, after all. He felt like a virgin who'd just unhooked his first bra. He even had the throbbing stiffy to prove it.

He *was* a virgin, much to his chagrin. Girls aren't usually excited about jumping out of their panties and into bed with sweaty, disheveled gingers. Not to mention speckled gingers as creepy and as mean as Stevie Croft.

But maybe that would change after tonight. Bev Simmons from down the street had grown up quite a bit over the last few months. *Grown up*, Stevie thought. *It's more than that. Them jahoobies have bloomed and come out to play. Love to get me a double handful of those puppies.* If his mission tonight was successful, maybe Red would whip him up a love potion. Or, at the very least, a wild animal sex potion. That would do just fine.

Stevie slowly pushed the window open and climbed into Ed Dalton's trailer.

♉

What a fucking chode, Stevie thought, as he observed his surroundings. *This guy's into crosses like Hugh Hefner's into tits.*

He crossed himself—inverted, of course—and nodded down at the ground. He pictured Hugh underneath the earth's crust, amidst fire, brimstone, and a whole lot of ass, raising a glass of bourbon and nodding to acknowledge Stevie's respects. Stevie made a mental note to get his hands on a crushed velvet smoking jacket at some point.

His mental notebook more closely resembled a mental sticky note. Just one sticky note; there certainly wasn't enough room for a whole pad between his ears.

On the bedside table sat a porcelain statue of Jesus, with his hands together in a semblance of prayer and bent slightly at the waist. This interpretation of J.C. had flowing chestnut hair, which was held in place by a scarf that had been knotted like a bandana. Stevie thought he looked more martial than pious, ready to come out of the bow and deliver a Bruce Lee roundhouse to the nearest cranium.

Shit, I might have joined up with His side if He was snappin' necks instead of healing people and turning water into wine. Nobody drinks wine, asshole.

A well-loved Bible rested beside Jesus Lee, ready to be picked up and leafed through each night before Ed counted sheep. Rounding out the bedside accoutrement was a picture of Ed and his wife on their wedding day. They looked happy. Stevie thought they looked too fucking happy.

Newspaper clippings are filled with details on the various triggers of psychotic episodes. Open your local rag on any given day and you are sure to be met with a story on the mother who drowned her toddler in the bathtub because the little bastard had the nerve to spit up on her sweater. Or the businessman who put a stir stick through the barista's eye, popping it like an amniotic sac during labor, after discovering his latte had one shot of espresso instead of two. For Stevie, the knife that cut his tenuous hold on reality was the picture of Mr. and Mrs. Ed Dalton, smiling out at him and rubbing their happiness right in his goddamn face.

The plan was out the window; it was now just as gone as Stevie's mother, his chances to ever make it out of Troon's Perch, or his opportunity to live some version of a normal life. Stevie snatched the picture off the bedside table and burst into the living room.

Ed wasn't watching TV, but was instead sitting with his back to Stevie in front of a computer on the other side of the room. Not to be underrepresented, a painting of Jesus hung above the card table desk, housed in a gaudy picture frame and tilting his face down toward where Ed was seated. Hay-zeus Creesto had his lips pursed and his left eyebrow raised in an expression of thorough disappointment.

The old man didn't even turn around when Stevie made his theatrical entrance, which only served to further enrage the gangly ginger. Ed wore corded headphones and was wholly absorbed by whatever he was watching. Ole' Joel must have really been getting after it. Modern day Brimstone Buffs can't limit their messages to television or radio; they've got to push their product on streaming platforms as well.

Stevie cocked his arm and rifled the wedding photo at Ed's skull. The Devil had helped his pal with a lot of things, but athletic ability was not one of them. The framed picture missed the geriatric by a healthy five feet and exploded against the wall like a dove connecting with a Randy Johnson fastball. Ed's ass caught Tony Hawk air and the headphones were jostled off his ears.

Now the prick comes back from La-La Land and turns around.

"How's your wife, Eddie? How's she doing these days, big guy? You still have the hots for her, now that she's got worms crawling in her eye sockets and dirt in her downstairs?" Stevie's head was canted to one side, so that his ear almost touched the top of his shoulder. "Does that get your member in motion, you sick bastard? Why don't we split a big bowl of Raisin Bran and talk it over?"

Stevie's line of questioning was clearly rhetorical, as he rushed Ed without giving the surprised senior citizen an opportunity to affirm that he did, in fact, want to dip his pen in putrefied ink. The Devil, observing the happenings with mild curiosity, thought that the younger Croft ran the risk of overusing this recently discovered literary device.

Ed dove out of the chair with the agility of a much younger man—or, as Stevie would later think, a man who had spent much of his life looking over his shoulder in anticipation of being caught—and narrowly avoided Stevie's first swing of the paperweight. Stevie's momentum carried him into the vacated folding chair, knocking it over and pushing his blood pressure past its boiling point. He briefly caught a glimpse of what appeared to be four separate closed-circuit television feeds on the computer monitor, arranged in a quad-panel manner so that the user could observe all movements simultaneously.

"You had the dream, didn't you, Eddie? You made happiness look so easy, you and the dead bitch," Stevie whirled around to face Ed, who was on his ass and crab walking away from his attacker. "You chose a happy life with a happy wife. The only thing I get to choose is who to chop up, and guess what, Ed! I choose you, Pikachu!"

Ed was moving as fast as he could, but he had apparently used up all of his dexterity with his first evasive maneuver. "What… what do you want?" His bottom lip trembled as he spoke. "Take anything you want, please, just don't hurt me. I don't have much."

"No, but you had it all, buddy." Stevie leapt forward and cracked the old man on the jaw with the quartet of weighted, smiling faces. The back of Ed's head rebounded off the living room floor like a speed bag that's just received a good wallop. Stevie, now on his knees and straddling his prey, leaned back and allowed the paperweight to tumble out of his hands. He was breathing heavily, his chest rising and falling in stiff, abrupt movements.

"You got to have it all."

♉

Stevie bent over the emptied contents of the duffle bag, beaming at his assortment of murder tools. He wore an expression of pride, not unlike a new parent watching his squirming rugrat blow snot bubbles and fill its diaper with *just the cutest wittle poo poo*. Ed Dalton was sprawled out on the floor behind him, unconscious and patiently waiting to be put down. Stevie had taken particular pleasure in noticing that the crotch of Ed's jeans was dark and damp.

The next sequence of events was scribbled on the Sticky Note in Stevie's mind. First, he would cover the den from floor to ceiling in plastic sheeting. Next, he would duct tape Ed to the coffee table in the center of the room, putting him on display like a turkey ready to be basted. If Ed didn't wake from his slumber while being strapped down, Stevie would shove smelling salts up his nostrils until the old man roused. He would bend over and look into Ed's eyes as he regained consciousness. He wanted to watch the geezer transition from fatigue and disorientation to the realization that he was in quite a pickle.

Stevie thought that would be the bee's tits.

He wiped the drool from his mouth with the back of his hand. He assumed this was what little kids felt like while they sat at the top of the stairs on Christmas morning, waiting on the go-ahead from their parents to rush down to the living room and tear into the loot that the Fat Man left behind. He could only assume, because Stevie had never actually had a Christmas himself.

It was at that exact moment, with Stevie staring off into the ether as his tongue lolled out the side of his mouth, that Ed Dalton wrapped his liver-spotted hand around the young man's ankle and tugged with all the strength he could muster. Stevie's face came down hard on the jug of bleach, cracking his two front teeth and filling his mouth with a warm rush of blood. He thought that it tasted like someone had stuffed an eight pack of batteries into his cheeks.

Ed rolled the dazed intruder over, reached up, and ripped the ski mask off of his head, revealing the shocked face of a child. Not really a child, but Ed never stopped thinking of the kids that he helped as children, even after they grew taller than him and moved on with their lives. The blood that ran from the corners of Stevie's mouth was just slightly darker than the dirty red hair that hung in greasy ringlets over his eyes.

"St-Steven?" Ed stuttered in disbelief. "What's wrong with you, boy? What are you doing here? I don't understand why you would want to hurt me."

Stevie did not respond, but instead stared back up at Ed with wide eyes and a mild smirk. He ran his tongue along his bottom lip, hungrily collecting runaway blood and bringing it back into his mouth.

"I don't want any trouble with you, Steven. Or *for* you, for that matter. I don't know what you've gotten yourself mixed up in, but I know that we can get this straightened out. I understand things are tough at home, so let's get you cleaned up and talk about this. Sometimes, all it takes is a good chat session to clear the bad gunk out of our heads. Come-"

"I know something you don't know, Ed. I know something you don't know. I know something you don't know," Stevie chanted, working himself into a lather. "I know something you don't know. I know something. *Iknowsomething Iknowsomething* I know something!"

SPTOO

Stevie spat blood into Ed's eyes and laughed hysterically. He continued cackling as he stretched his arm out amongst the items that had been dumped onto the floor and gripped the kill knife with his right hand.

"I know something you don't know, Eddie! The scales! The scales, Eddo! *WE GOTTA BALANCE THE MOTHER SHITTIN' SCALES!*"

Ed was frantically wiping the blood from his eyes when Stevie buried the knife in the side of his neck. The sharp point traveled through flesh, muscle, and trachea with the ease of a garden spade penetrating wet top soil.

The old man's eyes bulged and his head jutted

backward, as though he had just observed something that mightily offended him. He opened his mouth to speak, but all that came out was a moist gurgle. Stevie thought he sounded like a running garbage disposal that'd been clogged with the hand of an unfortunate soul reaching for a lost ring. Blood bubbled out of Ed's mouth and spilled down his chin.

There was no need to be quick now. Stevie sat up deliberately, his head returning to the side-cocked position that it had assumed when he first encountered Ed upon entering the living room. From that angle, he took a moment to observe the old man holding his hands to his throat and gasping for air. The blank stare that had overtaken Stevie's visage indicated the same clinical detachment with which a scientist might observe a rat in a maze. It didn't matter if the rat was rewarded with a big hunk of cheese or the cold snap of a metal trap to the spine, the scientist's demeanor would not change. The same was true of Stevie—the only thing that could have shaken him from his Zen state would've been Ed Dalton making a miraculous recovery from a blade to the jugular.

It wasn't *exactly* the slit throat that the Devil had requested, but Stevie thought it was close enough for government work.

Ed Dalton's hands dropped from his throat and his knuckles rapped against the floor. His wide eyes no longer looked at Stevie, they looked through him. He uttered one final choked remonstration before succumbing to either loss of blood or lack of oxygen stemming from the fluid that had made its way into his windpipe. The old man fell forward from his position on his knees and landed nose-first with a dull thud directly in front of Stevie.

There was no questioning the fact that Ed Dalton was quite dead—dead as a doornail, a dodo, or disco. However, just to be certain, Stevie found great joy in removing the knife from Ed's neck and repeatedly embedding it up to the hilt at various points on the dead man's body. He lost count of the number of thrusts; he merely stabbed until the muscles in his shoulder screamed for him to stop.

♉

Well, fuck, Stevie thought as he stood up and surveyed the room. *That didn't exactly go according to plan.*

Both Stevie and his surroundings were covered in Ed's blood. There had been no time to lay out the plastic sheeting, and there was far too much gore to be cleaned up with bleach. He tossed the knife down on Ed's body and turned to look at his reflection in the glass of the frame that hung above the computer. He thought he resembled Sissy Spacek after she had a bucket of pig's blood dumped on her at prom in that old movie from the seventies.

"I am becoming something," Stevie said, to no one in particular. "I have a purpose."

He brought his gaze down from the painting with the intention of gathering his belongings and hitting the road, but his eyes caught something on the computer screen that gave him pause. He had noticed the camera feeds before, but he hadn't really seen what was being monitored. He approached the computer with apprehension rising quickly in his gut.

What he found on the late Ed Dalton's computer made Stevie want to vomit. Not because of the nature of the content itself, but rather, the implication of what type of person might want to watch it. If this was what it appeared to be, then Stevie might have just scored an own goal.

Displayed before Stevie on the computer monitor were four separate children's bedrooms, neatly organized two by two like televisions at a sports bar. All four kids—three girls and one boy—were tucked into their beds and seemed to be at various stages of sleep. Stevie noticed the dressers, which were visible in all four feeds, and remembered that kids do more than sleep in their bedrooms.

Ed Dalton was a perv? The same Ed Dalton that volunteered at the soup kitchen and rang the Salvation Army bell outside of Walmart?

"This isn't going to balance shit!" Stevie raged, sending spittle and blood spraying from his mouth. "Why would he send me to whack Ed Dalton? The guy was a fucking kiddie diddler!"

He picked the monitor up, ripping the power cord from the wall and the VGA cable from the back of the computer, and hurled it across the room. The box landed with an unsatisfying thump against a cheap shelf that was situated against the wall and dropped to the floor. Rather than a cathartic explosion, Stevie was treated to an anticlimactic crack in the screen. The magnetized latch on the storage compartment at the bottom of the shelf clicked open.

Curious and without direction—the ship had veered so far off course that Stevie was relying solely on ad libs at this point—he walked toward the shelf. What he discovered in the opened storage compartment confirmed his suspicions about the old man. Inside the shelf were stacks of porn magazines and printouts, some of it vanilla and some of it decidedly… not. He now knew with certainty who had been putting the porno in the Little Free Library that the Boy Scouts had built at the front of the neighborhood.

I just killed the most rotten sonofabitch in the whole goddam trailer park. How did Red get this so wrong?

Furious, confused, and crying, Stevie stormed out of Ed Dalton's blood-spattered trailer. He didn't bother to gather up his things or attempt to clean the mess. It didn't matter, anyway—Stevie thought this would be his last mission for the Devil.

♉

By the time he got home, the predominant emotion that Stevie felt was disappointment. It was a piercing, empty feeling that sat in his stomach like a brick. He found himself wishing he had never met Red. He would have preferred to live out his days in drunken anonymity, rather than get a taste of the good life and have it ripped from his grasp. He supposed this was how child actors who had flamed out felt; they ended up with all of the substance abuse problems and daddy issues, but none of the wealth and fame to show for it.

He had trusted the Devil completely, had been thoroughly devoted to him for the last six months. When Beelzebub told him to jump, Stevie asked him to specify a building. And so, when the Devil sent him to murder an upstanding citizen in order to piss off The Man Upstairs, the postmortem discovery that the victim was actually a dirtbag was a breach of trust akin to a father giving his son a birthday gift filled with angry wasps.

There is no pain deeper than that which is leveled upon an unsuspecting child by a parent. Although Stevie was not the spawn of Satan, he had come to think of himself as somewhat of a surrogate son. They didn't toss the pigskin around out back, but there was a give and take there, a mutual admiration that is commonplace in a typical father-son relationship. Red had helped him build the wings and had encouraged him to fly close enough to touch the sun, knowing full well that the damned things would melt and Stevie would come crashing down to the earth's surface like the Space Shuttle *Columbia*.

Stevie trudged through the front door and made a beeline to the refrigerator. He opened the door to the fridge, smearing a bloody handprint on the handle, and couldn't help but smile when he saw that at least one thing had gone right this evening; there were no less than a dozen beers staring out at him from their chilled home, ample stock with which to get solidly shitfaced.

Unless Red filled these up with tighty whitey tea, Stevie thought. *The way this night's going, I wouldn't be surprised.*

After removing the coldest looking Schlitz and popping the top, Stevie traipsed over to the television in the living room. He sat, with his ass on the floor and the back of his head resting against the TV, and wondered what jail would be like. Dealing with other kids around town was one thing, but protecting himself against violent adults was another proposition entirely. He was wholly lost in his thoughts when Christy Cans, the Minx of the Month who graced the cover of the copy of *Saucy Minx* laying on the coffee table, turned her head and began to speak to him.

(Hey Stevie-weevie, you better take a good look. Take a nice, long look, and maybe grab your ass and imagine its mine for good measure. Because the only thing you'll be grabbing in the clink will be the pillow. Did I say grabbing, Stevie dear? I meant biting. You'll be biting the pillow while Rufus grips both your shoulders and checks your prostate.)

"Shut it, bitch," Stevie's head ticked twice after he spoke; quick, jarring motions that shook his eyes in their sockets. "You just shut it right the hell up."

(You're gonna wanna shut it up, Stevie-weevie. You're gonna wanna shut it up and throw away the key. Because if you leave it open—say, when you drop the soap in the communal shower— somebody's gonna clog your drainpipe, big boy. Somebody's gonna cram your colon!)

Christy Cans bent forward, pressing her substantial breasts together and penetrating him with her icy blue eyes. Her irises resembled whirlpools speckled with flakes of shimmering crystal. She pursed her hyaluronic acid-filled lips and blew him a kiss.

(Nighty-night, Stevie baby! Keep your butthole tight!)

"You BITCH!" Stevie kicked the coffee table from his

seated position, and Christy Cans and the rest of her salacious sorority went flying across the room.

"Steven. We have discussed the name calling."

The Devil's ambling timbre typically had a cowing effect on his protégé, and this moment was no different. The pendulum that controlled Stevie's erratic emotional state swung promptly back and placed the young murderer in a more somber mood. His face took on the expression of a little tyke who'd just sent his beloved pet fish to a watery grave via the porcelain portal.

"Why would you do this to me?" Stevie spoke meekly to Gang Green, knowing that his mentor was lounging in his typical spot on the other side of the cushions. "I could have been a good soldier for you. There's nothing I wouldn't have done. I… I loved you, and I thought you loved me."

"Love is a strong word, Steven, and I do not venture to use it lightly." There was a rustling behind the couch, and Stevie's two-sizes-too-small heart skipped a beat. He had never seen his master in all his glory; every glimpse he'd gotten had been in the cramped space between the wall and the couch. The Devil continued: "What I love is the superior display of efficiency that I have witnessed this evening. It's not often that one gets to dispose of two birds with one stone, but I do believe that's what has occurred tonight. Bravo, young man."

The angel purporting to be Lucifer stepped out from behind Gang Green, placed both hands on his face, and ran them up and over the back of his head. As he did so, the maroon tint of his skin faded and was replaced by a smooth alabaster hue. The horns that had poked out from the forward part of his skull disappeared beneath his fingers and were supplanted by locks of luscious platinum hair.

"Edward Dalton was a living, breathing monster, far worse than anything from the horror pictures that you watch on late-night television. He preyed on the helpless and, in doing so, permanently altered the trajectory of many lives for the worse. Fiends like Edward Dalton leave behind immeasurable tragedy and devastation, and I and others like me will be dealing with the fallout for years to come. And you… you, Stevie, are irreparably broken," the angel spoke matter-of-factly, as though he were imparting wisdom that was quite plain to the naked eye. "Contrary to popular belief, our Father does not seek to forgive and forget. That was his primary strategy for many years, and for many years, people like you and your deceased neighbor Edward consistently thumbed your noses at His grace. The lesson was learned—the Lord is nothing if not observant—and He has decided to pivot to a different tactic."

Stevie stared, mouth slightly ajar and fire-red hair matted with the blood of a prolific pedophile, and struggled to determine how to respond. He decided on self-preservation.

"You gotta help me," Stevie implored the deceitful celestial being. "I did your dirty work. It doesn't matter who you are—Devil, angel, or fucking Jimmy Fallon doing a bit—I did you a favor and now *you* owe *me*. You gotta clean up Ed's trailer. Make it look like he skipped town or got scooped by ass-probing aliens, I don't care. Just make it so that shit don't get back to me."

"Your lack of intelligence has betrayed you once again. The very same ignorance that allowed me to guide your actions as if you were a marionette." A look of amusement overtook the angel's face. He broke into a toothy grin and snorted. Stevie didn't know angels snorted. "You're the second bird, my dimwitted friend. The gullible second bird. You *have* been a good soldier! You've dispatched with a notorious predator, sent him down to live with the one who you thought you were chumming with this entire time! And now, you'll end up in prison or dead by your own hand. If I were to place a wager, I would put a considerable amount on the latter. The behavior that I've observed over the last half-year suggests that self-harm is an inevitability. It matters not, however. You are not at a crossroads, Steven. You, my cretinous friend, have arrived at a dead end.

"You have been a useful tool—nothing more than a pawn in a conflict that is far beyond your level of understanding. Look at it this way: you've been damaged and destined for nothing since birth. Your environment has not helped your cause, but your composition has always been rancid. The Lord has plucked you from an aimless existence and blessed you with an accomplishment. As appreciative citizens say to members of the armed forces—thank you for your service, Steven."

With that, the angel looked expectantly toward the ceiling and turned his palms so that they faced outward toward Stevie. A ray of light washed over the holy being— for a moment, Stevie thought aliens really *were* coming— and he evanesced, returning to his divine home to receive congratulations from his righteous colleagues and the Big Guy himself.

Stevie sat and continued to look vacantly at the pea green sofa. He turned the beer can up and gulped down the remainder of the contents, relishing the carbonated burn as he chugged well over half of the suds soda. The boy let out a sour belch and tapped the tab of the can like he was sending an SOS with Morse code. He was still drumming away when a blood curdling, high octave shriek reverberated off the walls of the doublewide.

(Somebody's ass is getting probed, Stevie-weevie! But it's not Dead Ed! No aliens going after our cold, clammy buddy! It's not gonna be Deadie Eddie!)

Christy Cans shouted from her resting place against the wall, where the crumpled issue of *Saucy Minx* had landed after being forcibly relocated by Stevie's tantrum. The pages of the skin mag vibrated as Christy reached a fever pitch.

(Old Dead Ed is gonna get a kick outta watching you get your

shitter swizzled! They got TVs with all sorts of channels where Ed is now. You know how Deadie Eddie always liked to watch!)

"Shut your shit-filled bitch mouth!" Stevie fired the empty can at the magazine, missing his target by a mile. Christy Cans got the gist, however, because she shut her shit-filled mouth. The loquacious magazine reverted to its previous inanimate state.

Christy's message had been churlish, but she was right; he wouldn't survive jail. He was going to have to off himself. He thought that maybe he could steal enough smack from Jim Avery's pop to catch a hell of a high before his eyes closed for good. Rockers and other celebrities OD'ed all the time; shooting up with too much junk was a lot more metal than looping a belt around your neck.

Stevie Croft had visions of suicide dancing in his head when the front door handle began to jiggle. He turned to face the sound, and when he did, the fumbling ceased. His initial thought was that his drunk father had returned home and had forgotten his keys on the sticky bar counter. He was getting up to open the door when three authoritative knocks rattled the doorframe.

♉

When Stevie turned the knob and swung the door open, he was not greeted by his soused pa. Instead, he found himself face-to-face with a tall, slender man wearing a three-piece suit. A quick glance to the Coors Light clock on the wall told him that it was 1:12 A.M; too early for dear old dad to be home—they didn't give you the boot at the local watering hole until 2 A.M.—but far too late for a stranger to be soliciting.

The man was dapper, certainly the most well-dressed visitor that the Fairview Heights Mobile Home Community had ever welcomed. His suit was a deep charcoal, offset by a gold tie adorned with dancing medieval jesters. Most of the jesters held tambourines, but Stevie noticed with fascination that a few of them wielded silver-handled daggers that were tipped with blood. The gentleman wore rimless John Lennon glasses with clear lenses that provided a view to heterochromic eyes, one green and one hazel. The pupil swimming in the emerald iris was much smaller than its counterpart. He gripped a walnut leather attaché case in his left hand and thrust his right hand forward. Stevie vigorously shook it without hesitation.

The visitor did not mind that Stevie's gloved hands were not exactly clean.

Stevie tugged at the neck of his black cotton sweater; the temperature in the Croft household had risen significantly since he had opened the door to the gentlemanly caller. The walls of the trailer seemed to swell with piping-hot moisture, like a tank water heater that'd been filled above capacity and cranked up to eleven.

"Hello, friend," the visitor spoke with clean, non-regional diction. "I've been made aware that you've recently fallen victim to a nasty case of manipulation. For as long as I can remember—and that is a very, very long time, Mr. Croft—malicious imposters have been attempting to take on my appearance and use it to further their own selfish interests. It disappoints me to find that such an aged stereotype continues to thrive. Horns and red skin? I'm not sure if you noticed, sir, but this particular rapscallion even had a forked tail. A tail! As you can see, the individual who swindled you got the look quite wrong."

Stevie listened to the Devil with rapt attention and a look of pure admiration. His eyebrows were up and his lips were pressed together in a toothless smile. A single tear fell from the corner of his left eye and pinballed down his freckled cheek, cutting a streak through the dried blood of Ed Dalton.

"I've got some ideas on how we can get even, Mr.

Croft. More than a few, in fact. Why don't you have a seat, my friend? I'm anxious to get started."

ABOUT THE AUTHOR

CHRISTOPHER COOK lives in South Carolina with his wife and daughter. He is currently at work on a novel, but continues to be drawn to short fiction. Not unlike a certain character in his tale, he has quite a few ideas and is anxious to get started.

I DON'T EAT CHILDREN

Michael W. Clark

"I don't eat children." The creature handed the baby to Maggie.

"You were to get rid of everyone!" Maggie took the child. It was extremely calm considering its entire family had just been killed by the creature.

"Not children." The creature started eating the child's mother.

The crunches made Maggie flinch despite her hatred of Shelly. Maggie hated her for being so nice. "I paid you for all of them."

"I will pro-rate the invoice." The creature laughed, or at least that's what it sounded like.

"What will I do with the kid?" Maggie held the cooing child out at arm's length.

"None of my concern," the creature muttered through its full mouth.

The creature was difficult to see. It was large but indistinct. Maggie should have been afraid but wasn't. She had been right there when it murdered all the other adults in the forest clear cut. They had all gone on a camping trip into the great Oregon forest. Pelton had joked about running into Bigfoot. Maybe he had? The creature must have big feet. It had big everything else.

It was a Craig's List ad that had connected them, Maggie and the creature. Maggie thought this odd. "How do you get the Internet out here?" she asked as she pulled the baby closer to her chest. She didn't like children, or women who made them.

"Did you have difficulty in school?" The creature seemed to chuckle as it ate.

"Is that an insult?"

"You answered my question."

Maggie hugged the child. It seemed to have fallen asleep. It made her calmer too. "Why would you need money if you lived out here?" Somehow the bodies were disappearing. It must be eating them.

"We are not wolves," something said. "But wolves are good enough."

"Wolves took them?" Maggie just realized the answer to where everyone went.

"Not completely ignorant," another something said.

"Wolves get blamed for so much," something said. "And the drug dealers."

"Poor wolves," another something said.

♉

"Falmath Falls?" Jason's suit was more expensive than his car. He wore the suit to impress the clients. His car was just to get him from here to there. "The wolves of the Falmath Wildlife Reserve." He frowned. "Ran off with everybody except Margaret Blame."

"And a baby." Anna added.

"Baby on a camping trip?" Jason asked only for completion's sake. People up here did all kinds of outdoorsy things that didn't really make sense.

"You wouldn't take your baby with you on a vacation?"

Anna was their private investigator. She had only just started working for the law firm.

"Two comments. One, camping is no vacation. Two, no baby is either." Jason folded his fingers down. He had that tone. The other partners had warned him about his tone—that condescending tone. They thought it a bad thing. Jason didn't, but the partners wanted him to watch it. He was watching it.

"Ah, well." Anna poked at her e-tablet. She used a stylus. It made her feel more comfortable in public. Poking at something with her finger didn't seem polite, certainly not ladylike. She had enough of that in her life with her career choice, she didn't want to add to it unnecessarily. "It was a tech start-up, small, with some secret widget or something. Ms. Blame wouldn't say what it did. Still a big secret." Anna motioned in the air. "Like I could do anything with it if she told me?"

"Egocentric, thy name is tech startup." Jason rubbed his upper lip.

"She should change her name." Carlyle rolled his eyes. His suit was cheap, but his car wasn't. "If we have to go to court."

"No charges." Anna rolled her eyes back. "Camping accident is what the rangers say. Some rumors though. A disturbance in the force. Partners didn't get along. Ms. Blame wanted to be prepared."

"Like any good boy scout." Carlyle nodded.

Jason sighed dramatically. "If the client wants preventative protection, we can provide it." Jason left the conference room.

Anna turned to Carlyle. "Why the sigh? She has the money to pay your fees easily."

"Just not much fun in prevention." There was a dog yelp and then another. "Sorry, my phone." Carlyle smiled at Anna's confusion. "It gets my attention." He looked at his phone, looked at Anna and then pointed out the door as he answered the phone.

Anna shrugged as he left the conference room. New clients always took getting used to. Her business kept her on the move all over the northwest. She grew up in Portland and had a condo there. It was home enough, still she had only just heard of this law firm, C.L. Associates. They had been in Portland since the Shanghai days over 150 years ago. It puzzled her. Not knowing something she should know annoyed Anna immensely. Crystal Lane, the lead member of the firm, was much older than she appeared. It was all she would ever say about her age. She had hired Anna. The reason for that was also unknown to Anna and too was annoying. The Margaret Blame case didn't appear to need her type of investigation skills, but a paying client wasn't to be turned away. Anna had enough of the unpaying kind to make her appreciate that.

Margaret Blame hadn't been the CEO of ComPacSion, hadn't even been a founding member of the company, but she *had* been their first accountant. Preston had first insulted her with his reply to her wanting substantial stock in the company by saying he would never let an accountant run a company, not even an accounting firm. But she had saved the company. She was the one who brought in the major investors. Without funding, the technology was valueless. Preston H. Dodge, Ph.D. was so pompously full of himself. He hadn't invented the tech; Stewy and Louie had done that. But they just followed Preston as if his shit was marijuana smoke. They did smoke a lot of weed in the company. It relaxed them, Preston said. Ha! Margaret didn't know what Preston had a doctorate in; bullshit maybe?

Why she had taken Louie and Shelly's kid, Margaret didn't know. The creature had just handed it to her, and she took it. She didn't even know its name. She kept it, though. It made her appear a victim, too; or sympathetic at least. It was a wilderness accident, everyone agreed. Too many wolves, not enough wild prey. Tourist campers were easy to prey upon anyway. Margaret laughed at having thought this would be hard. She was now the sole executive of ComPacSion. Preston and his bullshit doctorate could suck on that in whatever intestine he was in.

The investigator from the law firm, though, asked too many questions. Margaret was only being cautious in hiring them. She hadn't planned to do such a thing—only a guilty person would need a new law firm. Looking at the baby though, that first night, Margaret felt protective. A high-powered law firm seemed to best way to achieve security. The logic didn't track well in her accountant mind, especially now with Detective Anna nosing around.

♉

Anna was a bit disturbed with the background of the ComPacSion executive staff—former executive staff, she corrected herself. Preston Dodge wasn't a Ph.D. He wasn't even Preston Dodge. He had many names, and had run many confidence games. The company's technology was real, but had been pilfered from another startup. Dodge had bankrupted the previous company and immediately started ComPacSion. He had had funding all lined up for the new endeavor. He could have saved the other company, but he didn't have controlling interest in it, as he did with ComPacSion. Louis Strand and Steward Bigger were engineers at least, but they had helped Dodge scuttle the other company. Anna always attempted to stay positive about humanity, but these guys made her struggle. "Death couldn't have happened to a more deserving bunch," Anna added to the discussion section of her written report. "This could easily have been a revenge killing as anything if it weren't for the camping angle and the wolf tracks.

Carlyle snickered as he read her last sentence. "You

think there is more to this than an accident? The police don't."

Anna stood by the office window. She looked off into the volcano smoke in the distance. "Yes, the police usually don't." She shrugged. "What they want is a neat package with a bow on it. Another closed case."

"And what's wrong with closing cases?" Carlyle smiled. Anna was an attractive woman for a P.I. They had hired a few women P.I.s in the past, but none had made him fantasize about them. Simply seeing her sweaty was on his mind.

Anna shrugged her strong shoulders. "Not with closing, but getting it wrong is an issue."

"Thought you had been a cop." Carlyle had imagined her in a police uniform already.

Anna quivered a little. "Military police. Not city or state."

"You enjoy the military?"

"No!" Anna shook her head turning to look at him. She seemed both angry and sad. "Not important."

"OK." Carlyle looked into her sad eyes. She didn't look away, but rather through him. " What do you want to do about your suspicions?"

"They're not suspicions, just…alternative explanations." Anna scratched her head with her e-tablet stylus. Her blonde hair was thick and full.

"Then keep at it." Carlyle smiled at her hair. "The more we know, the better protection we can provide."

"May be nothing."

Carlyle smiled at her eyes. "May not be. You can train wolves."

Anna smiled back but walked out of his office. Carlyle watched as she walked away.

Maggie didn't want to talk to P.I. Anna. Anna kept

sending emails requesting a meeting, and each one made Maggie feel sick. The police had stopped talking to Maggie long ago. This latest email made Maggie furious as well as physically ill. It was a simple question. It said. 'Do you usually hire from Craig's List?' She had fired back, 'Why are you investigating me?' 'Routine' came back as a routine answer. 'Just following leads the police might grab onto.' Then came, 'Did you get along with the others?'

Maggie nearly panicked. She called Jason first, though. "Why are you investigating me?" she barked as Jason picked up the call.

"Routine." He answered immediately. "Who is this I am speaking to?" He asked pleasantly.

"Margaret Blame. Do you have a different answer now?"

"No."

"You should."

"I don't. And it is routine." Jason stood looking out his office window. The clouds intruded on the blue sky. "Client privilege is important here."

"But I am a very private person." Maggie's anger was gone, although the nausea wasn't. "I, ah, I have, well a, ah, past."

"Don't we all?" Jason's laugh was reassuring.

"It won't affect the way you represent me?"

"Why should it?"

"It just won't, will it?"

"Of course not." Jason laughed again. "It is part of the lawyer business. The representation is the same no matter what. And it is the best we can provide."

"You won't pull off the P.I.?"

"No, it is just part of our service. We need to know your vulnerabilities."

"I don't like it." Maggie said, feeling the nausea subside.

"Sorry to hear that. Would you like us to return your retainer?"

Maggie sudden felt the panic again. "No! Ah, no. No,

ah, it's OK. Sorry."

"I am sorry to have upset you, but we will do our job."

"Yes, ah, sure. Certainly, you will."

"We will take care of you."

"OK, ah, good."

♉

There was something in her house. Maggie had bought it when she assumed control of the company. The banks were literally begging her to take an excessively large loan from them for the excessively ornate house she wanted. So she did, and got a very good rate. The house was in a gated community. It was ornate—and secure. That had been the point of buying it, protection, both for her physical self and her reputation. But there was something in her house, and Maggie gasped when she realized it.

The baby was calm and quiet though; the something was being discreet. It was the creature. It was so big she couldn't really see it. The baby may be calm, but Maggie wasn't. "It's you." Maggie whispered out of fear.

It laughed its familiar laugh. "It is us."

Maggie's mouth immediately dried out. It was difficult for her to speak. She tried to control her breathing. "Have you come to kill me?" It was the only thing on her mind. "I am caring for the baby."

"The baby. Yes, we are here about the baby." Its breath was massive and oppressive.

"I, ah, it is fine."

"Just fine?"

"It's a baby. It's healthy and calm. It doesn't seem to miss its mother." Maggie felt cold and hot at the same time.

"No one would, you said. Apparently, you were correct," said the creature.

"How unfortunate," said another voice that was still the creature.

"People can be so disappointing," said the creature to itself.

Maggie forced herself to swallow. It was a dry swallow and hurt. "I am not responsible for that."

The creature laughed. "What a thought. Someone responsible for humanity." It seemed there was a chorus of laughter.

Maggie became colder than she had ever been. The laughter faded away, as did the creature. She wanted to be with the child, but she didn't move. Rather she *couldn't* move. There was no mist, but her vision was impaired. She felt dizzy, but she couldn't sit down. There was nothing she could do, so she did nothing. It was a long time before she felt like she could move; still, she waited a little longer before she did. When she walked into the child's room, its baby snoozes reassured her, but of what she didn't know. It was just comfortable to be with the child. Maggie sat in the chair beside the crib and thought about what she should name the baby, since she had decided to adopt it. Certainly, her new lawyers must be able to handle an adoption?

♉

Anna never felt balanced on a bar stool. She always thought she would tip over. She did wonder if she would feel better if there was a back to it. Then it would just be a tall chair. She laughed at herself. She probably would feel different. It was irrational. It was why she was laughing. Her career was all about people doing irrational things that needed investigating. She raised her glass of scotch in the air. "Here's to irrationality!" she toasted.

The older man next to her chuckled. "Sure. Irrationality is what makes the world go 'round." He then drank whatever was left in his glass.

"Man, doesn't it?" shouted a man somewhere in the not-so-crowded bar.

"That Dodge fella. Bad piece of work," the older man nodded. "More I looked, the more came up. Cons, all kinds of nastiness. Untrustworthy with a capital 'UN'! Ha! Never do business with such a sort." He tapped the bar for another drink.

"I'll get this round." Anna told the female bartender.

"Thanks, lass," the older man said. "Why you want to know about the Preston Dodger?"

"Did a preliminary on him for a job I just got." Anna sipped her scotch. "Want to get some more depth on it."

"But he and his band are dead." The older man rolled his eyes. "Some sort of wildlife incident? Sure! Sure crap!"

"You know that?" Anna watched his face in the mirror behind the bar.

"Damn skippy. Why I quit my last paycheck. Uh, you know anyone need an aged but effective detective? That's me, the old effective detective. Poor should be added in those descriptors, too. Ha!"

"Ah? If you don't mind me asking for details on this? You think there was, ah, *more* to the disappearances?"

" Uh? Well there was a non-disclosure thing-a-me-bob." He twisted his hand in the air. "But…"

"But?"

"Screw that." He looked over his shoulder. "The, uh, client. Nothing specific. It, well, it creeped me silly."

"A lot of clients do that." Anna nodded smiling at his reflected expression. He seemed concerned.

"Yeah, well, not usually the highbrow law firms."

Anna laughed. "Lawyers can be pretty creepy though."

"Guess you right." He drank half of his newly poured drink. "Maybe it was just a bunch of coincidences? Yeah, that happens." He nodded.

"Not that often. Usually things are linked. Somehow."

He sighed. "Yeah, that was my feeling. Just… I'd investigate, background checks, more in-depth than you are doing. It's just, well, the creeps and criminals that popped up. The real bad guys, well…" He swallowed.

"Not that I'm a coward or anything like that, but ya don't get old in this biz by being stupid. The bad guys would die or disappear. The normal Joe's and Jane's stayed OK." He drank the rest of his drink. "No proof, just coincidence. Like I said."

"But creepy enough to back away." Anna nodded.

He nodded in return. "Caution is the bitter part of valor." He made a face.

"Is the name of the firm off limits?" Anna leaned over.

He tapped on the bar. Anna looked. He traced on the wet bar a large C and then an even larger L. He then knocked on the bar. "Another is needed. I buy." He pointed at the invisible letter traces. "Don't approach. Not them. Drop whatever it is. Too creepy even for lawyers."

Anna nodded. "Good advice. Thanks for talking business with me. Now tell me some more stories about working vice with my grandfather."

♉

"Oh? Him?" Carlyle rolled his eyes. They seemed to be blue now. Anna could have sworn they were brown. Carlyle made a mock drinking movement with his hand. "He was getting a big monkey on his back. Too bad. I liked him. He was funny for a P.I."

"I guess I am not that amusing, true," Anna nodded. "He used to know my grandfather."

"Gone now, I guess? Sorry." Carlyle looked directly into Anna's eyes. Hers were always blue. "Well, we haven't really gotten to know each other. You could be amusing enough."

Anna laughed. "Thanks. I'll try harder."

"Don't try, do!" Carlyle grunted. "Sorry, never been good at imitations."

♉

"Aren't emails private?" Maggie stood behind her desk.

Anna stood at her office door. "Not really. Not the free email accounts."

Maggie shook her head in disgust.

"Just background. You know this. In case the police have a change of heart." Anna stepped into the office. "This cleaning service? Did you ever use them? It sounded as if you were very interested. 'Mystery Life Improvements: All Round Cleaning.' I can't find a web site for them."

Maggie breathed in. "They, ah, were just a little service. Low overhead."

"Web sites cost next to nothing these days. Mine does." Anna walked further into the room. "You had a meeting with them, it appears."

"What does this have to do with wolves?" Maggie snapped back.

"That's what I am attempting to determine."

"How could there be any connection?" Maggie's voice was stressed.

Anna shrugged. "Attempting to be thorough." She looked into Maggie's eyes. "Is there any?"

"No!"

"Did you use their services?" Anna stepped closer.

Maggie took a deep breath. "No, ah, well. I did meet with them. But, ah, they were too busy to accommodate my needs."

"Did they threaten you?" Anna asked.

Maggie frowned. "Why did you ask me that?" Her face reddened.

Anna tipped her head to the side. "I ask everyone that. Especially, people with money. Did they?"

"I didn't have any money."

Anna waved her hand around the office. "You do now. And a company and a baby."

Tears came to Maggie's eyes, but no words to her mouth.

♉

Margaret Blame was hiding something. Anna knew she was lying about a whole lot of things, but what modern executive didn't these days? Intrigue, getting around people, putting one over on your adversaries—it was all just part of the game. Anna knew this all too well. If she talked to an executive and that individual seemed honest and straightforward with her, Anna thought them just a very good liar. Anna was sometimes disappointed in herself for being so jaded and cynical, until her jaded attitude saved her ass. The real world was a dangerous and disappointing place, and she had learned to live with it. Her entire career was based on it. Anna wasn't surprised about Margaret; she just wanted to know just how bad she was. Was Margaret Blame bad enough? If her grandfather's friend was even close to correct, Margaret Blame might just meet with an accident soon. Maybe she was meant to go with the rest of the company's execs? The whole circumstance seemed ridiculously crazy, but Anna's experience showed her ridiculously crazy was often possible in this hyperbolic world of the Internet. She just had to make a plan to deal with any possible, ridiculously crazy event. She also knew she had to keep her plans to herself.

"Blame was… *is*… ambitious and annoying, but not very strong," Anna said to Jason and Carlyle. They were in the conference room. The lighting there was intentionally irritating. Comfortable people were better liars. Everyone knew it, so the lighting was a bit of a cliché. "Big dramatic moves are not in her history. The Dodge fellow though, the not-a-doctor Dodge, he was a major con artist. Not one to rob from the rich and do anything other than keep it."

Carlyle laughed. "A double not. Not a doctor and not a Robin Hood. Not not not. Ha! Ha!"

"No paper trail on Ms. Blame at least?" Jason stood up. He seemed taller, generally bigger to Anna.

Anna shook her head. "Not of excessive wrongdoing, no. Nothing the police could use." Anna scratched her nose with her stylus. Maybe it was the lighting. Anna felt very uncomfortable, almost irritated. Her skin seemed itchy. She could distinctly hear both Jason's and Carlyle's breathing.

"Is there anything else?" Jason's voice commanded.

Anna shook her head. "I have a few loose ends to tie up, but there doesn't seem anything substantial in them."

There was an unrecognizable noise. Anna intentionally didn't look for it. She watched Jason move out of the room.

"OK then." He said as he walked out their door. "File it and move on to other cases." He moved like an animal. It was the only way Anna could describe it.

"Can I take a few personal days before I pick up another investigation?" Anna asked, but only Carlyle was left in the room to hear it.

"Just started and you want a vacation already?" Carlyle snickered.

"Just a few days." Anna shook her long blond hair. "Not very long."

"A hot assignation?" Carlyle's voice seemed different now too. "You have met someone?"

Anna smiled. "I meet people all the time. It is part of the job." She shook her head. "But being alone is what I envisioned."

"Oh! No fun at all. I have had way too much of myself." He laughed deeply.

♉

Maggie held the baby close to her chest. "Her name is now Elizabeth Blame." Elizabeth was awake but calm. Elizabeth was always calm around the creature. Maggie felt a little guilty, because she had picked up the baby when she realized the creature was near, and realized she was using the baby as protection. She didn't want anything to happen to Elizabeth, either. Maggie knew the creature wouldn't harm the baby. The baby apparently knew it too. "I changed her name as a first step in her adoption. It's what you wanted."

The creature's laugh came from everywhere in the house. "We asked nothing of you."

Maggie kissed Elizabeth's smooth forehead. Elizabeth was a pretty baby, not like most babies who Maggie thought nondescript and mostly ugly. "It's what you wanted. I just knew."

"What we didn't want was visitors!" The creature grunted in another voice. It moved immediately to the adjacent room.

"I told her not to stay!" Maggie spoke, trying not to upset Elizabeth. "She wouldn't listen to me."

"She will listen to us," said a different voice.

Anna pointed her .45 at the creature. "Whatever you are, stop now!" Anna shouted. The creature laughed. Anna fired three shots in reply. The immensity of the creature overwhelmed Anna. "Don't hurt the baby!" Anna shouted as something like paws stood heavily on her chest. She didn't realize until that moment she was lying on her back. The weight on her chest was immense. She could barely breathe. Something hot and furry was in her face, too close to be recognizable, but its breathing was familiar.

"We don't eat children," the creature stated.

263

"Adults, though, are another matter," stated another voice.

Anna gasped. Now she couldn't exhale. The creature seemed to get even closer, its heat overwhelming Anna's senses. At that moment her consciousness disappeared just as her breath had.

♉

Jason and Carlyle sat in the conference room. Jason was reading his e-tablet. Carlyle was looking out the window at the cloudy sky. "I have stopped liking clouds," Carlyle commented to no one.

"The Wildlife Service has found the wolves," Jason said to no one particular.

"They exterminated them, right?" Carlyle stated.

Jason nodded silently.

"Poor wolves." Anna said from the conference room door.

Jason looked up from his e-tablet. "Most things die, eventually." He placed the e-tablet on the conference table. It made a scraping noise as it settled in.

Carlyle turned around toward Anna smiling. "Most things do."

Anna stepped up to the other side of the table. She placed a card key and a flash drive on the table. They settled down without any perceived sound. "Everything dies."

"Whatever you say." Jason looked at the key and flash drive. "Leaving us?"

Anna nodded. "I think it's for the best. I have other clients needing my services."

"They are very good services," Carlyle added. "You needn't go." He smiled with green eyes.

"Yes. With the wolves taken care of, Ms. Blame doesn't need our protective services." Jason stood up. "We will have other investigations. You are very good at them."

Jason's voice deepened. He seemed to get taller.

Anna didn't feel fear, only irritation and annoyance. The overhead lighting doing its job, maybe? "There are other P.I.s." Anna shrugged.

Jason sighed as did Carlyle. Jason nodded. "Yes. There is always someone else."

"Just some are better than others," Carlyle said.

Anna felt warm now. Not annoyed, not frightened, just warm. "Thank you, but I have other cases. Maybe later. If you need extra help." Anna's finger pointed to the card key and flash drive. "That's everything I did."

"Not everything," Jason said.

Anna frowned. "I didn't make copies, if that's what you meant."

Jason shook his head. "It is not, but I am not concerned. Thank you."

Carlyle stood up suddenly. "I can walk you out."

Anna suddenly became hot. "Ah, no, thank you. I don't want to disturb you further."

Carlyle smiled with blue eyes. "It is no trouble at all." He glided around the table. "You needn't worry. You need not worry at all."

Anna didn't know what to do other than smile back. "Alright. That would be nice of you."

Jason nodded. "It is unusually nice of him."

Carlyle laughed as he took Anna's hand. "Yes. Maybe this is a better situation. No longer your employer. We could go to an early lunch. Yes! You wouldn't mind, would you?"

The pressure of his hand was immense at first and then it became as light as a feather. Anna breathed in deeply. "No, not at all. That would be good." She said in a low voice.

Jason sat down and picked up his e-tablet from the table with a scrape. He started reading. Anna followed Carlyle out the conference door, away from the always irritating lights.

ABOUT THE AUTHOR

MICHAEL W. CLARK, PH.D. is a former research biologist and college professor turned writer. His stories have appeared in *Lost Souls, Surprising Stories, Morpheus Tales Magazine*, UC Berkeley's *Imaginirarium, Black Heart Magazine, Tracers and Infernal Ink* and *365 Tomorrows*. He also has stories in the anthologies *Fat Zombies, Creature Stew* and *Future Visions*. His sci-fi adventure novella *The Last Dung Beetle* appeared in SerialPulp.com. He is the editor and content provider for the website www.ahickshope.com.

ALL TO PLAY FOR

Wondra Vanian

"Read 'em and weep, fellas."

Courtney slapped her cards down with such enthusiasm that the stacked chips shook and nearly toppled over. A few of her companions groaned aloud as they threw their own cards down in anger. Some of the worst card sharks and scoundrels in history, they were not used to losing so many hands in a row.

Especially to a teenage girl.

Especially to a teenage girl who also happened to be the cockiest, brashest, and most self-assured person any of them had ever met.

And, unfortunately for them, the best card player they had ever had the misfortune of facing.

Courtney had won every hand they'd played and planned to win however many more it took to get back what she had lost. It was a tiny thing, amid a pile of similar objects in front of their current owner, the Lord of Gambling himself.

To, as they say, add insult to injury, Lucifer played with the stacks of chips piled in front of him. He flipped them over, stacking and restacking his winnings. It was easier to think of them as that, as nothing more than colorful wooden chips, than what they really were.

Souls.

Courtney's soul, and the souls of other poor fools unlucky enough to make the wrong deal with the wrong person. Dozens of souls trapped in red, green, blue, and black discs; the color of the chip indicating the value of the soul. Her chip was green—hardly worth playing for, in The Devil's eyes, but the most important thing in the world to Courtney.

She watched her soul surreptitiously, keeping an eye on it as it moved up and down the stack Lucifer played with. His fingers moved casually, almost lazily, but with the swiftness of a much-practiced maneuver. *Flick, click, stack.* The chips moved up and down again.

It should have been hard to tell her chip apart from the other green discs but, somehow, Courtney knew exactly which one belonged to her. Or, rather, *used to* belong to her. She could *feel* which soul was hers, calling to her from across the table. She could also feel its absence like a dark chasm inside that grew larger every day they were separated.

There were still three other players between Courtney and her soul. Not that she was worried. Courtney was confident she would win her soul back. After all, she couldn't lose. It was the time it would take that bothered her. Her father thought she had stayed over at Paige's house and would be expecting her back the next afternoon.

Rumor had it a poker game in Hell could last months. Courtney really hoped they wrapped things up quicker than that; she'd be grounded until her thirtieth birthday if her father found out she'd been out all night gambling. Again.

Seventeen was much too young to have a gambling addiction. Her father, teachers, and the bevy of therapists she had been dragged to all agreed on that one. Courtney disagreed. She didn't have a gambling problem; she had a winning problem. It was the winning Courtney was addicted to. She couldn't get enough of the rush of victory, the thrill of walking away with everyone else's money. All the fun stuff she bought with it was just a bonus.

"You're up," she told Lucifer, reminding him that it was his turn to deal.

The Devil shuffled the cards, his claw-tipped fingers making surprisingly quick work of it. Without bothering to look at the cards he dealt her, Courtney shoved a stack of chips forward, trying to think of them as only that. It was easier that way.

"Call," she told the others.

One by one, the others placed their bets. One by one, they lost it all. It came down, as is was always going to, to Courtney and Lucifer.

"Cheating bitch," snarled the last player Courtney had beaten. He loomed over her, full of fury. Courtney didn't blame him. She'd be awfully furious, too, if she'd just lost her soul to a kid. But she wasn't about to let *any* man intimidate her.

She pushed her chair back and rose. "Call me that again," she challenged, lifting her chin defiantly, "and I'm going to kick you in the balls so hard they-"

"That's enough," Lucifer interrupted in a deceptively calm voice. "Miss Miller, if you don't return to your seat, I will have to assume you no longer intend to play."

Reluctantly, Courtney sat down.

"Mr. Devol," Lucifer continued, "we will discuss your lack of manners another time."

The Devil snapped his fingers and Devol disappeared, presumably sent back to whatever region of Hell he inhabited. Courtney failed to hide the shudder that ripped through her at the thought.

"It would appear that it is just us," Lucifer said.

One player left to beat, she thought.

If it weren't for the enchantment guaranteed to make her a winner at any game she played, Courtney would have been too terrified to face The Devil. As it was, her stomach rolled as she lifted her eyes to meet Lucifer's crimson ones. For the first time since she'd entered the game, Courtney wondered if The Devil could nullify a contract put in place by his subordinates. If so, she was in very big trouble.

She needn't have worried. A few hands later, Courtney's soul sat amid the large pile of chips at the center of the table. They were all in and everything hinged on the cards Lucifer had just dealt. Courtney was no longer cocky, brash, or self-assured; she was straight up terrified. *Worse* than terrified, if that was possible. When she got home, she was going to find a word that meant "so scared one can barely draw breath and doubts the ability of their sphincters to perform the function for which they were created."

Assuming she made it home. Assuming Lucifer didn't laugh in her face for trying to trick him, snap his fingers, and send her straight to the very depths of Hell without waiting for her to die first.

Courtney dragged the cards toward herself, picked them up, and glanced down. Her heart thudded painfully.

Two of Diamonds. King of Spades. Ten of Spades. Six of Hearts. Ace of Spades.

There was only one hand Courtney could have hoped for if she wanted to beat The Devil—and it was the rarest hand of all, the one most professional players finished their careers without ever having seen.

A royal flush.

Trying to hide the fine tremor shaking her hands, Courtney removed the two and six from her hand and placed them face down on the table. Lucifer's face was expressionless as he drew two cards from the deck and tossed them down in front of Courtney. He kept the hand he'd been dealt.

She was almost too afraid to look.

Lucifer placed his cards on the table, face up, without so much as glancing at them. He watched Courtney and waited.

She looked at The Devil's hand. Seven, Eight, Nine, Ten, Jack. All Clubs.

A straight flush. Almost impossible to beat. Almost.

Courtney took a steadying breath before reaching out to flip over the cards on the table. Still, she couldn't look at them.

Come on, she told herself. *This is what you've been playing for. This is it. Look at them. Look at them. Look!*

She glanced down…

…and laughed.

Jack of Spades. Queen of Spades.

The infamous royal flush.

The only hand that could possibly have won her back her soul.

Hysterics threatened to consume Courtney as she reached out to drag the massive pile of chips toward herself. She'd done it. She'd beaten The Devil and won back her soul.

Spectators, no doubt afraid of the wrath of their master, inched away. No one congratulated Courtney on her victory. Even Lucifer remained silent as Courtney grabbed the backpack at her feet and started shoving chips inside. The chip that contained her soul, however, she kept clutched tight in her fist. She was never letting *that* out of her sight again.

Finally, as Courtney pulled the zipper closed, Lucifer spoke.

"That won't keep you from coming back here, you know."

Courtney froze. Her heart leapt to her throat, then dropped through the soles of her feet. "What?"

"There are plenty of people here," he told her, "still in possession of their souls. Most of them, in fact."

That was the moment Courtney realized she'd been tricked. No, worse, that she had fooled herself.

"Naberius failed to mention that," Lucifer continued, "when you made your pact." It wasn't a question.

Courtney, dumbstruck, could only stare at The Devil. "You knew," she said. "You knew I couldn't lose but you played anyway. But... *why?*"

Lucifer lifted one shoulder in a shrug that spoke volumes. "I enjoy the game."

That was something Courtney couldn't understand. How could anyone enjoy a game they knew they couldn't win? It was beyond her.

As if he could read her thoughts, Lucifer said, "And that is why you will never win."

At a loss for words, Courtney could only shake her head. She told herself that she didn't understand The Devil's words—but, truthfully, she only *wished* she didn't.

"Go now," Lucifer said. He waved a hand and a door appeared in the air next to the table. It looked a lot like the door to Courtney's bedroom. Exactly like it, in fact.

Courtney rose mutely and, clutching her soul in one hand and her now-heavy bag in the other, walked to the door. She turned the handle, then pulled. The door swung open to reveal her bedroom. The moment Courtney stepped into her room, the door disappeared. As it faded, she thought she heard The Devil speak again.

Courtney told herself she had imagined The Devil's parting words. She had to; they would haunt her for the rest of her life if she hadn't.

See you soon.

Dropping the backpack on the floor, Courtney went to shower off the stench of Hell.

♉

Courtney spent a long time staring at the green chip in her hand. Too late, she realized she should have asked how to return her soul to her body. Though it belonged to her once more, Courtney's soul was still trapped inside the small, wooden disc. Eventually, she used the X-Acto Blade she usually used for art class to chisel out a hole just big enough to slide a ribbon through. Then, Courtney tied the ribbon around her neck. Tight.

It was never leaving her sight again.

Despite the horrible thoughts racing through her mind, Courtney eventually fell into a fitful, nightmare-fueled sleep. She woke with a gasp, nearly falling out of her chair. For a moment, she thought she could still smell the unmistakable scent of sulfur.

Courtney rose with a shudder. She turned around… and screamed.

Her room was packed—*packed*—with people. Boys, girls, men, women; young and old. They stood crammed together between Courtney and the door. Some looked sad but more than a few looked angry.

"You!" one of the men accused, pushing his way through the crowd. He looked like he ought to be dealing cards on a riverboat somewhere, not standing in a teenage girl's bedroom. "You've got it, I know you do. I want it back!"

The bedroom door flew open. It passed right through several of the people standing near it.

"How rude," one old woman complained as the doorknob punched through her abdomen. Her sequined dress sparkled in the light spilling in from a nearby window.

Courtney's father burst into the room, baseball bat in hand.

"What?" he said, eyes swinging wildly around the room. "What's wrong?"

A dusky-skinned young man near Courtney rolled his dark eyes. A young girl reached up to tug on Courtney's shirt.

"He can't see us," the girl told her, wide eyes filled with

tears.

It would have been obvious, anyway, since Courtney's father let the bat drop to his side as he breathed a sigh of relief. "You okay, kid?" he asked.

Courtney nodded. "Bad dream," she told him, hoping it was true. It *had* to be a bad dream. The only other explanation was that she was losing her mind.

Or I never made it back and I'm still in Hell. A shiver ran through her body.

"I didn't hear you come in," Courtney's father said, running a hand through his hair. He wore the heavy cargo pants and tee-shirt that made up his work uniform, but they were rumpled, as if he'd fallen asleep on the sofa waiting for Courtney to come home—which he probably had.

"I, uh, teleported in," she told him, too rattled to think of a convincing lie.

He laughed before turning to leave. "Well," he said from the doorway, "See if you can teleport some of these clothes into the washer, 'kay?"

"Sure, Dad."

When her father had gone, the strange… apparitions? converged on Courtney.

"You have my soul," said the riverboat dealer. "I can feel it. You've got it and I want it back."

"Please," the little girl said woefully.

The desk cut into Courtney's back as they closed in on her. She bumped a can full of colored pencils in her hurry to evade the ghostly figures. The pencils hit the floor and rolled through the crowd.

"They're in the bag!" she said desperately. "Just take them and go! I didn't want them, anyway," she added.

A teenage boy with a nose ring and heavy eyes snorted. "Doesn't work that way, genius."

A young woman spoke up from the back of the room. "You can't just give them to us," she explained. "It doesn't work that way." She rung the edge of the apron she wore between her hands.

"Okay," Courtney said. "How *does* it work?"

"We have to win them back," the aproned woman explained. "We lost them in a game, so we have to win them back."

Uh oh.

"You have to *win* them?"

There were nods and murmurs of assent.

Boy, are they gonna be pissed…

"And, uh… what happens if you can't win them back?"

Pierced-and-Moody answered. "Then we keep trying until we do."

"Or," the glitzy old woman added, "until you lose them to someone else."

Courtney pulled out the chair behind her and sank into it.

"Well, excuse you," an elderly man muttered when her knees went through him.

"Where do you go when we're not playing?" Courtney asked. A bad feeling spread through her even before the old woman answered.

She looked around. "Well," she said, "here, I suppose." The others nodded their agreement.

The old man looked at the band posters on her walls and added, "I miss Hell already."

"Wait, no," Courtney said. "You can't stay here. I have… school and… and… *life.*"

The riverboat dealer leaned over to say, "Then I suggest you start losing, girl."

Courtney buried her face in her hands and groaned. "I *can't!*" she admitted miserably. As the room erupted in angry discourse, Courtney thought she could hear The Devil laugh.

ABOUT THE AUTHOR

WONDRA VANIAN left the madness of America behind for the valleys of Wales where she lives with her husband and an army of fur babies. Her career as an author began in 2014 when she left her job working for The Man to learn how to live with chronic illness. A Top-Ten finisher in the 2017, 2018, and 2019 *Preditors and Editors* Reader's Poll, Wondra was also named a Notable Contender for the Bristol Short Story Prize in 2015 and was shortlisted for the *Twisted Tales* Flash Fiction Competition in 2016. A writer first, Wondra is also an avid gamer, photographer, cinephile, and blogger. She has music in her blood, sleeps with the lights on, and has been known to dance naked in the moonlight.

DEMON'S PINT, DEVIL'S JUG

Steve Oden

The damned imp tried to hornswoggle me.

I had heard the spiel before, all the false pledges and promises the hell spawn dangle in front of mortal folks to file a lien on their souls. Only I wasn't some rummy conjuror from the backwoods who would trade his eternal spark for a bauble not worth a rotten turnip.

No sir, I owned power enough to force the minor demon to accept my first and final offer. The little scutter would settle for my right big toe, minus the nail, in exchange for the recipe—or nothing.

The digit already was in a Mason jar full of white lightning, lid tightly screwed down and locked with a ward. I had set the container just outside the pentagram drawn in red clay dirt, then hobbled away a safe distance. My foot was swathed in a dirty flour sack and my mood ornery. I wanted what the imp claimed to possess.

Blasto was the thing's name. A red-eyed snarly little

beast, he resembled a snapping turtle on two bowed legs, but even uglier. The thing stank like a fart and oozed pus from its warty piebald hide.

Tube-like nostrils sniffed the air. The imp could smell blood, even inside a canning jar that recently held pickled okra. Blasto leaned forward, greedy eyes on the amputated appendage that had already turned gray.

I had pulled the toenail off with pliers. The imp would have used occult essence stored in the nail to hex me. Hair, nails from fingers and toes and sex juices are three ingredients demons can build curses and spells around. Blood too, of course.

Interrupting his lick-lipping reverie, I declared, "This ain't no auction. You want to make a deal or not? Some other infernal critter is bound to be interested. That toe is fresh but won't be for long."

The pickled digit really wasn't mine, in the first place.

A fresh corpse had been buried a few hours ago with the right foot missing. Nobody at the funeral commented on the empty sock and boot. I fairly compensated the widow for selling me part of her dead husband, a womanizing rogue if there ever was one. I needed only the big toe to protect myself from a double-cross but wound up buying the whole shebang.

Blasto was too stupid and hungry to notice it wasn't my blood and my limp was fake. The thing hissed, "Done!" I carefully erased part of the pentagram so the imp could reach out and drag the jar inside. A puff of smoke and flame followed. When the air cleared, a parchment remained.

The recipe.

I turned at the thing's triumphant screech. It had removed the toe and was gnawing the meat down to the bone. Reminded me of a deformed child eating cob of sweet cob. Blasto looked smug when only the bony phalanges remained. He spoke a spell and declared, "Have the taste of ye now, fool!"

The last I saw of the imp was his ugly mug showing consternation and surprise at the consuming fiery tongues invoked when the casting went awry. Wrong toe, wrong victim—the latter already being dead and his soul fled somewhere else.

My hand closed around the parchment. I felt its power and knew it was Harley Sink's infernal recipe for spirit water. Wouldn't be long now until people in these mountains spoke my name—Durrell Hotchkiss—with the same reverence as the legendary moonshiner. I aimed to be the best who ever lived.

♉

First, I had to obtain one more piece of the puzzle.

This involved dealing with the other side. Angels, cherubim and seraphim can be devious and dangerous in their own ways. However, they can't do anything—neither promise, buy, sell nor trade—without the knowledge and permission of the omniscient Creator.

He who sees through time and space can't be fooled, neither can anything happen that hasn't been ordained. I had thought up this scheme, but if my heavenly contact wasn't allowed to seal the deal…well, it would be because God disapproved. All my planning would fall apart.

Seraphim are hard to disguise in their natural state. The multiple wings and seven-foot tall segmented bodies draw stares, even while garbed in white bed sheets with hoods. Lots of mountain folks mistake them for KKK'ers or ghosts when they're out and about on holy errands. Drunkards have been known to take potshots at such heavenly messengers.

A few days after I got Harley Sink's recipe, two seraphim stood on my shack's rickety porch at midnight, buzzing with impatience when I was slow to answer the door. You know when they're angry by the light generated at the end of their abdomens. Like monstrous fireflies.

They almost crap burning white beams when really peeved and put out.

Oh, they'd come on a mission, alright, but you can't always trust them to shoot straight. In this case, they were working a side deal. The terms included me kicking back a percentage pf the moonshine sales profit to them. Everybody, high or low, in the spirit realm has an angle.

"You durned buzzers! The Big Guy approves of this venture, else your cockroach carcasses wouldn't be standing in my doorway with dirty bed linens draped over your ugly noggins," I shouted.

"You ain't negotiators. You are messengers, so hand over the map to Adam's forgotten spring or haul ass back to heaven and tell the Boss you screwed the golden mule!"

These words caused the seraphim to run out their stingers. There was nothing they could do. One of them squeezed a white lozenge out of its sphincter. It fell with a clatter on the weathered planks. I hoped it caused heavenly hemorrhoids.

The seraphim launched into the night sky with angry humming and not so angelic curses. Their sheets and pillow cases drifted down on my roof. The fabric lasted forever and was always starched, ironed and clean.

I squatted to poke the lozenge with a kindling stick. Wasn't soft, rather hard like bone. I tried every way in my book of incantations to open it, but the armor wouldn't yield to my magic. Lusting for what was inside, I cradled the prize in my arms and trekked four miles to my nearest friend and neighbor.

♉

Bull Childers was an iron-monger and blacksmith. Even in the pitch blackness after midnight, I could see the forge glowing red in a shed behind his cabin. He never allowed the fire to go out. One of his seven sons stayed up all night feeding the forge with coal from the shallow mine on the hillside.

The kid was goggle-eyed when I stepped into the light with a seraph's egg. "What's that?" he asked. I told him never mind what it was, just make haste to fetch his pappy.

Bull took his time. He was never someone to be rushed. Deliberate, sober and big-hearted, he towered over me and had arms and shoulders that store-bought clothing would not fit. This was why he went bare-chested summer and winter, with only a thick neck-to-ankle leather apron to protect against flying metal slivers and skin-searing sparks.

"You had visitors," he grinned, scratching the thick black beard that draped his hairy chest.

He knew my scheme and was pledged to help. The smithy turned to his son: "Get on the bellows and make that forge hotter than the Devil's asshole!"

Bull fed the fire with a bucket of coal. In minutes, the heat was almost unbearable. He took the lozenge from me. With a pair of tongs, he thrust it into the heart of the furnace.

"Just wait and see what happens," he said, filling a cheek with burley tobacco.

"It won't explode?"

The large shaggy head shook side-to-side.

"Naw, it's a sacred message carrier, not a bomb. I read up on these things in the Lost Book of Enoch that you lent me." My blacksmith friend was also a part-time preacher, fascinated by apocryphal and Old Testament literature.

Even in the inferno of the forge, the lozenge remained white. Bull used tongs to remove the object. Turning to me, he said: "Catch!" Without thinking, I snagged the tumbling lozenge in mid-air. The surface was cool, almost icy, when it should have burned flesh.

"Put it down on the anvil," the blacksmith instructed. I obeyed. He unfolded a pocket knife and excised a tiny cross in his palm, recited whispered words while blood oozed on the angelic container:

"My name is engraved on the Creator's palm. I will never be forgotten, no matter what evil or danger threatens. I follow the Son and wait for His return. Amen."

The lozenge fissured without a sound and the surface fell away like a boiled egg shell. Inside was a bronze reliquary encasing a crystal chamber in which clear liquid sloshed.

"Adam's lost spring," I said, wonderingly. "Pour out a drop anywhere, and the sweetest, purest water this side of heaven will bubble out of the ground."

Bull Childers chuckled, "I believe this means we are in business!"

♉

Lemuel Battler was the high sheriff of Cherokee County. Folks called him "Bat" because he could whistle so high, the sound would pain your eardrums. He watched as Bull and his sons helped me with the first run from our new still, using Sink's white lightning recipe and angelic spring water.

When clear liquid started to flow from the condenser, I filled a tin dipper and passed it around. Bat took the first sip and his eyes opened wide. He drank down the dipper's contents and gave it back to me.

The sheriff smacked his lips and gave out a piercing whistle. "Hoo-eee! I swear on my mama's grave, this is the smoothest white liquor ever passed over my tongue and down my guzzle," he said.

Bat was an expert when it came to moonshine, having busted up mountain stills on both sides of the Tennessee-North Carolina state lines.

His victims usually were recalcitrant illegal distillers with stubborn streaks. 'Shiners prospered if they were wise enough to accept his offer of security and shipping assistance. The sheriff would help them deliver and sell their product in return for certain consideration. Having a network of deputies watching out for federal revenuers or riding shotgun in trucks to ward off high-jackers was worth the kickback.

The sheriff and I had already worked out a deal. He would guard our stills, located not in the isolated hills and hollows but at a peckerwood sawmill outside of town, the recently closed county poor farm, an abandoned cotton seed mill and defunct schoolhouse.

Access to water and the need for secrecy no longer were obstacles to making our moonshine. Anywhere I sprinkled the holy water, one of Adam's springs bubbled up, an inexhaustible supply of the sweetest, purist water on earth or in heaven.

Under the watchful eyes of Sheriff Bat and his deputies, we planned to haul the ingredients—bushels of corn meal and rye meal, hundred-pound bags of sugar, barley malt and yeast—to the still sites and make the runs. When the condensers started flowing like hoses, the moonshine would be jarred-and-jugged for loading on the trucks.

The deputies would shepherd the cargo to destinations in North Georgia, Alabama, Kentucky, West Virginia and the Carolinas. From those states, a lot of the white lightning was bound for big eastern cities.

This was our plan. But everything depended on our product.

Bull took the next dipper of new whiskey. His Adam's apple glugged, nary stopping until the last drop was gone.

"Lord-a-mercy," he said. "Is it possible to work off two-hundred proof 'shine that won't blow off a man's head? This is almost pure alcohol but the best I ever tasted. I know it sure 'nuff is potent. My eyeballs are crossed!"

I didn't share my secret. This wasn't Harley Sink's supernatural recipe. It was my own, but using water from

Adam's spring. The product would make us rich, but another version would give me power to complete a task long contemplated.

When I added infernal ingredients to the recipe, no human would be able to drink the dark lightning, only demons and servants of the Evil One. Definitely that unholy concoction would be for consumption by the cruel, soulless and damned.

♉

We called the moonshine "Hotchkiss's Angel Water" because it was a taste of heaven. Remarkably, folks could drink it with no ill effects.

No one got mean drunk. No one woke up the next morning with a hangover. Hard men became forgiving. Sinners gave up their vices, except drinking our 'shine. Gamblers turned their backs on their cards and dice to save money for their families—and the best white lightning ever distilled.

Me, Bull and the sheriff began getting rich. This wasn't my purpose. I still lived in the shack and walked or rode a mule to town. Wore old clothes, sewn with patches on the elbows and knees. Didn't have electricity, indoor plumbing or a telephone.

So, it took a while for the sheriff to get a message to me. The spring rains had come, flooding mountains creeks and turning slopes slick. The deputy bogged out his patrol car, a 1949 Ford, and had to walk up the hollow to knock on my door.

"Sheriff says to tell you some shady characters been around asking 'bout Durrell Hotchkiss, what you look like an' where to find you."

"Feds?" I wondered.

"Naw…real peculiar folks. All bundled up in long coats with floppy hats over their heads. Couldn't make hide-nor-hair of their faces. Some of 'em must've been circus midgets, not tall as a goat's back. Others stunk like a week-dead hog. Whew!"

Mountain hospitality dictated that I should invite him inside to dry off and warm up. I gave him a jug of Angel Water instead and closed the door. He'd be happy as a cricket when he got back to town, even if his patrol car floated away.

If my ruminations were correct, I was due to have other visitors before this night was over.

♉

The thunderous knock came at midnight. I thought the pinewood-planked door would bust to flivvers at the impact.

"You can't enter!" I hollered. "Bust my door down and I will bust your heads."

I was prepared, having chalked a pentagram from wall-to-wall inside the shack. My grandpa's rabbit-ear hammers, double-barrel shotgun was loaded with black powder and silver pellets. Old Bo-Whoop, what we called the 10-gauge cannon, rested easily in the crook of my arm. Just in case, within reach was a bucket of Angel Water

Using a string tied to the latch, I pulled the door inward. Dense blackness that constituted more absence of light than darkness seemed to flow like fog, sending shadow tendrils across the threshold. The tips sparkled blue fire close to the chalk pentagram border and drew back.

Now, they knew I enjoyed protection. Just to make certain, I cocked both hammers of the gun. The clacks made a sound of dry bones breaking, but the old iron-forged firing mechanism was good as the day it was blessed in church.

I loudly boasted, "All I got to do is wait until the cock crows. It won't be boring. I'll just sit here a-whittling white oak heartwood into conjure stakes while polishing a few parting hexes for your putrid hides. You'll go back to your master to make him even madder than he is now."

The black fog swirled and coalesced. Standing on my porch, a short figure dressed in a trench coat topped by a wide-brimmed hat dripped water that steamed when it hit the warped wood. Plate-sized eyes blinked. A miasma of stink rolled into the shack that would put a skunk to shame.

Behind the little feller was a tall character covered in what looked like a scorched tent. My only clear glimpse of the thing revealed claws like the blades of a hay rake almost dragging the ground.

"What is it? Y'all didn't hear what happened to ol' Blasto?"

Short and stumpy jerked and blinked. News had gotten around in the nether realms of the demon's demise. I figured this pair didn't want to make a dangerous moonshining warlock angry, if they could avoid it.

"Boss sent us," said Short Stuff. His blubbery words slipped through slimy lips. "He ain't much happy. Said you'd know why."

My laugh made the hellions take a step backwards. Happy warlocks are the worst kind. They've got something up their sleeves, usually powerful incantations for sending lower-echelon demons, imps and monsters to limbo where roaming supernatural beasts will tear them apart, no matter the dark angel or demi-god they work for.

"Let me guess. My new moonshine is cutting into his soul profits. Bad people are turning good. Shootings and murders are down. More people are in churches, and folks are tithing more than ten percent. Widows and orphans are being cared for. Street preachers and prophets are drawing huge crowds. Sickness is in decline, and people are being healed by miracles—all because of my Angel Water!"

"Boss says you should stop making that stuff."

"Or what?" I asked.

"He said you'll be sorry. Don't know why. You know

he don't explain things to us."

If I wasn't a moonshiner and warlock, my career would be in drama or used car sales. I waited before replying, glaring at the demons with my best pissed-off, spell-caster attitude. Short Stuff started to tremble and sweated green droplets from under the trench coat when I explained the only condition under which I would stop making my mountain dew.

The green sweat became a puddle as the demon cringed. "You want us to tell that to the Boss? Might as well shoot us now with that blunderbuss," he said.

"Oh, I know. Bearers of bad tidings and all. But here's a little sweetener for the pot. See those crates of pint bottles and crock jugs sitting at the end of the porch? Take 'em to Old Scratch with my blessings. Sort of a peace offering until we get things worked out."

♉

Short Stuff swelled in alarm, like a toad frog about to get stepped on.

"Hey, we can spot a trick like this a mile away! Nobody's hauling any o' your angel booze down in the Pit. Nice try, warlock."

"Boys, I can see you are way too smart for me. Let me apologize for trying to fool you," I said, breaking the line of the pentagram and stepping out. The surprised demons backed up, wary of a magical attack.

"To make amends, I want to y'all to try my new 'shine. It's called Satan's Sewage. Made special for the other side of the coin, so to speak. Contains no ingredient harmful to inhabitants of the nether world, whether demons, earthly monsters, evil men and women or damned souls. In fact, they'll get meaner and nastier from drinking it."

Keeping old Bo-Whoop trained on them, I dragged three crates of black liquor from behind the door.

"This stuff is poison to humans, but tastes like

wormwood, snake venom and flesh rot on the tongues folks from the dark side," I explained, handing Short Stuff a pint jar of viscous liquid the color of hot asphalt. His jaws gaped, revealing multiple rows of jagged teeth and a forked tongue. He tossed in the jar, crunching the glass, metal lid and all.

He swallowed and was lifted off his feet like someone had lit a stick of dynamite underneath. Short Stuff landed out in the dirt yard, whistling like a teapot.

"Whew!" he hollered when he came to his senses. "I do believe the Boss will relish this here gift."

A much-relieved pair of demons disappeared into a hole of blackness that made midnight's darkness look plain cheerful. They were burdened with my moonshine. I wondered how much would actually get back to Old Scratch? Most of the pints would be filched by the lower-level troops. Many of the jugs would be appropriated by hellish officials, devilish governors or dark legion commanders.

What the upper echelon tasted might be enough to tickle their curiosity and open a new market for me. Satan's Sewage had the potential to become more popular than Angel Water…plus, it was cheaper to make. More profit for us.

There was another reason, of course.

I needed to see Bull right away and prepare for another midnight visitor. Production of our new brand needed to ramp up, and I wanted to confab with my partner about a special supply contract. The potential client was the slickest liar and most heartless negotiator that had ever existed. He'd be coming in person to see me.

Our legal document needed to be so tight that not even the tiniest spark of hellfire would cause a scorch.

You can't summon Satan in a pentagram. You can't

tempt the Great Tempter, either. Any being that spars with God All-Mighty already has covered the angles and familiarized himself with your weaknesses. Your only chance is to have something that Old Scratch wants and can't get elsewhere.

Barter is his game. He can't rob you or tear your head off and then steal from you. It's a straight up trade: value received for value given. Herein lies all manner of trickery, shyster-ism, cheating, falsehoods, smoke-and-mirror shenanigans, empty promises, slick talk, con games, card-up-the-sleeve gyrations, massive lies and broken trusts.

I prepared for the meeting the only way possible. I had the agreement, its legal terms inscribed on a sheet of iron that Bull had flattened in his rolling mill. Nothing else mattered more than the contract: no curses or spells, nothing to trap and hold the most powerful evil creature ever known (even if it had been possible) and certainly no way to call on the angelic host for help.

The cheap wind-up alarm clock on my mantle stopped ticking at exactly midnight. The fire in my wood stove whiffed out, and the oil lamps inside the cabin dimmed so only flickering shadows danced on the wall.

Outside, a tornado wind howled and buffeted the cabin. I thought the roof would come off. Everything shook. An earthquake, I thought, then detected rhythm through the plank floor and soles of my boots like the approach of gigantic footsteps.

Satan himself had come a-calling. I didn't know whether to say my final prayer and stand my ground or flee. The latter would have been futile. I would have been bargaining for my life and soul instead of a moonshine contract.

The squeak of my granny's old rocking chair near the hearth alerted me to the Archdemon's presence. I turned, expecting to confront the worst nightmare from hell but instead saw a handsome man dressed like a Baptist preacher at a funeral—all in black, clean-shaved, with a smile that showed sparkling white teeth.

I smelled pomade on his slicked hair. His fingernails were neatly trimmed, and his breath exuded the scent of cloves. Neatly pressed pants, a necktie knotted perfectly and red handkerchief in the suit coat pocket completed his ensemble. He looked like someone you could trust or would want your daughter to marry.

♉

I had to remind myself it was a glamor.

"Greetings, friend. I am told you are the inventor of a most amazing liquid refreshment and have come to talk about your future," Satan said in a mellow, comforting tone.

My hands trembled and my forehead felt feverish. I smelled brimstone, even after the cabin's interior temperature suddenly dropped below freezing.

"Mr. Hotchkiss, I am here to pick a bone and perhaps make a deal," said Satan in a that melodious voice pitched to make me at ease. He was a slicker, alright.

"The dark 'shine you sent via my not-so-worthy servants caused immeasurable trouble among the Hierarchy of Hades. Demotions, disciple, dismemberment and outright disintegration resulted. I am just now getting the organization whipped back into shape. I owe you for that, sir!"

Satan went on to describe drunken imps and demons, battalions of Hell's Legions unable to answer roll call and princes of darkness who refused to stop partying.

"I am a teetotaler myself, having inclinations and vices tending more toward the drinking of blood and consumption of seasoned human flesh. Both are healthful sources of infernal energy and immortality. However, I am told your distillation—which you have named without my permission and in absence of a branding agreement—is quite unique."

290

I nearly choked. The Great Liar was incapable of telling the truth. He indeed had imbibed Satan's Sewage, thereby setting my hook in his lying mouth. The trouble he described was what Bull and I had hoped: a full-scale revolt of alcoholic demons, devils, dervishes, dark princes and the assorted damned souls…the impending breakdown of everything in The Pit.

The evil hordes could not do without the black elixir once they tasted it. Just a drop on any monstrous tongue was like occult opium.

This was my bargaining chip. So, I lied right back to him.

"Sir, I accept your compliment and applaud your stand on spirituous liquor and other alcoholic distillations. I had hoped to honor you by attaching your name to my new moonshine. If I have offended, please accept my apology."

The rocking chair creaked as Satan crossed his legs. Something much heavier sat there. I couldn't see its true form and didn't want to peer in the Devil's own face. He knew what I was thinking. The smile widened until it seemed to split his head.

"I don't accept apologies, nor do I need honors. What I seek is dominance, the obedience of servants, paralyzing fear in those who defy me and the worship of all who occupy this mortal world," he said without raising his voice.

"Yet you need something from me?" I dared to croak.

Satan rocked to-and-fro, not that it improved his mood. I noted his jet-black eyes seemed to contain tiny red sparks. He wasn't accustomed to defiance.

"What I expect from you, sir, is an antidote for the concoction sent to Hades. One sip turns a raging hellion into a cowardly lump with no murderous ambition. The worst fiend in the lowest level of hell sings humorous ditties when he imbibes it. Our most alluring and depraved succubus wants to do nothing more than bake teacakes and embroider fancy napkins. Every daemon captain of the infernal horde is on sick call. They claim to have hangovers!"

I didn't respond. Satan rocked so violently that I feared granny's prized white oak rocker would burst into splinters. The eyes in his handsome face burned red now. His temper was growing and soon would be out of control.

Time to make a deal.

"You've not acknowledged all of the problem. Satan's Sewage is highly addictive. Without a steady supply, the hell-lands will explode in rebellion. They'll blame you. It will be another civil war but this time evil against evil."

In a blink, the prim figure in the rocking chair began the metamorphosis into his true form. The shadow on the wall foretold what would happen. Even before Satan stood, the shade was massive: an umbra of webbed wings unfolding, clawed arms with spikes and horns protruding from hips, shoulders and head.

I turned away, hoping Bull had guessed correctly.

Satan roared. Dust and cobwebs rained from the open-rafter ceiling. The walls shivered.

My blacksmith friend predicted that white oak magic and the iron magnet he'd screwed to the bottom of the chair would hold the arch-demon for the critical moments I needed to bring Satan to heel. If it didn't work, I was a walking dead man or worse

♉

The chair wouldn't hold Old Scratch for long. He didn't have any idea of my scheme, but being trapped in the rocking chair was about the biggest shock the devil had experienced since his stooges had failed to keep Lord Jesus in the tomb.

I couldn't stop his summoning, however. The call went out, a command for all evil servants to attend him. A split-second later, my shack began to lean, the floor humping like a caterpillar and old square-headed nails popping out of seasoned wood with screeches that would have done rabid tomcats proud.

The front door wrenched off its hinges and sailed away. All the windows blew out. I stumbled out on the porch, which undulated like a cottonmouth snake on a railroad track, to behold a legion of hell-spawned soldiers arrayed on the slopes surrounding my home. Taking a closer look at the malformed and monstrous warriors, I noted the obvious.

They were all drunk. Wobbly in the ranks, so to speak. Many were held upright by soldiers on either side. Sounds of retching, headache moans and arguments about whose turn it was to swig from a jug of Satan's Sewage arose from crooked files of inebriated demons. Indeed, they were not an impressive sight.

I pointed to my old wagon parked in the yard and issued an invitation.

"Hair o' the dog is what y'all need. The wagon is full of crates of infernal liquor that will calm the hop-toad in yours gut and put the hiss back in your snakes! It's on the house, boys," I hollered.

I imagine the Yankee retreat at the first Battle of Bull Run looked a lot like the legionnaires in Satan's army deserting from their lines to race for the booze. I stepped back inside before the fighting started.

Satan had regained his composure. The handsome, well-dressed man sat in granny's rocker, still as a totem.

"I underestimated you, sir! Accept my compliments for a strategy well-conceived, but what will you do now? This hybrid magic can't hold me much longer, then you will be at my mercy," he growled.

My face cracked in a grin. I couldn't help it.

"Why, I'm surprised you ain't already figured it out."

I got behind the rocker and scooted it to a window. The broken glass crackled underfoot and scraped with a spine-tingling noise. But when Satan looked into the yard, he whistled like an over-pressured steam engine ready to explode and lightning came out of his ears. His elite soldiers were capering and singing, playing peek-a-boo, wrestling in the mud, fighting, gambling—about anything enlisted ranks will do except follow orders.

Half or more were passed out, the others unsteady on their feet. They couldn't have answered roll call if Gabriel had tooted his horn and passed out free tickets to heaven. The Great Army of Evil was helpless.

♉

Our negotiations were completed satisfactorily—for me, at least.

"So, Satan snapped at the opportunity, huh?" Bull Childers chuckled.

"I wouldn't call it a snap. More like a choke. He bit his tail and almost swallowed it—he was so angry. But a deal is a deal. He just didn't come out on top this time. In fact, that durned devil might have lost more than he knows!"

In exchange for an exclusive franchise to supply Hades and the hell-lands with Satan's Sewage, I had agreed to revise the recipe to include a hangover spell. Only this one caused a demon's head to actually explode when too much was imbibed. The contract also prohibited me from bottling the dark-shine in gallon or larger jugs. These volumes would be reserved for Satan and his princes during their high-and-mighty parties.

They said Lucifer (I had started calling him Luke) was impossible to fool, that he was a master of contract language and hard-nosed negotiation. After watching his best goblin warriors playing stuff-the-imp in my outhouse, he asked for a pint of my elixir. Glad to oblige, I watched him tip up the bottle and drain it with barely a gurgle. Teetotaler, indeed. Ancient liar, more like it.

What he didn't catch was a paragraph of fine print, inserted among the "wherefores" and "to whit" language.

It simply stated that the supplier—me—would from time-to-time have the legal authority to adjust the recipe in order to improve Satan's Sewage, and reserved the right to do this without notifying the primeval customer.

Bull and I had already started lacing still runs of Satan's Sewage with Angel Water, expecting to eventually seeing the same effects on the demons that the recipe had with earthly alcoholics.

We sat in white oak rocking chairs on the porch of my rebuilt house, a two-story brick with colonial pillars on the front. His kids frolicked in the lake I'd had dug, swimming and diving while all of us waited for the hog to get done in the barbecue pit. A couple of bleary-eyed imps turned the spit. They were handy for such things and appreciated the fact that I wouldn't let their heads explode.

"Heard last night old Luke had a conniption fit when his folk started up a union and voted to go on strike unless he meets their demands," Bull said, refilling my tumbler of Angel Water.

"What are they asking for?"

"Paid vacation and sick leave. Overtime. The regular stuff. Oh, yeah. They want to form clubs."

"Clubs?"

"You know, sports and recreation. Arts and crafts. A book club and a quilting club."

I wondered how long it would take Luke to dig out his contract and go over it with a fine-tooth comb. This set me to speculating about his reaction. Since he'd been consuming a pint a day for months, the devil had become less curmudgeonly and almost likeable. Angel Water certainly had that flavor of fellowship and friendliness.

ABOUT THE AUTHOR

STEVE ODEN is a speculative fiction writer whose work has appeared in print and online magazines and anthologies such as *Constellary Tales*, *Harbinger Press*, *Black Veins*, *Scary Snippets* and *Tales from the Canyons of the Damned*. He retired after a 40-year career in newspaper and magazine journalism. He now writes full-time from his home in Wartrace, Tennessee.

DEVICES OF JUSTICE
Andra Dill

Dara supposed a better person would feel guilty. A good person wouldn't be crouched down on a garage floor contemplating how best to sabotage a mountain bike. A soft yellow beam from her miniature reading light played over the front wheel. Thin shadows from the spokes stretched across the oil-stained concrete and were swallowed up by the tar-black dark. Being good wasn't a priority right now. If she didn't want to be grounded until she was sixteen, she needed to finish this job and get home before her parents realized she'd snuck out.

She frowned, studying the bike. Indecision along with the mingled fumes of gasoline and weed killer made her stomach churn. Her plan had seemed simple enough when she'd been snug in her bed two hours ago. Now she wasn't sure that it would work. The temptation to just steal the bike nudged Dara but remembering her little brother crying she easily pushed it aside. Righteous fury burned through her veins. Pain for pain. It was the only thing that would appease her. If it didn't work… well, she'd worry about that later.

After casting a quick glance at the lone exterior door, Dara loosened a bolt.

Overhead in the rafters, she heard tiny claws skittering. Despite the oppressive heat, she shivered, hoping that whatever raced across the wooden beams didn't lose its grip and fall on her. Dara touched the back of her t-shirt and pulled the stretched-out collar up. She wiggled the wheel then loosened another bolt.

A new sound, a soft click, had Dara extinguishing her light. Holding her breath, she stared into the dark toward the closed door. Every muscle in her body coiled, waiting for it to swing open. Seconds ticked by. Sweat trickled down her temple but she didn't dare move to swipe it away. Dara exhaled and began counting. She strained to catch any other sound besides the pounding of her heart. When she reached 100 Dara turned the reading light back on.

And screamed.

A woman stood on the other side of the mountain bike. She waved at Dara.

Dara fell backward, landing on her butt. The small light slipped from her fingers. It clattered to the floor and spun. Its soft glow cast a merry-go-round of wavering light around the claustrophobic space.

Between alternating shadow and light, Dara stared wide-eyed at the nearly six-feet-tall, black-haired woman. Where had she come from?

"Shh." The woman held her index finger up to her scarlet lips. "We don't want to wake up the entire neighborhood. Do we?" Dressed in a dark pencil skirt, a frilly white blouse, and red stiletto heels that matched her lipstick, Dara thought the woman looked like one of the starlets in the old black and white detective movies her dad liked to watch.

Dara clamped her hands over her mouth, stifling a

hysterical laugh. She had to be dreaming this. Didn't she? Maybe she'd slipped and hit her head. People just didn't pop into existence.

The light halted on the bike like a ball landing on a roulette number. The woman tipped the bike from side to side. "I think he'll notice the wheel is loose. Don't you?"

The woman sounded real enough. The pleasing scent of cinnamon wafting from her drowned out the garage's nauseous chemical smell. Dara couldn't remember ever smelling anything in her dreams. Heart thundering in her chest, she pinched herself, hard. Dara yipped.

No. Not a dream.

The woman cocked her head to the side, a smile flitted over her lush mouth.

It took Dara long moments to gather her wits. A dozen questions snarled in her throat until one broke free. "How did you get in here?"

Ignoring her question, the 1940-esque dame asked one of her own. "How old are you, child?"

Dara bristled at being called a child. She stood up, brushing off the seat of her ragged blue-jean shorts. Lifting her chin, she said, "I'm twelve."

"So bloodthirsty. I admire that in one so young." Between one breath and the next, the woman's pearl-white skin morphed into reddish scales. Blue-white flames danced in her eyes.

Stumbling back a step, Dara whispered. "What are you?"

"Not what…who. Don't be rude. You may call me Vanith." The scales disappeared leaving smooth pale skin. "Now. Let's talk about what *you* are doing."

"You're the devil." Dara ran for the door.

In the blink of an eye, Vanith blocked her exit. "Not *the* devil. *A* devil." Shining the reading light up onto her face she stretched her lips into a feline grin. "You can't possibly think that Archangel Lucifer can be everywhere at once, do you?"

"Ar… archangel?"

Vanith arched a slim black brow. "What? He has many titles. Don't get hung up on the little things." She aimed the light at Dara. "I've been watching you for a while. You're an interesting girl. Tell me. Did you have a backup plan?" She tapped the bike wheel.

Watching her? The walls of the garage seemed to close in on Dara. She clawed at her throat, trying to get enough air.

"Let's go for a walk and you can tell me all about it." Vanith opened the door. "Shall we?" The light she held vanished.

Sultry August air mugged Dara as she lunged out of the garage. Heavy clouds obscured most of the stars and bracketed the fingernail moon. The house where he lived was dark as were the neighboring homes. Dara glared at the house then followed Vanith to the sidewalk. Somehow, she doubted she'd get far if she tried to run from her new acquaintance.

The bugs quieted and only the soft click of Vanith's heels against the pavement broke the night's stillness.

A light breeze ruffled Dara's short, blonde hair but didn't seem to affect Vanith's Lauren Bacall hairdo.

"A devil?" Dara warily watched to see if red scales would appear again. A tendril of cinnamon tickled her nose.

"Yes. And you are a sneaky creature of delicious mayhem." Vanith rubbed her slender hands together. "In the past two years you've engineered one broken collarbone, one sprained wrist, and though I don't think the last one turned out the way you expected, seeing that college brat doused in fake blood was entertaining." Her laugh tinkled like delicate windchimes.

Dara froze, anxiety pinging through her. Would Vanith tell her parents? She'd been extra cautious since the super-glue incident four years ago. It hadn't been fair that they'd grounded her for the entire summer when she'd only been trying to get back at Mrs. Smith for drowning those kittens. What would they do if they found out about her other… incidents?

"I was just balancing the scales." Dara thrust her hands into her pockets.

"Ah, justice. A girl after my own heart. If I had one."

In the distance, Dara could hear motors but nothing stirred along the street they walked. They passed one darkened house after another. Ahead of them, a street lamp emitted an orangish glow.

"What did the bike's owner do?" Vanith asked.

Anger scalded Dara's blood. She clenched her jaw, fisting her hands inside her pockets. "He thinks it's funny to hit little kids with his bike. His buddies think it's a hoot. The adults won't do anything about him." She rolled her neck and unballed her fists.

"I can help you."

Dara barked out a derisive laugh. "I'm doing just fine on my own. I don't need your help. I'm not an idiot. Any help you give would cost me more than it's worth."

"Humans." Vanith stopped walking and turned to face Dara. She planted her icy hands onto Dara's narrow shoulders, making Dara shiver. "You read Marlowe or Goethe and you think you know it all."

Dara had no idea who either Marlowe or Goethe were, but her mother was a huge fan of Brendan Fraser, so she'd seen *Bedazzled* more times than she'd ever admit.

"I'm not giving up my soul." She crossed her arms over her chest, thrusting out her chin.

"See? That's what I have to deal with." Vanith gently shook Dara once then released her. "I'm not really that horrible. Why do you think God allows Lucifer's continued existence? People forget that there needs to be balance. To appreciate the good, happy times you have to experience the sad, low times. Without pain, adversity or temptation," Vanith waggled her eyebrows, "mortal life wouldn't have any true meaning. You seek justice. Balance.

Yes?"

Dara's thin arms dropped to her sides. What was Vanith's angle? There was always an angle. "Yeah," she said cautiously.

"So do I. And all I ask is that you let me help you."

"What do you get out of it?" Dara narrowed her eyes.

"Do you like chocolate?"

The question took Dara by surprise. "Sure." She drew the word out as if it had three syllables.

"Pizza? Pop? Cake? Tortilla chips?" Vanith spun Dara about and, linking their arms, resumed walking.

"Cinnamon rolls." Dara's stomach rumbled.

"Well. Chaos. That's my favorite treat."

"Is this a trick? It is, isn't it? You really want my soul."

"Oh pish. We leave the big contracts for Archangel Lucifer. I vow to you that I have no designs on your soul." Vanith squeezed Dara's arm and patted her hand. "I'm all about balance."

They turned the corner. A black cat darted out from under a parked car. It paused for a moment, glaring at them, then zipped across the street and disappeared beneath a row of hydrangea bushes.

Dara glanced up at Vanith. It would be handy to have a devil help her out now and then. The sprained wrist payback had ended up costing Dara two cracked ribs. Thankfully no one noticed the tree branch had saw marks. Dara's mom had drilled her for hours afterward. Mom had a suspicious mind. If Vanith could keep her under her parents' radar that would be a huge advantage. She hated being grounded.

What would happen if she refused Vanith's offer? Would she rat Dara out to her parents?

"If I accept your help would I be…" What was the word she wanted? Dara chewed her lower lip. Condemning that was it. "…condemning my soul?"

"I don't want your soul, little girl."

There had to be a catch. She wished she could talk to

her dad. He'd freak out, of course, if he even believed her, but he always had the best advice.

"Eventually you'll get caught. You can, of course, give up your little retribution hobby. But somehow—" Vanith chuckled, a light mellifluous sound, "I doubt you could give it up for long. Think of it this way. We are helping each other." She smacked her lips. "Mmm. Mayhem. It's delicious and it keeps me rejuvenated. Take tonight. I made sure that the wheel won't come off until your bully is going at a good clip."

"You did?"

"Consider it a gift."

Another black cat, or maybe it was the same one as before, slunk out of the shadows and stalked through the grass. Dara noticed that it moved parallel to them, matching their pace.

"What's the catch?" she asked.

"Dara, I vow to you this is a straight-up tit for tat. I help you and in exchange, I reap the sweet aftermath. We are both devices of justice. No signatures in blood. No damned soul."

Tempting. She felt sure that Vanith could teach her a great deal. There were a few other people on Dara's to-do list. But this wasn't a Hollywood movie that had a clever happily ever after ending to save her from a tricky devil. If she knew all the angles and was confident she wasn't being taken for a fool, Dara would jump at this opportunity. She might be a kid, but she didn't trust—

"You can't make any binding agreements as a minor."

Dara stopped walking. "What?" Could Vanith hear her thoughts? The cat halted and sat on its haunches.

"You aren't a legal adult. Any contract would be null and void. I told you this is—"

"How about a one-year trial period?" Dara blurted.

"A trial?" Vanith tapped her lips with a well-manicured nail. Blue-white flames flickered, obliterating her pupils. "Yes. A one-year trial." Grinning, she extended her hand.

"We have a deal."

Dara knew she'd have to be careful. Working with Vanith might become addictive. Visions of ultimate paybacks danced in her head. Yeah, she'd pace herself.

She clasped Vanith's hand. "Deal."

"I think this might be the beginning of a beautiful friendship. You are such a bloodthirsty creature. Delicious."

ABOUT THE AUTHOR

When not daydreaming about plot lines and characters ANDRA DILL practices yoga, reads voraciously, and drinks too much coffee. She loves road trips and going off on wild tangents. Andra writes in multiple genres—including but not limited to—urban fantasy, steamy romance, paranormal romance, and horror.

Follow her on FaceBook
(www.facebook.com/andradillauthor), Twitter (@aedill)
and Instagram (andradillauthor).

THE DEVIL HIS DUE
Gerald A Jennings

To say Arnold Walker had experienced a run of bad luck would be a considerable understatement.

His beloved wife, Vera, had died suddenly and unexpectedly; he had lost his job of twenty years when his employer's company was bought up by a foreign competitor; his 401k had been looted by an identity thief, and his dog had run off. To top it all off, he had just returned from the doctor, where he had been told the abdominal pains he had been suffering recently were stage four stomach cancer.

Which was why he was currently sitting in the living room of his house (though his mortgage was in the process of foreclosure) considering whether it would be an overdose of pills, filling his garage with carbon monoxide by leaving his car running with the door closed, or, quick and simple, the pistol he had bought for home protection.

He had just about decided on the overdose of prescription pain pills when there was a knock on the door.

"Go away. I don't want any more damned insurance or

Tupperware! And I already own an effing vacuum cleaner!"

The knock was repeated, more insistent this time.

Angrily, he threw down the bottle of pills, strode to the door, and wrenched it open. On his doorstep stood a tall, elegant, nattily dressed man he had never seen before. The stranger's suit was tailor-made and obviously very expensive. Under one arm, he was carrying a gift-wrapped box adorned with a varicolored bow.

Nonplussed, Arnold blustered. "Well? Who the hell are you and what do you want?

"Mr. Walker, I am aware you have suffered a series of misfortunes, and I have a proposition for you that you may find interesting and to your advantage. May I come in?" Without waiting for permission, the man stepped in. He reeked of expensive cologne, but with an underlying note of something unpleasant.

Walker was angry at this presumption. But the man had an air of authority that made him hesitate and choke down his choler. Suddenly, he found himself more curious than angry.

He eyed the man owlishly for a long minute, which seemed to discomfit the stranger hot at all, who just sat looking at him, a smile on his face.

Walker made his voice brusque, but the brusqueness was hollow and lacked conviction. "Well, what's the pitch? What do you want? If it's money, I don't have any."

"As I said, Mr. Walker, I am aware of the misfortunes you have recently suffered. And I am in a position that I may be able to remedy them." At this, he sat the gift-wrapped box on the coffee table between them.

Arnold Walker snorted at this. "Yeah, sure, you're gonna bring my wife back to life, find my dog, get me my job back, put the money back in my 401k, and cure my cancer. You're bat-shit crazy. Piss off! Get the hell out of my house!"

The stranger demurely put out his hands, closed his

eyes, and nodded his head, mutely asking to be heard.

"I can understand your skepticism, Mr. Walker. And bringing your wife back…let's just say under other circumstances, even that might be possible…I have, ah, certain *connections*, but currently she is unfortunately beyond my reach. All the other things, including your cancer, however, are manageable."

At that point Walker stiffened with shock, because where a nanosecond before there had been a expensively dressed stranger sitting across from him the sofa, now there was a creature—only vaguely human—with red skin also dressed completely in red, with horns growing out of his forehead, carrying and swishing a long, barbed tail from side to side like a cat. Now the air reeked, not of expensive cologne, but of Sulfur.

In another nanosecond the elegant stranger was back, smiling apologetically. "Sorry to be so crude—I hate catering to the absurd parodies of me your churches have inculcated—but are you now convinced I have, ah, the resources to better your circumstances?"

All Walker could do, still numb with shock, was nod his head.

"Good. Now we can proceed. First of all, I am ready to remedy your problems, and I do not want your soul in payment. My accountants have assured me that your years of regular attendance at church—insisted upon by your late wife—have left you beyond our reach unless you would commit some heinous atrocity beyond your current capabilities."

Walker thought for a long minute, then mentally shrugged. What did he have to lose? The guy was obviously legit. And he didn't even have to sell his soul to get his life back.

"Okay, Mr…"

"No need to be so formal. Just call me Lucius, a name I use in this form, short for my formal name, Lucifer."

"Okay, Mr…uhh, Lucius. I've read my Bible. I know

you don't make deals unless you get something in return, and you say you don't want my soul. What's the deal? And how do I know you'll deliver?"

"Oh, I'll keep my word. I always do. Because it pays me to. The rewards of honesty are manifest, even to the devil."

At that point there was a scratching at the door. 'Lucius' strode to the door, opened it, and in came a Golden Retriever, happily wagging its tail. The dog proceeded to jump into Walker's lap and began licking his face.

Walker was overjoyed. "Brutus! Where have you been?" Content, the frenzy of licking done, and happy to be home, the dog settled next to Walker on the couch.

"I guess I gotta thank you—"

He was cut off by the beeping of his cell. He answered, listened intently, nodding and giving assent to the message at intervals. When he hung up, his face registered total astonishment.

"That was my financial advisor. He said they've caught the guy who raided my 401k and they've got all my money back. Not only that, but one of the stocks I'd speculated in has more than doubled in the last week and I've made an additional twenty grand. Incredible. How the hell did you *do* that?"

Lucius laughed. "Sorry. Trade secret."

Walker sat for long moment in stunned silence, taking in the look of satisfaction on Lucius's face. Then he leaned forward and spoke.

"Okay—I'm convinced. And damn! I just realized my stomach doesn't hurt anymore!"

Lucius nodded. "And it won't. Your doctor will discover you've had a miraculous spontaneous remission."

Walker was silent again, but he was smiling, to use the bromide, from ear to ear.

"So what do I have to do to keep my end of the deal Lucius?"

"It's simple. The only thing you need to do is unwrap this package for me."

Walker was instantly wary again. After all, he was literally dealing with the devil.

"Why can't you just open it yourself? Is it booby trapped?"

Lucius shook his head. "No, nothing like that. Read the card attached. I'm certain my former associate—actually my former employer—wouldn't resort to anything as crude as that. Let's just say there are certain constraints that have been placed on me that I can't undo."

Walker took the card and read it, shocked by the business memo format.

"Ah, bureaucracy—one of my finest, lasting subversive achievements," Lucius said, smirking. "Along with my invention of the MBA degree, of course."

> **TO:**   Lucifer, former Light-Bringer, now the Fallen One
> **FROM:**   Jesus Christ, Savior, Messiah, Lamb of God, Lion of Judah
> **SUBJECT:** Terms and conditions regarding residual benefits still available to former employees

As he read it, Walker saw mixed expression of anger, grief, and yes, fear on Lucius's face.

"Okay. Do I do it now?"

Lucius nodded, clearly steeling himself for whatever unknown was to come.

"Okay, I'm ready, Lucius. Anything I need to do first? Any precautions I should take in case you're wrong about your employer not being so crude?"

Lucius was silent for a long minute, finally responding in a voice full of infinite weariness and choked with sorrow.

"No. Just open it. You have nothing to fear. The

burden is solely on me. The only thing you need to do is show me what's under that wrapping paper."

Walker shrugged, tugged at the bow. The wrapping fell away, and Walker gingerly lifted the lid off the box,

The only contents were a tiny decanter of red liquid—wine?—and a small piece of unleavened bread.

It is a fearsome thing to see the Prince of Darkness completely break down and weep unashamedly for the first time in countless millennia, convulsed by huge, wracking sobs and shedding scalding tears that steam as they course down his face.

ABOUT THE AUTHOR

GERALD JENNINGS lives amid the corn, wheat, and soybean fields of rural Northwest Ohio with his wife, his daughter, and three young grandsons. The town they live in is literally one of those that if you blink driving the speed limit, you'll miss it. He graduated from Ohio University in 1966, after which he spent a less than delightful year serving with the army in Vietnam. He's been a teacher, a communications specialist for a large electronics company, and currently works full time providing services to disabled adults. He's previously been published by the Wild Rose Press (romance) and the Punkin House Press (poetry.) He's an avid reader, and cites as his biggest influences J. R. R. Tolkien, H. P. Lovecraft, Richard Adams, and Robert Heinlein.

DOMINION
Cara Fox

Portia Courtenay's evenings of gambling, drink and debauchery were legendary. Their infamy had attached a near legendary status to the monthly meets, and the neat little calling cards she delivered were treasured amongst her circle, more valuable than the gold and diamonds they wore with reckless abandon.

This evening, though, the dowager duchess was on edge. Every nerve was heightened and her eyes narrowed as they swept across the dozen men in her parlour. Tonight there was a cuckoo in their midst; an interloper taking on the guise of an invited guest. The clean-shaven man with long hair and pale, watchful eyes was perfectly cordial, taking his place in the card games and obeying every societal rule, but the incontrovertible truth remained that Portia had not invited him.

The stranger had not acknowledged his intrusion. He did not even introduce himself to her as he took his seat at the table. His conviction made her doubt herself, but the longer she stared at him, the more certain she was that they had never met before tonight, for he was impossible to forget. There was something altogether captivating about him, a sense of breathless intrigue that danced in the air around him, dark and entrancing all at once.

Portia was so caught up in watching him as the hands of whist played out to their conclusion that she only realised the men were talking when someone drew a sharp breath. It was the man nearest to her; Jack Sewell, the youngest son of one of Queen Victoria's closest advisors.

"Pray tell me more about these rumours, Mr. Fitzroy," she heard him say curtly.

Douglas Fitzroy leaned forward, clicking his fingers to summon a refill as his eyes darted from side to side to ensure all those present were watching him before he spoke. "They are deeply scandalous, sir," he said. "Indeed, I am not certain I should recount them in the presence of the duchess."

Portia lifted one eyebrow and allowed him a smile, hard though it was to look away from the stranger. "Sirs, as well you know, I am notoriously difficult to offend. If the gentleman wishes to hear the rumours, then please speak freely without fear of offence."

"With pleasure." He slowly cast his gaze across all twelve of them, waiting until the entire assembly was enraptured before he quietly spoke again. "*Demons. Demons, my friends, right here in London.*"

Fitzroy's breathless words had the intended effect on the company. A shiver of thrilled, fearful anticipation chased around the room, the tension all but tangible. Clearly emboldened by the reaction, he pressed on.

"Lucifer's soldiers lurk in the shadows, making mischief and dragging our beloved city down in readiness to strike. Who knows how long they have been lying in wait?" he said, his voice low and his eyes wide. "Months? Years, perhaps—but they are here, friends, and the rumours I heard assert that they will soon leave the shadows behind and stake their claim on our beloved England."

Portia stared at him as silence fell and stretched out its skeletal hand over the company. She hesitated, caught up for a moment in the spell his words weaved, but her rational side rode to the fore.

"Tosh!" she said laughingly.

"My sweet duchess, I swear it is not so." He sunk into a sweeping bow. "Demons are real, and they are very much here. The proof of their presence is unmistakable."

Sewell slapped Fitzroy on the back and pulled him back into his chair, gesturing expansively at the younger man's empty glass by means of explanation as the rest of the men joined Portia in a fresh volley of laughter to defuse the tension. However, the long-haired stranger was not laughing. He merely surveyed the merriment, his eyes narrowed until he realised she was watching him in turn. When their eyes met, he bowed his head slightly and ran his thumb across his lips, lifting one slender eyebrow in a challenge that was impossible to mistake.

Portia rose to her feet, circumnavigating the tables with ease to touch her dark-haired little maid on the shoulder. "Alice, with me," she said under her breath, keenly aware that the stranger's eyes followed her still as Sewell leapt up.

"Your Grace, has our conversation troubled you?" he said.

"Not in the least, but I am afraid I must step outside for a moment. Pray excuse me." She forced a smile. "Play out your hands, gentlemen; I will be back for the next."

The simmering sense of unease settled in the pit of Portia's stomach to nest there uncomfortably when she stepped into the entrance hall. To her relief, Alice was only two steps behind her.

"Portia, are you feeling unwell?" she said quietly.

A swift glance proved them to be alone in the unlit hall, and so Portia laid her hand over the maid's. "No, not unwell, but troubled nonetheless. The gentleman with the long hair, Alice. Did you admit him, or is it Mr. Lowther I must rebuke?"

"Rebuke?"

"Aye, rebuke!" she said, her voice far sharper than she intended it to be. "My apologies, Alice, but I find myself on edge. That gentleman was not invited, so I am concerned as to how he found his way in here—and for what purpose."

"Forgive me for eavesdropping, your Grace, but I know the man of whom you speak, and it is I you must rebuke, not Miss Maynard."

Portia whirled towards the newcomer descending the carpeted staircase; John Lowther, the butler she inherited from her husband along with the handsome London townhouse. Steadfast and unerringly reliable, she had no reason to doubt his capability until now. "Mr. Lowther, you admitted the stranger?" she said, her eyebrows shooting up towards her hairline as she spoke.

"Yes," the elderly man said. "Though I did not recognise him, he had your calling card, ma'am. I saw no reason to think he was not invited."

"You are certain of that?"

"Entirely so." Lowther grimaced. "Should I send a runner to the inspector, your Grace?"

"No, Mr. Lowther, we need not trouble him for this. If the stranger is here for ulterior purposes, I doubt he will show his hand with so many gentlemen surrounding him. I confess myself curious to discover his motives."

"As you wish, your Grace."

Though clearly troubled, Lowther bowed neatly and retreated, leaving Portia alone with the maid once more. When her eyes flickered back to where the enigmatic stranger waited for his secrets to be revealed, Alice sighed under her breath and reached out to entwine their fingers.

"Be careful, Portia," she said, her words for the duchess alone.

"I always am."

Portia briefly considered retreat, but the mystery was impossible to resist. Slipping back into the midst of the rowdy parlour with Alice at her side, the duchess refilled her own glass and retook her seat, content merely to observe the stranger whilst she mused on his motivations.

Many of the men present had hinted to her about marriage, some more strongly than others, but Portia had no intention of marrying again. However appealing a prospect the young, well-connected duchess was to them, she received a handsome annuity from the duke's estate until such a time that she married again. Francis ensured she was fully able to support her lifestyle without needing to throw herself on the mercy of the sharks that swam unchecked amongst the ton. Her self-reliance, though, was no deterrent to the men around her. She suspected it was for that reason that the stranger had employed subterfuge to win himself admittance tonight.

Portia's smile failed to reach her eyes when she eased back in her seat and watched him over the top of the empty glass, startled to realise how swiftly she had polished off its contents. The wine did nothing to soothe her unease, but it had at least lubricated her mind, for she belatedly realised that it must be Harlow's card that the stranger had somehow acquired. The portly barrister was the only man absent from the invited company.

As that conclusion clarified, the stranger rose from his seat at the whist table and made a direct line for her. Her breath quickened. She stood to meet him with her head held high and a spark in her eyes that invited no deceit. Perhaps he recognised it, for a ghost of a smile played around the corners of his thin lips as he gestured towards the whist tables.

"There are large stakes at play tonight, my lady, but I suspect it is the banker who is victorious," he said directly.

She inclined her head, her voice kept low so that only he could hear her. "Of course. Why else would I offer to host these evenings, if not for profit?"

Laughter danced in those eyes that seemed to see so much. "I thought as much. However, I am afraid you will not empty my purse tonight, for my preference is for games that favour intelligence over luck. Do you have a chessboard, my lady?"

Portia exhaled, forgetting everything but that gentle challenge she could not resist. "Would you care for a game, sir?"

"Indeed."

The chess board was produced, the pieces in place for the game to begin. She sent two pawns forward and the stranger accepted the gambit. Somewhere behind them the raucous games of whist played out to their final conclusions, but she cared nothing for that now.

The game was swift. Portia had always favoured a bold gamble over the tedious monotony of playing her hand with caution, but tonight it proved to be her undoing. After less than ten minutes, the stranger leaned forward. His right hand hovered over his rook as he clicked his tongue.

"You have overreached, my lady. Your queen is exposed, her defences too thinly stretched."

"My queen?"

"Forgive me. I mean the king, of course."

He smiled and advanced his knight to checkmate Portia. The game was won, her gamble lost—but she had one more hand left to play. As the company began to dissipate, the night's victors crowing over their substantial triumphs, she cut across to stand in front of the stranger and spoke before she could change her mind.

"Would you care to take dinner with me tomorrow, sir?"

He inclined his head. "An invitation perhaps more suited to another of my brethren, Portia, but I find myself inclined to accept nonetheless."

"I am glad. Until tomorrow, then?"

"Until tomorrow."

With that they parted ways, but even in his absence Portia thought of the stranger. When she retired to bed and curled into the reassuring warmth of Alice's soft body, it was his face she saw in her mind's eye. Perhaps it was foolish to invite him to dine alone with her when she knew nothing about him, not even his name, but she always had been partial to a gamble.

The hours crawled past in insolent monotony, but eventually the appointed time arrived and brought the long-haired stranger back to her door. Tense with anticipation, she waited throughout the course of the meal for him to say something to illuminate his intrusion into her life, but though he conversed with perfect cordiality, he let nothing slip until they retreated to the smaller of the two parlour rooms, where the butler had laid out the evening papers for her perusal. She had no intention of attending to them tonight, but the smudged black print caught her eye. The names imprinted on the leading article leapt from the page to demand her attention.

Portia's heart began to beat faster when she turned back towards the stranger and lifted one trembling hand. "Sir, did you see the evening papers before you came here?"

"No, my lady," he said, his low and sonorous voice the only sound she heard. "Has something in their pages disturbed you?"

"Indeed it has." She lifted her head to look him in the eye, and almost instantly wished she had not done so. "Of our companions last night, you and I are the only ones who remain."

"How very unfortunate," he said, his voice steady despite the news she imparted. "If I believed in conspiracies, I would caution you to seek out a defence, my lady. Were that so, I would be happy to share with you the cloak of my protection against the horrors that roam the streets of London—at a cost, of course, but nothing you were not willing to pay."

The stranger posed his words as a gentle jest, but some long-forgotten instinct made Portia hesitate. Her head was spinning as she answered him in like whilst she fought to decipher his true meaning. "You speak of these horrors as if you know them intimately. What have you experienced, sir, that you think I need protecting from?"

He circled around her to lead her away from the papers as he tilted his head to the side. "I have experienced wonders—and horrors—beyond your comprehension. Never in this age have mortals had to confront them, but the time is nigh. Here in Britain, defences are stretched perilously thin. In the backstreets where misery runs rampant and men prefer to look the other way, Portia, it is all too easy for my kind to slip through the cracks unseen."

"Your kind? You speak of yourself as if you are separate from mankind."

"And you are most astute."

"Astute enough to know that your words remind me of something altogether…infernal."

He took the nearest seat and stretched out his legs. "Are you a theologian, Portia?"

"A student of religion, yes, but only as a product of my childhood. I am what is referred to in hushed tones as a lapsed Christian, you see. It distresses my youngest brother greatly, so in deference to his tender feelings, we tend to avoid the subject entirely."

"And why is he particularly sensitive to the subject?"

"Sir, my brother Aubrey is a man of God. He is the vicar to a sweet, sleepy little parish in the heart of Surrey. My exploits scandalise him, but as Monty often reminds him, the law is a thin line that I take care never to cross."

The stranger's eyes narrowed. "Monty?"

"My twin brother, Montmorency. He is an inspector with the Metropolitan Police, and he keeps a fraternal watch on the little entertainments I so like to indulge in."

"Both of them are therefore lined up in opposition. How unfortunate."

Portia's heart picked up its pace once more when she chanced a look into the stranger's pale eyes. They narrowed as they locked onto her, almost seeming to dare her to seek further. She never had been able to resist temptation.

"Opposition?" she echoed. "I am afraid I do not understand your meaning, sir."

"Oh, I rather suspect that you do, even if you prefer not to admit that to yourself yet," he said calmly. "Tell me, Portia, what does Mammon mean to you?"

Not for the first time, she wished she had paid more attention in the schoolroom. It was not that she lacked the aptitude for the lofty ideas expressed in her brothers' textbooks, but rather that their logorrheic delusions of grandeur failed to impress her. Even as a child she recognised mankind's ability to fool themselves into believing in their own exaggerated value. Portia had always preferred a more tangible kind of worth.

As she sought deep into the recesses of her childhood, though, the stranger's words sparked a memory she grasped with both hands, for the lavishly illustrated descriptions of the seven deadly sins were easy to recall now her mind settled upon them.

"Avarice," she said. A shiver chased down her spine and the stranger leaned forward, his breath quickening and a spark dancing in his eyes that seemed to reflect the candlelight back towards her as she continued. "Mammon represented greed; not mere physical hunger, but the vice or sin of craving wealth and power in all its forms."

The stranger exhaled and eased back in his chair once more. "Indeed," he said, but before he could elaborate on his enigmatic words, the door to the parlour was opened from the outside.

Mr. Lowther bowed as he moved into the void, his neat, slender moustache twitching slightly when his eyes flickered past Portia for a moment before he spoke. "Ma'am, Inspector Talbot is in the hall."

"Now?"

The butler grimaced. "Yes, ma'am. Shall I send him

away?"

"No. No, of course not."

Portia shook her head in a futile attempt to clear it, disturbed to realise that she was so preoccupied by her companion that she had not even heard the door knocker. In fact, for a moment she had even forgotten the grievous news the papers imparted upon her. Flustered, she rose to her feet and smoothed down her skirts as she started towards the butler and the doorway, then abruptly turned back to the stranger.

"I must attend to my brother. Will you wait for me?" she said impulsively.

He languidly waved one hand through the air. "Oh, it is not as if I am needed elsewhere, not yet," he said. "I am as eager as you are to conclude our conversation, my lady, so I shall entertain myself until you return."

Despite that implicit permission to retreat, though, Portia found herself lingering still. His words whispered at something dark and dangerous, mysteries that were hers to unveil if only she dared seek far enough. The way he steered their conversation towards theology reminded her of the rumours Fitzroy described to them all last night, and her breath quickened at the memory of the theistic Satanism he spoke about. She opened her mouth with one more question for the stranger hovering unspoken on her lips until she heard her brother's voice from the hallway. Breaking free of the thrall, she shivered and closed the door firmly behind her, convinced she heard the faint strains of the stranger's laughter following her as she moved through the hall and lifted one hand in greeting to her twin brother.

Montmorency Talbot's lean face was drawn and pinched. The weight of the day was worn clearly upon his furrowed brow. A smear of dirt marred his clean-shaven face, and his polished black boots were muddied on the soles.

"A man's body was discovered only a few hundred

yards from here, Portia," he said directly, relinquishing his worn greatcoat to the butler. "I have been investigating the scene all day, so I thought I would impose upon your hospitality for the night, if you do not mind. The thought of hailing a hansom back across London only to return to my empty home—and cupboards—does not particularly appeal."

"Of course I do not mind," Portia said automatically, her heart still beating far too fast when her eyes roamed over the hall. Finally relaxing when she saw the shape of her maid amongst the shadows, she beckoned her forward. "Alice, could I trouble you to enter the rear parlour and ask whether my guest needs anything in my absence whilst I attend to my brother?"

"Of course, ma'am," the maid said.

Monty stilled, his hand frozen in the motion of handing over his hat as well. "You have company?" he said. "Portia, you should have told me. I am surely an imposition -"

"Never, brother," Portia said. Ordinarily that was the truth, but tonight she found herself quietly resenting her brother's presence, despite her cordial words.

Perhaps he knew. His eyes narrowed, his nostrils flaring when he took a step closer. She tensed, perfectly aware that he was sifting the air, searching for any unfamiliar scent that might illuminate the mystery for him. Even now he could not separate himself from the profession he loved so fiercely.

"Does the lady need an escort home?" he finally said.

Portia rolled her eyes, but a faint smile curved her lips even as a flush rose to heat her cheeks. "There is no lady, Monty."

"A gentleman caller, Portia? You never fail to surprise me."

"I do my best." Portia took her twin's waiting arm as Alice entered the parlour, closing the door behind her. "Come through to the dining room, Monty, and let me see you settled with dinner before I return to my guest and bid him farewell for the night."

"You must not feel obliged to dismiss him on my account—"

"Monty, dear, when have I ever done anything on your bidding?"

He laughed, some of his cares seeming to lift away as they walked into the dining hall and she guided him to the seat at the head of the table. "All too true, Portia. Be that as it may, though, as little as I expected you to ever seek out a gentleman's company, if he pleases you, I would not want to be an obstacle to your happiness."

"A wild leap of logic, brother," she said firmly. "You are entirely correct in your supposition that I have no want for a gentleman's company in that sense, and even less for any kind of entanglement. The gentleman is a friend, no more, and he never intended to stay here overnight."

High time the subject was changed, for despite her insistence, Portia felt her flush deepen, her brother's intent stare seeming to see far too much. The easiest thing would be to confide in Monty about the stranger and everything he said, but there was something about him that made her want to guard him with avid jealousy, to keep the dark secret of him all to herself for a little longer. Bustling around her brother to conceal her reaction, she evaded his eye until a plate full of steaming meat and potatoes had been set before him. Finally she felt safe enough to take a seat next to him and speak again, seizing upon his day's work as a safer topic of conversation.

"I presume you have been able to identify the unfortunate person whose body was found. One of those named in *The Times*, I venture?" she said.

"No, another man entirely," Monty said with a sigh, pushing his food listlessly around the plate. "A gentleman of some repute, Portia, with a wife and a young son too; a Mr. Jonathan Harlow of Pembridge Place."

The world slowed to a crawl around them, the power

of the handful of inconsequential words Monty spoke far greater than he knew. Just another man, one amongst many. His death meant nothing to Portia, but his absence last night came into sharp focus through the lens of his death—for it was the calling card given to him that the stranger used to gain absence to her home last night.

Now Harlow and the other men were all dead, and the stranger was sitting in her parlour.

Portia gripped the table edge tightly. "You are certain about his identity, Monty?" she said.

"Entirely so; his brother confirmed it an hour or so ago. But come now, Portia, you seem troubled by my news! I was not aware that you knew the gentleman."

"A…a passing acquaintance, no more. He was supposed to join my dinner party last night, Monty, but he never arrived."

Alert once more, Monty reached into the pocket of his trousers and withdrew a well-thumbed notebook and fountain pen. "Here?" he said sharply. "Portia, Harlow was murdered sometime between five and nine o'clock last night. Tell me, did he send a message to excuse his absence?"

"No." Staring past him into the distance, Portia rose to her feet. "Monty, excuse me. This cannot wait. Finish your meal, brother mine. I fear you shall be in need of its sustenance before the night is through."

She heard her twin call after her, but she left the dining room without looking back. Anticipation thrummed through her veins, the furtive thrill of the threads coming together quickening her step as she returned to the parlour where the stranger awaited her. But he was not alone there. Too late Portia remembered.

Alice.

She had sent the maid into the parlour, the parlour where the stranger was—the stranger who she now suspected was capable of cold-blooded murder for something as insignificant as a calling card.

There was not a moment to waste. Her mouth too dry to call out for Monty to follow her, Portia dashed down the hall and threw open the parlour door.

Too late.

The door swung shut with a soft thud in her wake as she stumbled forward, the world whirling around them as the terrible diorama emblazoned itself across her mind forevermore.

Alice was dead. Her body lay sprawled on the burgundy carpet, her head lolling loose at an unnatural angle, her mouth gaping wide and her eyes staring unseeing at the ceiling.

She was dead, and Portia had sent her to that fate.

Barely able even to breathe under the crushing weight of her deep, bitter grief, Portia snatched up the closest weapon to hand. Wielding the long, thin poker with a hand that shook so wildly she could barely keep her grip, she whirled towards the sombre-faced stranger, but he spoke before she could fire her accusation in his direction.

"She was a mere pawn," he said as his top lip curled back. "Waste not your time mourning this insignificant creature, Portia. Save your tears for when you truly need them."

"A *pawn*?!" Near dumbstruck by the height of his cold dispassion, she advanced on him, but then the poker slipped through her fingers as the final piece of the puzzle fell into place. If Alice was a pawn to him, disposable and meaningless in the grand scheme of the game at hand, then Portia was a game piece too—and London was the chessboard.

The truth was hers to grasp now. Impossible, terrifying and magnificent all at once, it rocked the very foundations of the world she thought she knew. Two worlds were colliding, and neither of them would ever be the same again.

Portia lifted her head to look him in the eye. "You are the Devil himself," she said simply.

The demon did not deny it.

"My game plays out to its conclusion tonight, Portia," he said instead. "You may refute your culpability if it makes you feel better, but the truth remains that you sent your pawn into danger. She fell, as will all the others until eventually only the queen remains."

She stumbled back as the poker slipped through her fingers to fall to the carpet at Alice's side. "You are mistaken again. You mean to say the king."

"I said precisely what I meant." Lucifer turned to the left and a slow smile spread across his face. "Hark, Portia! Did you hear that?"

Portia shook her head without looking at him, powerless to tear her eyes away from Alice's body on the floor at her feet.

He advanced once more, closing the distance between them with an inhuman rapidity. "More of my brethren have joined me in your realm. I hear the evidence of their presence in the distance. You would do well to consider my offer, for time is fast running out."

"Your offer?"

His long fingers closed around her wrist and his free hand came to rest beneath her jaw, tilting her head inexorably upwards until she had no choice but to meet his darkening eyes. "Protection, Portia," he said softly. "Few mortals will be offered such an honour, but my offer will not stay on the table forever. Consider it carefully. When next we meet, I will have your answer."

Portia jerked back. He let her go.

She retreated towards the door, not taking her eyes away from the devil all the while until she grasped the handle, fell back into the hall and slammed the door closed in her wake. Leaving Alice's broken body at Lucifer's feet tore her heart in two, but her lover was already lost. Monty, though, was mere feet away. She could not save Alice, but Portia could still fight with everything she was to save her beloved twin.

As she dashed towards the dining room and doubled over as she burst in through the doorway, she realised that she could not tell him that Alice was dead. If he had any idea what happened here tonight, he would not walk away. Her fierce, stubborn, valiant twin would never turn his back and let a murderer walk free, but nothing she could say would convince him of the breathtaking power of his foe. She believed in Lucifer with a faith she had never known until now, but her brother would never understand without proof—proof she could not risk him finding.

"We need to leave London, Monty," she said without preamble.

His fork fell to the plate with a loud clatter. "Is this some jest, sister?"

"I only wish it were!" Pacing back and forth, she strained to hear any sign of the demon in pursuit, but all was silent in the hall outside. "Monty, there is no time to explain. If you trust me, then do as I say."

"Portia, you know I trust you, but this is absurd! You know I cannot abandon my duties -"

"And you know I would not ask this of you without good reason. We cannot even wait for the morning mail coach. The dear duke's brougham is still maintained for when I have need of it, and the horses are stabled only two streets away from here. I suggest we utilise them to make good our escape."

"Escape?"

Portia dared not stay any longer. They were running on borrowed time. Trusting that her twin would follow her despite his doubts, she dashed back into the hall and near collided with the butler as he emerged from the kitchen.

She seized him by the arm. "Mr. Lowther, take whatever money you need from the safe to put yourself and the staff up in a hotel for the night—and for the love of God, do not enter the parlour!"

His eyes widened. "Your Grace, whatever is the matter?!"

No time. Onwards, away. Without a moment's hesitation she threw open the front door and left the house of horrors behind, desperately relieved to hear her twin following in her wake. He did not question her or even speak a word of protest until she had given the order for the horses to be tethered to the carriage.

"Where are we going?" he said, his mouth drawn in a thin line and his eyes darting ceaselessly from side to side.

"Surrey," Portia said instantly. "Monty, I want you to promise me something. Whatever we see tonight, whatever we encounter as we leave London, do not stop driving until we reach Aubrey and the vicarage."

What little colour remained in his face drained away. "Portia…"

"Swear it, Monty!"

"I cannot pretend to understand this, sister, but never have I seen you like this before," he said heavily. "Very well. I swear it."

She exhaled, but then he reached up to touch his head and made to turn back.

"My hat -" he said.

"Fuck the hat!"

"Portia!" His eyes wide, her twin jerked away from her. For a moment she thought he intended to admonish her uncharacteristic curse, but instead a visible shudder passed across his face as he leapt down onto the road, mounted the driver's seat and cracked the whip to spur the horses without another word.

They left with barely a moment to spare. Fierce flames licked the London night sky as their carriage hurtled through the city. She was under no illusions. They were only able to escape because Lucifer permitted it, and if his strange words were the truth, then this was no act of charity. London and the demons that so surely stalked its shadows faded rapidly into the night, and finally the achingly familiar skyline of the Surrey countryside where Aubrey resided came into view.

The slumbering, docile village was always a vivid contrast to the city, but never more so than tonight. Barely able to breathe under the weight of all they left behind, Portia leapt down from the carriage before Monty brought it to a halt outside the vicarage, then hurtled along the neat, precise garden path with no care for the carefully cultivated spring bulbs that lined it as she threw herself towards the door to hammer upon it.

In less than a minute, her bleary-eyed brother appeared in his nightgown, a flickering candle held aloft in his left hand and his mouth hanging agape as she spoke with no words of greeting.

"Aubrey, what weapons do you have here?"

"Portia, it is three in the morning!" Aubrey stared at her and then turned to Monty for help. "Brother, what is the meaning of this?"

"I am not quite sure that I know myself, Aubrey, but something is afoot," Monty said behind her. "I do not think we should linger outside. May we come in?"

Portia did not wait for his answer. Pushing past her brother, she plucked the candle from his hand and walked straight into the parlour, ransacking each drawer and cupboard she found there. All her search yielded was a tarnished pair of howdah pistols, devoid of ammunition and sorely lacking in maintenance.

Despair flooded her body, sapping her strength as she leaned back against the wall. "Aubrey, is this really all you have?" she said in frustration.

"Good God, Portia, this is Surrey, not the bloody Sudan!" he said as the brothers followed her into the parlour. When neither Portia nor Monty laughed, Aubrey's attempt at a jocular smile faded away and he spoke again, his voice low and intent this time. "Very well. I fear I shall regret this, but what in the name of God is happening?"

Monty sighed. "I am not entirely sure that I know myself, but there was much mafficking as we drove out of London, Aubrey. Had I not been escorting Portia, I would not have left at all. I hope my superiors will forgive my dereliction of duty when we return."

"Return?" Portia swiftly shook her head, setting the candle aside in favour of the pistols, empty though they were. "Brothers, it is my belief that there will soon be no London to return to. Aubrey, what do you know about earthly manifestations of Lucifer?"

The last vestiges of sleep left the vicar's face as his eyes widened and he took a step backwards. "The devil himself?"

"Yes." Speaking that simple word brought the height of the danger into sharp relief, and that made her remember all she left behind. "Brothers, he killed her."

Her twin tensed, pushing past their younger brother. "Who?"

"Alice. She is dead, Monty," Portia said bleakly. "She was murdered in the parlour whilst you and I were in the dining room mere feet away."

Monty stood rooted to the spot, his jaw working but no words emerging from his mouth. Instead it was Aubrey who spoke.

"Sister, did her assailant name himself as the devil?" he said under his breath.

She did not answer him. Instead she swiftly crossed the room, her heart thumping wildly out of time all the while and her eyes fixed on the crack in the white window drapes. Somewhere in the distance Aubrey was speaking still, but she could not comprehend his words. All she knew was the face she saw fleetingly pressed up against the glass, intruding upon the family scene to bring the horrors of London down upon them once more. The last vestiges of hope flickered and died as Portia stared into the night, looking into Lucifer's eyes for no more than half a heartbeat before she turned back to her brothers.

"He is here."

Her stark words rang out clearly. Both men paled, glancing at each other to exchange a look of fraternal comprehension before Aubrey whetted his lips and put voice to the thought they all shared.

"If it truly is Lucifer…if you are right, Portia, then we are already lost."

"Yes."

It was him. She was certain of that. The fight was over before it began, but her brothers were readying themselves for battle nonetheless, taking out their weapons of choice; Monty his pistol and baton, and Aubrey a small cross from the pocket of his nightgown. Side by side, the men advanced and opened the front door to reveal six creatures standing in the village square, arranged in a semicircle facing the vicarage. Their faces were unnaturally pale, and the gleam in their dark eyes told Portia everything she did not want to know. There was no sign of Lucifer, but he was pulling the strings tonight.

Without saying a word the demons spread out and began to move towards the three siblings. Monty spoke first. "Halt, in the name of the queen!"

The first demon's face twisted into a mocking smile. "Your queen holds no dominion over me."

The constable fired. The demon flinched when the neat, precise little bullet lodged in his abdomen, but though he stumbled, the shot did nothing to halt his advance.

Aubrey twisted towards Portia. "Sister, go!"

"Go where?!"

But even as she spoke, she realised she already knew. For one so determinedly agnostic, the compulsion to turn to God in her hour of need took her breath away. She instinctively sensed that the church held the answer.

"You'll follow me?" she said desperately.

Monty smiled, though the reassurance was belied by the fear that clouded his eyes. "We shall be right behind you, sister mine."

Portia veered right. Tossing her useless pistols over her shoulder towards the demons, she hurtled in through the open doors of the church and doubled over to catch her breath, one thought burning bright in her mind. The villagers were sitting ducks, fast asleep in their beds whilst the only line of defence was about to fall.

Divine inspiration struck. She seized hold of the bell rope and pulled with all her might. The church bell peals roused the village, and in less than a minute hundreds of men, women and children spilled out into the square as she dashed back to the doors, but even their massed force was nothing against the demons.

"In here! Monty, Aubrey, bring them here!"

Though the vicar's face was deathly white, he did not falter in the face of damnation. His clear, melodious voice rose high as he squared his shoulders defiantly and urged his congregation on.

Aubrey ushered the woman and children towards the consecrated ground, a shepherd shielding his flock as the fires of Hell began to rain down upon them. Led by Monty, the men held their line and the villagers flooded into the church, spilling down the aisle towards Portia. She could not bear their silent accusations, all too aware she had brought Hell itself to their doors, and so without a word for her younger brother when he burst through the doorway and sank to his knees in weeping prayer, she slipped into the vestry and closed the door to act as a shield.

She did not find the sanctuary she sought there. Someone was already present.

"I see the pawns are lined up in formation to protect their queen, Portia," he said.

Lucifer.

Portia glanced at the clock on the wall. Four in the morning. Dawn was some time away yet. She sensed none of them would see it arrive. "Good morning, Lucifer," she said, relieved to hear how steady her voice remained. "How did you get in? I thought we would be safe inside the church."

"A clever defence, granted, but such earthly barriers are nothing to me." The devil moved forward to stand between Portia and the door. "You are protected against my lesser brothers here, granted, but those of my age and power can pass onto consecrated ground unrestricted."

Portia's breath hitched wildly. "Then why have you not already led your brethren into battle?"

"The fight outside is meaningless, a mere amusement to pass the time. My sole purpose here is to find those worthy of preserving when the new world order dawns, and that is why I sought you."

The demon's words took her back to London and a proposal made back when life was simpler, when mortal danger was all she had to face. Now it was not only her soul, but the fate of the world in peril, and she did not think she had the courage or wit to play out this hand and defeat this greatest of foes.

Lucifer surely knew. His half-smile widened when he spoke again.

"You have had enough time to consider my offer now. I urge you to accept. I feel like you and I could be allies in this war, Portia. Swear your allegiance and give me your fealty, and I promise you will survive the war unscathed. When the queen falls and the country is mine, you will be safe at my side."

She did not flinch away from his intent stare. "A tempting offer, Mammon, I admit that much."

"Yet still you do not accept my proposal."

"No." Aware her answer would seal her fate, Portia hesitated, but the words tumbled forth regardless. "I fear that the incontrovertible truth, Lucifer, is humans and demons are, and always will be, on opposing sides."

"I sense that your mind is made up, Portia. In that case, there is only one course left open to us."

She swallowed hard. "And that is?"

Lucifer produced her chessboard with a flourish. "Would you care for a game?" he said with a smile.

There was nothing else to do whilst she waited for her world to end. Numb, Portia bowed her head and seated herself cross-legged on the cold stone floor whilst the devil set out the board before her.

Their pawns in position, the game began.

ABOUT THE AUTHOR

CARA FOX is an English author trying to write her way out of the dark. She favours steampunk, horror and Gothic romance, but you can find her anywhere that the stories sink their claws into you and the wine flows freely. Her work has been published by *Tales To Terrify*, *Empyreome*, *Broadswords & Blasters* and *Horror Addicts*, among others, and she is working on her debut novel, *The Strange Case of Doctor Magorian*.

A NIGHT AT SATAN'S PALACE

Damascus Mincemeyer

Twilight was nearing and the Las Vegas lights were blinding in the Winnebago's side-mounted mirror when Stuart pulled the RV into the nightclub's parking lot. In the passenger's seat Bruce grumbled as the vehicle's brakes hissed before coming to a full stop.

"Why the hell did you insist on renting an RV for this road trip, Stu? We should've come out here in some style instead of this glorified station wagon." He sighed. "I swear I've never felt like such a fogy in my life."

Stuart turned the Winnebago's engine off, shook his head and chuckled at his friend's grousing. "You just turned seventy-two, Bruce. If you feel like a fogy, *that's* probably why. So don't blame the RV. And if you remember, you're the one who chose to come to Vegas. *I* suggested going to Florida. What I'm really interested in knowing is why you wanted me to stop *here.*"

He pointed to the nightclub. It was far from the shine

of casinos and tourist hot-spots, but a gaudy, glowing spectacle all its own, an electric-red sign above the parking lot bearing a pitchfork-wielding devil with a wide, wicked smile on its neon face.

"Satan's Palace?" Bruce cracked. "How can you *not* be interested in visiting a place named that?"

Stuart adjusted his bifocals. "It's a strip joint."

"I know. That's an added bonus, isn't it?"

"I don't think Deborah would like me being here." Stuart said, nervously fingering the small silver cross necklace his wife had bought him. Bruce tapped his arm.

"Oh, come on, you old goat. What's it going to hurt to see some cute young thing shake her ass for five minutes, huh? Give a few dollars. Have a few drinks. Deb will never know. And besides, what's the saying about what happens in Vegas?"

"It weighs on your conscience." Stuart sighed. "I don't know, Bruce. It doesn't feel right."

"Five minutes." Bruce goaded. "One drink. Make-believe your twenty-one again."

"I was in Vietnam when I was twenty-one. I don't want to make-believe that *ever* again."

"And I got arrested protesting the DNC in '68. That's not the point. Remember last year when we joined that guided motorcycle tour? Remember how fun it was?"

"I remember almost dying when those two biker gangs went at it after we stopped at their sleazy roadhouse. That *wasn't* fun."

Bruce rolled his eyes. "Not what I meant." He gestured to the club. *"Live* a little, Stu."

"Fine." Stuart submitted, rubbing his aching lower back as he clamored out of the Winnebago behind Bruce. The lot was half-filled with vehicles, the first refrain of The Doors' 'Light My Fire' audible even outside the building, where a thick-muscled, ponytailed doorman barricaded the entrance with his body.

"You lost, Pops?" He asked sarcastically. "Bingo hall is

down the street."

Bruce pulled a wad of bills from his cargo shorts. "We want beer and babes, my man." He smiled, slipping the doorman some cash. "That about cover us?"

"Bingo." The man said, stepping aside. Once through the door, Bruce caught Stuart's expression and answered the question he knew was coming.

"I withdrew some extra money from my IRA, okay? I wanted to have some fun out here. Play the tables. See some showgirls."

"Well, I'd say you succeeded at that," Stuart muttered; around them the club was alive with dancing women, the interior bathed in garish crimson light, the air thick with a heady perfume of cheap alcohol and stale sweat. To the right of the door was a long bar tended by a bald, goateed brute, and at each stool and table men sat, lonely, vacant eyes focused on the main stage, where a flame-haired woman covered in tattoos and little else gyrated around a pole while the song played.

"Damn," Bruce said. "Haven't seen a pair like those in thirty years."

Stuart ran a nervous hand through his thinning silver hair. "This is *embarrassing*. She's young enough to be my granddaughter."

"Yeah, but she's *not* your granddaughter, now is she?" Bruce said with a wink and a leer.

Still eyeing the dancer, Bruce accidentally bumped into a man in a rumpled black jacket and fedora who sat at the end of the bar smoking a cigarette and nursing a drink that splashed on the countertop with the collision.

"Watch where your goin' there, Don Ameche," he snapped.

Bruce apologized, but as soon as he and Stuart were out of earshot he said, "You hear that guy? Skid row Humphrey Bogart calling *me* Don Ameche. I'm getting buzzed off of his second-hand beer breath."

Stuart tugged at Bruce's sleeve. "Come on, a table's

opened up. Let's get this little experience over with."

No sooner did they sit than a smiling woman approached them, blonde with fishnet stockings and a serpent tattoo slithering around her bare torso to a skin-tight top.

"I'm Sindy. Drinks?"

Bruce smirked, pointing to the bar. "Give me whatever Bogie back there's having. And bring some prune juice for my friend," he prodded Stuart. "His sense of fun needs some flushing out."

Sindy's smile widened and she turned away just as another stripper—tall with auburn hair, a short sequin skirt and skimpy halter top—led a hefty, middle-aged businessman in an expensive-looking suit to a cordoned off back room. Bruce chuckled. "Guess *he's* going to see some dirty dancing up close."

Stuart shook his head. "I've got a bad feeling about this. Something's not right here."

"Spare me. Just because we ran afoul of some shady characters last year doesn't mean *every* joint's crawling with creepers."

'Light My Fire' ended, the red-headed dancer scurried behind a closing curtain and an emcee with a microphone took to the stage. He was nearly identical to the bartender—shaven head, black goatee—and in the nightclub's scarlet lighting seemed to Bruce as much a devil as the cartoon Satan on the sign outside. The resemblance didn't end there, either: his voice was deep and gravelly, like he'd seen too many horror films and was aiming to spook an audience less interested in menace than booze and bare breasts.

"My name is Anton, and I'm proud this evening to deliver unto you a *very* special guest for Satan's Palace. One of our most exotic and enticing featured dancers has finally returned after far too long. A true mistress of darkness, a seducer of saints, one who has turned holy men away from the cross and nuns from their vows…" Anton let his pause build before announcing: "Welcome back the alluring…*Desdemona.*"

He left just as dry-ice fog billowed from the rear of the stage and the first licks of AC/DC's 'Hell's Bells' kicked in over the club's speakers. When the curtain opened a shapely, statuesque woman emerged from the haze wearing thigh-high leather boots and a pair of black cherubic wings extending from a shoulder harness, the rest of her encased in a tight-fitting, curve-accentuating bustier. But it was her face where the true tantalizing beauty lay: high cheekbones and come-hither eyes and bee-stung lips, all framed by luxurious dark mane.

The woman danced, and mesmerized men sitting close to the stage began throwing money, whistling, calling her name, and Bruce's heart fluttered when she shed her bustier, revealing an inverted cross carefully painted down her naked cleavage. As the song reached its first chorus Desdemona grabbed a bottle of whiskey from the nearest table, drank a mouthful and held it in, revealing a Zippo concealed in her other hand. With fiery gusto she flicked the lighter to life, spewed alcohol from her lips, a crescendo of flame arcing in the air while the audience cheered.

"This is too much," Stuart said, pushing away from the table and pointing to the restrooms at the far end of the bar. "I'm going to the bathroom. And then I want to *leave.*"

"Don't get lost." Bruce jibed, but Stuart didn't even look back.

♉

Like the rest of the club, the men's room of Satan's Palace was awash in ambient red, and standing at the urinal Stuart noticed the flagrant deviltry decor on display even there: a pentagram was patterned in the floor tile, and each paper-towel dispenser bore a set of mock chrome horns. After washing his hands, Stuart splashed water on his face and stared in the mirror.

"What are you doing here, you old fart?" He asked, but his reflection staunchly refused to answer. Putting his bifocals back on he went to the hall; from where he stood he saw Bruce sitting enrapt by Desdemona's performance, and exhaling a deep breath Stuart was about to return to the table when an anguished wail floated through the corridor.

Just some kinkster getting their jollies, he thought, and pictured a paunchy, pale pervert tied up, gagged and whipped by a plastic-wrapped dominatrix, though why anyone would shill out cash for treatment a prisoner-of-war received for free was beyond him.

A second cry, louder and more agonizing, changed his mind. It sounded less like a libertine's revelry than pain, pure and undiluted by pleasure. Stuart glanced down the hall; at its opposite end was an unmarked door, and when another shrill scream echoed from behind it he chided himself for the desire to investigate. Yet something altogether more chilling killed the idea he was hearing common debauchery: the ill-natured chorus of chanting, faint and rhythmic, rising and falling like ocean waves.

Ignore it, Stuart. He thought. *Maybe a high-roller paid for the full Caligula treatment, sexy slave girls and Gregorian monks included. None. Of. Your. Business.*

Satisfied the mental debate was settled, he went to turn away when fast footsteps closed in behind him and Anton was there, a sinister cudgel in one hand. Taken by surprise, Stuart didn't have time to react before Anton slammed the weapon into his stomach, leaving him breathless on the floor. The bald man grabbed Stuart's arms, pulled him up and shoved him towards the door; Stuart struggled, called out for help, but his captor's hands were younger, stronger, and he had no choice but to go in the guided direction.

The door opened onto a descending stairway that continued further down than Stuart would've expected a flight of steps leading to a basement to go. When finally it ended, the passage expanded into an area far different from the boiler room his mind conjured—a floor of granite blocks spread across a space as large as a baseball diamond, stone columns inlaid with lit torches supporting a high-vaulted cathedral ceiling, at the center of which sat the statue of a winged figure with cloven feet and a goat's head, female breasts and a prominently erect penis, an open, circular pit of dancing flames situated directly in front of it casting the sculpture in flickering, shadowy geometry.

The chanting reverberated throughout the chamber, and Stuart soon realized the source: assembled around the pit were a dozen hooded, black-robed figures, hands clasped and heads bowed in reverie as they sang their dark dirge. But the voices did nothing to conceal the screams, and dangling upside-down from a chain above the chasm was the middle-aged businessman Stuart had seen earlier being taken to the VIP area, except now he was naked, bound, writhing to escape, his overweight belly carved with a bleeding pentacle, the auburn-haired stripper who'd led him lamb-like to the slaughtering floor gently caressing his face. Watching the scene, hearing the unnerving choir, seeing the monstrous statue, Stuart chastised himself a final time.

Shit, he thought. *I knew we should've gone to Florida.*

♉

By the time Sindy returned with Bruce's ordered drinks he scarcely noticed her. His attention was concentrated solely on Desdemona as she seductively shimmied about the stage, wriggling from the rest of her meager clothing. As he was about to take a sip, the stripper worked her way to the edge of the platform near Bruce's table, and the alcohol never made it to his mouth. Desdemona crawled towards his seat, gaze fixed upon him, and Bruce felt a hum in the air as she slid closer, an electricity he couldn't explain deadening every urge except the one to stare.

"Am I not all you desire? Am I not all you could want?" She asked, reaching out to him; there was a heavy, drowsy tone to her voice, like a swarm of bees, that fingered a chord deep within, and Bruce tried to maintain his composure despite the fact that he suddenly felt like a bumbling teenager on a first date.

"Jesus," Bruce whispered.

"Not even," she said, the energy of her touch, the hypnotic allure of her voice overriding what sense remained in him. Desdemona smiled then, leaned in, kissed Bruce hard on the lips, the sensation wild and violent enough that, for a second, he thought he was going to pass out. An instant later, her tongue flickered into his mouth, brushed against his own, and inexplicably he tasted strawberries, honey and a dozen other things that blurred into pure ecstasy.

Bruce was so enthralled he didn't see the fedora-wearing man rise from his barstool, didn't hear the cries of alarm from the audience as he withdrew the shiny, nickel-finished Beretta .380 from within his rumpled jacket and shouted, "Get *away* from him, *bitch!*"

Only when the first gunshot rang out was the spell broken; Desdemona screamed as one bullet ripped into her face, three more shots pumping her torso in quick succession. She crumpled to the stage, the nearby patrons scrambling from their chairs and away from the gunman.

"Don't let them look you in the eyes!" The man yelled, still firing; with Desdemona down, he shot at Sindy, clipped her in the arm, then kept on his rampage, aiming at the other strippers while seeming to avoid the men in the room.

Trance shattered, Bruce jumped from his seat and tackled the man to the floor; the gunman flailed, and Bruce expected any moment to be peppered with holes.

"You crazy son of a bitch!" Bruce shouted. "What the hell's wrong with you?"

"I had to *see*," the gunman cried. "I had to *know*."

"Know *what?*"

There was a low, bestial growl from the stage, loud enough to hear above the panicked clubgoers, and as Bruce looked over his shoulder he saw Desdemona slowly crawl to her feet, *faux*-wings lopsided, the flesh where she'd been shot hanging in tatters. Something that reminded Bruce of fish scales shimmered bloodily beneath the ruptured skin, and the stripper's eyes radiated a sickly green. Beneath him, the man bristled.

"That."

Bruce stared with open-mouthed shock as Desdemona leapt from the stage, a gnashing dervish landing amid the horde of fleeing men; like the rest of her, the flesh of her fingers had torn, exposing scalpellic talons, and she worked her way through the throng, wolf among frightened lambs, shrieking, slicing, slitting. Bruce saw the carnage in snippets—one man's throat left gaping, another's jaw removed, a third spilling his opened belly to the floor, but what he noticed most was the luminous intensity in Desdemona's eyes, her abruptly inhuman focus fixated wholly upon the man who'd attacked her.

Distracted by the mutilations, the gunman scrambled from Bruce's grasp and yanked him to safety behind the bar.

"What the hell *is* that thing?" Bruce shouted, ducking down.

"A demon." The man answered assuredly. "The strippers? They're *demons*."

♉

Stuart watched as the auburn-haired woman stroked the hanging man's cheek, her voice throaty, sensual, smooth as a purring cat when she spoke. "Look at me, Wayne."

Pleas answered: *"No!* God, *no!"*

"You're *right.*" She smiled. *"No* God. Not *here."*

Anton pushed Stuart forward then. "Mistress Angelique? I've another sacrifice."

She glared at Stuart, studied him; against the gothic medieval trappings she seemed farcical with her skimpy outfit, curled hair and French-tipped fingernails, but the malevolence on her perfectly made-up face cut through any mirth. She ripped Stuart's shirt open, her fingers uncomfortably warm against his sagging chest.

"This one hungers. For lust. For liberation. Yet he lies to himself and claims he doesn't." She paused, licking pouty lips. "Come to me, enter *my* kingdom, and the freedom you seek shall be yours."

"Should we chain him beside the other?" Anton impatiently asked. Angelique shook her head and motioned to the hanging man.

"This is the last soul we need, Anton. Tonight, the Lightbringer rises."

"The Lightbringer rises!" The gathered men repeated in unison, and Stuart tensely giggled.

"You *need* some light down here, honey," he said to the stripper. "So you can see how *ridiculous* all this garbage is. Good God, what's next? Play some stupid heavy metal records backwards? Drink the blood of a virgin?"

Angelique seized Stuart by the throat, too fiercely for anything human, and this time her touch wasn't merely warm, but scalding. Stuart struggled for air, gaze helplessly drawn to her suddenly scorching eyes, and only an abrupt cry from the stairs staunched the spiritual suffocation she was attempting.

The bald bartender rushed from the steps and across the stone floor, frantic to the point of hysteria: "Mistress! Desdemona's been attacked! Sindy and Damiana, too."

"Impossible! None may attack our sanctum." Her tone was furious, but the sounds of gunfire upstairs resounded into the chamber, and Angelique hesitated. Stuart stole the opportunity, stomping on Anton's foot and elbowing him

in the gut. The man yelped, slackened his grasp, but Stuart still couldn't find escape; Angelique's vise-grip was too strong and he clawed at her arm, unable to break the hold until—the cross! *The cross!* The one Deborah had given him for their anniversary. Ripping it from his neck, Stuart pressed the jewelry against Angelique's face, forced it hard onto her cheek. There was a steaming, sizzling sound, like fat rendering in a skillet with a smell to match, and Angelique screamed, pulled back and shoved Stuart to the floor.

"Christ's fucking maggot!" She rasped. When she looked at Stuart again, he saw her left cheek had seared and blistered, revealing rippling, reptilian flesh beneath.

Stuart heaved himself up and ran, ignoring the agony in his back, his mind in overdrive and swearing: *Shit. Shit! SHIT!* Behind him, the hooded men broke ranks from around the pit to give chase until the hidden thing below Angelique's pretty facade stopped them with a stern command: *"No! Complete the ritual! Open the gate."*

Her entire body quivered then, split from groin to gullet, something blackened and charred with its bones on the outside and bird's beaks for hands stepping from the shredded skin to pursue its quarry. Dashing up the endless stairs, Stuart thought every step would be his last; his chest heaved, his knees wobbled like jelly, but he kept going, adrenaline propelling him to the main floor, the howling jabberwocky Angelique had become snapping at his heels.

The sounds of violence—gunshots, terrified screams, smashing bottles and overturning tables—were wild in the air, and huffing for breath Stuart looked around, saw a fire extinguisher on the wall beside an embedded, glass-encased axe, the words BREAK IN CASE OF EMERGENCY written above it.

"Shit, if this isn't, I don't know what *is.*" Stuart hit the glass so hard he thought his elbow broke, but succeeded in shattering the case with a second sharp strike. He took the axe and swung just as the creature burst from the stairwell, buried the blade in the thing's skull before wrenching it out again, but even then it still moved, still screeched and came at him, clawing down the hall as Stuart ran.

☿

"Demons?" Bruce scoffed. The gunman nodded.

"Every last one, straight from the abyss and sucking Satan's own cock for all I know. Fucking bitches have been hiding in plain sight for years, collecting the souls of men who come here. That's why I warned you not to look into their eyes—it's how demons enslave you. Some poor bastards they keep as servants, but most they put on the short bus Downtown. No passing go. No collecting two-hundred dollars. *None* of that shit. And once the demons gather six-hundred and sixty-six souls they can open a gateway and bring forth Lucifer himself. Then it's Hell on Earth for *everyone*, not just punters who like a little Saturday night titty-shake."

"How do you know all this crap?"

The man reloaded his pistol. "Name's Ray. Ray Zaceki." He pulled his coat open, revealing a priest's collar around his neck. *"Father* Zaceki. Used to be an IRS agent until I investigated a brokerage firm that traded human souls in some kind of paranormal Ponzi scheme. That's when I discovered the supernatural isn't just bullshit meant to scare the kiddies at bedtime. Lives were lost. Vengeful oaths were sworn. Now this is what I do. "

There was another guttural growl and Desdemona appeared at the end of the bar holding a patron's severed head in her cerise-stained hands. Sniffing the air, she tossed the decapitation aside and glared at Ray.

"A man of God in our house of sin? I should've smelled it earlier." She traced a clawed finger along the inverted cross between her bloodied breasts. "Come to me, priest, find a new destiny in my arms, my kisses, my wet thighs."

Ray chuckled. "No offense, babe, but I've crawled over better than you to take a piss."

He stood, firing, again and again, and with each shot Desdemona howled until one bullet struck dead center through her forehead and she dropped to the floor.

"Holy *shit!*" Bruce cheered. "You *killed* her!"

"Not even close," Ray said. "Rounds are packed with blessed salt. They'll sting like shit in their eye, stun 'em, but it won't kill the bitches. These, though—" Ray opened his jacket once more, unveiling rows of small interior pockets stuffed with hypodermic needles. "These'll do the trick. Holy water. One jab and it's along the highway to Hell they go."

He passed some syringes to Bruce. On the other side of the bar a last few, desperate men were making for the exit; one of them—squat, flabby with a ripped flannel shirt and cowboy boots—wasn't fast enough and fell prey to the red-haired, tattooed stripper Bruce had first seen whirling around the pole. Unlike Desdemona she still resembled a kittenish vixen, but any part of Bruce doubtful to Ray's story died when the dome of her head shivered and split wide as a bear's maw, a viperous tongue flicking from the toothsome gap. Bruce watched, horrified, as the row of incisors tore at the cowboy, devouring him face-first.

"*Shit!*" Bruce yelled, and the stripper—the *demon*— heard him, dropped the corpse and jumped upon the bar top, reeking of brimstone, flayed skin flapping against the exposed, mottled muscle of her true guise.

There was a shout from the front entrance, and the muscular doorman rushed over, holding a machete that he brought down on the demon's neck with two-handed force. The thing yowled, and Ray pushed Bruce aside, leveling two rounds into its chest.

"Pin her down!" He ordered, and Bruce held one of the demon's writhing arms while the doorman restrained the other. The creature bellowed an excruciating, pained roar when Ray plunged a syringe into its neck, and Bruce cringed as a foul-smelling black tar spewed from every open orifice, the fabric of the demon's flesh disintegrating into a putrid, viscous mass of unraveling muscle and bone. When it finally stopped moving a retching, sulfurous smoke streamed from the remains that turned Bruce's stomach.

The doorman looked at Ray. "You okay?"

"So far, so good, Rufus."

"You two know each other?" Bruce asked.

Ray nodded. "After I traced all the disappearances and otherworldly activity back to this place I needed an inside man. Rufus has been working here the past week, screwing with security monitors, interfering with their protection magick, salting the exits so those evil bitches can't escape."

"How could you work here without them putting the demonic whammy on you?" Bruce asked Rufus. A sly grin stretched the doorman's lips.

"Oh, they thought they did, Pops. But they *can't*." He admitted. "I'm *gay*."

"Well, lucky for you, then. I guess."

There was a screech from the end of the bar as Desdemona again rose from the floor; far from the ravishing beauty Bruce had ogled, she had molt the last vestige of humanity, a nightmare alone remaining: eager eyeballs where nipples should've been, layers of shimmering scales along the torso, but most blasphemous of all was the long, slime-slathered tentacle birthed from the vaginal gash between the demon's legs, as thick as Bruce's arm and ending in a mouth of snapping, sharp shark's teeth.

Bruce froze at the sight, but beside him Rufus lunged for the demon; Desdemona nimbly avoided the machete and counter-attacked, the doorman reeling clear over the bar from a single harsh hit.

"*Fuck!*" Ray shouted, popping off two furious shots. Against its true form the salt rounds did little besides enrage the demon, and Desdemona's labial tendril struck, cobra-like, taking a chunk of meat from Ray's abdomen before it sent him careening into a liquor shelf.

Terror clenched Bruce's guts as the demon turned to him next, wagging a malefic finger. "Come to me..." It demanded. "Give me your *soul.*"

Bruce let out a fearful chuckle. "Sorry," he said. "But I was already married. *Twice.*"

He went to stab with one of the syringes, but the demon was too agile, the tentacle coiling instead around his neck and raising him from the floor, its teeth clicking in his face. Bruce kicked and spit, desperate for breath, and tried to thrust the needle a final time. His limb refused the command, and quickly—too quickly—a stifling asphyxia crept throughout his body, drawing darker with each passing heartbeat.

♉

Stuart raced into the main area of the strip club, the tableau greeting him as gruesome as any he'd witnessed while a combat photographer—the blood, the fire, the mangled bodies—only these atrocities weren't the handiwork of night-raiding Viet Cong. The grotesque gallery of creatures around him bore that responsibility, profanities to reason each, the worst being the one that had Bruce in a stranglehold, so outrageous a thing Stuart couldn't discern anything lucid from its anatomy.

Stuart yelled, wedging the axe deep into the creature's flank; the shock of the attack forced it to relinquish Bruce, and Stuart chopped, frenzied, at the thing's tentacle, a gangrenous ebony bile spraying from the wound. Once amputated the appendage was a headless asp, its mouth still attempting to bite even as Stuart kicked it away.

Bruce scampered upright, braced his forearm under the creature's chin and stabbed a hypodermic needle into its neck; there was an inhuman bawl, and the body—skin, muscle, bone—dissolved to a stenching, sticky bulk.

There was a crash behind Stuart then, and the shrieking locomotive that once was Angelique tore from the hall, knocking the axe from his hands and Stuart from his feet. As the thing swept down for the killing blow Bruce pulled the plastic applicator from another syringe, aimed and tossed it, dart-like. The needle stuck tight into the monster's chest and soon, too, it's body burst, a revolting, gelatinous mess spattering Stuart with inky ichor.

"Bull's-eye." Stuart said as Bruce hoisted him up.

Bruce laughed uneasily. "I guess all those nights at the rec center weren't wasted."

Stuart looked at his friend; Bruce's clothes were ripped, saturated with sweat and blood, but the fear in his eyes had disappeared.

"Thank God, Stu," he said. "I thought they got you."

"Demon strippers?" Stuart asked.

Bruce nodded. "How'd you know?"

"Figured it out."

There was a moan, and the man in the fedora Stuart recognized from earlier in the evening leaned on the edge of the bar, his features curdled with pain.

"What's *he* doing here?" Stuart asked.

"That's Ray," Bruce said. "He's an exorcist. Sort of."

From across the room, the ponytailed doorman staggered up to them, forehead lacerated and bleeding. He touched a hand to where the demon's tentacle lanced Ray, fingertips coming away crimson. "Fuckin' bitch got you good."

Ray grimaced. "I'm still breathing, ain't I? Means I'm not done yet, Rufus."

The floor trembled; liquor bottles smashed to the floor, the red-hued lights crashing from ceiling to stage soon after.

"Earthquake?" Bruce asked.

"The Hellgate," Ray said, wincing. "It *can't* be opening. Not *yet.*"

Stuart snorted. "Look pal, I hate to break it to you, but

whatever ingredients these things need for their Devil's Food Doomsday Cake they've already got."

"Shit," Ray spit as another rumble rattled the building. "Time for the Armageddon Contingency." He pulled something small from his coat's interior and tried passing it to the doorman. "Take it."

"No," Rufus refused. "I'm not leaving you here with half your spleen hanging out."

Stuart looked at what Ray held; it was an ornately carved wooden box, the intricate designs long worn with age. "What is it?"

Ray's legs buckled and he slid to the floor, swearing all the way. When Stuart repeated his question, Ray finally answered, "It contains a shard of the true cross. We have to place it within the sacrificial seal. It's the only way to truly close the portal forever."

"Mighty convenient of you to have *that,* isn't it?" Bruce snapped. Ray grimly smiled.

"I was a Boy Scout as a kid. Always prepared."

"But we don't know where the portal *is,* Ray." Bruce argued. "Damn thing could be anywhere."

"It's in the basement." Stuart said, and when Bruce cocked a disbelieving eyebrow, he continued with: "Trust me. I was just there."

Bruce shrugged. "Alright then. Basement it is."

"There's not much time," Ray said as the building shook again.

Stuart took the box from him. "I'll go. I know where the gate is."

"Not alone you're not, geezer." Bruce retrieved the fallen axe. "We go down, we go down together."

They were almost to the hall when Ray called out. *"Here,"* he said hoarsely. "You might need this."

Ray tossed Stuart the Berretta; once caught he noticed the well-worn walnut grips were inscribed with religious icons. Hefting the pistol, he looked at Bruce.

"I'm twenty-one again after all."

The ground quivered and Ray yelled, *"Go!"*

Stuart led Bruce to the descending stairway only to collide with a dark figure rushing through the door in the opposite direction. Stuart fell, seeing the bald bartender on the floor a few feet away similarly dazed from the impact. Far from being a sinister satanic servant, the man was beside himself with bewilderment.

"What's going on?" He asked, standing. "Where am I?"

Before Stuart answered, the bartender pushed past him, screaming away down the hall. He wasn't alone, either—with most of the demons dead, the other robed men were emancipated from their thrall, and as Stuart and Bruce traversed the stairs they had to dodge more of the fleeing cultists.

The subterranean temple was different than when Stuart last was there; the stone floor had cracked, the sacrificial pit in front of the obscene statue expanding as the ground gave way. The hanging man was gone, his offering a trigger to the unfurling events, but as Stuart came to the bottom of the stairs he noticed that not all the worshipers had escaped; some dangled perilously from the edge of the fiery sinkhole, desperately trying to claw their way to the surface. Anton was one of them, the man's evil leer supplanted by terror, but when Stuart went to pull him up the earth shivered more violently than ever, the chunk of masonry Anton clung to collapsing into the flames.

This time the quaking didn't cease. Stuart felt something shift deep within the bowels of the world, and from the flaming cauldron there came an unearthly, blood-chilling cacophony, so loud he hardly heard Bruce above the din:

"Stu! The cross, Stu!"

Stuart opened the box. Part of him expected it to be empty, the rest was unimpressed with the simple shard of wood that fell into his palm, looking no different than barbeque kindling.

Is it really from the true cross? Stuart wondered. He'd never been exceptionally devout, but as the ground shuddered he spit prayers to Mohammad, Buddha and Elvis Presley, placed the shard back into the reliquary and heaved it into the pit before darting back the way he'd come.

"Upstairs, now!" He shouted, pushing Bruce up the steps. On the main floor the sounds of inferno died away, replaced by the chattering of cracking ceiling and walls. Stuart's lungs protested with fatigue, and in the confusion there wasn't a way to perceive how close the remaining demons were—in the wriggling shadows, around the next corner—and the unknowing set his teeth on edge.

When they arrived in the main area of the nightclub, the unfolding destruction was worse than anywhere; a layer of the second-floor terrace had fallen onto the stage, dragging sections of the roof with it. Half the room was engulfed with a burgeoning fire, and behind the bar, past the greasy, uncoagulated remains of Angelique and Desdemona, Rufus struggled to pull Ray to his feet.

"Is it done?" Ray asked weakly.

Bruce stooped down, shouldering one of Ray's arms. "I hope so. Let's go."

All four men shrank towards the exit, but failed to make it ten feet when Ray shouted in alarm. The demon who'd masqueraded as Sindy spider-crawled from behind a portion of roof, body covered in pus-weeping legions, her head twisted backwards, twin venom-spitting vipers bobbing from the eye sockets, a chunk of what had been the bartender swinging from her mandibles. She spat the meat out and lurched up, reaching for Ray, but when Rufus blocked the demon's path her claws instead latched around his throat.

"...*Invert*..." She hissed, one of her eye-serpents removing a chunk of his neck while the other plucked off his lower lip, petal from a daisy. Rufus screamed, tried to bring the machete to bear, but the creature swatted down the blade, clamping jaws tight around his hand.

Stuart emptied the Berretta into the demon; it howled,

more, he suspected, from surprise than pain, and when Rufus freed himself what remained of his forelimb was a gnawed, bone-pierced wreck. With the pistol useless, Stuart swept up the machete, hacked at the creature, but its advance refused to falter.

"Screw this." Stuart tossed the blade aside, clutched a wad of Rufus's shirt and retreated towards the door. There was another earth-spasm, and this time everything—floor, lights, stage, the demon—spiraled into the ever-expanding cavity devouring the building. Ahead of them, Bruce and Ray had reached the parking lot, and just as Stuart led Rufus across the threshold the entirety of Satan's Palace convulsed, a house of cards plunging into a black hole, the energy of the implosion laying each man low.

When the ground stilled, Stuart found the after-silence as equally unnerving as the chaos itself. He was face-down, glasses missing one lens, head and heart pounding, and when he lifted himself up half the parking lot was gone, the asphalt eaten away by the crater that swallowed the strip club. Only the wobbling devil-sign remained until it, too, toppled thunderously into the pit.

Next to him, Bruce rolled over, a head-to-toe coating of white plaster-dust fallout making him seem more ghost than man. Looking at where the nightclub had been he gravely chuckled. "Well, I guess Satan doesn't have a palace anymore."

"You okay?" Stuart asked.

"I'm *alive.*" Bruce smirked, slapping Stuart on the back. "We made it out of another one, Stu."

Nearby, Ray stood, fedora gone, face ashen, groaning as he clutched his wounded belly. "Shit, the whole place is Downtown now, isn't it?" He winced with pain. "Where's Rufus?"

Stuart glanced to where the doorman lay unconscious; his mangled arm was seeping blood and Stuart unfastened his belt, tautly securing it around Rufus' limb. "He needs to get to a hospital. *Both* of you do."

Ray shook his head. "No. No hospitals. There's a shitload of evidence the medical community's been infiltrated by necromancers, and I'm not about to take that risk. I've got a safe house a few miles from here. One of my associates was a sixty-eight whiskey in Iraq. He'll fix us up."

Another tremor rippled the ground then, followed closely by a second, and uncomfortably Stuart looked at Ray.

"What's *that?*"

"Fuck if I know," Ray said as the rumbling continued. "But I don't like the sound of it."

In front of them the wreckage from the crater swelled, sank, then erupted into a high-arching pillar of fire that illuminated the pre-dawn sky, the concussive force knocking the men back to the pavement.

Above the deafening roar of the spire came a sound, like the shrill concerto of a million tortured teeth, so intense it made Stuart's ears ache. Shapes—shadowy, inhuman, malformed—flitted from the flames, yet their arrival was mere preamble to the blackened entity that soon crawled from the caldera, large as a city bus and boiling with brimstone.

Stuart shielded his eyes as the thing burst from the maelstrom's heart like a whale breaking the ocean's surface, every feature visible in exquisite, burning detail—its horned head and hoofed feet, those leathery, veined wings that propelled it upwards and left a massive slipstream of trailing embers as it ascended over the Las Vegas skyline to the horizon beyond.

The column of fire sputtered, swirled, dissolved, leaving the air coarse with sulfur. Slowly, Bruce sat up.

"What. The *hell.* Was *that?*"

"It looked like...It looked like *Satan.*" Stuart said, remembering the idolatrous statue. "Did we just release Satan? I thought the gate was closed."

Bruce glanced at Ray. "You said that was a shard of the

true cross."

"I thought it was. Guess I was wrong." Ray said, a frown shifting quickly into an angered scowl. "*Fuck*, I paid eight-hundred bucks for that, too. Son of a *bitch*, I got ripped off!"

In the distance a symphony of sirens played, reached crescendo, and Stuart pulled Ray up. "So, what do we do now?"

Ray's bitter expression didn't soften. He pointed to Vegas, the shining neon lights lonely, tired and out-of-place in the dawning desert daybreak. "We get our asses out of here and figure the rest out later." He looked to Bruce. "You got a ride? My Durango's probably somewhere near the eighth circle of Hell by now."

The Winnebago was one of the few intact vehicles in the parking lot, though a bent stripper pole thrown aloft by the devastation skewered its siding. Stuart wondered if the RV still ran, but after he and Bruce hauled Rufus, then Ray, into the Winnebago, Bruce slid into the driver's seat and effortlessly started the engine. When he clicked the radio on, The Rolling Stones' 'Sympathy For The Devil' was just starting; Bruce's face soured and he turned the dial right back off.

"I'm not in the mood for music."

"I've always been a jazz man myself," Ray said. "But right now, I'd settle for some morphine."

The sirens were growing closer, and as he guided the RV from the parking lot, Bruce said, "You know, Stu, we should seriously think about going to a retirement community."

Stuart rolled his eyes, took the first aid kit from a small cabinet drawer and cut some gauze. "We could, but we'd probably be stalked by a body-snatching mummy or something."

Bruce laughed, driving away while the morning sun rose, just like always.

ABOUT THE AUTHOR

DAMASCUS MINCEMEYER has had stories published (or set-to-be published)in the anthologies *Fire: Demons, Dragons and Djinn, Earth: Giants, Golems and Gargoyles, Air: Slyphs, Spirits and Swan Maidens, Hear Me Roar, Crash Code, Hell's Empire, Appalachian Horror, On Time, Bikers Vs The Undead, Psycho Holiday, Monsters Vs Nazis, Mr Deadman Made Me Do It, Satan Is Your Friend, Monster Party, Wolfwinter, A Tree Lighting In Deathlehem* and the magazines *Aphotic Realm, Gallows Hill* and *StoryHack.*

ALSO FROM CRITICAL BLAST

GODS & SERVICES
edited by R.J. Carter

When old gods need new worshipers, they offer their divinity for sale. Put a little god in your life with this collection of short stories from authors Ross Baxter, Ira Bloom, Laura J. Campbell, Aristo Couvaras, Jon Del Arroz, David J. Pedersen, Zach Smith, Michael Tierney, and Katherine Traylor.

BULLETPROOF: ORIGINS
by Stephen J. Mitchell

Kody Haywood is a freshman at Bannerville High School, struggling to maintain focus. Every day he finds himself getting lost in his thoughts, the hallways at school, or even in conversation. Having a mind that wanders makes him an easy target for the school bully and all-star athlete, Brett Walker.

As his birthday approaches, Kody discovers a genetic change in his body that renders him indestructible. When a mysterious letter from his deceased father arrives on his doorstep, it puts him in the crosshairs of an international terrorist!

Facing trouble in and out of school, Kody must find his focus and deal with two very different enemies or else there will be terrible consequences for being…

Bulletproof!